SKIN DEEP

Jacqueline Jacques

HONNO MODERN FICTION

Published by Honno
'Ailsa Craig', Heol y Cawl,
Dinas Powys, South Glamorgan,
Wales, CF6 4AH.

*The author would like to stress that this is a work of fiction and no
resemblance to any actual individual or institution is intended or implied.*

ISBN 1 870206 67 3

Published with the financial support of the Welsh Books Council.

Cover design and image by Jo Mazelis.

Back cover photograph of author
by Suzanne Bosworth.

Typeset and printed in Wales by
Dinefwr Press, Llandybie.

SKIN DEEP

Newport
CITY COUNCIL
DINAS
'd

*For all those who suffered under the Nazis
and died for their beliefs*

Acknowledgements

Thanks to everyone who believed in my 'brainchild' from its conception: to my husband, Peter, who kept me focused, to Marisa Merry, who has been so generous with her time and insider TV knowledge, to Joan Emery, who encouraged me to speculate, to writing friends, for their probing questions and continuous support, and to Janet Thomas and all at Honno, who saw its worth and patted it into shape.

1

As he recoils from the studio glare, his arm a shield, for a moment, for the first time, I glimpse the anguish of the torture-victim and wonder if what we are doing is right. But it's too late now for guilt or pity. Cameras are rolling. My stopwatch is ticking. I glance down at the running order and follow my thumbnail, a shiny black beetle creeping down the clipboard. Check, check, check. I cue the presenter. 'Standby, Tom.'

I still think we should have gone for the extension. Forty minutes might be long enough to 'in-depth' your everyday icons of sport, screen and politics, but this is once-in-a-lifetime stuff. We should have leaned on the sponsors in my opinion. But who listens to the mumblings of a mere Production Assistant? 'Get back in your box, Clare,' was the gist of what Alison said, with a smile so acid it must have furred her teeth.

Over a jangle of title music, I count Tom in, 'Three, two, one . . .'

'Welcome.' He beams smugness. 'My guest tonight was born in Hanover, Germany, eighty-five years ago. He grew to adulthood in poverty and oppression, witnessed the rise of Hitler, but unlike many of his fellow countrymen, set his face against Fascism. He fought against Franco in the Spanish Civil War and, in 1942, while risking his life as a British agent, was captured by the Nazis and interred in Buchenwald concentration camp. Incredibly, sixty years on he has hit the headlines with a story that must give hope to millions . . .'

My heart bumps against my ribs. I lick my lips.

'Ladies and gentlemen, please give a special *Way of the World* welcome to Ma-a-ax Zeiler!' The audience takes its cue from his emphatically outstretched arm and applauds madly. They want this, more than anything.

'Now!' I click my fingers. Nothing happens. Tom waggles his hand which, losing the effect, droops impotently.

'Get him on!' Still nothing. Oh, please! 'Come on, Max! What's the matter?'

He's frozen, that's what. Our hero has stage fright. The Stage Manager has him by the arm but he's dug his heels in. I'm whimpering, 'Don't do this to me, Max,' almost biting through my lip. Oh Lord, it's all going to go wrong. The programme will be a disaster; the press will have a heyday; I'll be out of a job . . .

There's Jay now – Jason to the rescue! Jay can do it if anyone can – Production Assistant and altogether nice guy. But Max isn't used to the racial mix, even now. There's a resistance. As the dark hand reaches his shoulder, Max flings it off. Seconds tick by as Jay talks him down with you-can-do-it, we're-all-behind-you reassurances. (Oh come on, guys . . . the applause won't last forever.)

He's on! We can breathe again in the draught from the audience's roar of hope. Because this eighty-five year old is gloriously young: as tall and straight as a tree. Tom Farrell catches his arm to anchor him, pats it as you'd pat an old friend while, in the wings, Jay looks up at me and rolls his eyes, wipes away the sweat with the back of his hand.

'Max . . .' Tom could gobble him up, the scoop of the year. He rubs his hands in delight. 'Looking good, Max, looking good!'

A single nervous titter from the stalls. He'll have to work harder than this. Not that they're bored at all; they're spellbound.

The guest backs off. You can almost smell his panic. 'It is, em,' he swallows the tremor. 'I am glad to be here.' His English is formal, as you'd expect.

'I'll go with that!' Dig-in-the-ribs guffaw, but it's not a joke.

Poor Max. All he's been through and Tom's full frontal fawning to boot. There's Alison's voice, a flea in my ear-piece, telling Tom to 'sit the man down before he fucking falls down.' This is accomplished with nods and prods and Bambi's awkwardness as he folds down his strange new limbs. Anxious fingers rake his hair as he retreats down the sofa. He watches the tilted monitor at his feet as though it might bite.

But it's all right, they understand.

He takes it far too seriously, pondering the questions too long and answering in monosyllables. You'd think we hadn't rehearsed this. Alison squints over white knuckles at the bank of monitors above us. She's not praying; it's gum she's chewing, the spearmint vying with several brands of perfume, hot microchips and the emissions of half a dozen nervous people sealed into a control pod.

After some heavy digging Tom manages to turn up a cloddish yes, Max has been to London before, staying with relatives, in the thirties, on the run from the Nazis.

Silence, and Tom's beginning to look desperate. I prompt him: 'Traffic, Tom.'

'You'll have found the city very changed from those days. Busier, obviously.'

Max frowns and, ah yes, remembers that he's meant to be telling us how, that first morning in Oxford Street, he'd cowered on the pavement with his fingers in his ears at the little green man's urgent summons, while buses beeped and taxi-drivers roared abuse. Audience laughter feeds into his muscles, relaxing him imperceptibly, and he launches into a halting little speech about how he'd been utterly dismayed by the noise, the bustle, the aggressive clothes, the loose talk. He'd had to remind himself that all that pushing of things to their limits was simply an expression of, a celebration of, freedom and equality, the very things he had been fighting for.

Good. That's the warm-up over. 'Thirty seconds to film-clip,' I announce.

Switch to auto-cue. Close-up of the presenter, speaking to camera, jowls heavy as he settles down to the script.

'There can't be many of us who are not still reeling from the news, last week, of Max's resurrection, sixty years after his body was committed to a Nazi grave. Not least Max himself, I should say.'

Whose eyes are dark wells, the depth unfathomable. You think you glimpse the suffering and then the light changes and it's gone.

'Cue VT.' I count back from ten as Tom reminds the viewers about the discovery made, seven years before, by workers constructing the *Metro* linking East and West Berlin.

'Two, one. Run VT.' On cue the screens flood with videotape. This is the first showing of these particular shots: the ancient Nazi bunker with its desks, maps, overturned chairs, old-fashioned telephones, the litter of papers from the open filing cabinets, and the next room where the charred bodies had been found. Nick unearthed the reels from the Berlin film library. He's surpassed himself this time.

'And in a chamber under the floor –' Tom is delivering his lines like a horror film heavy – 'they found what seemed to be a large concrete chest which they broke open, hoping to find the answer to the mysterious disappearance of Hitler's body.'

We can't see anything much through the curling smoke of liquid nitrogen, until a lens adjustment shows us that the Fuhrer isn't there, only six amorphous lumps wrapped in waxed paper. An anonymous hand carefully removes the parcels from the top, showing us another six below them, and the same on the bottom. They might be anything. Cabbages, even.

'They turned out to be brains: human brains,' he intones. (Boris Karloff, eat your heart out.) 'Each neatly packaged and labelled. The brains of selected concentration camp internees, removed and frozen by the Beast of Buchenwald, the notorious doctor Klaus Hofmann.'

There's a movement of air, as the audience sucks breath through its teeth. My ears tingle. Hearing yet not hearing. A hook that's been missed. Or a link. Nobody else looks worried. Forget it, Clare, I tell myself. It couldn't have been that important.

'Today, four of those brains have been successfully transplanted into donor bodies. Max is one of them.'

They know all that. It's why they've made the trip, why they've braved the Underground, queued in the hot sun. They can lay claim to him. He's almost a Brit. He was on our side in the war. It was in all the glossies on Sunday. In the few days since the news broke, every presenter on every channel, every expert in every field, has examined brain transplants and the Buchenwald survivors, from every conceivable angle. But they still like to hear it said, to see the pictures that make it a little more credible, and to behold the man, of course, the walking-talking resurrection freak.

'Cue photo, thirty seconds.'

'We can only speculate,' observes Tom, 'on the outcome of emergency meetings in Washington and Brussels, called to discuss the moral and practical implications of the controversial new surgery. In the meantime *Way of the World* has invited Max Zeiler to tell us what it has meant to him to have another crack at life. I should mention, at this point, that parents might consider some of the more, ah, *harrowing* aspects of Max's experience, unsuitable for children and people of a sensitive disposition.'

He doesn't really expect them to switch off? After that build-up? This is compulsive viewing. History in the making. Oh God, my fingers itch, what couldn't I have done with this material! But God saw fit, at the time of the most thrilling event in the history of television, to relegate Clare Russell to the lower ranks of the production team.

'Cue photos,' I say, dutifully. And gnaw on that missing *something* that refuses to translate into words. A niggle, a feeling, nothing I can put my finger on.

Tom leans back in his chair and winks cheerily at his guest, mouthing 'Relax' while his voice-over smoothes and glosses the torn and faded photographs that come flickering across our bank of screens. But I can't. What was it? Oh come on, Clare, it's too late now, the moment's gone. Forget it.

Max, a blond and beautiful toddler, stares pale-eyed in sepia from the knee of a long-skirted woman with dark, fluffed-out hair. Behind them her dark-suited husband and his moustaches stand stiffly to attention. We hear Tom's recorded voice explaining that Max's mother was Annie Stephens, a schoolteacher from Surrey, who met the prisoner-of-war, Gustav Zeiler, in 1916, while he was working in the fields near her home. She brought up her children to be bilingual.

Now a little gap-toothed boy beams, in *lederhosen* and feathered cap. His sister Berthe's dimpled face is framed by wispy braids, which become thick ropes in the next photograph, wound round her head, while Max's big boy grin is not for the photographer. He doesn't care that his pullover is frayed or that his trousers are too short. Boys will be boys and scuff their shoes in good times and bad. He and his cousin Harry examine their nets for tiddlers on the banks of an English river, oblivious of Berthe paddling in the shallows and hyper-inflation back in the Weimar Republic. It doesn't bother him that Gustav is out of work or that Annie has to teach German to rich English kids in order to make ends meet. At least her money is worth something here. In Germany the exchange rate is 4.2 trillion marks to the dollar.

By the next photo, American aid has improved things a little, and the employees of the Gratz tractor works are out on a summer spree, with Gustav and his brood in the forefront of the picnickers. Annie looks plumply happy, but then everyone has orders to smile. Only Max is scowling – moody teenager. Perhaps he has just learned that he is to join his father on the assembly line.

'Cut to newsreel.'

The Depression. Shuffling queues of men outside a soup kitchen, avoiding looking at the camera. Women with sunken eyes, pushing prams of firewood. Banners with slogans, police with batons raised, scuffling with workers outside a motor factory. We thought it was bad in Britain, Tom says, but it was ten times worse in Hanover.

A talking head next – an old woman with apple cheeks and a tight silver perm – Max's sister, Berthe, though she looks like his granny. In the studio, Max's lips are a thin line. There's no telling what he's thinking.

'Ve vas sitting around ze table.' Her accent is thicker than Max's, more guttural. 'Papa was in his shirtsleeves, mending a shoe on the last. He had nails in his mouth. Max looked up and confessed, "Papa, I do not know vezzer I can stay on at Gratz. It is unbearable. You are vorking so fast it is dangerous, and you dare not slow down or talk, even, because zey are just looking for an excuse to sack you. What zey want is to take on somebody else at a lower rate." Papa took ze tacks from his mouth. He said, "Max, you hef two choices. If you leave, you vill be one of those poor creatures at the gates, so hungry for vork you will take vatever zey offer. Or you can join ze union." Max hesitated before confessing, "Papa, I *haf* joined." He fetched his coat and turned back the lapel, und zere vas a yellow union button. Zey both roared with laughter when Papa turned back *his* lapel to show another. But it was somesing zey had to keep very secret, *very* secret. Zey would beat up on you or sack you for organising against management, and you had to feed your family.'

During Hitler's rise to power things got much worse, she explains. Trade unions were not only banned: socialists, communists, all daring to oppose the fascist regime were put into a labour camp or shot. Millions of left-wing sympathisers simply disappeared. So you bit your tongue if you had any sense, and watched with horror as the rest of Germany fell under Hitler's spell.

Here's another photograph to take away the bitter taste. Outdoors on a balmy day. A long table is spread with food; everyone's dressed in their glad rags, toasting a blushing bride and groom – Berthe and Helmut – with foaming tankards of beer. Max, nearest the camera has his arm round a pretty, dark-haired girl. She wears a flower pinned to her dress and a hat on the hypotenuse. All smiles. No hint of the risk Max is taking by staying on in Germany for the wedding.

'Where's camera two?' Alison demands. 'Let's get a reaction.' She wants a frown, at least, to tug at the heart-strings. But he's done all his weeping.

In hindsight, of course, we should have had a camera on him the day the photos arrived from Berthe. Missed opportunities, no excuses. Buck your ideas up, Clare. Then he was so upset Nick and I had to take him for a drink before he could face the bus ride back to Bayswater.

'Ah, good boy,' Alison is crooning with spearmint breath.

Look, look, the hero is hunting for his hanky. At last. His timing's off, but better than never. Eyes salting, mouth a-quiver, lovely stuff. And, with magnification adding its own poignancy, there's a nice 'still' for the morning papers.

Good, camera three is picking up *moues* of sympathy in the audience, tissues polishing noses. That'll go down well with the viewers. I mean, when you think – of all those people at the wedding feast, only old Berthe is left. Parents, brother, aunts and uncles, cousin Harry over from England, the girl Sophie, all his friends, gone, and only, like, *yesterday* in his terms.

I mean, fancy waking up one morning and discovering that everyone you love has, well, died. Overnight. How would I feel if Mum and Kate and Nan weren't there? God, it would be horrible. What would I do, all alone in a strange new world, with everybody who knew me, cared about me just wiped out, gone? And Nick, what would I do without my darling Nick? Without anyone to turn to? Not Jay, not any of my friends. Not even Sid. He's not the best dad in the world but I wouldn't be without him. It must have been devastating for Max when he first found out. And then to discover that he had a different body into the bargain – it's a wonder he didn't go mad and top himself, though I suppose they'd have taken precautions. Couldn't lose their national treasure. I think he's taking it bloody well, considering.

I would hate to have someone else's body foisted on me. A couple of inches off the five foot nine wouldn't come amiss but the rest is, well, it's never going to make my fortune, according to Nan, but it's mine, it's me, what I am. She takes responsibility for my looks, my Nan, having been ginger herself once. She's the one paid for me to have my nose pierced, bought me my first coral stud, said I put her in mind of Jean Simmons in *Blue Lagoon*. Next year she's going to have hers done. It's always next year. Now she keeps coming round with lipsticks and blushers and eyelash dye and things. 'I bought these in the High Street, Clare, but they make me look like an old tart.' So what does that make me?

But I know she means well.

And I suppose the medical people meant well with Max and the others, giving them a second chance, and that. Beggars can't be choosers and I suppose they did their best. But it doesn't make it any better. I mean, according to him, he's very different from the body he's been put into. Age is about all they've managed to match, give or take a year or two – and the blood group. That has to be right or the brain won't take – immune responses or something. And sex. It would have been a bit of a blow for poor old Max having to deal with periods and PMT on top of everything else.

That's what the audience is thinking, most likely, their heads on the slant, their eyes slitting and sliding between the wedding guest on the screen, with his raw Slavic cheekbones, and the rugged Englishman beside Tom; I can almost hear them comparing the two, whispering, 'Nothing like.'

This Max has a body honed by posh games at public school, not 'footer' with a tin can on the cobbles of Hanover's back streets. He's never bunked off school because he had no shoes to wear; he has never gone hungry. But the lodger, inside, *has*. That's what's hard to remember.

Next picture. This is the last photograph he managed to send home from Spain. A single-decker bus, a real old bone-shaker with a boxy bonnet and a driver's cab, and two young soldiers in greatcoats, laughing and squinting into a winter sun. Max seems to be toasting the cameraman with a bottle of wine. He has a hunk of bread in his other hand, held up to shade his eyes. The taller man is chomping on a huge length of sausage. A rifle is propped between them.

'Where was that?' asks Tom.

'The road to Madrid. We, volunteers, were called to defend the city after the government moved out and left the people to their fate.'

'And just remind the viewers, would you, Max – what year was this?'

'It was 1936. November.'

Tom inclines his head. Correct. 'You saw some action, then?'

'A little.' He doesn't smile.

Over cynical footage of Republican and Nationalist posters burning side by side on a crumbling house front, Tom trots out the statistics. Thirty-five thousand foreigners from fifty-four countries volunteered to fight for the republicans in the International Brigades, German dissidents among them. In the end, though, with Hitler's help, fascism triumphed and Max fled to England, writing articles and pamphlets for the German resistance movement and then, when our government took him up, taking a more active role, behind enemy lines, helping Jews and others to escape the Nazis. But as everybody knows, he was eventually captured and taken to Buchenwald.

'Where you were tortured, I believe.'

Max nods, his face unreadable. He used to have the scars to prove it.

'But not shot?' The words are loaded. What is he implying?

'No,' he looks straight into Tom's eyes. 'I do not know why they chose to keep me alive, Mister Farrell.'

'There are worse punishments than death.'

'Yes.'

'Three, two, one,' I say, 'and cue music, cue film.' And there's the footage of shaven-headed prisoners, lying exhausted and hollow-eyed on their bunks, after a day's gruelling labour. They look so thin and ill, in their dirty convict stripes. Some hold out skinny arms to a stunned cameraman, to display inhuman tattooed numbers, sores and bruises, some to beg for food and help. Some simply curl in a thin blanket, too numbed by cruelty to move.

Max's nostrils flare and his fingers creep over his mouth, over his nose, as though he can still smell the stink of the place. I remind myself that he hasn't seen this clip before.

When the camera moves outside at last, silently, so as not to startle the fragile skeletons who move in the shadows, empty spindles, with the last threads of life slipping away, Max's fingers slide up to massage his forehead, cover his eyes but then treacherously part and he is forced to look. Is he there, perhaps – one of those living cadavers? Will he know himself, or anyone else?

Silly me, of course he won't: this isn't even his camp, and it's after his time. This was filmed by the Red Army when they liberated Auschwitz in January '45. Nick, who did most of the research for the programme, gathered this horrific material from all over. He'd had to keep reminding me that Max was dead by then, or rather his body was. And buried.

'We do appreciate how distressing this must be for you, Max.'

Do we? Really? Can we imagine what it's like for him, seeing it all again? For the first time, I doubt our intentions. This is cruel, isn't it? Callous? Couldn't we have spared him this?

Putting the programme together there was never any question of leaving this bit out. This was the high point, the whole point. The Nazi labour camps were vile, sickening, an unbelievable horror. Showing the depths to which a depraved regime could sink. And the eye cannot look away. So, say what you like, it's great television. The audience is deeply affected, biting their lips, frowning, shaking their heads. At the Nazis' callousness or the media's? I wonder. Certainly they won't forget, in a hurry, the look of sheer disgust on Max's face before he slipped back behind the mask.

'One morning,' Tom goes on, back on script, 'instead of being escorted as usual to his work in the salt mines, Max was startled to find himself being marched in a different direction.' He nods at the younger man. His cue.

But Max has downed tools. His face is set hard. You can hardly blame him. I remind myself that he is used to interrogation.

'Max?'

Alison's jaw drops in a silent groan and her eyes roll whitely up. We all hold our breath.

He squares his shoulders, and to everyone's relief, says at last, 'I thought I was about to face the firing squad.' Another pause before he can bring himself to tell us that, instead, he found himself being prodded at gunpoint towards the camp hospital.

'And you finished up in the office of *this* man, Klaus Hofmann.'

Don't. Poor guy. Don't put him through this. I want to run down there, put my arms round him, kick away the monitor. He can't bring himself to look, to confront his peak-capped persecutor, but like a child behind the settee, he has to peep. And then he's caught, turned to stone by that reptilian stare. An unquenchable thirst for knowledge has dried the face to a husk and the eyes are pale with abstraction. Muscles curve the lips but you can tell that Klaus Hofmann's smile was never sweet.

'Max?'

There's a rustle as contempt moves through the audience, twitching lips, puckering brows. Hasn't the poor man suffered enough? Why torture him further? Yet I know they'd howl if Tom were to stop now. It's there in all of us, the beast.

'Take it easy, Tom,' mutters Alison, but not for him to hear.

'Max, did you have any idea why Doctor Hofmann should have wanted to see you?'

He frowns as his senses return, and moves his head, slowly negative.

Tom prompts him to speak, 'Can you tell us what happened, Max?'

He clears his throat obligingly. 'There were four officers sitting behind a long table . . .' His voice is strong now. I needn't have worried; he can cope. He's a survivor. Quietly he lists his inquisitors: Hofmann and his associate, Professor Gisela Weiss, and two other men in white coats, more doctors. He had to stand before them, he says, answering questions like a schoolboy.

'What sort of questions?'

'Mathematics, general knowledge, literature, that sort of thing. It made no sense. It was like a kindergarten spelling bee, but I realised that there was far more at stake than coming top of the class. They seemed pleased with my answers. It occurred to me that they might be considering me for work at the hospital. Record keeping or something. I, I . . .' For the first time, he falters, perplexed, at his own stupidity.

Tom observes, 'Record keeping would have been a welcome change.'

He raises eyes that are haunted, and blinks. 'I beg your pardon?'

'You were hopeful.'

'*Hope*ful?' he considers the question. 'Hope was something you did not allow. I knew Doctor Hofmann to be single-minded and ruthless. I knew he used certain prisoners for testing out his theories.'

'Jews?'

He nods. 'I thought he might want to try something out on an Aryan, for comparison.'

'Did he speak to you?'

'After the questions he said, "I see that two years in Buchenwald have not dulled your wits, Herr Zeiler." I was startled to hear my name – I had grown used to being a number. It was then that I noticed the doctor had a file open before him. My photograph was attached and I could see personal documents – scruffy old school reports, medical records, even my union card. They must have raided my parents' home. I could not understand why he had gone to all that trouble. Then Professor Weiss wanted to know my family history, what my grandparents had died of, whether there had been mental problems. I answered as truthfully as I could without putting my family in danger.'

'What happened then?'

'I was taken to another room and given a written test. It was strange to use a pencil and paper again, to think about trivialities for an hour and a half. Some questions simply measured numeracy, literacy, spatial awareness, that sort of thing; some involved ink blots and optical illusions, designed to gauge the balance of my mind, I think.'

'But you still had no idea where all this was leading?'

'None.'

'And after all the tests?'

'They took me to an empty side-ward and strapped me to a bed.' He stops speaking, breathes steadily, composing himself for the ordeal to come. 'I could not move,' he continues at last, 'not even my head. After a few minutes the doctor came in, capped and gowned to perform an operation. I tried to scream but a gag was forced into my mouth. A nurse wheeled a trolley to the bedside. It chinked over the uneven floor. There were tools – a hacksaw, drill, things a carpenter might use – jars of liquids, one made of metal, which must have contained a freezing agent. It gave off steam and frost had formed on the outside.' He closes his eyes briefly. 'They shaved my head completely and laid it in a scoop of crushed ice. They stuck straws in my nose so that I could breathe for as long as possible and then they packed ice all over my face. I couldn't see, or hear. Everything ached with cold. And then,' he says, without expression, 'someone started drilling a hole in my skull.'

In the silence someone shouts, 'No!' and Tom edges forward on his chair. 'You were *conscious* during the operation?'

'Long enough to register the most violent and unbelievable pain,' he says evenly. 'Not just where they were drilling,' he pauses fractionally, 'all over my skull. The grinding vibrated through the bone and every nerve in my head was protesting. My teeth loosened, I am sure, and my eardrums exploded. And then, the drilling stopped and, something, some liquid must have been pumped into my brain. I felt as though my head would burst, and then I couldn't feel anything, just a sensation of trickling cold, of darkness and gloom, and – and heaviness, my head being too heavy for my neck to support. I began to shake, so violently they had to hold me still. I do not remember when my heart stopped beating, but I knew that it would . . .'

There isn't any more to tell. Not for another sixty years.

He mentions snatches of consciousness when he was told to turn his head this way, that, flex certain muscles, raise limbs and fingers. He says he remembers violent headaches, and wondering about the smell.

'The smell?'

'Clean linen, fresh air, soap, disinfectant. I lived with the stench of filth in my nostrils for more than two years. You miss it when it is not there.'

Farrell's laugh is harsh, ill judged, and there's a beat as he waits in vain for his audience to respond. Unperturbed by silence, he resumes his air of compassion and coaxing. 'And then you opened your eyes.'

'There was something over them. Bandages. I was conscious of a woman's perfume, and her voice in my ear. She said I must prepare for a shock. I thought it was Professor Weiss. I could not understand why she was speaking in English. "You have been asleep for a long, long time," she said. "The war is over and you are safe. When you open your eyes you will find changes that will be difficult to assimilate, changes in your surroundings and changes in yourself, in your appearance, in your voice, but you are not alone, Max; we are here to help you."

'When she was sure that I had heard and understood she took away the blindfold. I was in a pleasant hospital room and the woman sitting beside the bed introduced herself as Susmeta Naidoo, the surgeon who had performed the operation. She held my hand and explained that this was the twenty-first century.'

2

By the time the show went out I was beginning to understand the science, the reason Max and the others had
survived in spite of everything. Though when Susmeta told
me I'd passed my hand straight over my head. I'd never
heard of a cryoprotectant.

'A form of anti-freeze,' she'd explained, her eyes gleaming
with what I took to be scientific fervour. 'No, silly, not the
stuff you put in your car!' she smiled, quite mistaking my
look of horror. 'This was a biological concoction.'

'And that makes it all right? God, Susmeta, it's, it's vile
. . . it's . . .' I shook my head, too disgusted for words.

'It's barbaric,' she agreed quietly. 'Well, I know that's
what it must look like to the layman. But to be honest,
Clare, we do similar experiments today.' I stared at her in
disbelief. 'How do you think we got around to freezing
embryos and sperm and transplant organs? We had to
experiment, make sure we could resuscitate them safely.
You can't afford to make mistakes with living tissue.'

'But you don't experiment on living people.'

She bit her lips, and I looked at her sharply. 'Animals,'
she said quickly. 'We use animals . . . and cell cultures. It
just so happened that Hofmann lived in a political climate
when it was all right to think of certain people – Jews and
gypsies – as inhuman. As animals.'

'But *Hofmann* wouldn't . . .' I began.

'It's a historical fact. That's what they believed.'

'No, that's what *Hitler* believed. He was mad. It suited
Hofmann and a few million others to go along with it. He
used Hitler's hatred of the Jews to his own ends.'

'Well,' she shrugged, 'I don't know. Possibly. No, you're right – he must have known it was wrong. Which makes what he did all the worse, I suppose. But,' she sighed, 'he was a scientist. He had to know, had to find out.'

'What, by pumping anti-freeze into people's brains?'

'If you want those brains to survive the freezing process.' A frown flitted across an otherwise untroubled brow. I wondered if she was having qualms about the morality of it all. Certainly it would take a particularly warped sort of mind to come up with the notion of freezing human brains in the first place, and burying them, like a grisly sort of time capsule. Her hands and shoulders made mystified gestures and she sipped her drink thoughtfully before speaking. 'He knew that without his cryoprotectant they would deteriorate. Like strawberries when you freeze them. Their structure would change – they'd turn soft and mushy.'

Apparently ice crystals form inside cells on freezing, absorbing all the water and leaving the cells with too high a concentration of salt. These two mechanisms damage cell membranes and cause cell death. This must have been a real problem for Hofmann, Susmeta said, until he'd hit on the 'anti-freeze' idea, infiltrating the cells, at a temperature close to zero degrees Celsius, with something called dimethylsulfoxide, (she spelt it out for me). I couldn't help wondering how many brains had turned 'mushy' in how many experiments, before he'd got the concentration right. All those poor people. I wiped my hands on my shorts as his image slid into my head. I'd only seen a photograph, an official pose, and I shuddered in the heat of the day, remembering those still, hard eyes, challenging the camera. Yes, he would have an affinity with ice. Had that thin face cracked, melted into a smile the first time he'd packed a brain with ice to cool it rapidly, doused it in anti-freeze, removed it from the skull and quickly frozen it in liquid nitrogen? Had he grown hot with excitement when he realised that, at last, unbelievably, this one could work, could survive? He must have flung his arms round his sidekick, Gisela Weiss, swung her off her pretty feet, cried 'Eureka!' or the German equivalent. Must have.

I rocked my Pimms, watching the cubes clunking against the side of the glass, their edges smoothing in the sun. Susmeta's words, lightly spoken, drifted onto my notepad like thistledown, delicate tufts and tendrils of shorthand that translated into butchery. In describing how the demon surgeon would have removed the brain from the skull, she spoke in grudging awe of his skill and technique, given the primitive tools at his disposal. No moral qualms, no qualms at all.

I wished the guys would come and rescue me. But the pock, pock of ball against racquet, intermittent applause and excited gasps and groans continued to drift out to us. They were glued to Wimbledon where, of course, straw-berries were the traditional fare. I suppressed a slightly nauseous yawn at a vision of Mum's Pavlova waiting for me at home. Frozen or fresh I doubted I could fancy it now.

I wondered if Susmeta had crisps or Bombay Mix in her silver cupboards. A bag of Bombay Mix would have helped soak up the booze. Funny how, a month before, I'd expected her to be some sort of cottage loaf Indian matron, with white hair and specs. Instead this delicate naiad had ushered us into her gleaming marble-tiled hallway. She was beautiful, in her late thirties I would guess, radiating intelligence and the sort of inborn grace and charm that make people like me feel like galumphing idiots.

That was where I first met Max Zeiler. I must admit, I was completely unimpressed by our producer's proposal that I should be Max's bosom buddy for a month. I'd rather hoped he'd begun to see me as director material rather than nursemaid to a freak, or whatever else it was he had in his dirty little mind.

'Clare!' he'd bristled unconvincingly when I'd voiced my suspicions. '*Would* I do that? To *you*?' Most definitely he would. All was grist to Barry Giddings' mill. What he wanted, of course, was for me to bed 'Billy No-Mates', ferret out all his dark secrets, and pass them on to him. Our Barry was up for pimping, blackmail, any kind of bent deal so long as it resulted in juicy material for his show, though 'All I'm asking you to do is take the lad under your wing,' he insisted. 'Show him around. Cheer him up a bit. For God's sake, Clare, he doesn't have a friend in the world!'

'What about the doctor? Can't she show him the sights?'

He tutted irritably, 'She's too old,' and stopped long enough for me to form the cottage loaf idea, but of course, that wasn't what he meant. He wanted Max's escort to be mid-twenties and pliable, not mid-thirties and starchy. 'She doesn't have time,' he said finally.

'Me neither.'

'Look on it as a working holiday. We'll call it research. All expenses paid,' he weaselled. 'Double time weekends.'

Brightly I said, 'Okay,' surprising him, too, as an idea occurred to me. 'I'll do it if Nick can come too.'

'Nick?'

'Nick Robinson,' and, as he continued to look blank, said, 'Researcher on the programme?'

'I know who Nick Robinson is, thanks, and I don't think I can spare him.'

Oh great. He could spare *me*, no worries. I said, huffily, 'Well, I'm not doing it without him.'

He said 'Oh really?' in that nasty snide way of his, meaning *you'll do as I say, sunshine, or you're out. I am the Fat Controller.* The only way we ended up perched at either end of Susmeta's chaise longue, my boyfriend and I, offering to puppy-walk her protégé, was because Nick had put in his two pennyworth, and persuaded Barry that he really needed a skilled researcher on the job. Otherwise I would have been shark bait.

I don't cry easily – unlike other members of my family who have been known to get through an entire box of Kleenex over some neglected poodle on *Animal Hospital*. Not that I'm a hard case. I feel things as keenly as they do; just that emotion doesn't get as far as my tear ducts. Mum puts it down to when I was little and used to suck my fingers. Anything remotely sad or nasty and I'd pop two pale and soggy digits into my mouth. And because it's impossible to suck and blubber simultaneously – some baby reflex, I believe – I gradually trained myself to cope without tears, as men do.

But they rolled down when I heard Max's story that first time. Nick was blinking furiously; even Barry was biting his lips, and he'd heard it all before.

He didn't cry – Max. He had discovered the uselessness of tears a long time ago. Instead, as he told us tales of unimaginable horror, he gripped the arms of the oriental chair he sat in as though it was about to take off. As though he wished it would. He was no storyteller, I have to say, but we were very kind and encouraging, smiled as we asked our questions, and gently peeled away his defensive layers. His knuckles gradually lost their craggy look and his fingers began to trace the beautiful, intricate carving of the ancient wood.

There was rejoicing now from her lounge. 'Two sets to love! Blinding! The other guy didn't have a leg to stand on.' Nick and Max came out onto the terrace popping cans of beer.

'I mean,' Susmeta was saying, ignoring the interruption and my flagging interest, 'the very notion of using the Berlin sewers to generate electricity seems crazy to us. But what choice did he have? The brains had to be kept frozen. Transplant skills of any sort were beyond him. He would have had no idea how to reconnect the spinal cord, the nerves or the blood supply come to that.' She shook her head at the primitive past. 'Augmenting deficient chemicals, repairing diseased tissue, that sort of thing, was way beyond him. He didn't have the technology or the measurement techniques. He had to leave all that to us, sixty years in the future.'

'Bastard,' growled Max. 'May he roast in hell!' And then, surprisingly, 'But I suppose I must be grateful. Were it not for him I would be dead meat, as you say, Nick. Were it not for him I would not have seen London from a big wheel today, or the paintings in the British Tate Gallery or had lunch in a splendid French bistro. You, too, must feel indebted to him, do you not, Susmeta?'

'Indebted?' She was taken aback. 'Well, I suppose if I'm honest,' she frowned, 'I mean if we hadn't had the Buchenwald brains to work on we'd never have got it right. Heads we could transplant but only in a limited way. The organs functioned properly but the animals were paralysed from the neck down. Experimental material was restricted, always will be, of course, to animals and human cadavers. You can't mess about with the brains of living, breathing people. No, you're right, Max, the Hofmann brains were a gift. We learned from our mistakes. Sad but true.'

Of the eighteen brains in Hofmann's cache only four had been successfully transplanted. There was one still in storage, waiting for a donor with a special blood group. Of the remaining thirteen, several were damaged beyond repair by mishandling back in 1944 or from irreparable freezer burns sustained in the interim. Others had been lost in the resuscitation process through lack of oxygen or because of rejection by the host's immune system. But half a dozen perished during the transplant operation, three while they were trying to find the antidote to the poisonous cryoprotectant Hofmann had used, three through surgical error. *Trial* and error. There was the faintest tinkling as

Susmeta's earrings moved in sorrow. 'But yes,' she said, looking up at him almost apologetically, 'each setback, each failure added to our store of knowledge, Max. So I must be grateful.'

He managed a tight smile.

Among the things that suck-a-thumbs acquire, apart from a corrective brace and ridged fingernails, are good powers of observation. Max was Susmeta's pride and joy, I could tell. Maybe not her first-born but her favourite, surely? Her dark eyes were full of him, her slender fingers twitched to touch him, probably just to check his pulse or reflexes, but even so . . . She was attuned to his every breath, every flicker of every muscle, every nuance of mood.

But he wouldn't meet her eyes. There was something – what Nan would call 'an atmosphere' – almost as though he resented her, his dependence on her. It was a strange set-up, certainly, doctor and patient living under the same roof, albeit in different parts of the house – *her* house, the woman to whom he owed his life. He had no money of his own and no family, of course, unlike the other survivors, and coming from a male-dominated society it would certainly jar, this indebtedness.

He was a funny guy, very private. I mean, he realised that we needed to know what he'd been through, his history, and that's what he gave us. But that was all he gave us.

'You're having a laugh, aren't you, Clare?' Nick demanded, when I complained that I couldn't get through his 'touch-me-not' barbed wire fence. 'Jesus, think how you'd feel, pitched into a whole new scene in a whole new body. All he's been through he's not going to trust anybody yet. That's what we're for.'

The truth was I resented dragging this guy around London. I'm not a great one for museums and sightseeing.

I've got the T-shirt, to be honest, after a childhood of Mum taking us on recces for her school trips. I'd have been far happier at work, doing something creative. But, clearly, the establishment had decided it was time to let the fledgling leave their stuffy nest and try his wings with people his own age and, give Max his due, he *did* lighten up after a while.

London helped, having changed somewhat since the time he was here in the thirties when Saint Paul's was the tallest building. The skyline now just about blew his mind. Though he didn't appreciate my remark about architects and their erections. Being German, Nick said, he had a different sense of humour. But I got the impression he thought I should wash my mouth out with soap, a nice young girl like me. And that sort of thing hurts, you know? Nick said I had to remember that they were all chauvinists where Max came from. I think I said, 'Bollocks.'

He wasn't too sure about the Mayor's new gaff, the Norman Foster building. 'This is considered beautiful?' he wanted to know. I said the German Bundestag had been Fosterised, too, that his influence was worldwide. He pulled a face. And when we took him to the Saatchi Gallery, he said that he'd been too busy fighting his corner to take much notice of what was going on in the art world. It was probably asking a bit much to expect him to get his head around unmade beds and cows in aspic.

We took him to the War Museum to try and jog a few memories. That turned out to be another mistake. I suppose it *was* a bit of a downer, sitting in the bomb shelter, but I hadn't expected him to come over all pale and sweaty, like he was about to throw up. We had to get him out quick. And I'd quite enjoyed sitting in the dark, with the thud of falling bombs and cement dust sifting down through cracks in the brickwork – it was very atmospheric. Nick was really pissed off. He'd been hoping for some usable anecdotes.

The Science Museum was much more to Max's liking, especially the Space Age section. He was sparking and fizzing like a visiting Martian. *'Ach du meine Gute! Was ist denn das?'* What was it for? Why? Who? When? How did it work? Mostly how did it work?

He was the same at Nick's mum's one rainy afternoon. We watched a DVD of *Schindler's List* – just to let him know how the western world viewed the horrors of the Third Reich. He sat like a coiled spring, tight and unmoving, staring at the screen, hardly blinking. Afterwards, he seemed distracted. We thought that perhaps we'd overdone it, like we'd stirred up too much pain. And then he said, 'You can buy these films in the shops? I will ask Susmeta to purchase me such a machine.'

When we called Berthe in Hanover I don't know what moved him more, the technology of the mobile phone or the fact that he could see and hear a younger sister who was now sixty years older than him. Not that they spoke for long – the old lady was too upset, he said. He promised to write, to send her an email but with the help of her next door neighbour and his scanner, she got in first. Dozens of photos arrived via the Net, pages and pages, of his family and friends, of Annie and Gustav, English relations, German, of them all at Berthe's wedding (the one we used in the show), his girlfriend, Sophie, so alive and pretty. All long gone. He just sat there shaking his head, pale and dumb with grief, so we showed him how to print them off and left him to it. He didn't need us intruding. After an hour or so he came out and thanked us. So I gave him a hug as you do. He was surprised and touched, I think, but if you can't be there for a mate . . . And he *was* a mate by then. It was strange how it had crept up on me, my liking for him.

Susmeta was really pleased with his progress. We were washing up in her sleek, silver kitchen. She agreed that we'd been good for him. After a month he was much more relaxed, far less introspective. He'd grown in confidence and was beginning to come to terms with the person he now was.

I shut the kitchen door now so that he wouldn't hear. 'But he's the same person he's always been, surely?' I said, and handed her a glass, which I'd washed and then dried, hoping she would, at least, put it away. (The dishwasher was in mid cycle, and the housekeeper went off at six.)

'No he's not,' she said, putting the glass onto another work top, 'he's taller, fitter, better looking. He has a better diet, a better life-style, more interests, more exercise, *friends* . . .' I gathered from her gesture that that's what Nick and I were. 'It all impinges on an individual's psyche. He's not even the Max I operated on six months ago. He doesn't have us running around at night any more because of his nightmares. He doesn't blame himself any longer for the death of his comrades.'

'What?'

She lowered her voice. 'Survivor guilt syndrome,' she explained. 'If his brain had been put at the top of the chest instead of the bottom, we'd have made all our mistakes on *his* brain instead of someone else's. He blames himself, or he did, because by the time we'd got to him, on the bottom layer of the freezer, we'd perfected our methods, sorted out the antidote to the poison and he lived.'

'That's silly,' I said.

'People in trauma are rarely rational,' she said.

'But he's better now?'

'Getting there. There's still the physical thing. His muscles are not yet attuned to the signals his brain sends them. He is coming to terms with his bulk and strength – he became very weak in Buchenwald – but his fingers still want to hold spoons and pens in their own way, as I'm sure you've noticed. It has taken him ages to get his signature right.'

'How are the others managing?'

Susmeta pursed her mouth, weighing how much she ought to tell me. 'I suppose it'll come out in the programme,' she said at last, while I opened and shut cupboards looking for somewhere to put the glasses she'd piled up. 'We have in counselling, at the moment, a man who was an accomplished pianist before the war. Unaware of the implications, I chose as donor someone who didn't know one end of a penny whistle from the other. The awful thing is, I should have known from his inferior parietal lobes. They're so much wider than average.'

'Ri-i-ight,' I said.

'Axel Schlager is – was – a musical genius, Clare, and we – I've – ruined his chances of a musical career.'

'You're saying his brain can only function inside a musician's head?'

'He could function well enough inside *any* head, but he needs a pianist's *body* in order to play the piano. A pianist's *hands*. The ones we've given him are not only smaller than Axel's, they span the keys differently and they have the completely wrong muscle-memory. The donor's hands were versed in a million skills, tying shoe-laces, doing up buttons, shaving, holding a golf club, but not the one thing that matters to Axel. He is being very good about it but it's no life for the poor man if he can't play. I feel terrible about it.'

'Well, maybe a piano player will die soon and you'll be able to transplant his arms or something.'

'Legs too. The poor chap can hardly reach the pedals.'

I clapped my hand to my mouth but it was too late. My snort of rude mirth echoed round the kitchen. She looked aghast and then she too saw the funny side. 'A *tall* piano player,' I managed to blurt out, before more laughter overtook us. 'Oh poor guy,' I said, coming down like badly cooked soufflé. 'It must be doing his head in.'

She said the chances of finding a suitable donor for Axel

were remote. People weren't too keen on leaving their entire body to science. Sans eyes, sans heart, sans kidneys, sans liver, the corpse could still be laid to rest and properly mourned, but not if there was nothing to go in the coffin or only butchers' scraps.

'When we were looking for someone for Max there were just two card-carrying corporal donors in the entire country, around his age and with his particular blood group. One was black. A car accident had left him brain-dead and he was being kept alive on life-support. The other was a woman with an incurable brain tumour. Knowing Max as I do now, I am sure he would have risen to either challenge but I felt at the time that it was asking a lot of a man who had already been through incredible psychological trauma. The only other man in the same age range was suffering from the early onset of Alzheimer's disease. There was no knowing when he would die. In fact, he deteriorated so rapidly that, two weeks later, his was the body we used to house Axel's brain.'

'The little guy! Gosh, talk about the luck of the draw! If it had been the other way round Axel might have been six foot two and . . .'

'Able to reach the pedals,' she chorused, nodding. It was worse than that, she said. It was a Saturday afternoon and a horse had thrown its rider during a point-to-point and kicked in his skull. The man was rushed to hospital but no one expected him to last the night. Lo and behold he was a card-carrying donor. He was the right age, O-positive and male, a real catch. (O is the one blood group that will not reject other blood groups, apparently.) She made a wry face.

'Don't tell me,' I said, 'he played the piano.'

'In a jazz band.' She tutted regretfully. 'But we weren't to know. We had him brought to Meredith's, where I work, and placed on life support.'

'Does Max know?' I meant about Axel.

'He knows what I've told you. He doesn't know who his donor is. That could lead to all sorts of complications. Eh, Max?' she said, fondly, as he padded over the marble floor to the fridge in his socks. 'And we wouldn't want to add to all your other worries.'

He shrugged, not in the least bit interested in women's talk, took out two cans of beer and was padding back to the lounge when she stopped him.

'Show Clare your scar, Max.'

The famous scowl was back immediately and he clicked his tongue impatiently. Nevertheless, when she gestured with her elfin chin that he should bend down he did so, and she lifted up a lock of fair hair to reveal an ugly zigzag scar where the horse's hoof had smashed through his temple.

Ouch. That blow had killed somebody. He admitted, ruefully, that it was still quite tender to the touch after six months. She could have spared him that, I said, left a few nerves un-knitted so that he wouldn't feel it. They both shrugged. She was a perfectionist.

'What about the other brain transplants?' I said, when he'd gone back to watch the day's highlights. 'Are they happy with the way things are?'

'Seem to be. Ellen Sauerbruch has gone back to live in Germany, Willi Greff to Austria. He has family there. Ellen, we're not sure about. And Friedrich Liebl you know about – the brain is still in a frozen state.'

'The man with the rare blood group?'

'And I stand about as much chance of finding a middle-aged male donor with his blood type as I do of making a snowball in hell.'

3

It was when she said it again, in front of God knows how many million viewers that my heart rolled over. 'While I have the chance, Tom . . .' her thick blue-black hair brushed his shoulder, pretty-please, as she wound him round her finger . . . 'you don't mind if I take this opportunity to make an appeal?'

How could he refuse? She was irresistible, wholesome as fresh baked buns, and as spicy. Wicked burnt-currant eyes flicked over him, promising all sorts of treats. Helpless, he gestured. 'Feel free.'

'I get the feeling that many in the audience would now seriously consider a brain transplant, if not now then at some time in their lives. Am I right?'

There was a buzz of assent and Charlie, on camera three, panned the rows, passing over the doubting Thomases blinking dimly in the dark, and focusing on the bright faces of the converted. You didn't have to suffer old age or disability. You could have the operation. The ayes had it.

She nodded thoughtfully. 'Hmm. I'm sure you can see the problem. Unless more donors come forward, we are going to have to disappoint an awful lot of people. So I'm asking you, please, to at least *consider* becoming a corporal donor –' twinkling as an afterthought – 'on death, I hasten to add!' Once they understood it was a joke, they laughed. 'I know it's a momentous decision to make and many of you will have scruples of a religious or moral nature, or maybe you're just squeamish about the idea of someone else using your body after you've finished with it.'

I wondered whether I could do it – sign away my right to rot in the ground or be burnt to ashes. I thought I probably could. But what about someone else, someone close? Suppose Nick were dying and they asked me to give permission for *his* body to be used in a brain transplant? Could I? Knowing I might bump into him on a train afterwards? Knowing how I'd feel when he looked through me, not recognising me? It would be heartbreaking. I wondered how hard it had been for the parents of Max's body donor to give their permission.

Now she was talking about Friedrich Liebl whom she described as a freethinking German, a young sculptor with a somewhat cynical turn of mind. Grainy old photographs of leering wooden gargoyles flickered over the screens, followed by more serious stone forms, but all with the distinctive crude chiselling you'd associate with whittling. Her eyes slid over them and back to camera, as her expression became more impassioned. 'But because there are no full-body donors on our lists with AB negative blood, it looks as though he will have to remain in limbo, in the hospital freezer.' She'd never mentioned the blood type before, just that it was rare. 'Simply a matter of signing a donor card,' she assured them. It wasn't nearly as time-consuming as giving blood and involved no needles.

Sid and I used to go in for that, father and daughter doing their bit for a cup of tea and a bickie. We'd lie side by side in the Assembly Rooms and discuss heady stuff, like childhood games and seaside holidays and how he'd met Mum at the School of Education. 'She was very superior,' he'd say with pride, 'a two-one in English, and me the pits, in her eyes – a dabbler in paint. But I got round her, by God, and here you are to prove it!'

I remember watching his tube flowing with the red richness of his blood and thinking how superior it was to my poor offering. For his was rare, special, and how he loved having them come round in the middle of the night begging for a pint or two of his life-giving AB negative!

Uh-oh! There was a hitch of some sort. Tom seemed to be ad-libbing, red in the face, and getting that pop-eyed frantic look he got when the cue-board stuck.

It took Alison's sharp elbow in the ear – 'Pull your fucking finger out, Clare!' – to bring me to my senses. I was the one they were waiting for! *I* was the hold-up! Oh God, oh God, I panicked, blinking at the running order through a fog of words and times flying every which way. Where? What?

Seq. 52. Susmeta's appeal. 3 mins. Tom links to hospital clip.

Seq. 53. VT of transplant operation.

Stupid, silly cow! I cued in the video-tape and, as the operating theatre filled the screen, breathed again as Tom gave me the thumbs up under cover of the voice-over. 'Brain surgery, these days, relies heavily on computers . . .' The hiccup was sorted, only a few seconds behind schedule.

Even so my face was burning and I could feel the barbs of accusation glancing off my neck. What had happened? I'd never done that before – drifted off in the middle of a show. Damn Sid and his special blood. Damn him to hell.

'Where the fuck were you, Clare?' the director whirled on me as we hit the break. 'Poor Tom was wetting himself!'

'Oh, honestly, a few seconds, Alison. You couldn't see the join.'

'More like ten by the time he got his act together. I nearly had a fucking heart attack!'

'Forget it, Al, it won't happen again. Is there any coffee?'

'It'd better *not* happen again.' She changed tack, assuming concern. 'It's just not like you, Clare. You're all right, are you? I have to be able to *rely* on my PAs, you know.'

I told her a tale about the stopwatch sticking.

'That's precisely why you're supposed to have *two*, Clare. Failsafe. I suppose you *did* have two?'

I'd lent my other one to Sharon on *New Brooms'*, I said – a complete lie. No PA in the world has two stopwatches. How are you supposed to hold your running order, cue in your sequences *and* keep two stopwatches ticking over?

'You PAs!' She peeled a stick of gum and folded it between her teeth, then tossed back the grizzled hair, exposing her strong, bony face. 'If Charlie hadn't had his wits about him we'd all have been up Shit Creek, ducky. Well, you'd better send a runner to find you a fucking watch that works, hadn't you?'

'Yeah, right.' I puffed on a fag to calm my nerves and saw the runner off on her fool's errand, through twenty rows of chattering people. Snatches of *What if*s and *Just suppose*s wafted in through the open door along with cheesy smell of Pringles and orange peel. Someone said, 'Be on the Internet soon, I'll bet, shopping for a new body – better than going on a diet.'

The glass didn't rattle as Max raised it to his lips during Question Time. I hoped that he was feeling easier, or maybe it was just that the ice had melted.

Someone asked about the tissue samples Susmeta had taken from Max's brain. Presumably they'd yielded other information beside his blood group.

'We could tell he was male, highly intelligent, and that he was under-nourished, lacking in certain essential minerals and vitamins, as would be commensurate with a starvation diet or some wasting illness such as cancer.'

'But his DNA,' insisted Tom, 'surely that would tell you all you needed to know?' He did so like to air his puny knowledge. He clasped his hands in the pose of a doctor listening to symptoms, his index fingers to his lips.

'Not that much actually. Contrary to popular belief,' she

smiled a Canderel smile, 'we are still a long way from being able to divine an individual's looks, personality, life history from his DNA. We learned much more from the extensive CV that Hofmann had the foresight to include when wrapping each brain. He left nothing to chance.'

Tom's chubbiness puckered, a deflated balloon. Wisely he uncrossed his legs and turned to his friends, the audience, for more questions, so many of which Susmeta answered that Alison was forced to hiss, 'She's hogging the fucking screen, Tom. Give the head-case a look in.'

Tom rounded on him, 'Tell me, Max,' who looked up, startled, slopping water from the glass he was secretly sipping. He swallowed furtively and we all thought we saw, for a split second, the labour camp internee snatching at crumbs, lapping at puddles. More kindly, Tom repeated the question, which was about Max seeing himself in a mirror for the first time.

He frowned for focus. We'd been over this. 'It was not such a shock,' he recited, weighing the glass in his hands. 'Parts of my brain were still inflamed or numb. I did not know who or even what I was. If Susmeta said I was Max Zeiler, I had to believe her. I doubt I would have known my own – I mean my *former* reflection.' He paused, said carefully, 'It was not until my brain had settled down, a week or so later, that memory returned and I really understood that I was looking at another man's face. By then I had been counselled and knew what to expect.'

'Right,' said Farrell, pulling at his second chin. 'But it's not a bad face, Max.' His smile was a movement of flesh only. Women in the audience nodded. Oh yes. They liked the eyes, deep-set and shrewd, with faint, fading laughter-lines. When he learned to laugh again they would deepen. The nose was slightly aquiline, the bones were nicely arranged, the lips finely drawn and mobile. You could trust such a face. The close-up prompted a flurry of questions.

Did he know whose face it was? Not by name.

How he had acquired that scar? A riding accident, he believed.

Did food taste the same? Better than in Buchenwald, certainly.

Did he see things differently now? Were colours and shapes the same, seen through another's eyes? How would he know?

Susmeta leaned forward, anxious to explain the scientific reasons but Tom ignored her and took another question from the floor.

Was Max still a socialist? Would he do it all again? Yes and yes. He was giving nothing away.

'Mrs Naidoo,' a questioner hoping for a more revealing answer, 'there were tens of thousands of Jews in Buchenwald, transferred from Auschwitz, and yet there are none among your transplantees. Were no Jewish brains frozen?'

'No,' she said, as shortly as her protégé.

Tom took it upon himself to enlarge on this, 'Not in the Berlin cache. All eighteen were prisoners of conscience.'

'Political dissidents,' Susmeta confirmed. 'Anarchists, communists, all with an IQ of at least a hundred and twenty on the basis of Hofmann's tests.' Her voice honed to an edge of sharp irony, 'And Aryan, good German stock. Quality material for his grisly experiments.' Distaste grooved her lips. 'He was an opportunist.'

'Makes you wonder what he had in mind,' said Tom. 'Do you think he meant to resuscitate them after the war?' I didn't trust that innocent air. He was up to something. Better watch out . . .

'Without question.' The earrings jangled certainty. 'He had the brains stashed away so that whatever the outcome of the war, whoever the victors, he could dig up his cache and continue his research into brain transplantation at leisure. In fact he was so far along there is no doubt that he would have been a forerunner in the field and reaped the glory, had he lived.'

This was the answer he wanted. His eyes narrowed with

cunning. 'But he didn't "reap the glory", as you put it. He was killed in the inmates' uprising in April 1945. I put it to you, Mrs Naidoo –' he shifted, leaned into the camera – 'that we might owe more than we'd care to admit to this man's drive and dedication, and to the political climate that provided him and indeed, your good self, with unlimited experimental material. What do you say?'

What *could* she say? Trust old Tom to put his finger on the truth. The air sang like the wind in barbed wire. She said nothing, merely raised a quizzical eyebrow. He could '*put*' whatever he liked.

He pressed home his point. 'Now we can quit our body for one that is healthier or younger, like a snake sloughs its skin, again and again, until the brain wears out. Why bother with a sex change when a surgeon can slip your brain into something more comfortable? Criminals with cash can hide out in the bodies of innocent victims. It's the last word in recycling, Mrs Naidoo, and all thanks to Klaus Hofmann, wouldn't you say?'

The shrug of her shoulders, her spread fingers and her smile were enigmatic.

'Sorry, guys,' I felt I was intruding, 'thirty seconds left.' He knew. He always timed it so that he could have the last word.

'And on that disturbing note, we have to end this edition of *Way of the World*. Thanks to Susmeta Naidoo, for allowing us an insight into an amazing scientific advance and welcome to our world, Max Zeiler!'

I was counting, 'Ten, nine . . .' but Susmeta had already broken in, with danger glinting in her eye. 'I suppose, according to your lights, Tom, we should thank Klaus Hofmann for the success of both programmes.'

'Both?'

'Mine of medical research and your programme here, tonight.'

'Touché, my dear!' With open arms he acknowledged her prowess, his delighted 'Thank you for watching and goodnight,' drowned in applause.

'Kill overheads, cue signature tune.'

Tom could be heard muttering in the darkness, 'One for the archives, I think.' The switchboard was already blocked with calls.

After the show Susmeta insisted on taking us all to Angelo's to celebrate Max's 'coming out', as she put it.

'Really?' said Jay. 'Why am I always the last to know?' I pointed out his mistake and he touched my glass of champagne with his own, grinning hugely. 'No, no, sweetie,' he said softly, 'I know which way he leans. Did you see how he jumped when I dared to lay hands on him tonight? Old-school homophobic.'

'Was the appeal all right?' Susmeta wanted to know. 'People can't ignore it, can they? They'll have to donate now.'

We assured her that she'd be tripping over donor bodies when she turned up for work in the morning, half of them AB negative. Herr Liebl was on his way.

Nick said, 'I thought they'd got the blood thing sorted. I mean it's not the end of the world if a donor's and a recipient's blood or tissues aren't compatible, is it? Like they can put pigs' organs into humans without fear of rejection.'

'Drugs,' she said, simply. 'More red, anybody?'

'So why –?'

She continued pouring. 'Why not in a brain transplant? Side effects. Even in a heart transplant they can be pretty unpleasant. The immune response has to be suppressed. That's every white blood cell in the body. When the brain's the antigen it's horrendous. Best avoided.' She stared moodily at the empty bottle. 'In fact, two of our brains that died were wrongly cross-matched. The brains couldn't function properly with all the drugs in the system. Freaked out. I'd rather not try that again.'

'I suppose,' said Jay, dissecting his fish neatly and lifting out the spine, 'if you were desperate you could always customise a donor to fit your requirements.'

'How do you mean?'

'Well, it'd be a real downer if your perfect donor turned up – like, they were the right blood group and everything, only they were the wrong sex.' He had a mate, he said, who'd had bits chopped off and turned inside out. Breast implants. They could do wonders. The conversation took a turn for the worse. Everyone knew or had read about similar operations on women who'd had wombs removed, penises and testicles grafted on.

I had to push my red mullet aside. I'd been going to tell them about someone I knew who was AB negative and perfect, apart from his personality, but I thought better of it.

Sex change ops were someone else's territory, Susmeta hastened to assure us. The brain was her brief, never exceeded despite temptations. Surgeons had been struck off for performing life-saving abortions and amputations and suchlike, mid-op, without the patient's express permission.

'Bit difficult when the poor guy's brain-dead,' muttered Tom.

'Technically,' she informed him, 'the transplant recipient *is* the brain – it's the body that's donated.'

She was in her element, the eminent scientist, belle of the ball. The wine flowed freely and she and Tom Farrell behaved quite disgracefully, actually raising their glasses to the memory of Klaus Hofmann, whose frozen brains, they agreed, had been a godsend to them both.

'Off the record, Susie,' said Tom, 'how significant were his experiments?'

'Off the record, Tommy,' she mimicked, pouring herself another glass of red wine, 'I'd say not very.'

Heads turned sharply, forks hovered between plates and mouths. For a shocked second, no one moved.

'There were no constraints – that was the trouble. He was like one of the mad scientists in the Academy of Lagado. *Gulliver's Travels*', she informed anyone who hadn't done 'A' level English. 'They did outlandish things with dogs and stirrup pumps. Tried to extract sunbeams from cucumbers. Hofmann did the same things with people. As his belly guided him. Vile things in the name of research. Not that I know much about it, just what Nick has told me.'

But Nick wasn't prepared to enlighten us. Max, too, was scowling. You couldn't blame him. 'Well, anyway,' she said quickly, 'as far as I can ascertain, he made no lasting contribution to the human condition.'

'But I thought you said . . .' I said.

'Oh the brains were a happy accident. Working on them brought our programme forward in leaps and bounds. But we'd have got there sooner or later.' She paused, delicately, to sip some wine. 'No, it was a shameful waste of opportunity, if you ask me.'

'Susmeta!' Outraged snorts and squeaks of protest echoed my own. Someone choked and had to be banged on the back.

Tom said, 'That is a shocking admission.'

'What is?' She dropped her chin on her knuckles and her wrist gave way. But she righted herself with a giggle and beamed. 'I envy him his free hand, that's all. Most surgeons and researchers would say the same if they were honest. I mean he could have done anything he wanted. *He* didn't have to pussyfoot around red tape, with embryonic stem cells grown in Petri dishes.'

Max regarded her coldly. 'So you think it was a good time to be a doctor.'

She jiggled her head between yes and no. 'I'm saying that, given their opportunities, they should have made real headway in medical research.' She drained an already empty glass. 'And they didn't.'

The morning-after found us all one-eyed and droopy, jammed into the producer's office, listening to the voice-mail. Nick, propped against the filing cabinet beside me, started an epidemic of yawning, as Barry fast-forwarded over a squabble of plaudits and brickbats. At the beginning of the tape these would have been about the new title music or Tom's beer-gut, nothing we could work on. Barry was looking for outrage. Praise was good, outrage better.

Like the peppery old buffer who shook his fist at us over the wires. Science had overstepped the bounds of decency! Where would it all end, dammit? You'd get killed crossing the road and wake up to find they'd been playing Franken-stein with your *brain*. Popped it into some other Johnny's head. It was monstrous! 'And who's to know where Johnny's been?' mused Jay, with his own agenda.

Which was too heavy for Nick to fathom. He shook his head hopelessly and groaned as his brain jangled. 'Take mine. Please. Johnny's welcome to it.'

'They want them frozen, not pickled,' I told him.

'Dear oh dear,' chortled Barry, spiking his espresso with a slug of something from a hip flask. 'Out on the tiles, were we, Robinson? Or somewhere warmer?' He gave me a lascivious wink that curdled my breakfast. Instinctively I edged closer to Nick with an adoring, intimate little smile, and his eyes un-gummed in surprise. What was I after? A hug would have been nice but I settled for a cigarette. There were No Smoking symbols all over the place, put there by Health and Safety or the cleaner. But coffee and fags were our creative fuel, and in the privacy of our own office, between consenting adults, what harm did we do?

The programme had certainly stirred up the silt of people's prejudices. Some cried blasphemy – only God was the Giver of Life. Max Zeiler was, to all intents and purposes, put to *death* in Buchenwald. To add to his allotted span was to deny the Creator. The Naidoo woman was an instrument of the devil. She had incurred the wrath of a jealous God and would burn in hell!

At another extreme were the neo-Nazis who saw nothing wrong with what Hofmann had done. Indeed, according to them, he should be given some sort of posthumous award for his contribution to the human good. The Nobel was mooted. As for Max, it would be reasonable to suppose that, as a beneficiary of the regime he had once vilified, he could well be reviewing his political stance. If he should need further information on the work of the British National Party, he should contact the following number.

Others were more concerned about Max's soul. One guy insisted it had departed his body on death and Max was now soulless or was somehow sharing the soul of his donor. Another reckoned that Max's soul had spent sixty years in limbo and had returned when the brain was resuscitated. I imagined all the frozen souls, curling wisps of vapour, heading off for their holidays.

Then came the voice of reason. 'All power to your elbow, Mrs Naidoo!' she chortled. Lady Eaton of Barking Creek, this was, known to some as the 'Barking Mad' Labour peer, eighty years old and a regular *Way of the World* correspondent. Could she be next, please? she wanted to know. There must be any number of empty-headed nubile young bimbos lying about on mortuary slabs.

My cappuccino exploded. Nick took it from me while I spluttered and Jay peeled himself off the wall to thump me vigorously between the shoulder blades. By the time I'd recovered another voice was speaking, a man's, cracked with age and holding together with Dentigrip.

'Hello? Hello,' he enquired, 'can you hear me? Look, I'm phoning about that programme *Way of the World*? I don't suppose it's of any interest to you at all, but that's me in the photo, the one on the left.' Someone prompted him. 'Eh?' he said crossly and 'What?' and then, 'Oh right, yes – the one of the two soldiers on the road to Madrid.' He cleared his throat. 'I served with Max Zeiler in the war – the Civil War, not the big one. Anyway ask him if he remembers Mallory – Douglas Mallory. We were good mates once. The Eleventh Brigade were all good blokes, even if they *were* Jerries!' As his laughter deteriorated into a fit of coughing we all waited, politely, for him to explain that though the battalion was a German one, they had recruited a few British machine gunners. 'Not that I knew a thing about guns at the start but you soon learn!' Again the wheezy laugh and another aside. 'I *am* getting on with it. Hello? Look, what I'm saying is if old Max is feeling a bit low, he might like to get in touch, talk over old times. I'm on the Central Line. If you could give him my address.' I took it down and his telephone number. He was just up the road from us, in Loughton.

'I don't believe this!' Barry was appealing to the ceiling. 'A contemporary of Zeiler's and this is the first we hear of him? What do I pay you researchers for, for God's sake?' He sighed heavily. 'We could have made something of it, last night. Wheeled him on stage to 'Tipperary' or some such. Too late now.'

Jay was looking pensive. 'That old geezer's Max's age . . .' he murmured, a frown bulging the bridge of his nose. 'If Max hadn't been put into cold storage, he'd be, like, eighty-odd, close to death. Just when things are taking off, technologically. Like when *he's* eighty he could put in for another transplant. He could go on ad infinitum.'

Nick shook his head. 'If he hadn't been put in cold storage, mate, he'd be history. Probably wouldn't have seen the war out.'

Jay's frown deepened. 'He's one lucky son of a bitch.'

'Yeah, right. You'd think he'd act more, like, *pleased*.'

'He's lightened up a lot,' I said hopefully.

'*Laughing*-boy?' said Jay. 'You're joking! I must bring out the worst in him.'

'Ah, babe,' I said, stroking his arm. Jay was such a sensitive soul. But it was true. Max had a real hang-up about gays. He was surprised, he'd told me, that they hadn't found a cure for it.

'He's still adjusting,' Nick assured him. 'He'll get there.'

'Loads of people still can't handle it.'

'Like my old man,' said Nick.

'Ignorant bastard,' said Jay, meaning Max, presumably.

'Right,' said Nick uncertainly. 'I guess he needs to see a bit more of life, get out a bit more.'

'Your dad?'

'Ssshh!' hissed Tom. They were reading the emails.

'He was telling me last night how worried he is about his future,' Nick said, lowering his voice.

'How d'you mean?'

'Well, presumably when Susmeta's finished her research or whatever, she'll chuck him out, and then what's he going to do? He has no job skills that aren't hopelessly out of date. No qualifications, no prospects.'

'He'll have to sign on.'

'Don't social services do this retraining thing?'

'And how's he gonna live in the meantime? Sell *Big Issue*?'

'There must be something.'

'Put a sock in it, you lot,' snarled Alison.

But our friend's future was far more important than the opinions of a few old viewers, none of whom were pianists offering to donate their bodies to a good cause, or AB rhesus negatives responding to Susmeta's appeal. She'd be disappointed.

'Too much to expect old Hofmann to have provided for Max's old age. Left him a little nest egg somewhere.'

'It wouldn't even have occurred to him, Jay. He didn't think of his experiments as people, with needs.'

'Bet he forgot about them as soon as they were put into store.'

I had this vision of Nan laying down apples for winter, wrapping them up in paper, just as Hofmann must have done, placing them gently in their boxes, separately, so that they didn't touch one another and bruise, and labelling them 'Cox,' 'Russet,' 'Worcester Pearmain,' before carrying them down into the cellar. I shivered suddenly as someone walked over my grave, and then I caught a thought by the tail before it slipped out of my head again.

'Nick . . .' I said slowly.

But he was saying something about Hofmann being more concerned with covering his own back in the event of an Allied victory. 'Probably had his passage booked on the first flight out to South America and an alias laid on.'

'Shame he never made it.'

'You're joking!'

'Nick,' I said again.

'Yeah?'

'What exactly was on those identity papers that were wrapped round the brains?'

'Just that – their identity. Their name and prison number, age, sex, nationality, that sort of thing, IQ, politics, medical history.' His eyes narrowed as he burrowed deeper into his memory. 'The date they were frozen, oh yeah, and their classification. Political prisoners were mostly Class Three: Enemies of the Third Reich – Leniency Recommended.'

'As opposed to . . .?'

'Not. Undesirables and such.' He made a throat-cutting gesture.

'Was there anything about the operation? Like where it was done and by whom?' He pushed out his lower lip, and frowning, shook his head. 'So how do we know these were

Buchenwald prisoners? That Hofmann was the surgeon? I mean they could have come from anywhere. Anyone might have done it, Mengele, even.'

'No,' he frowned. 'No, there was a letter. At least . . .' He pushed his glasses further up his nose. Harry Potter aged twenty-seven-and-a-half. 'Yeah, I'm pretty sure there was a letter saying that Hofmann was, like, the brain behind the brains. I mean how else would we know?'

'There was no stamp on the freezer, like Property of Buchenwald KZ?' I said.

'Nope, just the make.'

'So where is it now?'

'What?'

'The letter.'

'Search me. With the German authorities? In some museum or other?'

'You never saw it?'

'Nope.'

'Hmm.' For some reason I wanted to see that letter more than anything.

'It was all in German, anyway. And it didn't say much, apart from, you know, the surgical details, how he'd gone about removing the brain from the skull, the freezing process – blow by gruesome blow. Oh and the fact that he hoped that by the time the brains were found someone would have come up with a way of reconstituting them. You know all that.'

I sucked the roof of my mouth. 'Yeah . . .' but how did I know? Hearsay. It was going to bug me until I saw Hofmann's letter with my own eyes. Don't ask me why. Something to do with loose ends.

We went through the reviews next. *The Times* accused us of milking the Holocaust for our own ends and 'rivalling The Jerry Springer Show for cheap sensationalism.' The *Sun* picked up on Tom's tough manner. 'Ve hef vays of making you talk!' made their headlines, with a huge photo of Tom, sporting a Hitler moustache and haircut. It was very good. One for the office wall, we decided.

But, for the first time in a week, there wasn't a mention of brains on any of the other front pages. The main news was the Lords' demo.

There had been tantrums in the House. Nanny would have been shocked! What a to-do. Grown men and women waving banners and baying for blood! No wonder they were having their titles taken away. Adopting a low profile would have been the most dignified course of action but luckily for *Way of the World*, keeping one's head down did not come easily. Tomorrow night's programme would practically write itself. But that was the end of the Brain Transplant story. The news is dead – long live the news.

This was the bit I liked, when the air crackled with creativity, when a dozen intellects brainstormed a programme into being.

We were going to try and get the ringleader of yesterday's fiasco, Lord Halifax, on the show, providing they let him out in time. And Lord Titherille was always good value. He had played merry hell when they'd kicked him and the other 'hereditaries' out of the Upper House back in the nineties. And when he'd failed to get himself elected back in on the BNP ticket, he'd accused the government of ballot rigging.

Nazim was the one to interview him – someone nice and provocative to bring out the old boy's racism. He and Alison would pop up to Ottley Place for the grand tour and then whiz round the motorway to Thurwell, home of 'Rocking' Lord Fittlewell. When he realised they'd be taking me along as PA, Nick acted really pissed off.

'Think of me, won't you, down in the bowels of the

British Library all afternoon while you're boogying the afternoon away.'

'Boogying?'

'Don't tell me it hadn't occurred to you the Festival is on this weekend.'

'Is it?' I'd forgotten. 'Oh shame,' I pouted, in mock sorrow.

'Bugger off,' he grumped, with the barest hint of a grin. 'Tell you what though.' His wire frames glinted as the idea caught. 'You could take Max. Get him to let his hair down a bit.'

'Nick!' I groaned. Surely we'd done our duty now that the show was over?

'Oh go on,' said Nick. 'Poor guy. Who else does he have?'

I thought it might be cool to get a life peer's angle and was ordering the car to bring Lady Eaton to the studio the following night when a hush fell over the office. I'd said we'd film her at home – she was pretty decrepit – but she wanted to be here, in the thick and buzz of it. She didn't want to have to spend all day exhausting herself, she said, trying to make the place and herself presentable.

As I pushed the CLEAR button, wondering vaguely why people were gazing towards the door, I realised we were being invaded. A stranger was breaching security, shouldering a knot of lately arrived technicians into a metal clatter of filing cabinets, a stocky middle-aged gent, wearing a cream cotton suit, and carrying a walking stick. There was an unreal familiarity about his sagging face, like it was the death mask of someone you knew. In fact, though his mouth was zipped tight to give nothing away, he radiated agitation and pain. He flung open the door to Barry's office and, through the glass, we could see him limping over to the producer's desk, leaning across, drawing back his arm as though to release an arrow, and flattening Barry's not inconsiderable nose. As Barry's feet came up, his wheelie-chair carried him crashing and howling into the wall.

For a moment we were all too stunned to move. The stranger's puffy eyes were bleary, and his mouth, pale in a stricken face, was twisted with grief. As Barry snuffled into a bloody hanky and moaned, we had no doubt who was suffering more.

The man's voice was foggy with tears. 'You don't care who you hurt, you people, you *media*!' He used his walking stick for emphasis. It had a point on the end, a steel tip for digging into loose ground. It occurred to me as he pointed it at Barry, that it would make a good weapon in a crowded tube. Rather like my grandmother's umbrella. 'Just so long as you can shock and disgust!' he was going. 'You're . . . you're despicable, *all* of you!'

Well, yes. What was new?

'That was my son, Leon, you had on there last night. His body. He died on New Year's Day at the point-to-point. Horse's hoof through his skull.'

And that, of course, was why he looked so familiar, this guy with his son's deep-set eyes, his nose and chin – he looked like Max. Or rather, he looked like the guy whose body Max had been put into.

'Fuck,' said Alison.

The man looked at her, through her, and continued, 'Imagine how we felt, Jean and I, switching on, halfway through the programme, and seeing Leon, alive again . . .' There was a gnawing ache in his voice and he swayed. Alison put out a hand, but he flung it off, steadied himself on the desk. His cheeks were wet. 'He seemed so like his old self, strong and well. We couldn't think how it might have happened but it didn't matter because there he was. Leon wasn't dead at all. And then,' he growled, breathing hard to smother a sob, 'and then we learned that it wasn't Leon at all, but some German, some Max Zeiler, strutting around.' His face twisted and for a moment he gave in to his grief, unable to help himself. Someone offered him a chair, someone else a tissue, but he sniffed for control and spat out the words, 'Strutting around in our son's body!'

Tom's eyes were popping. It was a pose we'd seen before, Münch's 'Scream' with the spread fingers of both hands held either side of a dropped jaw. It usually got a laugh. Jay, next to me, flicked his lighter and sucked on a tab with a troubled frown. Nick was breathing hard, eyes and lips shut tight against pain.

Alison said, 'But you knew he'd left his body to science?'

'Of *course* we knew,' he said scathingly. 'We had no body to bury.'

Nick blinked. 'They didn't tell you they were using him for a brain transplant?'

'They did, but . . .'

'But you had no warning about last night's programme?'

The man bowed his head, mouthed a silent no.

'Oh Christ . . .' I said, nothing more adequate coming to mind. What can you say to a man who has seen his child die, and seen him again six months later, large as life on some TV chat show, walking, talking, making a mockery of his loss? I'd never really been touched by death except in a vicarious, second-hand sort of way, by a film or a book or music. There was Granddad, of course, but I'd been very young when he died, and he'd been ill for ages. All the same I was saddened by other people's sadness. 'Oh poor Mister –?'

'Paterson,' he said. 'George Paterson. My son was Leon.'

'How is your wife taking it? Is she all right?'

He looked at me and a mirthless, hollow sound escaped his lips. 'My wife is in hospital. I've just come from there. The shock was too much for her.'

'Oh my God,' said Jay, 'she's not –?'

'She doesn't know me. It's a breakdown, they say.'

'Will he sue, do you think?' asked Tom, anxiously, when

Paterson had gone, escorted by Security men who couldn't think how he'd got past them, unless he'd slipped in with the crowd from the game show.

Barry sniffed, removed the hanky from his nose and examined it closely. With tender care, he dabbed again at the damage and had another look. The flow seemed to be staunched. The chair's backward journey had dulled the blow. There were no breakages. 'More to the point, will I sue him?' he sulked, nasally. 'For assault,' he explained when nobody spoke. He caught our eyes and shrugged. He wouldn't sue.

His secretary produced a mirror and tissues and he cleaned his face, grumbling all the while about having to take the brunt of someone else's slip-up. He'd assumed, he said, stupidly, that *someone* would have had the fore-thought to *warn* the Patersons. A fairly basic prerequisite in the circumstances. Alison? Clare? Nick? Wasn't that what delegation was all about? What the minions got paid for? Covering eventualities like this?

Stands to reason, Nick's eyebrows were telling me, there has to be a scapegoat. No point in arguing.

When it was clear that Barry would live to produce tomorrow's programme, the 'minions' began to steal away. Tom went off to fix himself a lunch date with Lord Halifax. Nick opened up the Internet to begin his search for truth. Jay and I thought we might just have time, if we skipped lunch, to pop along to the Summer Sales. Jay needed cheering up after Paterson. And you can't go to a rock concert in a T-shirt and last year's jeans.

4

I tucked in front of a bus, at the lights, to make a duty call on the car-phone. 'Hi, it's me. How you doing?'

'Badly,' he groaned.

He'd only just got up. Lightweight. One late night and he was done for. I suppose it took some getting used to, all that wine, and Angelo's wonderful food. Susmeta had had Max following her own strict regime: regular hours, regular exercise, a balanced diet and easy on the booze. But in celebration of the programme's success she had let him off the leash.

I'd caught him in the shower, apparently, and it was now around noon. But then Max didn't have to go to work like the rest of us. Yet.

Actually, he said, he had been reading up some ex-prisoners' accounts of Buchenwald, on the Internet. 'Excerpts from Behind the Wire.' It had brought it all back.

'Oh, not the war again.' I didn't mean to sound so dismissive but it's all he ever did, download stuff about the camps, the Nuremberg trials, who'd been caught and punished, who'd escaped. I could see the fascination, of course. He had to know what he'd missed, how the Third Reich had collapsed, how Germany had been governed by the Allies and Russia, about walls going up and coming down, how the world had evolved, but honestly, this was the twenty-first century. He should be trying to put all that behind him now.

I caught myself frowning into the driving mirror, checking my newly dyed eyelashes. (Nan was right – they helped.) And even while I was telling myself that I didn't want the responsibility, that the me-Nick-and-Max threesome was becoming too claustrophobic, I was glad I'd just bought the black lace crop-top. I'd been eyeing the skimpy, sleeveless affair all week on my way to work and a rock-concert was just the excuse I needed. It was so transparent I'd had to add a black bra to the bill, and a pair of leather hipsters that were now laced from waist to ankles with thongs. The three bondage belts had been an inspiration and the skimpy sandals. Jay had bought a hot-pink vest for himself, a dinky little plastic shoulder bag, and a romper suit for his sister's new baby.

Nick was right. Being shut away with the computer Susmeta had given him wasn't good for him. Max needed to get out and see what people our age were up to, broaden his mind. Susmeta wouldn't think of it. She didn't go in for western music.

He seemed keen to come on the shoot. 'Be with you in ten minutes,' I said, furiously indicating right. 'Wear something casual.'

The guy in the builder's van made a dreadful fuss, giving me the long finger, blamming his horn and yelling, 'Silly bitch,' and suchlike, out of his window. But, hey, it's a girl's privilege to cut across. For all they knew I could have been a midwife answering an emergency call.

Susmeta was at the hospital, he said when he came to the door. That was the housekeeper I could hear, buzzing away with the vacuum cleaner in the basement. Come in, come in. He would nuke us some hot food in the micro-wave. It would only take a few minutes. He loved all the new gadgets and wanted to show off.

I *was* hungry. There was a Mars bar in the glove com-partment, but the call of real food was almost irresistible. Almost.

'Uh, no, it's okay, thanks,' I said, retreating down the steps, ignoring my stomach's protest as his eyes bored into my belly button. 'The crew will be halfway there by now. They'll only get into mischief if they have to hang around.

And Alison will blame me.' Alison and Nazim were travelling together in his Porsche, so they'd linger over lunch in 'La Belle Etoile' and then do a ton up the outside lane, catch us up.

If ever they were late, Al liked to think she could trust the crew to occupy themselves gainfully, shoot a few general views until she turned up. But I knew if I wasn't there to chivvy them, they'd be in the nearest pub, no worries. That was the reason I was in a hurry to get away from Bayswater. It really was. Nothing to do with a different sort of mischief that was turning me on, the sort that had to do with towel-dry hair and aftershave, with a skin-tight T-shirt and jeans, with a level, appreciative gaze and a mouth that twitched at the corners, with shower-fresh pheromones that were playing havoc with my senses.

That walk to the car was like wading through Southend mud. I had to grit my teeth and think how sensible and grown-up I was being. Or how truly pathetic. OK, so it was the first time I'd ever really been alone with Max but he was the old-fashioned sort, the perfect gent, who opened doors for you and gave you his seat on the bus. He could be trusted not to take advantage of a situation to poach a mate's girlfriend. I mean, that slightly sozzled leer over the panna cotta last night had been well out of order and we both knew it. He was still grieving for Sophie, his girlfriend of sixty years ago.

As for me, I was with Nick, and as comfortable with him as in a pair of old trainers. But Max was intriguing. War-hero, torture victim, political prisoner, it was all in there somewhere, behind tawny, lion eyes, so still and watchful they gave you goose bumps. In any case his room was up three flights of stairs, at the top of the house. Not worth the climb or the complications, I told myself firmly.

'I thought you were finished with me,' he said.

60

'Sorry?' Getting onto the M25 was taking all my attention. The traffic was thick and fast. It was like jumping onto a whirling roundabout in a kiddies' playground.

'Now that the programme is over, I didn't think you'd want to see me again.'

'Not true,' I said. I didn't tell him it had been Nick's idea. (We were onto the motorway, and that lorry had only given us a token horn-blast. God, why do they have to sound like ships coming into harbour? Now we were sliding across to my favourite spot on the outside lane, I could relax.) 'You don't get rid of me that easily.'

'Why is that, Clare?'

Careful, I thought, keep it light, impersonal. 'Well, you're an interesting guy. Been through the mill and – and like now you're making a go of it.'

'You don't know the half of it,' he said darkly.

'I *know* . . .' I said, deliberately misunderstanding him, sounding like Prunella Scales in *Fawlty Towers*. 'It was *so* a waste of material. I mean a great story like that? You could have done *so* much more with it. I told them it should have been a full-length documentary – an hour, hour-and-a-half, excluding breaks. At least. Forty minutes simply doesn't do it justice.' I flashed the guy in front, who grudgingly pulled over and let me through. 'I suppose now you'll sell your story to the tabloids. Or write a book.' I gathered, from his expression of distaste, he wasn't particularly up for that. 'And Barry will gnash his terrible teeth and roll his terrible eyes at another missed opportunity.'

'You think you could have done better?'

'I know so, baby. *I* can direct. They've let me do bits and pieces – back-story and stuff – and I reckon I've scored a few brownie points.' I nodded firmly, though I had wondered, at the time, whether 'gutsy and innovative' were the most flattering ways in which Barry could have described my efforts. 'They're supposed to be grooming me for higher things – and Jay – it's in the contract, but Alison's not likely to drop dead suddenly and give either of us a chance. Our only hope is to try another company or,' I floated a last resort through my brain, 'go freelance. Come up with a really brilliant idea, and some funding.'

'You have the idea.'

'Yeah?'

'Me. And the others, of course. The other frozen chickens. You could tell our stories, direct the film. From battery-farm to table, as it were.'

I made a face at his analogy, for my birds were already up and flying. Between junctions four and five we'd come up with a rough kind of story-line, the main character, Max Zeiler, and possible locations – Hanover, his home town, was a must, and Buchenwald, of course, the salt mines, where he had worked for a while, and wherever else was important to him or home to his fellow survivors. I was afraid he'd say no, that it would be too harrowing, revisiting these places, but he was up for it, surprisingly so. Presumably, having faced his demons in the chat show he'd come to realise that they weren't so bad, mildly therapeutic, in fact, and was now ready to scotch them once and for all. In fact I could never be sure whose idea it was, his or mine.

'Now all we need is the backing,' I said.

He was quiet for a while and when I slid him a glance found him deep in thought, pressing his knuckle into his lip and nibbling at the soft skin.

'Perhaps I *should* write a book. Make some money for you.'

I smiled. It was a kind thought, but I sure as hell wasn't going to have him give away all his secrets before I got my hands on them. Any books would come out of my documentary. For the structure was taking shape. Images, camera shots, were flooding into my head – the bunker in Berlin, the freezer filled with intriguing packages . . . and the letter. Hofmann – I'd have an actor, of course – writing the letter, putting it inside some waterproof skin, and slipping it down among his grisly handiwork, before shutting the freezer lid and sealing it with concrete.

The Mars bar had melted by the time I got round to it, and was impossible to eat without forceps and theatre gowns. Never mind, we'd eat when we got there. These stately homes always had restaurants.

I thought I'd better warn him. 'The guy we're going to see first, Lord Titherille?' I made an apologetic face. 'He's a bit of a fascist, I'm afraid – well, more than a bit. He makes no secret of his connection with the far right. He was one of Mosley's Blackshirts, I think, in the war.' Muscles tightened around his eyes as he replayed scenes from his recent past, confronted his enemies. 'But you don't have to meet him,' I assured him. 'You can have a wander round the grounds 'til we're ready to leave.'

'And this is allowed?'

'What – wandering round the grounds?'

'For such a man to have high office?'

'Oh yes – freedom of speech and all that. As long as he doesn't actually frighten the horses, he can think what he likes, even get up and spout his horrible beliefs in Parliament. Or he could. They kicked the hereditary peers out of the House of Lords a few years back. He has no power now, no voting rights at any rate. And his title's about to go the same way.'

'He is to be stripped of his title?'

'No. He'll be Lord Titherille until he dies. But it'll end there. His son won't inherit the title. He'll just be plain Mister. There will only be life peerages from now on. That's why we're interviewing him – to get his reaction.'

'There will be no more aristocracy?'

'Just a few close relations of the monarch, I think.'

He thought about it. 'But he will still have influence . . .'

'He was never a threat, you know, Max. They aren't, in this country, the fascists. I mean you find them on street corners, looking ugly and shooting their mouths off about asylum seekers and Jews and blacks but they're mostly ignorant thugs and, although one or two might get elected, accidentally, onto local councils, when there's a low turn-out, no one takes them seriously. Except the poor sods they beat up. It's not like Austria where the Freedom Party actually wins seats in their national elections. I mean that's scary. France and Germany have actually banned them, you know. And so they take to the Internet, hateful people.'

'They did not learn from Hitler's mistakes?'

'Hitler's *mistakes*? You're joking, aren't you?' I said.

Ottley Place was a spread and a half, boasting a deer park, kiddies' playground, plant centre, maze, every sort of garden, a restaurant. 'Vee haf vays of making you pay and dogs to bite you if you don't.'

We saw four being exercised – mean and slavering German Shepherds, guard dogs presumably. A couple of mean and slavering skinheads in black polo necks and leathers were straining to hang onto their leads. You could almost imagine Nazi uniforms and barbed wire. I thought I wouldn't interfere with them.

When the mobile rang, it was Alison to tell me that a tyre had blown and the lovely Porsche was even now being prised off the crash barrier. Nazim was hysterical and Al wasn't too coherent. 'All he wants to do is go home,' she wailed.

'To Tooting?'

'Madras! You'll have to do it without us, Clare,' she said.

'What!' My heart turned over.

'I have every faith in you. You know exactly the sort of

thing we want: one or two shots of the house and grounds, and a few talking heads.'

'Talking about *what*?' I squeaked.

'Oh, you know, their opinion about whether the country has suffered from the absence of the hereditary voice in Upper House . . .'

'Hang on!' I was doing the shorthand.

'Any bitterness.'

'Yes, I'm bloody bitter, Al, I'm not ready for this . . .'

'Silly girl, you can do it on your head,' she said. 'Get him to gripe. You know, a good old moan. How does he feel about his title dying with him? Democracy, that's always good for a laugh. Wind him up. Dictatorships, that sort of thing.'

'Shit, just a minute.' I scribbled down the key words.

'And Clare?'

'What?'

'Be nice to him – he's got shares in our fucking company.'

'Oh great. That's all I need.'

Max insisted on coming with me to meet the Titherilles. He was curious, he said. I wasn't too keen, myself. Having said I could direct I was now going to have to prove it.

Lord and Lady Titherille tottered out onto the steps, all ready to be broadcast nationwide, wearing some sort of Victorian tropical gear (he only needed a pith helmet) and a frumpy sundress that looked as though it had last seen life as a sofa cover. They eyed my lace and leathers with undisguised suspicion.

It felt rather cheeky, I have to say, asking an aristo his views on his own demise, but it was clearly his hobbyhorse and he went straight for the groin.

'What do they know about running the country, all these jumped-up actors and novelists?' I smiled nervously, not immediately catching his drift. As he went on about the scum rising to the surface and greasy palms, it dawned on me that he was referring to the meritocracy. 'What the PM wants are advisers, not spin doctors and sycophants – people with breeding, whose judgement he can count on, people with experience of managing affairs of state, making crucial decisions. It's what we've been doing for generations. *Generations.*' He paused to let that sink in. 'And doing damned well, I might say. *Damned* well.'

'I see.' That seemed fairly bitter. Encouraged, I grasped the wind-up handle. 'They're extremely well thought of,' I said, 'the novelists and actors who make it to the Lords. Revered, I would say – I mean they're all experts in their chosen fields and they have, em, informed views on a broad range of topics . . .'

He gave me dead, tortoise eyes under scaly lids. His wife shifted her spectacles down her nose, the better to observe me. I didn't dare look at Max. I could hear Charlie tutting behind his tripod. Presumably Nazim wouldn't, in a thousand years, have said anything so crass and obvious.

I swallowed over a dry throat and continued, 'There are ex-cabinet ministers, ex-*prime* ministers. Very experienced in running the country. And all those heads of industry and commerce, university professors,' I was having to think now, 'churchmen, scientists, em, high-court judges . . .' My voice gave out. Coffee would have been nice.

His eyes simply closed and clicked opened again to a pitying gaze. He spoke quite kindly. 'Look around you, my *dear* . . .' His chin inscribed a creaky semi-circle, down through parkland and woods and meadows, to a quiet river caressed by willow trees, and curving up again to fields of pretty sheep and cows. 'Ottley Place has been home to the nobility for more than four hundred years. Four *hundred*,' he reiterated. 'It is a monument, a *monument* to, ah, to traditional values, to stability, to the Titherilles' guiding principles of decency, truth and honour, loyalty, duty . . .' You could almost hear the accompanying strains of some rousing march. 'They may take away our voice in government, they may take away our titles, but they cannot take away what we have been, what we will be again, the moral voice of the country. All this wishy-washy democracy will pass, you'll see, and with it crime and unemployment. People want to be *told* what to do, what to believe. Firm leadership, that's what's needed. A firm hand.'

It was a prepared speech and his purple lower lip quivered as he paused for a fanfare or a cheer, maybe, from his audience. Sadly the only sound were the ducks on the lake, until someone calmly said, 'Bollocks!'

It was Max. I don't know where he picked up such words. 'Truth and honour?' he went on, smiling like the snake in the Disney film. 'Decency? I do not think so, Count. The only guiding principle the English aristocracy lives by is self-interest.'

My own self-interest nudged his elbow, but he ignored me, sailed on, his face taut, his eyes dangerous, the scar at his temple ticking away like a time bomb. 'You are afraid that people will ask themselves, "Just what is it that entitles one man to all *this*?" His own noble chin parodied the old man's earlier gesture. 'You have managed to erect a *rauchwand*, a smoking screen of manners, hoping that we do not peer too closely and find out that your right to have your feet on our necks died out with feudalism. It is no longer, em, no longer legitimate. It is a mighty bluff.'

Lord Titherille hooked a tufty eyebrow. And your point is? He raised his head. 'If every bluff were called, young man, the world would implode.' And he and his wife both stretched up necks like knotted tights, to see how he would take that.

Max shook his head in despair. Her ladyship was thought-ful; around her eyes and lips papery skin began to crinkle. 'Haven't we met before?' she demanded at length.

I explained that it was unlikely, though he had been in the news. They might have seen his photo in the paper or . . .

'Dashed if it isn't that actor-fellow, takes the part of the doctor, tall one in the green overalls, on that programme about the hospital. Without the spectacles, of course.'

'No, dear, it's the brain-transplant – the Buchenwald person. He was on last night. On this young lady's programme. Don't you remember you thought they were talking about the brain drain?'

'Exactly so, they'll have to dig deeper into their pockets, pay them what they're worth. Can't have them all running off to America, doctors *or* actors.'

Oh dear. I asked whether, in view of our limited time, they would mind giving us the guided tour *now*.

Max said, 'Thank you, no,' and was already crunching gravel in the direction of the restaurant when the champion of good manners saw his own chance to escape and hallooed after him.

'I say, young fellow. Mind if we have a chat?'

'Max . . .' I wanted to warn him, beg him to be careful. Whatever the old boy wanted to talk about it was likely to be something tactless and offensive, like the good old days of the Third Reich or an insider's view of the Hofmann set-up. I hoped Max wouldn't hit him.

He winked, which didn't reassure me in the least.

We did the guided tour, upstairs and down, following my lady through one chamber and another, Ez with his lights, Jo humping the reflector screen, Charlie and Bryn with camera and sound equipment, while I clicked away the minutes, jotted down the time, the words, the action and the replays, occasionally darting out to move a chair into focus, a picture into the light or to re-position Lady T's hand for the umpteenth time, for continuity's sake. I could have done with a PA.

There were more rooms than I'd bargained for: saloons and parlours, long rooms and short, above and below stairs. By Queen Elizabeth's bedchamber I sat down and wept, just about. The room was so called, her ladyship recited, because Her Virgin Majesty had stayed one night *en route* to somewhere else. The love and devotion with which the family had showered their sovereign were so considerable it was felt apposite to frame and display the household accounts for that week beside the *very* four-poster she had slept in. While Charlie changed the lens to do them justice, I took myself to the window seat and used the clipboard to fan myself with sweet fresh air, just as Max and his lordship emerged from the door to the private apartments across the courtyard. Max seemed to be smiling. It must be fairly amusing, ironic maybe, to discover that the enemy had had its teeth drawn, was a batty old dog, baying at the moon.

I was shattered. In fact I must have been looking pretty grim because Lady T asked whether I was feeling unwell. I admitted to a headache but said I'd be fine once I'd had a cup of coffee – hint, hint.

'Come with me,' she said, 'I think we might do better than coffee.' And I distinctly heard her muttering something about a 'few sandwiches'. Thank the absolute Lord, I thought, food at last!

She took us to the Physick Garden. The old man was already there, dead-heading chives. Max had disappeared.

It turned out to be *fever*few sandwiches that she'd had in mind for my headache. She picked leaves from a white, aromatic weed I recognised from Nan's garden and off she went to get Cook to put some bread and butter round it, while Charlie, Jo and Ez sniggered nastily. They'd had a fry-up at a Little Chef on the way in.

When it arrived, my dainty white sarnie with the crusts cut off, everyone fell about, spluttering into their light meters. I had to spit it out behind the sundial while my hostess was rooting around in the border. It was like chewing arsenic between cardboard. When she presented me with a dozen mixed and muddy herbs wrapped up in damp newspaper I was speechless with gratitude.

By now, of course, the restaurant was closed. I was just in time to see Max emerging, fed and watered. He'd had chicken salad, he said, and a beer. I had to make do with Ottley Place fudge from the shop, at three quid a throw. *And* I devoured the Mars bar as soon as I had the car doors open. As Max was handing over his hanky for me to wipe my hands, he dropped his bombshell. He'd been propositioned, he said. The twenty-somethingth in line to the throne had offered to patronise him, as in days of yore – to pay for further education, set him up in business, whatever.

'Well, that's nice . . .' I began, but Max was shaking his head.

'It is not nice, Clare,' he said. 'In return, I am to use my influence with Susmeta to have his brain removed and frozen. Life is intolerable, he says, in the present climate. He wants to be resuscitated, into a younger body, at that time in the future when the monarchy has passed, democracy is failing and the country is ripe for dictatorship. He will step into the breach.'

I exploded with laughter, spraying him with chocolatey spit. 'Sorry, sorry,' I said, mopping his cheek and trying to straighten my face. 'Oh dear – I hope you told him where to get off.'

'But we need the money, Clare. You have to make your film, hire your assistants, pay me for my starring role.' He managed an elastic grin. 'Yes, it would be good for us both and wouldn't it be the ultimate in irony – the stupid fascist paying for a film against the Nazis?'

'I wouldn't touch his money with a ten foot barge pole. Don't even think about it.'

'But . . .'

'No, Max.'

He slumped, brooding over his dirty handkerchief. Women . . . I could see him thinking. I said, cheerily, 'There's more than one way of killing a cat . . .'

'A cat?' he spluttered in exasperation. 'Why would you?'

'You'll see.'

5

We arrived at the Thurwell turnoff around three and spent the next half hour bumping and grinding down rutted country lanes, in a queue of vehicles heaving with camping gear and heavy rock. Bikers racketed past in clouds of dust, dark outriders, deaf and blind to the common herd, who roused themselves from sweltering torpor to yell vigorous complaint. Then came the walkers, strapped like martyrs to their towering backpacks and clanking with billycans, taking such gibes as came their way with grim stoicism.

Max was still sulking. To get his mind off rich fascists with more money than sense, I thought I might as well improve the shining hour – get him talking about his work as a British agent. After the first few grudging sentences, I asked him if I could tape it. This was something I could use in the documentary.

It had been his job to get people out of Germany, he said. Jewish people, mostly. He thought for a moment, and decided to tell me about a family called Wolff – Shimon, a prosperous art dealer, and his wife Rebecca, their teenage sons, Isak and David, and Rebecca's elderly mother, Gerda. They'd been living in this big house on Leopoldstrasse, on the outskirts of Berlin before *Kristalnicht* 1938. Soon after, the SS forced their way in and stripped the house – all their art treasures, their precious books, most of Rebecca's couturier clothes, her furs, were loaded into a truck and removed to God knows where. The Wolffs knew they, too, would have to disappear or die. Friends hid them in a cellar for some time but, inevitably, it became too dangerous and they packed what jewels they had salvaged, precious papers and money, and a change of clothes, and, trusting to a stranger, a member of the German resistance, followed him down into the sewers with their shoes tied round their necks, to spend the next couple of days wading through the liquid waste of Berlin towards the overflow outlet in the River Havel. It was a slow, stinking, nauseous journey, without sleep and with food that had to be eaten from the paper it was wrapped in, not handled in any way, for fear of contamination. In any case, with indescribable sludge between your bare toes and foetid liquid swirling around your ankles, sometimes up to your knees, food was the last thing on your mind. It was more important to keep your footing on that treacherous bottom. Once down, your chances of getting up again were slim. You'd be washed forward by the current and lost in the dark.

It was hard, but they knew that discovery would be harder and that, eventually, they would make it, to a grating Max told them about, and blessed fresh air. They would have to wait for cover of night before prising the grid loose and climbing out onto the stony bank of the river. There they would bury their soiled clothes, clean themselves up as best they could in the river, and put on dry things before covering their tracks and making their way to the road bridge to hide, sleep and await transport to the coast. Having seen the family stowed into empty crates on the lorry, his job would be over. He would lie low for a couple of days in a safe house, recovering his strength, and then return to Berlin for the next pick-up.

Despite the awful stench and darkness, they set out in good spirits, paddling along behind Max, chatting quietly about what they would do when they reached their daughter in England. All except Grandma. She went quieter and quieter, deeper and deeper into herself. And when they stopped to rest and eat, she wouldn't. She'd picked up some sort of bug and by the second day, was so weak she had to be half carried between two of them. Oh God, she groaned, why didn't they just leave her there to die? Maybe the SS would find her – a labour camp would be better than this. They shouldn't have such a burden. She was holding them up. She would be the death of them all.

They certainly had no intention of abandoning her, despite being behind schedule. Perhaps they'd have to forego their wash in the river – a small price to pay. Be brave, Grandma, said the boys. In a few hours we'll be out of here and on our way to the coast. Shimon and David were in front, with the old woman, and Max was back marker, with her ridiculously heavy suitcase on his shoulder, when a spasm took her and she doubled over, moaning with pain. They hushed her. Sound travels along the tunnels, above the splashing of water, the confluence of streams, and who could say who might be listening to the subterranean echoes?

'Mother-in-law, you must be quiet,' Shimon cautioned again, in a hoarse whisper. 'We're nearly there. Try and hold on. Mother-in-law, don't struggle.' But she couldn't bear the two men to witness her pain and degradation and slipped out of their grasp. 'Gerda!' cried Shimon as, in throwing them off, she lost her balance and went down into the torrent. Their cries seemed to carry along the cold dripping length of the sewer, but they were useless. She was gone. Although Shimon went after her, his torch beam playing over the murky water, and he grabbed at maybe the hem of her dress, her bare foot, maybe some other detritus, he came back empty-handed. He would have slipped under himself if David hadn't caught him, made him realise that it wasn't his fault.

'It was too much to expect them to mourn her quietly, to sob, to grieve, to curse the regime that had brought them to this extremity, in whispers.' Max passed a hand over his eyes. 'When we reached the turn-off to the overflow duct, we dared to hope that all might still be well. It was very dark and very quiet. The drain was dry. The only water we could hear was behind us and ahead, the river, with a different, fresher sound.

'The grating was rusty and stiff and we had to hammer the edges loose with the heels of our shoes. Eventually it fell away . . .' His eyes had taken on a faraway look and I knew there wasn't going to be a happy ending. 'It slithered down the bank and the others followed, ahead of me. Immediately, searchlights blinded us and I saw my friends put their hands in the air. The SS had caught us like rabbits. Shots rang out and one of the boys fell to the ground. I kicked Grandma's suitcase into a crevice and came out with my hands up. Our truck was waiting for us, but the driver was dead. They used it to take us back into Berlin for questioning. I never saw the Wolffs again.'

My eyes were wet. Dear God, this man and his ability to make me cry. I said gruffly, 'That's when they took you to Buchenwald.'

'Eventually.' His mouth twitched as though there was more he wanted to tell me, but couldn't. I switched off the tape. He took a double deep breath that was more cleansing than a sigh, set his mouth in a grim line and spread his hands briefly. A helpless gesture.

The distant sound of music drifted in over the idling engine.

He sniffed, made a wry face, 'Well, now you know.'

I had to ask. 'So what became of Gerda's suitcase?'

'Well, I think that is the point of the story, isn't it? If it is still there, which I doubt, that would be my future taken care of and you would have your funding.'

'Ma-ax!' I was appalled. 'God, that is so, like, dishonest!'

'Clare, they are dead. I have checked. They died in Auschwitz. I would be taking from no one.'

'The daughter? The one in England?'

'Name of Goodman. She was killed in a bombing raid, and her child.'

He was nothing if not thorough. He'd checked without telling a soul. I shook my head, marvelling at how sly he'd become. That's what two years in Buchenwald did for you.

'Clare.' He took my hand. 'I want this film to be made, not just for my sake, but for the sake of all the forgotten prisoners – the Germans who stood up for their beliefs.' Muscles pulled his mouth into determined grooves; his chin jutted. 'And I want you to make it. I have to go after that suitcase.'

I pointed out that in sixty years floods and storms would have washed through those sewers a hundred times, dislodging suitcases and anything wedged in crevices. In any case, who was to say it contained anything valuable? Or that the case and its contents hadn't perished in the wet.

'I thought it would be worth a look,' he said glumly.

'You're pretty desperate, aren't you, poor old thing?' thinking that he deserved some sort of reward for all he'd suffered in the war. What comfort could I offer? I began telling him about my own search – for Hofmann's letter.

He gasped, startled out of his mood, demanded, 'You've found it?'

My 'No?' was a challenge, a query. Everyone I'd asked, like on the programme, had taken the contents as read, though no one actually had. It wasn't on any computer file or videotape. It hadn't even occurred to me that Max might know of it, let alone be interested.

His face twisted, his broad shoulders sagged. 'I – I thought . . .' he began, and sighed. 'I'd really like to see that letter.'

'Would you?' I couldn't think why. It wouldn't say anything he didn't know already. 'I mean we don't even know that one exists.'

But he was quite sure. 'There has to be something,' he said. 'Susmeta knew about Hofmann and his Buchenwald experiments before any of the brains were transplanted and able to tell her for themselves. Somewhere he must have set out exactly what he'd done to us, and how future surgeons should go about reversing the process. But I've seen my own case notes or whatever you'd call them and there's nothing there, no guidance about the right antidote to use.'

'Hang on,' I said, 'you mean there *is* somewhere? Some mention of the antidote?'

'Of course,' he frowned. 'Susmeta knew how to combat the poison in our brains before she began work.'

The lying cow . . . 'She told you this?'

'She did, yes.'

Yet she'd told me, and however many million viewers . . . or had she? No maybe it was just me she'd told – that people had had to die for want of the right antidote. And yet, surely, that would have been one of the first things that Hofmann would have wanted his successors to know. He may have been a heartless beast, but he wasn't irresponsible. On the contrary, he left nothing to chance. Think of those CVs, all the details about blood group, sex, IQ. He wanted his brains to survive and to be comfortable in their host bodies.

'So Susmeta saw a letter, you think?'

'If she didn't, she got hold of the information some other way.'

'Ri-i-ght.' This was so interesting. Why would she lie about a thing like that, about why some of her patients had died?

He turned those inscrutable eyes on me. 'When you – *if* you find it, I'd be grateful if you'd let me see it.'

'Sure.'

'You see, I'm curious. Such a letter might contain some clue as to why the bastard chose me. It sounds pathetic, Clare, but I need to know if he actually gave a damn whether I, Max Zeiler, lived or died.'

One by one the cars reached the stone gateway where sentries in shades and fluorescent yellow tabards stopped us and checked our credentials. Max and I had the backs of our hands stamped with the password: 'Press', which entitled us to peel away from the bubble-tent shanty town in the water meadows, and head up to the house, whose tall Elizabethan chimneys stood up in alarm like rabbits' ears. Max, too, was showing the whites of his eyes.

Music crept up the hill from the marquees of the festival fields and I found myself bopping quietly as I locked up. I couldn't help it – the sound came up through the soles of my spiky sandals. Radio aerials were quivering and polished metal shone with an unsteady gleam. We were in a car park reserved for *Officials, Press and Performers*, the great and the good. The groupie in me removed her shoes and spent a mad five minutes, dashing here and there to peer in roadie vans and minibuses, hoping to spot a crashed-out lead-singer or two, but there were just empty crisp packets and beer cans. I almost genuflected before a black cab with Bike Shed's logo on the doors.

'Their bass guitarist is so-o-o good,' I drooled, and Max gave me this wan, sorry sort of smile. He dared to pity me, sad man! I mean that was rich coming from someone who thought 'Lily Marlene' was hot stuff! I imagined Nick's hope was that, while he was here, Max would learn to appreciate the finer things in twenty-first century life, like hard rock, but right now I just wanted to see him smile. Our conversation in the car had brought him right down. As we threaded our way out between vehicles I realised, with a lurch, that one of the vans belonged to Hag Spawn, (none other), customised to look like something vomited up from Hell. More important, the back doors were open and there was Polly Gross herself, jumping down with a black devoré gown on a hanger, and a pair of killer stilettos dangling from two fingers. I hadn't realised how small she was; she looked about twelve in her vest and hot pants, nothing like her black-lipped stage persona. But even scrubbed and braided, she oozed oestrogen like a bitch on heat. I'd read somewhere that she wore a testosterone patch to keep her 'frisky'. It surrounded her, more miasma than aura, like you were looking at her through a dirty lens. She was the sort of girl mothers have to warn their sons about because the poor dears can't see it for themselves. (And that is so creepy.) But her singing voice gave you goose pimples for different reasons. Sharp like rusty razorblades, sort of scorched Streisand. I'd have asked for her autograph if it hadn't been so utterly naff in front of Charlie and the rest, who were just drawing up.

She rasped, 'Hi there,' with a coquettish smile at Max that aged her about thirty years. I imagine she thought she knew him from some place, like you do when you recognise a face from the box.

I was invisible.

He perked up enormously. If I hadn't dragged him away, I'm sure they'd have gone way beyond establishing that she was a singer in a rock band and he was a brain transplant – 'Catchy title for a song,' she cracked. As we watched her go tippy-toeing barefoot down through the grass to her public, I thought I'd better tell him what I knew about her lurid life style, that it was mostly media hype, the stuff about her doing drugs and S and M, but there's rarely smoke without fire and he was such an innocent.

We found Lord Jerry Fittlewell in the Ops Room, a one-time banqueting hall whose oak-panelled walls were now pinned with maps and timetables, rotas and lists. Baseball caps, a bikini bra, jock-straps and other impertinences hung from glassy-eyed stags' heads, and loud-speakers were propped on plinths and in fire-places, burbling wild snatches of instrumentation from whichever band or bands were currently performing.

A long refectory table groaned under a feast of modern

technology. Flickering screens provided continuous surveillance of concert areas, camping grounds, toilets, exhibition tents, zooming in, every now and then, on anything that looked remotely suspicious. Should a fight break out in a beer tent, say, the heavies could be there within seconds, sorting it.

Max's nostrils flared. 'What would the SS not have given for a system like this?'

Among a snaking scribble of cables and red-eyed multiple sockets, operators were turning out reams of colourful printed matter. At the far end, above the salt, a large microwave oven featured a carcass turning on a spit and presiding over it all like a vastly overweight and designer-stubbled Jesus-at-the-Last-Supper was Jerry Fittleworth.

'No-o-o,' he was bellowing down his mobile, 'they go on after Hag Spawn, like we agreed . . . No, *three* numbers. No. If they don't like it, fuck 'em.' He flipped the mobile, roared at a dumpy little girl bent on not tripping over the wires, 'Any joy on those extra Portaloos, honey lamb? Well, get it sorted!' Honey lamb's head sunk lower. Then he noticed us and scowled horribly, for the camera. 'Jesus, I don't need this.' I thought he meant us. 'Five years I've been running this fucking show – you'd think it'd get easier! Prima donnas every one of them.' His mobile rang and he turned away. 'Oh fuck,' he said to it. 'Look, *you're* Security – *you* deal with it!' He found the camera's eye and jerked his chin in exasperation. '*Gatecrashers,*' he mouthed. 'No, no police, what do you take me for? You know what to do, but do it quietly. No mess.' He waggled his eyebrows, but I wasn't sure it was a joke.

'Clare Russell,' I introduced myself. 'We spoke on the phone. These are Bryn, Ez and Jo.' They all bounded forward to shake the lordly paw. 'Charlie, on camera. And my friend, Max Zeiler.'

He told us he could spare us five minutes, that he couldn't

care less about being the last Lord Fittleworth. It would make no difference to him being dead. If it mattered to the son and heir, there was nothing to stop him calling himself 'Lord' if he wanted to. You had your 'Count' Basie and 'Duke' Ellington, 'King' Oliver . . . As for Thurwell, if there was anything left to inherit when the creditors and the taxmen had picked it over, the boy was welcome to it. Bloody place was a millstone. Scarcely broke even in a good year. Last summer had been a disaster, weather-wise, and takings had been right down. If the boy had any sense he'd sell up and get a trade – tree felling, that's where the money was. As for the reformation of the Upper House, we'd come to the wrong man. He'd only attended the once, back in the eighties; been bored out of his skull. In his opinion, Guy Fawkes had got it just about right. Except you wouldn't need gunpowder these days. With so many old farts you simply had to light the blue touch-paper.

Charlie winked at me. This was lovely stuff. Nazim would be over the moon.

Jerry told us to grab ourselves a beer from the fridge (in the corner, between the Chinese lacquered commodes) and a haunch of whatever was in the micro – venison, he thought, and he'd troop us down the hill. Charlie needed a few close-up shots and his lordship was going to get us onto the actual stage!

'Stick close,' I said to Max, 'and if we *should* get separated I'll meet you back at the car at five-thirty.' We were all on a tight schedule. I had to drop the film off at the studio for editing tonight *and* I had the shot list to write up. It would mean staying up late but, on the other hand, there was no way I was going to miss Hag Spawn.

Halfway through 'Burning Ambition' she noticed us in the wings. Just a flicker of spiky lashes, an icy gleam through mascara, and you knew she'd spotted the camera, or Max, or both. His eyes were on stalks. I mean her voice alone would have done it but the dress was more devoré than velvet and her thrusts and jerks and wiggles gave tantalising glimpses of nakedness – no black bra for her – making quite sure that she had his attention. And when she curled out her pink, pointy tongue and made love to the mesh-knobbed microphone, it was his groan I heard, though every other man in the audience was nursing a hard-on. It was all so disappointing, somehow, finding out that he was just like all the rest, he or Leon Paterson or whoever's testosterone was working overtime here.

At the end of the number it was impossible to make myself heard above the uproar. I had to pull his head down and put my lips to his red-hot ear, shout that we were going down to take some shots from the audience's p.o.v. He nodded with hardly a glance at me. I pulled at his elbow; signed furiously that he was to follow. But when I looked back over the madding heads, he was chatting her up at the side of the stage. I tried to catch his eye but among thousands of other waving arms, what chance did I have? And why was I bothering, anyway? I'd warned him, hadn't I?

Sod him, I was enjoying myself, moving and grooving to the best beat in the world, of one mind with this seething mass of easy, happy people, loving them all. There was Bryn with his beer gut, flailing around, hopelessly out of time, treading on people's feet and smacking them in the eye, Ez, with Jo on his shoulders, like a blissful totem pole, and Charlie having a job keeping the camera still.

It was a quarter to six when we returned to the car park and he wasn't there. Instead there was a note.

Do not wait for me, Clare. Tonight I stay here as a guest of Polly Gross. Do not worry. Thank you for the outing. I will see you soon. Max.

Fuming, I helped Charlie pack away the gear, saw him and the others on their way and crawled gingerly into my red-hot car to head off home. I burnt my bum on the seat and scorched my fingers on the steering wheel. God, I had such a lot to do tonight; the shot list was the least of it. Blow Max, messing me about like this. I'd already put the car into reverse when it struck me that I couldn't just abandon him. He'd come all the way from 1944 – a time traveller, precious cargo, and I'd let him fall into enemy hands. Susmeta would skin me alive. I felt absolutely, unreasonably, miserable.

'Lucky sod,' said Nick when I shared it with him on my mobile.

'Nick!

'Pulling Polly Gross won't do him any harm at all.'

'I can't believe you said that!'

'He's a grown man, Clare. You can't hold his hand forever.'

'But she's such a . . . She's not a nice girl.'

'What are you, his *mother*? For God's sake, Clare, this is probably just what he needs. She'll give him a crash course on life in the twenty-first century.'

'Not to mention a dose of clap and a cocaine habit,' I added, sourly.

'She's not that bad, Clare.'

'She had to go to that clinic and be dried out.'

'That was booze, not drugs, and supposedly she's cured. No, it'll do him the world of good. Poor bloke's never lived, what with the Nazis and then the war and everything. If I'd been in the freezer for sixty years I'd be gagging for it.'

'I don't doubt it.' He was always gagging for it. 'He won't even know about taking precautions,' I fretted. 'He'll get AIDS.'

'Even the Nazis knew about taking precautions.'

'He wasn't . . .'

'I know, I'm just making a point. Where are you now?'

'I'm still at Thurwell.'

'Oh for God's sake, leave the poor guy alone.'

I ground my teeth and gripped the wheel, bombing along in the fast lane, overtaking everything in sight, facing out cars that materialised on my tail flashing their lights, forcing them to go round on the inside lanes. What did I care if Max stayed the night at Thurwell? He was nothing to me. Nor I to him, it seemed. Of course, he knew I was with Nick, and wouldn't poach, gent that he was. All the same, I recognised jealousy when I felt it and the black cloud of gloom followed me down the motorway.

I cut to the middle lane, skinning the nose of a Volvo and thoroughly deserving every toot and blast of his panic. Then, blood sugar at an all-time low, I slid into the slow lane where I could wallow, safely, in my misery.

'Where are you, Clare?' It was my mother.

'Nearly home. What's for tea?'

'Spaghetti and meatballs . . .' Oh yes! I could smell the basil, or it might have been the newspaper packets in the back of the car. She did make a stunning tomato sauce, my Mum. But it wasn't to be. 'Clare, do something for me, love. Pop round your Nan's and steal her address book.'

'Do what?'

'I'm doing invitations for her seventieth.'

'What seventieth?'

'Next month. I thought we'd give her a surprise party. She's been dropping enough hints . . .'

'You've left it a bit late.'

'I know!' she wailed. 'That's why we have to crack on. Please, Clare, it's on your way.'

'Oh Mum!'

'It'll only take a minute.'

'Like "Oh, hi, Nan, just popped in to see you. Bye!" God, can you imagine? She'll know something's up.'

'Tell her . . . Oh I know, pick up a local paper. She was wanting to know the times of films at the UCI.'

'Mum, I really don't have time. Can't Kate . . .?'

'Kate's in rehearsal.'

'She's always in fucking rehearsal.'

'Clare!'

'Mum, I've had a lousy day and I want my tea.'

'You can heat it up in the micro. Go on, dear, you must be nearly there by now.'

It was useless to argue with my mum. Growling in frustration, I turned off towards Walthamstow. I wasn't going to pick up a newspaper. I had the herbs in the back, probably the worse for wear after broiling in the sun all day, but hey. I had been going to give them to Mum but what the eye doesn't see . . .

Nan was delighted. I made it clear I was pressed for time and was only dropping the plants off because they wouldn't last the night in my car.

'Won't your mother want to sort them through?' she said, adjusting her specs and examining the sage. How well she knew her.

'She's nowhere to put them,' I said quickly as we walked through to the garden to 'pop them in while they're still breathing, poor things!' She'd been sitting out there at the gnarled old table Sid had knocked together, years ago. Twisted chairs and benches in the same rustic style listed at various angles throughout the garden. Music from the radio soared to a crescendo in some far-off concert hall and a sundowner glinted in the evening sun. Nan's life was sweet.

'So, Clare,' she said, 'where has your exciting media life taken you today?'

'Exalted circles, Nan. The stately homes of the down-wardly mobile.'

'Lovely,' she said. 'So we're putting the boot in on the aristos, eh? I'll drink to that.'

According to photographs, Alice Russell had been quite

stunning in her day. She'd played the young heroine in local Am. Dram. productions, for years and years, well into her forties, and she still had presence and bearing even though her once lissom figure had ossified. The flesh had slipped away from the bone, the muscles sagged; her once red hair was now white and bundled out of the way in a sheep's wool topknot, and her freckles had multiplied until you couldn't put a pin between them, but if I was going to look like her when I was seventy, I wouldn't mind at all. Stray tendrils stuck damply to her creased brown-paper neck as she wandered about looking for suitable homes for the plants, placing her feet carefully on the path as though she found her height unwieldy, as though it were a balancing trick like twirling a plate on a stick. Knowing how she used to stride around the world, I worried she was becoming frail.

She insisted on digging the holes herself, planting her feet square and bending her knees, while I told her about Ottley.

'Feverfew sandwiches! The woman's living in the dark ages!'

'Absolutely. Both the Titherilles are.'

'Titherille? That's not the Blackshirt, is it? Friend of Enoch Powell?'

'Yep.'

'Clare! He's a horrible man! He and his cronies in the Lords were the ones sent all those poor Asians back to Kenya. They split families and caused no end of suffering. Oh I don't think I can accept anything from him.'

'Nan, I'm not taking them back, and they'll die if you don't look after them.'

'Oh dear,' she told the marjoram, 'it's a pity there's not a herb to make people kinder or wiser or to cure wrong-thinking. Never mind, I suppose it's not your fault. You just put down your roots and make yourself at home. We're glad to have you.'

When she stood up she wobbled slightly. Beads of moisture were strung along her lip. As I went to help, she shook her head. 'Phew, I can't take this heat, Clare. Not like you youngsters.'

Not for the first time I worried about her living on her own. When Granddad died she'd refused point blank to move in with us. 'We'd be at each other's throats in no time, Pam,' she'd told Mum, with brutal frankness. This was before Sid left. Maybe he'd have stayed if his mother had lived with us. Who can say? She'd opted instead to stay put in her own higgledy-piggle house in Walthamstow's 'village', surrounded by Granddad's watercolours and her lovely big old furniture. She had everything to hand – shops that would deliver, if necessary, and good neighbours who would answer to a bang on the wall. There were friends to visit, the elderly Silver Ladies' Choir with their quavery voices, the Spiritualist church, the library, and her beloved writing group, under whose auspices she'd had a book of erotic poetry published. At sixty-five, that was quite something.

She knew all the stall-holders in the High Street and on market days she would trundle down with her basket on wheels, swathed in an Indian cotton garment she'd saved from the seventies, in search of fresh fruit, cat's meat and gossip. She had her own life, she insisted. She could manage. Hang the hazards of decline and incontinence: she'd cross those bridges when she came to them. In any case she'd rather disgrace herself in her own home than among strangers. So we let her alone and, with Granddad's insurance, she treated herself to a Saga holiday and a cleaning woman. Life was too short to polish a horse-brass.

I helped her heel the herbs into their new beds and, while she was watering them, nipped in, on the pretext of going to the loo, and put her address book in my bag.

When I returned she'd poured me a glass of Madeira,

my favourite. 'Saw your programme last night,' she said, casually. 'That was the young man you've been telling me about, with the brain replacement?'

'Transplant, Nan.'

Her nose wrinkled along lines of doubt.

'What?' I demanded.

She sniffed. 'No,' she said shortly. 'Didn't take to him.'

'Why, what's wrong with him?' I was instantly defensive.

Thin shoulders hunched. 'He didn't ring true, somehow. I know he's damaged, an old head on young shoulders, all that. But even so, he seemed to me,' she hesitated, frowned, 'well, he seemed to be acting a part. Badly.'

I thought of the Berlin sewers, the story I'd been privileged to hear that afternoon. 'He's bottling up a lot of pain, Nan,' I said. 'Trying to put on a brave front.'

Scepticism screwed her mouth like a twist of paper. 'Mmm,' she said, wagging her head, her nose wrinkled in distaste.

'I mean,' I tried again – I didn't like her dissing Max, even if he was a bastard, going off with Polly Gross – 'when you think of all he's been through, he's probably having to work very hard to hang on to his sanity.'

She was unconvinced. 'He's hanging onto *something*. I wouldn't trust him further than I could throw him. Don't go getting mixed up with him, will you, Clare.'

Huh, I thought, a chance would be a fine thing.

6

Nazim's neck was in a brace for whiplash, one of those attractive prosthetic sponge things. I don't know who in the world has orangey-pink flesh but Nazim certainly hasn't.

I heard Barry telling him that, no way, was he to appear on camera in that state. If he was determined to make the story his own, he'd have to dub. 'No worries,' said Nazim, who has to be the vainest man on the box. He was prepared to suffer for his art. He'd take the collar off for a few studio-shots of intros and links and then he'd get Charlie to superimpose them onto recorded GVs of the locations. He was full of tricks.

Barry gingerly fingered his nose, which was still sore and swollen. 'The story's more important than your pretty face,' he said. He was in a foul mood.

Alison was worse. She had double vision. She didn't say a word to me by way of thanks, just snatched the shot list which I'd finished typing in the early hours and, with a face like thunder, shunted me into the edit suite to run through the digitized tapes. As if it was my fault Nazim hadn't checked his tyres.

Mostly she groaned. Even with jarred retina, she could see that the camera was wrongly angled and in too close. Good God, you could see up the old man's fucking nose. That was the idea, I said. She looked puzzled. And what was all that with the signpost? Couldn't we have *tried* to get it in focus? Oh God, now the tape was running fast. Couldn't she trust me with a simple bit of editing? I explained that it was a speeded up tour of the stately home – a joke. But she wasn't in the mood.

'It's no good, Clare. I know you did your best, but we can't use it. I mean, what is all this stuff – these close-ups of cobwebs and woodworm?' She winced, 'And the swinging camera, portrait-to-portrait, chandelier-to-commode. It's worse than *NYPD Blues*. It makes you feel sick.'

'Exactly,' I said.

'I happen to like *NYPD Blues*,' declared a rather nasal voice behind us. I don't know how long he'd been standing there. 'Just passing through,' he explained.

'Tell her, Barry,' she said. 'It's a fucking shame. She's obviously tried hard . . .'

'I like it,' he said.

'You don't!' she squealed, her jaw dropping.

'Yep. It's all there. And the fascist memorabilia – say no more. Hoist with his own petard, I'd say. The hereditary peers aren't worth diddly.'

'But Titherille's a shareholder.'

'He's also out on his ear. It's fine, kiddo. Don't change a thing. Now let's have a look at the Thurwell piece.'

In the end I trimmed the Titherilles down to two minutes thirty of good, gritty stuff. Barry nicked the sign-post shot for the opening insert, with Tom going, 'Whither the aristocracy, now?' The muzzled Alsatian peeing on it was elevated to Programme Close. (Tom had the rest of the day to think of some witticism to accompany it.) Thurwell got a whole three minutes twenty. An entire day's shooting, and untold angst and creative energy whittled down to six minutes of airtime. But it was always the same. Take the Buchenwald Brains. Six weeks of research, miles and miles of footage, for a forty-minute show. There must have been reels and reels on Max alone. We'd hardly touched on Ellen Sauerbruch and the others. I wondered what Editing did with all their unused film. Dumped it probably. It was of no use to them. Though it might be invaluable to a person thinking of doing a ninety minute drama-doc.

Alison seemed a bit happier when I went in with the revised running order, actually giving me a little smile. Lord Jerry was a great hit and, as for the 'Shrinking Violet' sequence with Gross going *'Fade, fade away, baby, wither and di-i-e . . .'* with full, pink-throated vampire snarl . . .

I couldn't believe she'd never seen Hag Spawn before, as I told her later in the canteen, when she insisted on buying me coffee. She was more worried about her eyes. The hospital reckoned they'd right themselves in time but she didn't see how she was going to do her job properly. She was sorry she'd been so crabby earlier. Barry joined us.

'Good job, good job, kiddo. Saved our bacon.'

'Some nice touches,' Alison acknowledged generously. 'We'll have to put her name among the *Directors* credits, won't we, Barry?'

'Indeed we will. Bit more in the pay packet, too, I shouldn't wonder.'

'Maybe we can find some more pieces for you as time goes on. By the way, I meant to say, I like the eyelashes. Dyed them, have you?'

'Is that what it is?' said Barry, while I blushed helplessly. 'Thought there was something. Very fetching, very fetching.'

I was flying high until Susmeta phoned. I'd actually managed to put Max out of my mind, but her shriek of horror when she realised he wasn't with me made my heart slam like a lead door. She wasn't too impressed to learn that I'd left him at the rock concert.

'You weren't supposed to let him out of your sight.'

'Isn't he allowed a life of his own?' I asked.

'No,' she said, flatly. 'Anything could go wrong. His progress has to be carefully monitored, you know that. And if he were to fall into the wrong hands there's no knowing what might happen.' To her research or to him? I wondered.

I knew he still had to be wee-ed and weighed every day, input against output, and his blood pressure had to be taken, plus regular brain scans and tests of physical and mental agility, but he wasn't on medication any more. His body was quite comfortable with its new brain. There had never been any signs of rejection.

But who exactly were these sinister 'wrong hands' and what would they want with a brain transplantee? I mean it wasn't as if he was the Bionic Man and they could steal any secret technological workings. They could admire Susmeta's neat stitching if they wanted but that was about all. Otherwise he was just like anybody else. On the old-fashioned side but catching up fast.

I told her that the last place they'd think of looking for him was Polly Gross's camper van. 'He's as safe as houses,' I said, crossing the fingers of both hands.

'Cla-a-are!' she wailed. 'What on earth were you thinking of?'

'More a case of what *they* were thinking of, Suse. Polly and Max. I was completely in the way.'

Her exhalation, 'Oh my God!' blew in my ear. Then, 'Can't you go and get him?'

'No I can't. He's a grown man,' I said, repeating what Nick had told me. 'He's managed to survive a war or two and goodness knows what else. I should think he knows how to take care of himself.'

But she wasn't convinced, any more than I had been. 'I need him here. Now.' She sounded like a jealous wife. 'How long does this festival thing last?'

'He'll be home Monday morning, latest,' I promised her, gritting my teeth with pain, my finger bones were crossed so tightly.

'Monday!' she shrieked. 'But he – Tch! All my figures will be – Oh Clare, you're impossible!' She slammed down the receiver.

I could picture the fierce contortion of her features, delicate nostrils flaring, jaw muscles bunching like pickled onions. No doubt she'd like to wring my neck with her clever little hands. But what could I do? As for her obsession with graphs, she'd have to put up with a few gaps. She could catch up when he came home. *If* he came home.

I put my plan to Nick as we ate our sarnies in the park. 'What about a documentary, a one-off special, about all five of the brains? Where they're coming from, going to. Be good, wouldn't it?'

'Ace,' he said. 'But you'd better get in quick. Other people will have thought of it or the book or something.'

'Get in where?'

'With the boss. Get the company to back you.'

'I was thinking of going freelance.'

'Why?'

Which is what Alison said too. 'Nothing ventured, Clare. You've got Zeiler eating out of your fucking hand, and Naidoo. You've got the photos, the footage. You can get that old war vet, the one on the voice-mail, to say a few words. And the crew will be glad of the work now the run's nearly over. Put it to Barry, first. I would.'

The idea had already crossed his mind. He'd floated it past Alison but she was tied up all summer. In any case, her dodgy eyes made it impossible. The documentary would have to be made quickly while it was still news. He'd get the guy under contract, and the other survivors, before anyone else came sniffing around. Yep, it would make a great story. He'd be glad to have me on the team.

'I want to direct it, Barry.'

'I assumed you would.'

'Really?'

'Sure, you did great with the Titherille piece. It's in your hands, kiddo. Pitch it to Colin on Monday. I'll put in a good word.'

Hmm, I thought, a little black eyelash-dye goes a long, long way.

The Lords' show was a judicious blend of live studio chat and pre-recorded inserts. We visited eagles and owls with Erin, attended Formula One meetings with Derek and were guided round stately and not-so-stately homes by Nazim. Virtually. You couldn't see the joins. We looked at library film of hospitals and centres for the homeless, with Tom linking, and it was clear that there were at least a few aristos worth their salt, especially the ones who went about quietly doing good. As the PM said, in a recorded broadcast from Number Ten, these were the ones who had earned life peerages in some future Honours List, the ones who would be returning to the Upper House.

During the live interview with Lady Eaton, there was the added excitement of the newly formed FABS – Families Against Body Snatching – a dozen or so angry men and women, dashing down the studio steps, from nowhere, onto the set, waving placards: DON'T LET THEM TAKE YOUR LOVED ONES! BAN BRAIN TRANSPLANTS, END THIS OUTRAGE! and SAY NO TO BODY SNATCHING!

George Paterson was there, head bowed over his walking stick, incoherent with grief. Someone else positioned himself in front of camera, shouting and gesticulating about Leon Paterson being an unwilling vessel. Unfortunately only those nearest actually heard him since he wasn't wired for sound. Security lumbered on, better late than never, blinking at the bright lights and looking self-important and, during the ensuing scuffle and scrum, poor Lady Eaton's wig was knocked askew. Eventually the intruders were 'persuaded' to take their complaints into the corridor, much to everyone's disappointment. Muffled thumps and protests continued to punctuate the programme until the police arrived, ten minutes later.

Tom treated it as a scoop, a late news item, and ad-libbed in tremendous style, about a 'furore' following Wednesday night's *Way of the World*, how a member of the public had accused the surgeons in the German brain-transplant case of using his son's body without permission. It was a slight deviation from the truth but never mind.

'Back to tonight's programme. Lady Eaton, in your long career in Parliament, in both houses, you must have had occasion to deal with similar contentious issues . . .'

And, bless her heart, she rallied. Tucked her hair in with a trembling hand using the monitor as a mirror, and talked shakily about the treatment of certain debilitating diseases and how it was only the House of Lords throwing out the government bill that had prevented appalling abuse of embryonic tissue.

We had to cut the other contributions for fear of over-running.

I drove home in a turmoil. Me and my big mouth.

Though the evening sun through the car window was cooking me pink, goose bumps prickled at what I'd done, as though someone had slipped a cold wet fish down my back. Because it wasn't just a fill-in for Alison any more. It wasn't just a run-of-the-mill showing of dear old *Way of the World*. This was a one-off, ninety minute movie and it had to be more than just good. It had to be very, *very* good. This was make-or-break, head-on-the-block time. Though it wasn't my *head* Barry Giddings was after. I could still see his piggy eyes glazing over, his smug chops slavering as he rubbed his hands and talked about collaboration.

Oh bloody, bloody hell . . . What had I got myself into?

It wasn't completely cut and dried, of course. Colin had to be persuaded to fund the project. What if he didn't like the idea, which I had until Monday to work up into a treatment? My heart sank. Of all the production managers in all the world, Colin Galloway was the absolute scariest, the most intimidating. Even Alison came out of his office in tears. Even Barry.

But then it wouldn't be my fault, would it? Not if the budget wouldn't run to it? But it would, it would. It had to. God's not such a tease. He wouldn't dangle this opportunity in front of me and then snatch it away. Would He? Not when He knew I wanted it so-o-o much. I shivered again, and this time it wasn't so much cold fish, as Leonardo diCaprio sliding his icy hands down my vest as the *Titanic* sank to the bottom of the sea.

The sun shone that entire weekend and I missed it all, shut in my room sweating over themes and paradigms. Four pages had never seemed so difficult. The story was given; I couldn't change that. It wasn't like a screenplay where you can add facets of character, riveting dialogue, or twists in the plot as you go along; this was reportage. It had happened, was still happening to four, and eventually five, victims of Nazi atrocities. I'd start there, at the removal of the brains, and bring in the back-story as necessary. The first plot point would be the discovery of the freezer. Or should I *start* with Hofmann packing the freezer, writing the letter, as I'd originally planned? Or with the transplant? If my main concern was the resurrection of the Buchenwald Five and their integration into the twenty-first century, perhaps I should begin with the transplantee coming round from the operation, and let the viewer see life beginning again from Max's point of view? He, or the actor lookalike, would be the main protagonist, looking back over events and forward with hope, bringing in the other four as also-rans.

Nick had other ideas. He came over for Sunday lunch and proceeded to trash my twenty pages of draft. The opening sequence, he said, should be where the five are all together, working around the camp. One by one they get called to the hospital, never to return. When it's Max's turn we follow him in and see him through the operation. I'd got the completely wrong plot point at the end of Act One; it should be where Susmeta decides to operate on the first brain. The second act should be about the four transplants, how their past experiences impinge on their present, how they cope with their new bodies, new possibilities, life without the threat of Fascism, how they integrate into modern society, and the second plot point, the point of no return, should be when Max decides to take off on his own. The third act . . .

I'd had enough. '*You* do it, then, clever-bollocks!' I shrieked, stamping my size seven and raising a mild show of interest from the sunbathers on our lawn and considerably more from next door, where sunglasses and newspapers were lowered and knowing looks exchanged. 'You know so much more than me – you make the sodding film!' I stormed out of the office to fling around the bedroom. 'I'm never going to get it right. It's the most boring and stupid story there ever was and I hate it. I hate it.'

When I came out eventually, raddled with tears and sweat, I could hear him downstairs, with the others, yelling 'Howzat!' at the television.

Sod him. I thought he'd come to *help* me!

I'd just about whittled the story down to eight pages when he called up the stairs. I didn't answer.

'Cla-are!' he repeated in a really oily, weasely way. 'Honee-bun!'

Yuck.

'Your Polly Gross is live on telly tonight.'

What! I managed not to go flying down there, and sat stonily on, face locked tight.

He took the stairs two at a time, kissed the back of my neck, and licked behind my ear, going, 'Mmm-mm, salty . . .'

'Did we win?' I enquired with dignity. We had to have done, he was in such a good mood. Fingers came round and cupped my breast, stroking the nipple through the cloth; more were moving my skirt up between my legs. He mumbled into my collarbone, 'Hundred and fifty-nine, not out,' or some such. It was very hard not to squirm . . . with irritation.

'What was that about Polly Gross?' I squeaked, feeling cross that I was being used to augment his euphoria.

'Tell you afterwards.'

'We can't,' I said, 'they'll hear,' gesturing feebly at the open window and thinking, irrelevantly, of sounds that carried along smelly sewers.

'We can.' He leaned on the door to close it, and pulled me to him. I really wasn't in the mood.

So I shut my eyes and thought of Max.

'Cup of tea, you two?' said Kate, knocking on the door a minute later. 'I'll bring it in, shall I?'

'No!' we yelled in unison.

'I'll leave it outside then. Have it while it's hot. The tea, I mean!' I could almost see her eyes rolling in innuendo, wagging her hair extensions. She's not bad as sisters go but, not for the first time, I longed for a place of my own – peace and privacy. But I couldn't see it happening, not while Mum was still so raw. It was two years since Sid had walked out but she still had fits of depression, still came down in the morning, puffy-eyed from crying. I couldn't desert her, too.

The sun had dipped down behind the curtain when 'Marching Beneath the Banner' percolated my dreams. It took me a moment to remember it was Sunday and time for the God-slot.

Ratatat on the office door and Mum, this time, sounding strained and not a little strident, 'You've let it go cold. I knew you would! Haven't you finished that wretched shot-list yet?'

Shot-list? Treatment, she meant. 'Shit!'

'Clare?'

'It's all right, Mum. Be down in a minute.'

I rolled out of Nick's sticky embrace, and stood up to pull on my pants. It was only then I remembered that he had interrupted me. What was it he'd wanted to tell me? I nudged him with my toe where he lay, curled sweetly on the rug, looking more naked without his glasses than without his shorts.

'Nick. Nick!'

'Ow! That hurts!'

'What were you saying about Polly Gross?'

'Um?'

'Something about her being on TV tonight?'

'Polly Gross? Oh yeah, they said. She's on *Pops and Popsicles*. Live. I thought she might be the one to know where Max is . . .'

I knelt down and kissed him hard on the mouth. 'Nick, you're brilliant! What time's she on?'

'Eh?' He yawned. 'How do I know? Eightish, I'd imagine.'

'We can catch her if we hurry.'

'Eh? Catch her?'

'At the studio. Come on.'

Which was how come we were both back outside Arcady House at seven twenty-five on a Sunday. Unheard of. The FABS had set up a picket-like demo on camping stools and deckchairs in the shelter of the wall and had erected a sort of shrine around a large photograph of Max. Candles were burning and joss sticks. *'Pray for Leon Paterson,'* placards invited. *'Light a candle for a soul in Limbo.'* A guy in a FABS tee-shirt handed us leaflets as I swiped my smart card in the door. *'Have pity on these souls in torment,'* it begged. *'Eternally damned.'* Half a dozen names were listed at the bottom, one of which I recognised: George Paterson. The rest were the relatives of the other donors. Apparently Max and Ellen, Axel and Willi were demons who had taken possession of their children's bodies and turned them into zombies. Leon and his fellows couldn't find rest until their bodies and their brains were reunited and given decent Christian burials.

'Oh shit,' I said to Nick once we were inside. I had a horrifying vision of our having to run the gauntlet of their jibes and curses every working day once they found out about the film. Life would be unliveable.

'Hang on.' He went back outside and I saw him talking earnestly to George Paterson, waving his hands about and throwing some money into their collecting pail. 'Sorted,' he said on his return.

'What did you say?'

'Just that I was surprised they were hanging round here when Saint Meredith's was where the deeds were done. The hospital's where they should be trying to make friends and influence people. Give the surgeons something to think about. Make sure they are aware of the moral issues.'

'Susmeta's going to love you,' I said.

'I also told them that FABs were Flavoured Alcoholic Beverages and that they might want to think about their image.'

It was a different doorman from any that we knew, one of the Sunday shift. We showed him our IDs but he still wanted to know our business. I said I'd left theatre tickets in my locker. 'The Tempest' at the National. Okay I know they start at seven thirty but it was the best I could do on the spur of the moment. We pressed the fifth floor button in the lift, because old Jobsworth would be sure to check, got out at our floor and tiptoed down the stairs to the dressing rooms. We found her in make-up, looking like a china doll, all porcelain-skin and glossy lips. She couldn't remember where she'd seen me before but she did remember Max.

'Why should I know where he is?' She seemed really puzzled. 'We had a nice time, a few drinks up at the house with Jerry, but then we had to go, me and the guys. Had another gig in Bath Friday night.'

Nick gave me the sardonic eyebrow. It's modelled on George Clooney but comes over as Popeye. I'd been so sure that she'd . . . that they'd . . . and they hadn't at all. Well, they might have but not all night, and that put a different complexion on things. Entirely. He must have been wandering round the festival the whole weekend.

'When you left, how did he seem?'

'Okay. I like to leave 'em happy.' Seeing my frown, she added kindly, 'No, he was messing about on a computer, as far as I remember, into the small hours. I left him to it.'

'A computer?'

'Yeah. One of Jerry's boys had fixed it so he could send emails.'

I frowned. 'Right.' Who did he know to send emails to? Oh, Susmeta, probably, telling her where he was. Though she never looked at her mailbox. Why couldn't he just pick up the phone?

We wished Polly luck with the show and got her autograph for my 'little sister'. Kate's in her third year at theatre school but hey, who's to know? She certainly wouldn't. Kate, I mean. We went back upstairs to the fifth floor and got the lift down again, waved a cheery goodbye to the Jobsworth, saying something like at least we'd catch Act Two, and bombed over to Bayswater.

Where Susmeta was tearing her hair out. Friedrich Liebl's brain had been stolen, some time during Saturday night while she was watching some Bollywood movie.

Hospitals are such easy places to infiltrate, almost as easy as recording studios. They'd been expecting us when we'd gone round to film for the show, but while Mr Bradley, the chubby pink manager of Saint Meredith's, had come down to the foyer to whisk us, personally, through squeaky clean corridors to the very operating theatre where Susmeta had married brains to bodies, proudly pointing out labs and wards and places of interest *en route*, Ez, having to go back to the van for a new bulb, had snuck in and out one of the back doors unseen and unchallenged. Visitors were in and out all the time. Once inside, the thieves would have hidden out in washrooms and cupboards until their way was clear. The CC camera in the ceiling had actually picked up two figures wearing all-concealing theatre garb: gowns, shower caps, wellies and masks, but had thought they were on legitimate business as they entered the Path. Lab, switched on the light and helped themselves from the freezer cabinet. Somehow they must have acquired a swipe card, the key to closed doors in a hospital, because there were no signs of forced entry, no fingerprints, no breakages, nothing for the police to go on. It was frightening. Mr Bradley was beside himself, apparently. Suppose the thieves had been after drugs or one of the more kidnappable patients?

In fact, they'd been so tidy it was unlikely anyone would have missed the brain if Susmeta hadn't been intending to fly it out to Manchester on Sunday morning. A full body donor had become available: a Kurdish immigrant in his late fifties, rather older than Liebl, but he was AB negative, the right blood group, and it was a one-in-a-million break-through.

The police, who had warned the FABS protesters against disturbing the peace on Friday night and sent them home, hung about outside various Surrey churches after morning service to haul them in again, they being the most likely suspects. But they had the best of alibis. Most of them had been camped outside Arcady House on Saturday night, and the police themselves had moved them on. George Paterson had been in Leatherhead General visiting his wife.

The police were stumped. Who else would want the frozen brain of some old concentration camp internee? Clearly the FABS could have used it to bargain with, to demand an end to 'body snatching' as they saw it. But they'd made no demands at the police station other than those regarding calls to solicitors and that they be released forthwith. They were respectable businessmen; they wouldn't stoop to petty theft, they said. A few seemed to be kicking themselves that they hadn't actually thought of it. On release they'd gone back to picket duty, where we had seen them.

So who? Students? Jokers? Heaven forbid it was some heavy mob about to demand a ransom for the brain's safe return, or else.

The police had Susmeta record a news item for later that night, in which she begged the thieves to keep the brain at precisely the right temperature, otherwise it would spoil and die, making murderers of them. This was a man's life, after all. She'd been advised not to say anything about the donor in Manchester. The police felt it would give the kidnappers more leverage.

And now here on her doorstep were Nick and Clare with the news that Max hadn't been holed up with Polly, after all.

She pressed her slender palms together and bowed her head as if in prayer. Her eyes, when she raised them to mine were wet with dark tears.

'So why hasn't he come home? He's a babe in the woods, Clare. So vulnerable. Anything could have happened to him. All those people taking drugs. Oh God. It would be so easy . . .'

Poor Susmeta. By the time we left she had convinced herself that he had been kidnapped, too, and that some terrorist group was responsible. Neo-fascists. Who else would fear concentration camp survivors? They were probably scared that the transplantees would be able to identify some awful old war criminal.

'Maybe Klaus Hofmann himself is still alive. Think of that.' If she'd said Jesus Christ she couldn't have looked more reverent.

Nick and I gave her withering looks. 'Wishful thinking, Suse,' he said, and she sighed. Too bad they'd found the Beast of Buchenwald after the uprising with his head bashed in. Brains spattered everywhere.

7

Far from tying up my tongue, interview nerves turn me into one of those toys on the long-life battery advert. You set it going and it trips over the rug, falls flat on its face and still its little arms and legs are pumping, its little voice is wittering on, giving out with all this crap, these unspeakable clichés.

'*Basically*, Colin, I see this film as having an essentially political content. What I'll try to show is that while Hitler swept to power on mass hysteria, there were, em, quite a few, em . . . German left-wingers who dared to oppose him, who were persecuted, sent to labour camps, starved and worked to death. Some were extremists, communists and anarchists, but many weren't. In this day and age . . . I mean, nowadays, they'd fit perfectly well under the old Labour umbrella. Trade unionists, like Max Zeiler, and intellectuals like Willi Greff and Axel Schlager.'

He might have *said* something, agreed or not, but he just sat there, like a huge brown toad, inhaling noisily through dark nostrils and turning down the corners of his flabby mouth. He stared with dead eyes, fingertips pressed into the desk for leverage, as though he were about to spring, or stick me with his long tongue. He lowered his head but it was simply an invitation for me to dig myself in deeper.

The new scarlet gloss was gluing my lips together. 'At this m-mom-ment in . . .' I cleared my throat. 'They have been forgotten,' I said, 'those m-millions the Nazis killed for their political beliefs. Beside the enormity of what happened to the Jews, their stand has been, well, overlooked, frankly. Now, by the strangest quirk of fate, modern technology has given us five survivors. Five, well, four really, (though five if Friedrich Liebl survives, fingers crossed.) Um, anyway four anti-fascist Germans have come back from the dead to find that the world has changed, but not necessarily for the better. It is neither brave nor new nor perfect.' (Nice one. I practised that in the car coming to work.) 'It's a mistake to think fascism and Nazism have been defeated. Racism is rearing its ugly . . . em . . . is rife in Kosovo, Africa, em . . . Northern Ireland and, em, Sweden – well, all over really. In Britain it is, officially, a dirty word, but you only have to scratch the surface to expose a festering sore. At the end of the day . . . I mean, um . . . well, we are all prejudiced. There will always be "us" and "them" – Big-enders and Little-enders.' (Susmeta wasn't the only one to have read Gulliver, though clearly, from his puzzled expression, Colin had not.) 'As we see where Max is coming from,' I concluded, 'and where he's going to, well, I hope, in the film, that our attention will be drawn to the, um, the dangers of complacency.'

Tick. Tick. Whirr. That was me done. I gazed at the executive producer, empty, dry, hugging my stomach. I knew I'd said too much, or nothing at all. 'Your theme in a sentence,' Nick had advised.

Colin looked at me, heavy-lidded and suspicious. 'Are you a communist, Clare?'

I shook my head, speechless. I wasn't anything really, but what had that to do with the price of bicycles?

'Because we don't want any rabble-rousing. Not when canteen racism is so fresh in our minds.' (Canteen? Ri-i-ight.) 'As long as you're clear.'

Fair enough, forget all that. Whatever you want, Colin.

He thought five protagonists were too many. The viewers liked to identify with one hero, two at most. It was like a tennis match. You had to care who won.

'You care who wins team events,' I said, with a final

suicidal flurry. 'Enid Blyton got away with it – 'Five' do this, 'Seven' do that.'

'Enid *Blyton*?' Like what planet was I on? Then he said, 'Those kids had the same goal, the same enemies. Your brain cases are disparate.' I thought he'd said 'desperate' and it took me a moment to work that one out, by which time he was saying, 'Best to concentrate on Max Zeiler.'

If only. Oh God, how could I tell Colin my leading man was missing? 'And the woman –' he glanced down at my treatment, that suddenly looked so dog-eared and tired – 'Ellen Sauerbruch. That could be your love interest.'

Eh? Max wasn't . . . Oh hell, why not? Colin was the boss.

'You think I should follow just two story lines?'

'At most. Touch on the others, of course. If one of them looks more interesting . . .' He shrugged. 'This poor guy, Friedrich Liebl – if we suddenly find ourselves handing over large sums of money to Osama bin Laden, that might be a good road to go down. But it's up to you. You're the director.'

Was I? *Was* I! I felt my eyes brimming. Don't you cry, you wooss, don't you dare. 'So. I can go ahead?'

The muscles of his wide skinny mouth bunched into a sphincter, and he nodded. 'It's an important story. It has to be told. You already have Zeiler's confidence, and the Naidoo woman's. And this old guy, Mallory? Follow that one up. Yes, I think you can do it and Barry agrees with me. You'll be working closely with him, don't forget.'

I hadn't. There was a whiff of BO, mine, but hey . . . I wiped my hands down my posh suit before shaking Colin's equally clammy paw.

His lips were stretched in a froggy smile. 'Don't hesitate to get back to me if you come unstuck, though I doubt you will. And Clare . . .'

'Yes?' I was falling over myself with gratitude.

'Don't thump too hard on that old socialism tub, will you?'

When I phoned the German Embassy, after lunch, flushed with success and clutching my phrase book, they stuck me on 'hold' for twenty-five minutes and serenaded me with a selection of Bach hits while they found out that Ellen Sauerbruch had failed to keep her last appointment at *die Krankenhaus*, Cologne General Hospital. The family she was staying with in the city, the Birnbaums, hadn't seen her for days. They promised to get back to me about Willi Greff.

'I wonder,' I said, desperately, 'whether the Birnbaums would talk to me? I need all the help I can get.' If I wasn't careful I'd have no one left to make a film about.

'They have no English, Fraulein.'

'Well, that's all right, actually,' I said. 'I might ask a friend to translate.' Fingers crossed. 'Do you have their telephone number?'

He hadn't returned when I called in at Bayswater. Susmeta was cool in floating turquoise, but her eyes showed white like a scared rabbit. I suggested that maybe I should go look for him. Too late. She'd already had the police go down to Thurwell early this morning, in the hope that Lord Jerry's video system would turn up something.

I didn't like to add to her woes with my news about Ellen Sauerbruch, but I did tell her I'd got the go-ahead for the film.

'What film?' she said, her eyes darting and distracted.

Forget it. 'How, em, how's the musician, Suse? Axel Schlager? Do you think he'd let me interview him?'

Her eyelids snapped shut in exasperation. As she slowly lifted them, she looked straight at me, her mouth a cartoon squiggle of crossness. 'You don't give up, do you, Clare? What are you planning to do? Hand *him* over to the fascists?' I was gobsmacked. Me? But I . . . 'And my name is Susmeta, not Suse!' she added for good measure.

My eyes smarted. I loomed over her, power-dressed from the interview and utterly forlorn. How could she think that of me? That I would have anything to do with Nazis? With betraying my friends?

She turned away to the drinks cabinet and began pouring herself another glass of vermouth. No sign of one for me and I sure as hell wasn't going to ask. The bottle clinked against the glass, and something, an un-sound, which might have been the house stretching in the heat, made her pause, look up. Her eyes were huge as a key turned in the lock.

'Where the hell have you *been*?' She flew at him and somehow restrained herself from the anxious mother's slap. But tanned and unkempt, with four days' growth of beard, grass and mud stains on his trousers *he was gorgeous*, his prodigal's twinkle quickly changing to a frown of concern as he recognised his patron's distress.

'Did Clare not tell you I decided to stay at Thurwell? Did you not find my letter, Clare? I put it on the, em –' his fingers wagged the wiper motion – 'the window-cleaners? But perhaps it blew away. Oh, you must have been worried.'

'*Worried!*' she squealed. 'I have been out of my mind, Max! You have no idea. I thought you'd been, you'd been . . .' and she burst into tears. I managed, with an effort, to control mine.

He wrapped himself round her and patted her chicken wing shoulders, and the smug look over her head told me that the guy had had one hell of a weekend, if not with Polly Gross, then with someone. Sex oozed from his pores. When he caught my baleful glare, he raised a mocking eyebrow. My fists clenched.

'We thought you'd been kidnapped,' I growled, 'or even killed.'

'But no. I was enjoying myself. I had a good time, with the music and the people and the, em, the demonstrations, is that the right word? The demonstrations – Ja – of crafts and magic.'

If I was suspicious, she was insatiable. What had he eaten? Had he slept under cover? Taken proper care of himself? He smelled like a farm dog.

'Madam Surgeon,' he said, holding her at arms' length, 'you forget I am an old soldier. I spent two years sleeping under the stars in Spain. I have been on the run in Germany. I think I am able to take care of myself for a few days in gentle England.' And, as he grinned, I thought I glimpsed the shadow of the old Max, the bright boy of the photographs.

He told us that he'd spent the first night curled up on a window-seat in the banqueting hall, sleeping off the effects of Lord Jerry's hospitality. In the morning his host had given him breakfast and told him he was welcome, at any time, to help himself to food, drink, anything else he needed. But he had money in his pocket. Had it been necessary he would have been able to purchase sausages in bread and pastries with vegetables from the vendors, and beer. There had been no need for us to worry about his going hungry. What happened, in fact, as he wandered around, was that people had invited him to share their meals, have a drink or two.

I couldn't shake off the feeling that his blandness was just a touch OTT.

Susmeta was wrinkling her nose. 'Max,' she reproached him, 'you've been smoking!'

It was wonderful, he said, quite unabashed. After two years' in Buchenwald on two cigarettes a day, and six months out on parole, it was wonderful to fill his lungs again with tobacco smoke. In Spain they had been given a daily cigarette ration. It was as much a necessity as food for fighting men.

'You'll kill yourself. It's poison.'

Poison. Poison. Little bells began to tinkle in my brain as he asked, like an innocent child, 'There is no antidote?'

'You can stop – that is the only antidote.'

'Which reminds me . . .' I was about to say, but she had the wind under her tail, going on about a whole range of tobacco-related illnesses including bad breath and black-heads. I shuffled my feet, having recently dogged my own fag on Susmeta's doorstep.

'It does not harm the brain?'

'What's the point of having a brain if your body's defunct?'

He grinned, 'You could always re-plant my brain in a new body.'

'I wouldn't waste my time. A new body just so that you can pollute it all over again? Tch! And Leon Peterson was such a clean-living chap.'

'Leon Paterson?'

'Ah.' She bit her lip.

And I thought I was a blabbermouth.

'Well you had to find out sooner or later,' she excused herself. 'Leon Paterson is your body's donor, and you'd better know, his father is hopping mad. Saw you on television and got together with some of his chums to raid Friday night's show. You didn't see it?'

'No.'

'They call themselves FABS – Families Against Body Snatching.'

'Body snatching?'

'They think I'm Burke and Hare rolled into one, because they didn't grasp the fact that their children's bodies would go on living. Walking, talking and appearing on television. I mean, what else did they think whole body donation meant? They were happy enough with the idea that their dead child's body parts would enable another person to live, and it was explained to them, it *was*', she insisted, 'that every part would be used except the brain. And now they're saying I'm the Devil's child or something. In their ignorance they're talking about possession and zombies.'

'The police think they're the ones who stole Friedrich Liebl's brain,' I broke in, 'but they can't prove it.'

'What!'

'You didn't see that either?' He shook his head quickly. 'You missed Suse's, em, Susmeta's appeal?' He looked bewildered. 'On telly, dope! She asked the thief to return it, to at least keep it frozen.'

'No, I know nothing. This is terrible. Poor Friedrich! Just when it seemed you might have found a donor. They must get him back.' So she'd shared that much with him. She must have been so excited.

Susmeta said dolefully, 'They can take their time now. The Manchester people took the man off life-support last night, in view of the scare-mongering in the media.'

'Scare-mongering?'

Wearily Susmeta hooked a strand of black hair behind her ear. 'The Patersons and their friends are spreading alarm. People are starting to withdraw their consent, changing the conditions of donation, stipulating "organs only". Pretty soon we'll have no corporal donors left for brain transplants. And that would be dreadful. Friedrich and Axel are not the only ones waiting now. Interest has been keen. We have had enquiries from all sorts of people, not to mention referrals from GPs and consultants. Cancer patients, all sorts of terminally ill people – they all want brain transplants. What are we to do?'

I shrugged. It looked to me as though the miracle cure was doomed and Max was one lucky boy, apart from now having the Patersons on his tail. Perhaps he should grow a beard or wear shades. Now there was an idea. Slowly I said, 'You couldn't, em, you couldn't disguise them in some way – the donors – like so their own mothers wouldn't know them?' I laughed, too flip by half. 'Sorry, sorry.' But it

112

was interest beading their eyes, not dismay, and I pressed on. 'I mean, after you'd done the transplant you could hand the patient over to the plastic surgeon. Couldn't you? I mean that might make them a bit keener to commit to a, em, "corporal donation", like if they knew they wouldn't be recognised.'

'Ye-e-es,' said Susmeta, lightening up. 'That's it, Clare. That would do it.'

Max was looking thoughtful. 'Presumably this plastic surgery would enhance the looks of the patient.'

'Max, really,' I snorted. 'Aren't you beautiful enough?'

'Not me. But it is not right to expect the transplantee to live with disfigurement or in a body they are unhappy with.'

'No, no, of course not,' she said absently. 'Excuse me.' She put down her drink, untasted. 'I'm just going to make some phone calls. Maybe we can get those donors who have withdrawn their consent to reconsider.' She stopped at the door. 'Thanks Clare,' and, as an afterthought, 'help yourselves to drinks.'

I took a Beck's and gave one to Max, who had flung himself into a chair. Now that Susmeta had stopped quizzing him, he looked more relaxed. He gave me a little smile and stroked his bristly chin with exploratory fingers. But he was still somewhere else.

'Well, cheers, Max,' I said, showing my teeth. 'Glad you're all right.'

He looked up at the snide in my voice and frowned. 'I am very well, thank you, Clare. Perhaps a bit tired.'

Oh bless . . . I thought. Never mind about us losing sleep, imagining AIDS and drugs and goodness knows what. 'Enjoy the break, did you?'

His eyes slid from mine. 'I needed to be on my own,' he muttered.

'Did you now?' And all my lost weekends flashed before

my eyes, when we could well have done without him, Nick and I. I said nastily, 'I thought you were getting it on with Polly Gross.'

'Getting it –? Oh no, no. Though she is an attractive lady, I think.'

'Lady!' I almost choked.

'She was very, em, kind, but she had to go back. She offered to give me a lift to London, but I saw no need to return just then.'

'You are a selfish git, aren't you?'

'Clare, I left the note.'

'Oh fuck off.'

He sighed wearily and then sat up, all smiling attention, as Susmeta wafted back into the room, a cloud of turquoise serenity. Her fingers were fastened around her glass. 'Well,' she said, as though we'd asked her, 'I have organised a press conference for tomorrow. I shall tell them how helpful they were in losing me the donor for Friedrich Liebl. I shall tell them how everyone wants a brain transplant, but nobody wants to be a donor. And I shall say that, from now on, we will perform plastic surgery on any corporal donor, unless they specifically request us not to. I suppose we might even eliminate finger-prints and tattoos and birth marks – any distinguishing features. Actually, it occurred to me that we might even pay compensation to the family . . . well, not *us*, but someone, the NHS or some such body. Oh, by the way, Clare, Axel Schlager would love to talk to you. He is a sad and lonely man, with only his music for company.'

'Axel Schlager?' Max had pricked up his ears.

'Oh that's great!' My black mood was dispelled as if by magic. Of course, Max didn't know. 'I got the go-ahead today, this morning,' I fizzed joyfully. 'For the documentary. I'm going to be a director, Max!'

'Wunderbar!' He clenched his fist like a tennis pro winning

a rally. I held out my cheek for a kiss, but he missed the signals. 'Now your career will take off. Congratulations. And when do you start?'

'As soon as, baby.' Now I was showing off.

'As soon as what?'

I'd meant I'd started already, booking the crew and cameras, working out some sort of a timetable, organizing the budget.

'So, are you still going to start with the letter?'

'What letter?' Susmeta demanded.

I explained that Max and I were both convinced that an egoist like Hofmann wouldn't have left the brains to posterity without stating somewhere that he was responsible for them.

'I agree,' she said, but she hadn't seen any letter from him. Not that it would have meant much to her if it had been written in German. They'd telephoned her at the outset, someone from a laboratory near Hamburg. The skills needed were beyond them. They'd been in favour of putting the brains back into store for ten years or so. But some bright spark had thought of her as a last resort. And of course, the rest, as they say, is history. The bright spark had come over with the brains and checked her out, explained how the things had been found, this that and the other. And left her to it. So a lot of the information had been by word of mouth. On his return home he'd sent her a letter confirming everything they'd talked about. All important telephone calls after that had been followed up with letters or emails.

'And was there ever any doubt as to where the brains had come from, who did the operations?'

'None at all. They were known collectively as 'The Buchenwald Brains,' and the doctor in charge at Buchenwald was Klaus Hofmann.'

'Ri-ight,' I said, making a mental note. 'And if there was

anything you didn't understand or were stuck on,' I tried to put it diplomatically, 'like about the cryoprotectant, and the freezing agent, you just picked up the phone?'

'Or sent them an email.' She nodded.

'Was there any more information about the victims, a list of their names, their personal details?' Max demanded, eager as a puppy for some sign that his tormentor had cared what became of him.

'I don't think so. Not in my correspondence with the Germans. They simply said that these were the brains of eighteen political prisoners, mostly communists. Everything I needed to know was taken care of in the CVs that came with the brains. They'd unwrapped one or two and told me the sort of thing to expect, their blood groups and ages, personal history, all that mattered. I'll show you the file. Hold on.' She sailed off, leaving my question unasked.

Max bunched his lips, resigned to disappointment. Then he took a deep breath and changed the subject, raising his Beck's in a silent toast. 'And Axel will be in your film also?'

'All of you. Ellen Sauerbruch, Willi Greff, Friedrich Liebl if he's up and doing by then. Your sister, Berthe. Anybody who knows you, really . . .' Which reminded me. 'We had a call the other day, from an old friend of yours. Douglas Mallory? Do you remember him – from the Spanish Civil War?'

He frowned, 'Mallory? Of course I remember. My goodness, he is still alive?'

'Very much so. He wants to arrange a get together, if you're willing.'

He was nodding by now and grinning broadly. 'Mallory . . . but that is wonderful. Ja, he was a good friend. I look forward to meeting him.'

Susmeta was quite right, there were whole paragraphs in the email printouts about the cryoprotectant and its toxicity, but no mention of an antidote. I was surprised.

Nick had got it wrong, for once. But we all make mistakes, even the great Nick Robinson. The antidote must have been one of the things Hofmann hoped they'd have discovered by the time the freezer was opened. Max was more concerned about the fact that no one mentioned the prisoners by name or even number. No one cared that these had been real people, he ranted. They were simply concerned with the medical challenge of reconstituting the brains. But, as I said, to comfort him, there might be more in Hofmann's original letter. I showed him the shorthand squiggles in my notebook – the people who'd contacted Susmeta – and told him I'd continue my search.

8

Ellen has stood for some minutes observing him, testing him, knowing she doesn't register, that he doesn't see her. This is how men are with plain or older women.

She saw his train arrive; has watched him, tall and splendid despite his rough, slept-in looks, casting an eye over every female traveller, trying to find her. Some return his glance boldly, some smile, thinking they know him. Of course, he is a media star and whereas she shunned the cameras and scuttled out of hospital into the waiting car with a blanket over her head, he hadn't minded them at all.

Now he is looking at his watch and up at the clock. Checking time and place. He knows he couldn't have got it wrong. How long would he wait, she wonders?

'Max,' she has to call, finally, steeling herself for his bright expectation changing to uncertainty to bitter disappointment to a final careful concealment of all three.

'Ellen!' he cries warmly enough, but his dry kiss tells her that he cannot believe what they have done to her, any more than she can.

No one would guess that she had been beautiful. It is as though her skeleton has been compressed somehow, making her once fine bones stunted and thick. She has gained a few years and her silky grace, her cynical flaxen purity, has been exchanged for swarthy peasant lumpiness that neither diet nor exercise nor the finest clothes can disguise. Top hairdressers in Cologne and London despair of her coarse black hair. They advise cutting it close to her head like a man's, or like the shaven heads of Buchenwald – quite unacceptable. Instead she wears it wildly permed, in corkscrew curls, which seems to be the fashion among the young. Even so it does little to enhance the coarse features. Her soul stares out of shiny inkblots on parchment skin. There is no telling what racial mix runs in her veins.

In the taxi they speak of his escape. He is so pleased with himself, his cleverness. He couldn't have asked for a more convincing alibi. Lost in a vast crowd of hedonistic rock fans, replete with drugs, sex and deafening popular music: he could hardly tear himself away! She must be beside herself now, the girl, thinking how she let her charge, her protégé, slip through her fingers, anxious that his old-world innocence is being corrupted by base women and baser desires. How little she knows him. How well he has managed things. He is glowing and preening, cock-of-the-walk. Ellen smiles, almost able to believe him young and carefree, without that terrible burden of responsibility. Even the taxi-driver's eyes in the mirror are amused.

She whispers caution. The man may remember driving a German couple from Victoria to Chelsea Harbour. He may even have understood them. They cannot take risks.

They should have gone separately into the hotel. The glass of the revolving door reflects the mismatch, the rugged male and his incongruously stumpy paramour. The receptionist's stare is hard and knowing. She will remember them.

'She thinks I'm your client,' he remarks, ignoring Ellen's deep flush of shame.

'And you let her,' she complains miserably.

'What could I do?'

'Put your arm round me. Something, anything to show that we're close.'

'What does it matter, liebling?'

'I have to live here,' she says. 'I cannot have them thinking I am a whore.'

He searches her eyes, asking her to forgive him, probing

the mask for his beloved, but she knows how hard it is. Even she cannot find herself in the mirror when she tries. And it is clearly an act of contrition when he takes her in his arms as soon as they reach her room and hangs the *Do Not Disturb* notice on the door.

His lips on hers are too polite, his hand too slow to fondle her breast. She gives him a little push, tells him gently to forget it, and turns her head away, but he comes back, his leg forcing hers apart. He kisses her again, and now she feels his tongue on her lips, probing and entering. This time his eyes are closed, shutting out the stranger and pretending that the girl in his arms hasn't changed. Following his lead, she begins to feel her way. Her hands move slowly, tentatively, over his eyes and ears, over warm, young skin, move down to his chin, his neck, and his bristles are rough against her fingertips. Under the tee-shirt are new wonders, a symphony of hard and soft, bone and muscle, smooth mounds, tender hollows, and springy hair growing like marram grass in sand. It is exciting, like making love to a stranger. Where her fingers lead, her tongue follows. She finds a zip where once there were buttons, finds a penis swelling to unprecedented proportions.

It isn't the same.

'Relax,' he whispers, stroking her enormous breasts, her rounded belly, sucking the bracelets of her fat neck. 'Relax.' But how can she when she knows how ugly she must appear to him? He keeps his eyes closed, and as she does the things she used to, that still make him groan with pleasure, he wants to hurry. But she is not ready and it hurts. She cries out for him to go slowly, gently, but he cannot stop. Now she knows he is simply fucking. It has been a long time. A whore would do as well.

When she dares to open her eyes he is leaning on his elbow, gazing at her sombrely.

'Don't,' she begs, turning her face into the pillow.

'Sorry,' he says. 'Sorry,' and looks away.

There is blood, virginal blood between her legs! Is there to be no end to her humiliation? She pulls up the sheet and leans out of bed to take her cigarettes and lighter from the glass-topped cabinet. In silence she takes two from the slim gold case, lights them both and passes him one.

He waves it away. 'I don't, any more.'

'No,' she agrees, sadly. 'You don't.' He knows that she isn't referring to his smoking habits. He begins to bluster.

'It's not your fault,' she says, taking pity. 'How could you love this?' She blows smoke away from him and indicates, with distaste, her breasts hanging heavy as melons, the sheet sculpted to a Rubens nude. In the old days it would have ridged on the bones of her pelvis.

'I'm getting used to it.'

'Liar. You'll never get used to it. I was lovely. Look at me now.'

'You're not repulsive, you know, Ellen.'

She shrieks, 'How can you say that? I'm ugly! Grotesque. Lumpy as a Potato Eater and I hate it, I hate it!'

'Ellen, Ellen!' He is trying not to laugh. She must have hit the nail on the head with Van Gogh. 'Stop it. Believe me, it's not as bad as you think. Really. She is not perfect but, by modern standards, this new Ellen Sauerbruch is charming. Her eyes are . . . lovely.'

She does not miss that merest flicker of a pause as he gropes for the right word, the apt gesture, eventually settling on brushing her eyelid with the softest of kisses. She tries to pull away but he persists, tracing with his fingertips the eyebrows she has tried to pluck into shape, the rounded child's jaw, the shapeless putty nose, the thick lips, murmuring nonsense. 'The look in your eyes is the same, Ellen; the way you do things – hold your head, frown, wrinkle your nose – that's you. That hasn't changed. I still

121

see grace and elegance. What you are, what I love about you, transcends all . . . this.' He cups her face in his large paw.

'Don't lie,' she retorts, jerking free. 'We are not the same, either of us.'

He sighs, defeated.

Sunshine dapples a reflection on the ceiling from the river outside. Exhaled, her smoke winds a path through the window and out into the summer blue.

She could, if she chose, live here forever like some of the hotel's other residents, ugly old women, bewigged, bejewelled and rouged to the eyeballs. She could go on pampering herself in this oversized bed, in this sumptuous suite of rooms, with windows dressed like chocolate boxes and a refrigerator stuffed with exotic booze and an ice-box big as a safe. Who would know or care apart from the maid, wanting to clean?

Not God, who deserted her long ago.

Not her parents, tired of waiting up. They are snug inside the family tomb, wrapped around with sticky weeds that clung to her clothes last week, as she ripped them from words announcing that they had died within a year of each other, soon after the war, brokenhearted and childless. Her name was there, too: their *'beloved daughter,'* in spite of everything . . . *'Killed at Buchenwald,'* then the date, and as a concession, *'May God have mercy on her soul.'* But what does it matter now? They are dead, taking their hurt and disappointment with them. Now there is no one to give a damn about her. Only him . . . And, until they judge the time is right, they must remain apart, strangers in the eyes of the world. For the media would have a field day if they knew. Jumping to conclusions, spreading lies. It would be intolerable – all those cheap speculations about love in Buchenwald, all those jibes and sneers about Beauty and the Beast.

'It's as bad for me,' he says, breaking in on her thoughts, 'I feel as uncomfortable as you, as though I'm wearing somebody else's badly-fitting shoes.'

'You?' she snorts. 'There's no comparison! Your looks are an improvement.'

'An improvement?' His face tightens, 'Well, thank you, thank you, *liebling*.' His sarcasm bites. 'And what if I preferred my former self to this lumbering oaf I'm saddled with – always bumping into things, hands like feet. Oh yes, sweetness,' he says, disdaining her incredulity, 'it works both ways. Am I to take it that you found the earlier model wanting, then? Good looks are an improvement, are they, in your eyes?'

'No, no, I didn't mean that! Of course, I didn't. It's just that you have the, well, the better bargain. Believe me, I don't care what you look like. It's you I love, your mind.'

'My point exactly.'

She wants to believe him but knows how different it is for men. Discerning women don't set great store by their lovers' looks. Men, on the other hand, whatever they say, prefer their women to be pretty baubles that they can dangle before the envious eyes of their friends. If she has a keen mind and can hold an intelligent conversation so much the better.

He continues, 'The others will be feeling as bad, if not worse. Think of Schlager, poor chap, never to play again.'

'Schlager.' Her lip curls. 'What do I care about him?'

'Willi Greff, then. He knew his own pedigree. He will always feel that his body doesn't become him.'

Greff seemed perfectly happy when she had left him at the airport. He may have bemoaned the fact that his hair was falling out, but had no complaints otherwise.

She shakes her head, vehemently, her eyes filling with tears, 'It's not the same. How can it be? I'm a woman. It hurts, it really hurts, to walk down the Kings Road every day and see all the wonderful clothes, so daring, so brave, and the shoes! My dear, they're amazing, and I could have worn them, I had the figure, the legs. They were *made* for me. As I was. But now . . . I look ridiculous. Just ridiculous.'

'Sweetheart, don't do this to yourself.'

'I want to be young again,' she wails, 'and slim and beautiful!'

'Ellen . . .'

'I wish I were dead!' The sobs well up from the pit of her grief and he has no choice but to hold her, try to still her heaving shoulders, comfort her in the only way left to him.

When it's over he forks the cigarette from her and, closing his eyes, inhales deeply. Gives it her back. 'When you . . .' he begins, pauses, begins again. 'You were an angel, Ellen.' She realises he finds it hard to say her name. 'I worshipped your beauty, treasured it as a precious gift.' He frowns, licks his lips, takes another drag of her cigarette. 'That's how you were, and how you *are*, how you will always be, in my head and in yours, but physically, you're . . . well you've stepped down among the mortals, to my level.' She stiffens. Less than an angel, he means. 'You've become more, em, more real,' he ends up, lamely.

'And does "more real" make me more or less lovable?' It's a cruel question. Worded to kill. There's no way he can answer and please her.

'My love,' he pleads, smearing her wet cheek with his thumb. He takes her cigarette, smokes it all and stubs it out in her ashtray, then he lies down to look at her, slipping a hand under the sheet to find her soft underbelly.

She sighs, her eyes still stinging with salt. 'What am I going to do?'

'When the time is right I'll tell her how you feel. Perhaps I can persuade her to do another operation, put you in a body more to your liking.'

124

'If she won't?'

'She will . . .' His lips are firm, his nod decisive. He kisses her. 'Be patient, my . . . Ellen. This will pass, will become nothing more than a bad memory. Meanwhile, try to make the best of things. It's all any of us can do.'

She catches his hand as it sets out on a downward path. It is too easy simply to smooth her feathers with slick promises. She won't let him. She has made too many sacrifices. He has to know how unhappy she is. But he persists, stroking, caressing, tracing the roundness, massaging stiffness, melting resistance. She can't help closing her eyes and drifting, giving in to his touch, becoming warm and liquid. 'It will be all right,' her seducer whispers again and, reluctantly, she gives in and lets herself hope. Dear hand, clever hand stroking around and across and up and down, and down between her legs, finding the nub of her desire. 'Trust me, *liebling*,' he murmurs. 'I love you. I won't let you suffer.' She thinks she believes him. He gently tugs the sheet from her grip and, as he lowers himself upon her, whispers her secret name in her ear.

They take tea outside on the terrace, whose designer cobbles run neatly down to the quayside. Max stretches his long legs and basks in the sun, while they wait to be served. He says he has to look as though he has spent the weekend out of doors, 'roughing it', and they laugh together, holding hands across the table, loving conspirators now.

Bright water dazzles them into sunglasses and visors, and Ellen begins to relax. No one knows them; no one is looking for them. Here they can be themselves. A slight river breeze and the constant trickle and splash help to make the heat bearable, as does the iced tea when it arrives, served by an attentive waiter. Lime? Sugar? More ice? What about something to eat? A pastry?

'No, nothing.'

'Ice cream? A blackcurrant sorbet?'

'No, really. Tea is fine, thank you.'

He gives a little bow and goes away, only to reappear a minute or two later.

'Everything to your satisfaction, sir, madam?'

'Yes. Yes, thank you.'

'I wonder, would you mind, sir?' He produces, from his trouser pocket, a small camera.

'What? Why on earth . . .?'

'If you have no objection, sir. You're the brain transplant, aren't you? I like to have a photograph of all the celebrities who visit our establishment. If Madame wouldn't mind . . .' He doesn't think her newsworthy, thank God. She is to take the photo of him standing beside Max. He has brushed his hair specially.

No one looks up when they push back their slatted garden chairs to take a turn around the marina. But they haven't reached the harbour wall before the slap of fiercely shaken linen makes them look back. The waiter, tight-lipped and affronted, is showing off for the benefit of the other diners, making a point of changing their pristine tablecloth. Everyone, but everyone, is gazing after them curiously. He was not mistaken and he knows it.

The railing at the water's edge is cool as they lean over and talk, watching reflections flicker over the bright boats tied, like nuzzling piglets to the mooring posts. Nautically attired playboys clamber over the craft while sun-oiled girls arrange themselves to best advantage on deck. Presumably they have all posed for the waiter's collection. Perhaps they don't need to keep such a low profile. Bottles clink, engines fart rudely, fouling the air with puttering smoke, and then they are gone, leaving a rainbow slick and water slapping nervously against the wall.

It is a modern development, smacking of ancient fishing

ports, but boasting no industry or craft other than those pursued by hoteliers and publicans. On a Saturday afternoon in the heart of London, it is quiet, exclusive and, until now, discreet. Now and again there's a stainless steel sculpture with an obscure title, or spring water bubbling over a contrivance of stones, or picturesque tubs of flowers or an artist, sitting at his easel, painting a river scene, part of the appointed fixtures and fittings.

Money certainly makes a difference, and, she has no illusions, money is what attracts him to her.

Any small sum wisely invested in the early forties would have blossomed and borne substantial fruit in sixty years. The amount Papa Sauerbruch felt constrained to put in trust for his daughter, back in 1944, was enough now to keep her in luxury for the rest of her life. It was lucky he had done so. Fortuitous, or so the manager of Tourniers Bank had said. To choose Switzerland over the Fatherland would have smacked of disloyalty in those days, though many, mostly Nazis, had taken the risk and used the money, he informed her, after the war, to create aliases for themselves, set up in new countries. He had only admiration for Ellen's father's courage and foresight, and his faith in her determination to survive the worst prison on earth.

Who did he think he was fooling, that bank manager? He must have had a fit when she turned up with her withdrawal form and her credentials intact.

It is ironic. What use is money if it cannot buy her a new face, a new figure, new hands? Silently, she studies her stubby digits, spread along the railing, thinking of the clever, tapering fingers whose tips he used to take in his mouth. These hands are clumsy, repel his own when they come too near – a revealing gesture which he attempts to camouflage by lighting another cigarette. Oh dear God, what good is it to be as rich as Croesus and as ugly as sin?

He has something on his mind. 'Ellen,' he begins. It's

money, of course. 'Not for me, *liebling*. I am taken care of,' adding with some bitterness, 'like a pet spaniel.' She rubs small comfort into his bare arm. It's for a television film, apparently – about themselves – a freelance project.

'A film? And what will that involve? More questions, more probing? Will they never give up?'

'We are famous, my love. It is to be expected.'

But fame is the last thing she wants. To be put on view for millions of people to mock and jeer. 'I can't, no. Please, darling. I can't go before cameras like this.'

A semblance of regret tightens his lips. 'The girl, the director, is determined to do it and, if we have control of her finances, rather than her studio, she will have to do as we say. It could be to our advantage.'

She pulls a face, spreads her hands. She can see no advantage in having their past raked over again. Who knows what will turn up?

'And she knows there is a letter – she has worked it out – she will find it for us.'

Ah, the letter. Of course. He would be interested in that. *He* is the determined one. But no letter is worth her humiliation. She will not give in.

'Please, Ellen.'

'No, no, *no-o-o!*' Something clatters on the stones behind them: a videocassette, cracked across and spilling entrails of tape. Looking up they see a woman, swathed in some sort of nanny's uniform, struggling with a small girl who seems intent on throwing herself off the balcony to join it. Aware of her audience the little demon grins in triumph.

A large man at a table below leaps to his feet, gesticulating and, after removing a cigar from between gold-capped teeth, shouts up at the two on the fourth floor, thinking the video was aimed at him. Whatever passes between the four, (the man's wife now adds her shrill voice to the tirade), they all seem to understand each other and it gradually dawns on Ellen that these two on the ground are the child's parents. At last their daughter is persuaded to climb down and go back into the room, followed by the nurse, and the parents resume their seats, their cocktails and their conversation with their friends. It falls to the waiter to clear away the wreckage.

Crack! Another videotape skids across the cobbles and into the water by Ellen's foot and a third, bouncing off a sunshade, narrowly skims her ear. Whipping off his glasses, Max heads, fists bunching at his sides, for the side entrance and the fourth floor, discretion forgotten. The man shambles after him, sweating profusely and appealing to him in English.

Max stops in the doorway, seething. As the exchange continues, Ellen is aware of its tenor subtly shifting from mutual abuse to grudging conciliation, to enquiry and reply, to interest and smiles, to slaps on the back and a final hearty handshake as they part. The man continues indoors to deliver a timely ticking off to his brat or, more likely, to her nanny, and Max to rejoin Ellen with the news that the man, an olive-skinned businessman, recognised Max from *Way of the World* and was anxious to buy them drinks later that evening. Max had declined, with apologies, explaining that they had another engagement. The man pressed his business card upon him. Give him a call, he insisted. Perhaps Max could set up a meeting with the illustrious surgeon lady?

Now everyone on the terrace is nodding and smiling and Max and Ellen wave a cheery farewell as they retire to their room. No sooner is the door closed than Max rips the card across and tosses it in the bin. There is no way the 'illustrious surgeon lady' is going to hear about this stolen weekend or about rich bastards and their dreams of immortality.

Two days have passed; Max has gone back to his surgeon to plead his lover's cause. If Axel Schlager can be found a new body so can she. Only then will she agree to take part in any stupid film.

But for the moment she will sit in her air-conditioned apartment and read and dream. If she gets bored she'll go for walks along the river, take in a museum or two, visit fine restaurants. And she'll come back to her lonely room, watch television and help herself to a drink or two – without ice.

9

Old Mr. Mallory was living out his days in Loughton, in Westering Park, housing so sheltered it took me ten minutes to find it. I pressed the bell to his flat and waited, passing the time in reading a Labour Party poster in his window – a voice crying in the Lib. Dem. wilderness. I'd forgotten about the local elections next week. After a succession of microphone scrabblings, a self-conscious voice bade me come in on the buzz. No 'Who is it?' or 'What do you want?' So much for security.

A wiry old gent met me in the entrance hall, trailing an aura of fish supper and soap opera. He wore a discreet hearing aid, loose-fitting dentures and a crumb of cod on his chin. Fumblings in his cardigan pocket produced a familiar black and white photo, like a pass. My nod assured him that I believed he was who he said he was.

'Where's old Max, then?' He slurred his words like a drunk or someone who was afraid of his plate slipping. But his eye was bright and his thick white curls bristled like a cockatoo's crest. He even sidestepped along his perch for a clearer view out of the lobby window.

I felt awful. I'd been so set on getting his story I'd for-gotten that meeting Max had been his only reason for ringing the studio. I had to mime abject apologies, doubting he'd hear me over *EastEnders*.

His crest drooped visibly. 'That's a pity,' he murmured, and closed the door behind him to a burbling crack, so that he could hear my explanation.

'Max is keen to meet you,' I assured him. 'But we thought we should make this an, em, an exploratory visit.'

'Exploratory?' He looked up hopefully. 'Oh I see, you're sounding me out. Well, you have to, of course. The man's a prototype. National asset. Yes, naturally you have to take precautions. Make sure he doesn't fall into the wrong hands, eh?'

'Ri-i-ght.' There *was* that, I supposed.

'Well, you'd better come in. Come in.'

With a final bob at the window to satisfy himself that there really wasn't a young man secreted outside in the dusty depths of my car, and a furtive glance up the stairs to where a Stannah chair-lift waited to bring the first floor occupant down to ground level, he waved me into his flat.

It was impossible to speak above the racket. Half a dozen characters were at it, hammer and tongs.

'Could we –?' I gestured helplessly.

He was all concern; claimed he'd only had it on for company. Couldn't stand the programme, truth be told. In the ringing silence after the click, the squish when I sank down into his *World of Leather* settee sounded like an invasion.

His eyes lit with interest when I told him about the documentary, and, as he rubbed his chin ruminatively, the fish fell off, unnoticed. I said I saw his role as the vital link between Max Zeiler now, and then, at the time of the Spanish Civil War.

He raised an eyebrow. 'I see,' he said, but his mind was on my well-being. 'Do you take milk?' he enquired.

I hadn't noticed the tray on a small side table, and the posh tea-set, all fluted bone china. Three cups, of course. He must have timed tea to coincide with my arrival. The pot was hot and heavy and his hand shook. A dribble of liquid ran into the saucer.

I sipped and tasted dust. The set hadn't been used for a while. Still, I drank it, and asked for more when I reached the dregs – 'First decent cup I've had all day.' This time he let me pour.

The room was leached of colour. The mistiest of Turner prints relieved the stark cream of the walls, and a few unglazed stoneware pots stood along the windowsill, in size order, with dried grasses and teasels in the tallest. A lonely bowl of brown-spotted bananas and wrinkly apples ornamented a scrubbed-wood table and clustering chairs, and silver-framed family photographs toed an invisible line on the sideboard. I could see no other keepsakes, no ornaments to dust, no magazines to tidy, no plants to water, no female clutter – an old man's trouble-free sterility.

Reading matter was a choice between *The Oldie*, jammed spine to spine in date order, or two shelves of *Readers Digest* condensed novels in forbidding maroon, but no walls a-tumble with paperbacks like at Nan's. There were a few solid tomes on socialism and politics on the lowest shelves, a few atlases and dictionaries and encyclopaedias, and the *Guardian*, folded back to the crossword. I suppose he might have had a mad tidy-up in honour of my visit, but I doubted it. No one could have achieved such pristine order in twenty minutes *and* made the tea.

'Have you lived here long, Mr. Mallory?'

A year or two, he said. He and his wife had moved to the country when they retired, but she had died some years before, and to be honest, he'd felt rather dismal out there in the sticks without her. His daughter, Felicity, had spotted the vacant property in her local paper and suggested that he move to be closer to her and his grandchildren. It had been an upheaval but Felicity had helped and it was all for the best, he was sure. They'd cleared out all the old rubbish. And she'd helped him buy new furnishings. A fresh start. He was getting used to it . . .

When I produced the mini DV camera his ears went back like a cat's. 'I thought you'd be taking notes,' he said, regarding the contraption nervously.

'Don't worry,' I said, 'you'll forget I'm using it.'

'That's all you need, is it?'

'It is, actually. And the sound quality on this model is brilliant. I don't need a recordist or anything. Say something.' I switched on.

'I'm not very good at ad-libbing. Better at writing things down.'

'That'll do.'

While I played it back to him he tugged at his long ear lobe, and then at his shirt-cuffs so that they showed a regulation half-inch below his cardigan, and turned Max's unused cup over into its saucer with a sigh. I noticed his shirt had a crumpled, unironed look, like his trousers, and his tie had a grease spot.

I switched on and Mr. Mallory (after a faltering start, when I had to ask him not to shout), said it was terrible, *terrible* what they'd done to Max.

'Really?' I said.

Interfering with nature – it just wasn't right. They'd created a monster, neither fish nor fowl. They should have left him in peace, given the brains a decent burial, not messed about transplanting them.

'But that would have been murder. The brain was still alive.'

In Douglas Mallory's opinion it would have been the kindest thing. Put it – him – out of his misery. To force him to inhabit another person's body, inflict all this stress . . .

'Stress?' I couldn't see it. 'A lot of people,' I pointed out, 'scientists, politicians, well, anybody really, would give their eye-teeth for Max's chance, to see what the future holds. Wouldn't you?'

Not even as a fly on the wall, the old man said, his face darkening with anger, his jaw knotting, not when everything he valued had been thrown out, turned on its head – morals, attitudes, respect for authority. Not when schoolkids were beating up pensioners, and killing each other just because of the colour of their skin. Not when the NHS was on its knees and teachers were leaving the sinking ship of education in their droves. Not when little girls were playing Mummies and Daddies with real babies. Not when skilled men and women were put out to grass at fifty. Not when it was 'Me, me, me!' and the devil take the hindmost. God knows what New Labour thought they were playing at.

No, the end couldn't come soon enough for him. He was sorry for old Max who'd had to come back and see all his socialist ideals being trashed, the world in a downward spiral of greed.

I didn't know what to say. Suddenly I saw the enormity of the burden Max was carrying – the horrors of Buchenwald banked up inside him, and all *this* piled on top. Mallory had been on a sixty-year journey, from the golden age of the Welfare State, through the Winter of Discontent, the destructive Thatcher years, up to the Blair government and his present despair. But for Max it was an overnight, Rip Van Winkle trip. I agreed that he must be strung pretty tight.

He nodded grimly. 'On the telly last week, anyone could see he wasn't himself,' quickly adding, 'aside from his appearance, I mean. The strain showed – in his eyes.'

'But you knew it was him?'

'Oh yes,' he nodded with wise certainty. 'But you could see the poor chap was going through hell. That's why I thought he could do with a friend. Someone who'd known him as he was. Help him get his bearings.'

He picked up the photograph of the bus to Madrid and smiled sadly at his younger self. 'I was twenty-one then – over sixty years ago. Hard to believe I'm the same person, the same Doug Mallory,' he said, examining his knob-knuckled hands back, front and back again, as though they didn't belong to him. He sighed, 'I am, though. I still think the same things are important – *From each according to his abilities, to each according to his needs.* Take care of each other, in other words. *He* said the same: *Love your neighbour as yourself.* Jesus Christ, that is, the biggest socialist of the lot.' He peered over the top of his glasses at the photo and nodded, settled his glasses back on his nose, sentiment dismissed.

'And Max believed that, did he?'

'Max? Certainly. Give you his last cigarette, Max would – and take yours!' He laughed. 'Oh he was a good pal, old Max. And he could tell a good yarn. Just about his family, people he knew, but he made them sound interesting, special, you know? He'd start off, "There was this old soak at work . . ." and you'd all settle back, forget the fascists over the hill, and warm your toes on his memories.'

This was brilliant, exactly what I needed. Someone who knew what Max was like before, how Buchenwald had changed him. 'He's only just beginning to open up,' I said, thinking of the other day and that story about the Wolffs. I suppose if you've read enough personal accounts of the war on the Internet, it helps to put yours in perspective, makes it easier to talk.

Sorrow clouded the old man's face. 'Shame,' he said, closing his eyes and lowering his head as if in prayer. Eventually he said, 'I expect I'd find him a bit on the quiet side.'

'He's seen a lot of death,' I said, 'more than most. He was part of the German Resistance, you know, captured trying to get people out of Berlin.'

'I never knew what it was he got up to. He never talked about it. But, I, er,' his grizzled eyebrows bunched over the tops of his glasses, 'I rather got the impression he was working for our side, our government, I mean. Something hush-hush. We met up a couple of times after Spain, before the war with Germany, but I knew better than to pry. And then I joined the regular army and we lost touch. Pity, we had some good times, me and old Max.' And then an uncomfortable thought contracted his features. 'Mind you, if he'd known then what lay ahead . . . '

We both turned back to the snapshot, probably sharing the thought that, incredibly, there was nothing in Max's laughing face, not a shadow, not a glimmer, not a clue as to the horrors he would have to endure. He was shielding his eyes against the sun, not the future.

What, I wondered aloud, had prompted Douglas Mallory to go off and fight in Spain?

He frowned, inhaling deeply, and stared unseeing at the ceiling where a pollywog danced in the sudden movement of air. He pursed his lips and nodded as the answer came to him. 'You have to remember, Miss, em . . .'

I told him to call me Clare.

'There was nothing for us here, in Britain, in the Depression. Gloomy faces everywhere you looked, tight belts. It gave you the pip.'

I said, 'You must have been quite young.'

'Twenty-ish,' he sighed again. 'Getting older by the minute. I was out of work like everybody else and looking for answers. So I started spending time in the library – well, it was warm in there apart from anything else.' He threw me a look of regret or apology, and went on, 'Suffice to say, I got in with a crowd of lefties. You know how it is – you're sitting in the pub, later on, having a chat, and apart from the length of the dole queue, what else is there to talk about but what's going on in Europe? Fascism rearing its ugly head.' He sniffed. 'There was Hitler in Germany, Mussolini in Italy. And now old Franco had come along with his army, trying to take over Spain. I mean they'd just voted the Republicans into government. That was what the *people* wanted but he wasn't happy, him and everybody else who'd been squeezing the country dry for hundreds of

137

years, the capitalists and the landowners and the church. So, of course, the Spanish people, the workers, tried to stop him, didn't they? That was the difference. In Italy and Germany the people just lay down under it; the Spanish were made of tougher stuff. I felt for them but it was all happening a long way off. Then this chap, Harry – Harry Stevens?' Twin suns flashed in his glasses as he studied my reaction but the name eluded me. Some politician, was he? 'Salt of the earth, old Harry. Bit of a hothead but that was part of his charm. He took me along to a meeting of the ILP – Independent Labour Party,' he spelled out.

'Independent?'

'More extreme. They believed in workers' control. Marxist revolution. The workers were going to take over the means of production and run things themselves.'

'I thought that's what communists believed.'

He gave me a pained look. All right so I'm not so hot on politics. He said, 'Communists believe in *state* control. Big Brother and all that. The ILP believed that the state would eventually wither away.'

'But they had a lot in common with the communists?'

'No, young lady, the only thing they had in common was a hatred of fascism. And in the end,' he murmured, his eyes hidden behind glasses mirroring images of windows, trees, blushing clouds, 'in the end, it wasn't enough . . .' A blackbird pink-pinked in the stillness and, in a neighbouring flat, a canned audience laughed. Footsteps creaked across the ceiling.

'It was at that last meeting in September they told us how Italy and Germany had been violating the non-intervention agreement all along, supplying military aid to the Nationalists, guns, planes, you name it. It had been *Hitler's* planes that had airlifted Franco's troops out of Africa and landed them in Seville. And still Britain and France wouldn't lift a finger. I mean, they *said* their sympathies lay with the Republicans, but sympathy don't butter no par-snips. The workers' militias didn't stand a chance. Well, there comes a time, you know, you can't just sit on your backside and we started sneaking into Fascist meetings, me and my mates, heckling, throwing things, starting fights. And then –' His chin jerked with satisfaction – 'and then we stopped them marching down Cable Street.'

'The Battle of Cable Street? You were there?'

'Oh yes. October 4th 1936 Where else would I be? You know what he was planning to do, old Mosley? March right through the Jewish area. I suppose he meant to frighten them with his three thousand bullyboys – and twice as many police lining the route. That's what got people's backs up. I mean what the hell did they think they were doing? It was an invasion. Bloody cheek. These were people's homes, their streets, their friends and neighbours. Of course they were going to defend them.' His glasses flashed again and a grim smile played around his lips. 'Once we toppled that lorry in the middle of the road, got ourselves a barricade, there was no stopping us. We were tearing up the cobblestones, paving stones, bricks, you name it, and there were bottles and slops raining down from upstairs windows. The entire East End was out there having a go. A hundred thousand in the end, they reckoned, damned if they were going to let a gang of Nazi thugs ride roughshod over them. *THEY SHALL NOT PASS!* That's what they wrote. On the walls, on sheets draped across the front of houses – the same slogan they had in Spain. We just wanted to keep them *out*! It makes you realise, some-thing like that, just whose side you're on. Oh yes, I was in the thick of it, fighting for my class.

'It's hard to remember exactly what happened when. One minute you were running, trying to keep out of the way of the horses, then you were lobbing bricks, then you were fighting hand to hand, in a scrum of helmets and cloth caps. Fists flying about, not to mention the odd frying pan. And toasting forks, copper-sticks, anything you could lay your hands on. And all the while this flaming autogyro racketing around over your head. What a din! But somehow, you know, I heard Harry yelling, 'Dougie, over here!' I could just see him over the heads, hanging on for dear life to this beefy flatfoot, trying to stop him beating some other poor devil to a pulp. It was only after we'd decked him between us that I realised the bloke at the business end of the truncheon was Harry's cousin.' He paused significantly, stole a sly look at me and, as sunset flashed a second time on his glasses, light dawned. Blindingly.

Harry Stevens. I *had* heard the name before. Harry was Max's English cousin.

I juggled with implications and consequences. 'So you . . . he was . . .' and why not? Why had I assumed they'd met in Spain? Max had *told* me he'd been in London in the thirties. He spoke English. He had family here.

'It was the obvious place to come,' I said.

The old man wagged his head up and down, pleased to have kept me guessing for so long. 'It was also the first place the Nazis would look for him. And they were relentless, those Secret Police. But it didn't stop Max pitching in with the rest of us against the Blackshirts. He *hated* them so much. "*The Beasts*" he called them. 'Course he'd seen what they could do at first hand, in his own country.' His eyes glinted at me over prayer-clasped knuckles. 'You know his girlfriend, Sophie, was Jewish?'

'No!' Instinctively I braced myself for tragedy.

His lips thinned. At the time of Berthe's wedding, Sophie was working in her uncle's dress shop. In fact, she made the dress in which Berthe was married, and it was during one of the fittings at the Zeiler home – Aryans were forbidden, by law, to enter Jewish premises – that Max and Sophie met and fell in love. They were young: he was nineteen, she two years younger. Both marriage and extra-marital relationships between Jews and non-Jews were forbidden, and her parents were against it because he was a Gentile but, in spite of, or possibly because of the opposition, Max was determined to have her. In other circumstances, Douglas said, it might all have blown over, but Max was a 'bolshie little git', who had already attracted the attention of the bosses, at the tractor factory in Hamburg, for his anti-Nazi views. He had been beaten up and it seemed that he'd got off lightly with cracked ribs and a broken eye socket: there were rumours that socialists and trade unionists were being shot or sent to labour camps. It was only a matter of time, his mother felt sure, before they realised that their 'warning' had had no effect. Max would go to her sister in England, where he would be safe, and Gustav was to stop wearing *his* union pin and learn to bite his tongue or he'd be next across the Channel. Sophie would follow once Max had got himself a job and the means to support a wife. Annie had it all worked out.

But whether Sophie ever made it to England Douglas didn't know. Max went off to fight in Spain, sure that the war there would be over in a matter of months, soon enough to whisk Sophie away from her tormentors. Back in October '36, though the Jews in Germany were being pitilessly mistreated, it never occurred to anyone on the streets of the East End that Hitler, in his madness, would see extermination as the final solution.

'We were more intent on keeping Max out of police clutches. He was an illegal immigrant. God knows we didn't want him to be shipped back home and shot.'

'They wouldn't . . .'

'We weren't at war yet. The Germans had every right to demand his extradition.'

'So you saved his life?'

'Oh, I wouldn't go so far as . . .' His forefingers lifted

and fell on his bony knees, lifted and fell with a life and rhythm of their own, 'Well, I suppose, but it didn't seem like that at the time. We were just pals helping each other out. He'd have done the same for me or Harry. None of us wanted to be arrested, after all. We got him away up a side alley and over the garden walls. Nobody stopped us, except a woman who insisted on taking us into her house to clean him up.'

'Was he badly hurt?' I cared.

'A few cuts and bruises, nothing to speak of. Right as rain after a drop of scotch – for the shock, she reckoned. And a drop more when they told us the fascists had had to turn round and take their wretched march along the Embankment. Not quite the same if there's no one watching you, is it? It soon fizzled out.'

'So you had a few bevvies?'

'I should say. It was a wonderful victory. Legendary. There was dancing in the streets that night and we were bloody heroes (oh, I'm sorry – you'd better bleep that bit.) Where was I? Oh yes, we thought we were God's gift, all right. There was no stopping us after that. When they called for volunteers for Spain, we were first in the queue.'

'The, em, the ILP arranged all that, did they?'

'Ah well . . .' He seemed amused. 'They couldn't be seen to be going against the "non-intervention policy of their own democratically elected government", now could they?' His tone was ironic as he quoted what seemed to be some party line. 'Know why? "In case they encouraged the fascists!" Would you credit it?' He laughed mirthlessly. 'But they did what they could. Gave us papers, letters of intro-duction, got us on board a packet-steamer to Bordeaux but, from there, we were on our own. Had to make our own way to Paris. I mean none of us could speak a word of French. We expected any minute to be arrested and clapped in irons, or what was it they had in France, the chop!

142

Anyway, to cut a long story short we got to Paris and found Comintern's office. Communist International,' he explained. 'Says it all, doesn't it? The only people willing to lend the poor old Spanish people a hand were the Commies. Mother Russia.'

'But, surely . . .' I remembered seeing a film on telly about the Spanish Civil War. The British had sent ambulances and all sorts.

'The *unions* did,' he said, putting me wise. 'People that cared. The government did sweet Fanny Adams. Writers and such clubbed together, raised funds for bandages and food and the occasional lorry, but it was the Soviets who gave us the guns to fight with, such as they were. They were the ones gave us International Brigade passports, and got us across the border, down to Albacete.' The lenses darkened as he bent to fidget with the photograph, realigning it with the edge of the table as though it were a picture on the wall. As he retreated into his memories, his wedding ring tap-tapped against the wood, tapped . . . and was still.

I cleared my throat in the darkening room, and turned up the light. 'That was in Spain, was it?'

'Mmm?' he enquired, frowning and blinking, startled by my appalling ignorance. And with a weary sigh and a discipline born of parade grounds, he dragged himself to attention, shoulders back, chin up. 'Albacete was our training base, down on the eastern side. Franco hadn't got that far.'

At that moment, someone rapped softly on the door. 'Yoohoo! Douglas, are you there? You've left your door open, dear.'

I switched off the camera.

'Damn and blast the woman,' he said.

'Shall *I* go?' I offered, as he began creaking to his feet, but a small, grey, bow-legged body was already scampering into the room, whiskers a-twitch.

'Oh you *are* in! I couldn't hear the television.'

'Sylvia!' He gestured helplessly in my direction and one shrewd look took in everything about me, from my crinkly red topknot to my scuffed trainers.

'Oh,' she said, apple-cheeked and quite unfazed, 'I'm sorry, I didn't realise. One of your grandchildren, is it?' She was waiting to be introduced.

He turned to me with pleading in his eyes.

'Hi,' I said, proffering my hand, 'I'm Clare, from *Way of the World*.'

'I'm supposed to be telling her about my pal, Max,' he said sniffily.

'The brain transplant?' she said. 'Terrible thing, terrible,' echoing Douglas' words. Ah, I wondered, whose opinion *was* this? 'Well, I won't interrupt you. I'll just wash those tea things up, shall I? While I'm here?' And ignoring our protestations she whisked away the tray and waddled, like a sailor on a rolling deck, out to the kitchen, and closed the door.

There was a faint clatter of crockery but I thought it would probably add a dash of background colour. I tried to steer him back to the Spanish Civil War by way of the photograph. 'They managed to fix you up with uniforms, then?' In the film I'd seen they'd worn fairisle sweaters and marched about with suitcases on their backs.

He explained that *'Land and Freedom'* had been about the militias. The International Brigades were something different and they'd worn dead men's clothes. 'French,' he said. 'Left over from the First World War.'

'Still had lice in the seams, didn't they, Douglas?' There was Sylvia, framed in the doorway.

'Oh please!' I wailed, switching off the camera again.

'Sylvia! Clare's trying to make a film, dear. If you're finished out there why don't you just sit quietly?' He patted a dining chair and, when she sat, her feet didn't reach the floor. We began again with him explaining that the uniforms had been fairly clean when they'd been handed out, but had soon become infested again.

'Just imagine, Clare . . .' I switched off again, smiling tightly. 'They had lice crawling all over their, you know, private parts.' She shivered with something like excitement. 'You had to burn out the eggs with your cigarette end, didn't you, Douglas? And tell her what you had to eat.'

'She's not really . . . Oh well, there wasn't a lot, of course. Bean stew and bread.'

'And rats!' she crowed triumphantly. 'And donkey meat! I wrote a poem about it, didn't I, Douglas? You might like to read it, Clare. The viewers would be interested. I'll pop up and get it, shall I?' She hopped down from the chair. 'Guaranteed to turn you vegetarian,' she chortled.

'Oh I –' I cast around helplessly. Douglas' face was unreadable. The silver-plated clock on the mantelpiece dinged a timely reprieve. 'I'd love to look at it, but I . . . Gosh, is that the time? I really have to go. Perhaps next time I come, Mrs, em, Sylvia. If I *may* come again, Douglas?'

'Of course. And you'll bring Max next time, won't you?'

'Definitely,' I said. Film of their reunion was an absolute must.

'You reckon we pass muster, then? You trust us not to kidnap him and sell him to the enemy?'

What a lovely old man. Max was lucky to have had such a good friend. I hoped, I truly hoped that Douglas was not going to find Max too changed. He had had enough let downs in his old age.

10

The house in South Kensington rippled with music. I assumed, as we mounted the stairs, that it was someone's CD player on full blast, and then, when Susmeta hushed us (me, and Richard, the interpreter), and made us wait outside the door, I found myself looking for the red 'On Air' light. There was a pause. A phrase repeated. And then a crash, crash, crash of discord and temper. It was someone practising the piano.

The melody began again and to my poor ear it sounded fine. I don't know many piano pieces – a few bits of Chopin and that one by Tchaikovsky, and Liszt's 'Hungarian Rhapsody', but I recognised the Rachmaninov because Mum had played the CD over and over when Sid left. He didn't have an orchestra to fill in the gaps, of course – the pianist in South Ken, I mean – and it was during one of these that Susmeta poked her head round the door and said we could go in.

Axel Schlager was a little gem. Perfect in every way. If I hadn't been picky I might have given him serious consideration. But he was a bit old – in his late thirties – and a mere dot at five and a half feet. When you thought of all that talent you wondered how they had managed to cram such a mighty brain into such a small skull. He was perfectly formed, like Tom Cruise or Michael J. Fox, but his hands had been travelling up and down the keyboard at full stretch. I say 'keyboard' because that's all it was, a common or garden electronic synthesizer that could as easily turn out Clarinet or Trumpet or Tubular Bells as Piano. Susmeta said it was the only instrument he could play with anything approaching his old dexterity, thanks to her. She had condemned a concert pianist to hands that had no muscle-memory of the instrument.

'It's as if I were to put a ballet-dancer's brain into your body, Clare. No matter how supple and graceful the mind, no matter how it visualises the movements, your body is not made that way. You would never dance to the brain's satisfaction.'

'Thanks, Susmeta,' I said, grimly.

'Oh maybe if you had been trained as a dancer from an early age.' She spread slender fingers. 'But starting this late, your bones, your muscles are set in their ways. It's impossible.'

She really had no idea what raw nerves she was twanging. Okay, so I was a beanpole with two left feet. No need to rub it in.

But I knew about muscle-memory. Axel had practised all day, every day, for over six months, and his fingers were beginning, *just* beginning to get the idea. On a grown-up piano he sounded like a good student. On a keyboard, a *very* good student. He was clearly not a happy bunny.

Not that he was ungrateful, I had to understand, as he dazzled us with a smile. He was very grateful to have survived Buchenwald, grateful that his music would be heard, that he was able, at last, to write down the score for an opera that he'd held in his head for over sixty years. When they'd removed his brain in the camp hospital, the second act of the opera was incomplete and he hadn't really thought about the third. And yet, when he was coming round from the operation he could hear it in his head, not in its entirety, of course, but the mezzo's aria, the chorus and the motif for the final duet. And once he got them down on paper the rest had just seemed to fall into place. His subconscious must have been singing to itself all the while Frau Doktor Naidoo has been stitching him back together. Unless she had had music playing in the operating theatre and he had picked up someone else's opus. Now wouldn't that be a hoot!

Susmeta's teeth indented her bottom lip and her brow furrowed. 'Oh, Axel . . .'

'You *didn't* . . .?' I gasped. Axel closed his eyes in despair.

'Ravi Shankar.' She made a face as though she'd bitten into a lemon. 'An Indian musician and composer. You wouldn't know him. I – I didn't like to tell you.' Seeing his look of sheer agony, she relented, her tinkling laugh rivalling anything the piano could produce. 'I'm so cruel,' she chortled. 'No, Axel. Music is a distraction. I need to work in utter silence. You needn't worry – your opera is original. All your own work.'

He rolled his eyes and clutched at his heart in not quite mock relief.

'You should hear it, Clare,' she said fondly. 'Quite, quite beautiful. Especially the lovers' duet at the end. Pure joy. Soaring music of freedom.'

She clearly doted on the musician. A mother's pride in a gifted child. I supposed he was as much her creation as Max, and the others, in fact. She had given them life. I'd thought Max her favourite, now I wasn't so sure.

'So your hands haven't stopped you writing music, Axel?' I waited while Richard asked the question in German.

By way of reply he took my arm and led me to a computer over by the window, where goldfish swam to save the screen. A touch of the mouse and there was a complicated musical score. This was how he composed, with another keyboard imitating all the instruments he could wish, even the voices.

'Ve hef ze technology,' he grinned. 'Senk you, Frau Naidoo.'

She smiled. 'Thank *you*, Axel,' and turned to me. 'Some of my Buchenwald patients came round from the anaesthetic still frozen with terror but Axel had a big smile on his face.'

He had known instinctively, he said in German, even before he regained consciousness, it seemed, that he was out of Hofmann's clutches and in a place of safety.

'Until I opened my eyes and saw this monstrous woman in her shower hat!' We had known a joke was on its way even before it was translated, from Richard's chuckle, but still it caught us unawares. It amazed me that despite his sadness and frustration, music-wise, he was still able to crack jokes, though perhaps irony would better describe his account of the life in Buchenwald.

Like other concentration camps it had had its own orchestra, and a marching band that drilled daily on the parade ground, no excuses accepted. What they had lost in humanity the Nazis made up for in culture. They encouraged art, too, and craft, and held exhibitions of the prisoners' work. Not to be compared with that ugly Utilitarian stuff that the Bauhaus had been churning out across the river in Weimar before the Fuhrer, in his infinite wisdom, had closed it down; nothing nasty or revolutionary. Indeed the commandant's wife, Ilse Koch, was quite an artist in her own right, even though she dressed in jodhpurs and boots and carried a riding crop. Axel's lips narrowed as he told us the story. She'd ordered the Jewish prisoners stripped and lined up, then she had marched down the rows until she saw a tattoo she liked. That man would be taken away, immediately, to the camp hospital where Hofmann and his colleagues would remove the patch of skin containing the tattoo, have it tanned, and patched together with others to make lampshades for her lounge. It had taken an artist's eye to see the potential. Found objects.

'Jesus,' I said.

The musicians were given special privileges. Because calluses and blisters might have interfered with their listeners' pleasure they were given less crippling work to do. Some worked in the hospital, some, like Axel, in the zoo.

'The zoo?'

Oh yes. The tender-hearted Nazis had a soft spot for animals and had created a zoo to amuse the guards. It was just outside the barbed wire fence, near the main gate, presumably for the creatures' own safety. Okapi on the hoof or crocodile steaks might have proved too much of a temptation for starving prisoners. As it was the keepers and their assistants were frisked at the end of their shift for the smallest peanut or sunflower seed. Theft was punishable by death. That wasn't to say that the parrots weren't sometimes given short measure, and the monkeys always had an edge to their appetite.

Axel cleaned out the pens for eighteen months and saw prisoners come and go. Shovelling animal shit was not as bad as some of the stuff the others had to do and, with a couple of hours off for piano practice, it suited him to keep a low profile. On the surface, at least, it looked as though he were a model prisoner.

In the evening small groups, quartets and trios, would serenade the officers as they dined. Not that many listened to the musical wallpaper in a hall already noisy with clattering and scraping and clinking, chattering and laughter. Klaus Hofmann and the medical staff tended to sit apart from the other officers, at tables some distance from the performance area, but he was one of the few who paid attention. Axel had recognised him, on his fatal visit to the hospital, as the doctor who had sat through every one of his performances, raptly listening. He hadn't been the only musician in Hofmann's programme, but he was the only one who had survived.

I wanted to know why he had been imprisoned in the first place. Was he Jewish?

No, he wasn't Jewish, he said, but many of his friends were. Musicians and their families. He had courted trouble, he admitted, by hiding David and Leah Blum in his attic.

From his raised eyebrows I gathered I was expected to have heard of them. He hadn't helped matters by playing music by Jewish composers the likes of Arnold Schoenberg, his old teacher, exiled to America by Hitler in 1933. He himself was greatly influenced by Jewish 'kletzmer' music.

Without waiting for me to show my ignorance he turned back to the Yamaha to show us what he meant. I recognised it straight away: the plaintive wail of the black notes, haunting and distinctive, reminding me of the Drama Soc's production of 'Fiddler on the Roof' in my second year at Uni. (I'd played the matchmaker). And then he showed us what he'd done with it, taken a melody or two, a combination of rhythms, and produced something amazing. I was whisked away from this spacious apartment, with its potted tree ferns and 'Past Times' settee-throws, to a smoky Berlin cellar where jazz played, where decadents danced close up tight in a sinister sexy smooch to a limping waltz that sent shivers up your spine. At the same time, up in the top notes, he'd managed to get a sort of two fingers 'Fuck you!'

'Brilliant!' I told him eventually, when I could breathe again.

He shook his head, sighing. '*Nein*,' he said. '*Es ist altmodisch.*'

Old-fashioned. Sixty years out of date. Melodies were very old hat, compared with the compositions of modern minimalists. He couldn't compete. As for the sentiments, no one was interested any more, they had no relevance in the world today. It was a hard lesson but he was learning.

At thirty-two he'd still been a spoiled child, a brat, a *wunderkind* who'd thought his musical talent gave him immunity in many ways. But one day he had come home to find the house ransacked, his friends gone, and the SS waiting in the hallway to arrest him for harbouring Jews. He had been sent to Buchenwald and had never seen his friends or his family again. That's how it was – his fault. He fell silent and hung his head, studying hands that were not quite big enough for all this.

'*Ich habe durst*,' he said at last, changing the subject. '*Was trinken Sie? Kaffee? Tee?*'

We opted for coffee and I followed him into the kitchen to lend a hand.

'*Kalte Milch*?' he said, waving the bottle at me.

'You don't have Coffee Mate, do you?' I love the stuff. I eat it by the spoonful when Mum's not around, that, or cold cooked pasta with sugar and full-fat fromage frais. Yum.

There it was on a higher shelf than he could reach and, without thinking, I passed it down to him, as though he were a little old lady in a supermarket. His wistful smile of thanks made me shrink with shame. I tutted and threw up my hands to show what an oaf I was, how utterly insensitive. In guttural German he waved my apologies aside and proceeded to make me understand, by patting his chest and stretching his arm high that he had once been taller than me.

It wasn't until we took the tray of coffee and biscuits through to the others that he was able to explain, through Richard, that he had only just learned to stop ducking in low doorways. He wished he had a photo to show me, or else how would I ever believe that his feet had actually touched the pedals? If I wanted to know what he'd looked like before the war, he believed that sheet music might still exist with his picture on the front or even film, tucked away in some music library in Bonn or Hamburg. Then I would see what a dashing figure he'd cut in coat tails and spats with his hair greased to his head. 'Like Gene Kelly?' I asked, but he didn't know who I was talking about.

Susmeta said, with even less tact than mine, that it had been sheer chance that they should have decided to transplant Axel first. If it had been the other way round then Max would have had the smaller body he was used to and Axel, with Leon Paterson's musical background, would have been saved a lot of heartache. They had both been of the same blood group, A positive.

'Couldn't you have swopped them over?' I enquired. It seemed a fairly obvious solution.

She shook her head quickly, saying nothing, but from her expression I gathered she had put it to Max and he had refused. Max's brain must already have been transplanted when Axel's problems came to light. Well I couldn't blame him, I supposed. He probably felt he'd been mucked about enough.

I said, through Richard, 'Did you ever come across Max when you were a prisoner?'

Of course. Max was on the resistance committee. They both were.

'The resistance committee?'

It was inevitable that they should organise, he said. They were the *avant garde* of the working class, *la creme de la creme*. Most of the big names had been murdered soon after their arrival at the camp, like Ernst Thälmann, the chairman of the Communist Party before the war, but many survived. Some were communists, some anarchists, some social democrats, some like himself had no political affiliation. They just knew, instinctively, that what Hitler was doing was wrong, and in such extremes of danger as they found themselves, put their differences to one side and worked together against the class enemy.

'You rose up against the Nazis?'

Not he, nor the men he worked with. Though theirs were the brains behind the insurrection, theirs were the brains that had been quietly removed from their skulls and frozen a year or more before the end of the war. The very same: Max Zeiler, Axel Schlager, and Friedrich Liebl. He had never met Ellen Sauerbruch though he had communicated with her. Notes scribbled in code and stuffed behind loose bricks for messengers to deliver to the women's section. All organised down to the last crossed 't' and dotted 'i'. But somehow the SS had got to know about their plans for an uprising. Somehow they'd taken out the ringleaders.

To me it smacked of betrayal.

'What about Willi Greff?'

Axel had never known him. He presumed that he came afterwards, in the last six months.

'But there was an uprising?'

'Ah,' said Richard, translating, 'was there? That is the question.'

'What do you mean?'

'He wants you to look at this.' Richard handed over a magazine open at a page showing the photograph of a monument outside the entrance to Buchenwald. Statues of a dozen or so thin, shaven headed men in prison garb, some with arms raised defiantly, stood before a Communist flag. Some held rifles. '"That is the myth," he says. That is the Communist version. You know that Buchenwald is the "Red Olympus" on which the German Democratic Republic was founded?'

He listened some more, and quoted, 'We didn't overthrow the guards. Those who came after us may have done so. But the Americans claim that *they* liberated the camp on 11th April 1945, that as General Patton's tanks surrounded the camp the guards either fled or surrendered, that there was no bloodshed.'

Axel shrugged and showed us empty palms. He wasn't the one to ask.

'Tell me about your life in the camp,' I said, flipping the page in my notebook.

'Life?' He made a sour face. 'It was not life.' He drained his cup for courage. 'No sooner were we off the Weimar train than we were hustled into the disinfection building, given a hose down, a drenching with DDT powder and prison uniform. Then it was down to work: a march through the woods for a spot of stone breaking before lunch. Except there wasn't any lunch, nor afternoon tea, and supper was a ladleful of disgusting soup and a third of a loaf of bread. There was meat, a whole two ounces, three times a week, and an occasional potato or two. Oh and coffee.

'I was exhausted by the end of the day. I was unbelievably soft, never having done a day's hard physical labour in my life. I smelled like a pig and would have given the world for a hot bath and a beer. Failing that I wanted to sleep. I'd spent the previous night in a cattle truck that hadn't moved from the sidings until morning, as more and more people were loaded on, standing room only, or sitting on an upended suitcase. There were no toilet facilities and the place soon began to smell. Everyone was frantic with worry and the guards, pacing up and down outside, refused to answer questions about what was happening, where we were going. I kept a look out for the Blums, expecting them to be on the train, but there were so many people, such a crush. I didn't see them. Perhaps they were sent somewhere else.

'Stupid things kept going through my mind. Would Mama remember to tell Marius that I wouldn't be able to do the concert tour? Would she remember to go for her eye test? Would she be able to cope on her own in Berlin? Such a silly woman, so highly strung. She'd continued to cling to me as the Nazi had prodded me into the street with his revolver. The war would soon be over, she insisted, and they wouldn't keep me locked up forever just for harbouring Jews. My brute of a captor knocked her to the ground.

'I knew, after all that had happened that day, that I wouldn't see her or – or my friends again. I was so physically and spiritually exhausted I wept from sheer self-pity. The old man next to me continued to sit. As far as I know he didn't move or even look at me until I had cried myself out, until I reached that point when I realised the futility of it.

'"I'm sorry," I said, cuffing snot on my zebra stripes.

'"Don't be." When he spoke I realised he wasn't the old man I'd taken him for. The grimy broken nails he was studying belonged to young hands. His exhausted stoop had given me the impression of decrepitude but he was probably no older than I was. And although his face was grey with deprivation and the flesh had fallen away, leaving angular cheekbones and eyes on dark saucers, the skin was smooth and taut over the bones, and his eyes held an intensity that the elderly do not have, unless they go mad. '"The time to worry," he told me, "is when you can't cry any more. But just as the fascists have hardened themselves against any feelings of humanity, so we, their class enemies must harden ourselves against their cruelty. Close off our minds and sensitivities and simply obey. Or seem to. It's something Germans are good at, I think you'll agree." He wanted to know my name and I told him.

'He introduced himself as Max. "We are in the thick of it here, my friend, at the heart of the class struggle. The crucible. We must fan that spark of hatred for the oppressor until it is white hot. And when the time is right we will rise up. Prepare for the Revolution, Axel. We have nothing to lose but our chains."

'"Or our lives," I said.

'"They are lost already."

'I knew it. I stared at him, at his pinched profile and sunken cheeks, at his desperado's eyes that had been blue and were salt-glazed and bleary like glass thrown up by the sea.

'"How long have you been here?" I asked, dreading the answer.

'"Seven months."

'"That long?" It was possible then to survive. Perhaps I would still be here in seven months. Heaven forbid.

'"Some of the comrades have been here for years. Kurt there helped to build the place." He indicated a scrawny creature on the bed-rack opposite, who looked up at his name. "When was that, Kurt?"

'"Nineteen thirty-seven, God damn their eyes. Broke into my studio, drank all my booze, burned all my pictures – bloody life's work. Sedition, they called it. Satire, *satire* is what it was. I'm a cartoonist, for God's sake. What did they think they were paying me for? No sense of humour, the Nazis. Shunted me off to this hellhole. Never even had a chance to say goodbye to my wife. Come the revolution, eh, boys, come the revolution!"

'Six years! And still his soul clung to his bones, peering at a world of misery from deep brown sockets. I couldn't see him lasting five minutes in the quarry. He said he would rather split stone than do what he did.

'"What is that?" I asked

'"Work for which a cartoonist is aptly suited. Making death masks in the hospital."

'"Why on earth would anyone want . . .?"

'He shrugged and wagged his toffee apple head. "There are some mad buggers about," he said, "not least the doctors."'

'"What work are you in, Max?" I wondered, thinking that it couldn't be any worse.

'"Sorting," he muttered, turning his head away.

'"Sorting?" I envisaged a rack of pigeonholes for incoming mail. In my innocence, I even allowed myself to entertain thoughts of sending and receiving letters. Perhaps I could get one to Mama.

'Sorting, Max told me, was the vilest work, involving sad piles of clothes and baggage, shoes and spectacles and false teeth; a dozen festering slag heaps built from the curds and clinker of genocide. There were grading trays for precious metals and stones, for coins and paper money. The sorting house was a stinking hole, where treacherous rats come into their own, plundering purses, prying into private places for hidden spoils, prising rings from dead fingers, earrings from cold ears. Recycling began there, in the first of many rooms on the way to the ovens.'

Richard asked him something in German.

'Nein,' came the answer.

It turned out he was asking about teeth – the gold teeth and fillings that the Nazis had reportedly extracted from Jewish mouths. Had Max had to do that?

Susmeta said that that was a job for the surgeon, who would have had the right instruments, known how to separate filling from tooth. Max had, at least, been spared that.

I closed my eyes against the images that arose during this account. How could men and women, the humans running the camps, sink to such foul depths? I was appalled. Max had conveniently left out this little gem. I said I thought he'd told me he'd worked in the salt-mines.

'The salt mines?' he winced, sucking sympathy through his teeth. 'Poor guy, I didn't know,' he murmured. 'I thought sorting was as bad as it got.' Axel had heard dreadful things about the mines, about slaves being worked to death. Nevertheless, it seemed to me that Max must have preferred even that to 'sorting.' It was like tinkering with your CV – you leave out the crap bits. Or the crappiest bits, in Max's case. You try to put them behind you, live a lie.

Axel was saying that through Max he'd learned about the Jews who were also brought to Buchenwald, many from Auschwitz, in order to die of overwork, disease and hunger, in medical experiments and executions. Of all the internees they were treated the worst. Categorized as Class

One prisoners, that is, undesirable Enemies of the Third Reich, they were there to be exterminated.

He went on with his story. 'Max spoke in a grating monotone, his nostrils flaring, his breath sour. Because of what he did I imagined I could detect the stink of death on him, the emissions of humans at the extreme edge of fear. I could hardly breathe. I needed to move away from him, but it would have been rude. It wasn't his fault. So I excused myself,' he continued, 'and I lay down, folding a piece of rag into a pad and placing it on top of the metal dish they had given me, as I saw the others had done. That was my pillow. Then I hitched the blanket over my head and very nearly suffocated. The smell permeated every worn strand of the weave. It wasn't Max at all, or not just him. It was the smell of the camp and I would have to get used to it. By morning I'd stopped noticing it. I probably smelled as bad.'

Axel took a moment to breathe, to pour more coffee from the pot, nibble a biscuit and reflect. I stared at him. Axel, the Mummy's boy, the musician, had told me more in an hour than Max had told me in six weeks.

Now he was listing the skills they shared, the things they did for each other. One guy was a tailor and repaired all their clothes; another cobbled their shoes. Max, apparently, managed to 'acquire' tongues of leather from the Sorting House, needles and thread and other small, concealable luxuries. Once he came back to the hut actually wearing a pair of large hand-made shoes over his own plimsolls. 'Ours was the best-shod hut on the block,' said Axel. He himself helped out on the food front, smuggling out fruit and nuts and vegetables. He wouldn't say where he hid the stuff, only that the recipients made sure to peel them.

The men were reeling when they arrived back at the hut but no one was allowed to sit with his head in his hands. The stronger ones might rock their weaker comrades or massage them or apply ointment to their sores – Kurt, he reminded us, worked in the hospital – or they might feed them mashed bananas or let them sip water. And then they would get on with their homework. Several of the prisoners had fought in the Spanish Civil War or, like Max, had been part of the resistance movement. They passed on their knowledge of guerrilla fighting and their skills in improvising weapons to their comrades.

'Nothing fancy, you understand,' said Axel with a wink, 'just how to make and use fuse-wire garottes, kitchen knives honed to razor sharpness, bows and arrows, coshes and axes. Primitive weapons but lethal in the right hands. There were hundreds, if not thousands of us. If we mounted a simultaneous attack, the element of surprise would be enough to throw them off their guard; we would kill a few, capture their firearms before the alarm was raised and then do some real damage. It was important therefore to have good channels of communication throughout the camp, to let other sections know what was going on, what support they could expect. Writing materials were at a premium but somehow we managed to get the information through: what was happening in the outside world, what was needed for our arsenal, plans of how to construct a crossbow out of wooden bedslats and spoons and twine made from flax or horse hair.'

Most of their spare time, it appeared, was spent scheming and tinkering with primitive weapons, like Iron Age Man. To be honest, he said, they didn't have a lot more in common.

Apart from their music, I suggested. I knew Max didn't play but he was dead keen on all that classical stuff. Richard passed this along and Axel looked startled.

'He had a good ear,' he said, 'but he seemed to prefer popular songs, music-hall, that sort of thing.' He shrugged. 'Perhaps, in a year, a little Mozart rubbed off on him.'

'He told me he loved to hear you play. He listened outside when you practised.'

'Did he?' He seemed pleased. 'I didn't know. We were not really that close, you see. Different backgrounds. Though he taught me a lot about Marxism, and I found it provided a sort of anchor in all that chaos.'

'What else did you talk about?' I said, looking up from my notebook. I needed to know about Max's work in the resistance. But Axel said that was something Max *didn't* talk about. Too many people's lives depended on his silence.

However, he did find out that Max and Friedrich – Liebl, whose brain had been stolen from Saint Meredith's – had known each other before they came to Buchenwald. Friedrich was a sculptor, imprisoned for sedition. He had used his artistry to forge documents for the people Max was helping to escape. Axel said the woman, Ellen Sauerbruch, was also a partisan, captured round about the same time. (I found that intriguing. Max had hardly mentioned them.)

'If we weren't talking shop we were reminiscing. I suppose it was living with death. You tend to treasure the moments when you were alive. Those jewel-bright childhood memories. Student days. People you've known. Lovers. Max told me about his family in Hanover, his work for the union.'

'He didn't ever mention Sophie, did he?'

'Sophie?'

'Sophie Muller, his girlfriend. She was Jewish,' I said. 'I just wondered if he managed to get her out of Germany.'

'He never mentioned her.'

'She was killed by the Nazis,' said Susmeta. 'I asked him.'

Even so, I ought to check it out. Find out exactly how she had died. I made a note to get Nick onto it.

We left the pianist deep in thought. As his door closed he was picking out, with one slow and tentative finger, the notes of a familiar piece. What was it?

Richard knew. *'Humoresque,'* he said. 'Beethoven.' He drew in his breath, mashed his lips together. When people do that they're usually trying to keep something back.

'What?' I demanded.

'It's his comment on the vagaries of life, isn't it? The irony of his situation?'

'How do you mean?'

'Well, he wouldn't admit it for the world, poor guy, he's far too decent, but he was probably happier in the dirt and deprivation of Buchenwald. At least he had his animals to look after and he could play his beloved music on a decent piano. Too bad they gave him a second chance.'

11

'So you'll find out about Sophie Müller for me?'

'I'll try, Clare. I can't promise anything.' His voice in my earpiece was doubtful. 'I mean even Berthe doesn't know what happened.'

'She thought Sophie was taken to Auschwitz.'

'She disappeared, like everyone else disappeared. It was a natural assumption to make.'

'You mean she might not have been?'

'I mean I don't know, and Berthe doesn't.'

'Maybe Max does. But he's not saying.'

'Why wouldn't he? I mean, he strikes me as a straight sort of guy.'

Did he? I found that surprising. Compared with Nick, compared with *Axel*, Max was impossible to read. 'A devious cove,' my dad would have said. Axel had shone out through whoever's body he was in, clear and bright. For reasons of his own, Max was muddying the water.

As I progressed from lights to lights round the 'Waterworks' roundabout, I put it to him that Sophie might not have been killed by the Nazis. 'It's possible, isn't it? I mean Max probably assumes the worst and that's why he never mentioned her to Axel. But she could have escaped.'

'Not many did. Don't get your hopes up, Clare.'

It was true, I wanted her to be a survivor. I wanted to find her and have her in my film. So much. 'There are records, aren't there, of the people who passed through Auschwitz and those other places? It shouldn't take you long to search if it's on the Web. We need to know what happened.'

'What else did Axel say?'

I extricated myself from determined North Circular traffic and headed off down Forest Road towards Walthamstow's town centre. 'That he, Friedrich Liebl and Max plotted to overthrow the guards at Buchenwald. Apparently Max and Liebl were in the Resistance together before they were captured. *And* Ellen Sauerbruch.'

'Blinding! Why didn't he say, I wonder? Jesus, he kept that well a secret.'

'Apparently they used to send messages to her in the women' section.'

'What sort of messages? "Meet me behind the bike-shed after the Revolution?"'

'Nick!'

'I wouldn't have thought she was his type.'

'Me neither.' From what I'd seen of her on the newsreel, a hump-backed blanket on muscular calves, ducking into the hired car as cameras whirred and flashed, she wasn't much to look at. 'But love is blind, they say.'

'I meant socially,' said Nick. 'Her people were his class enemies. The Sauerbruch electrical company? It was big in those days. She'd have been to public school, travelled the world. She wouldn't have looked twice at a tinpot trade unionist.'

'She was imprisoned for anti-fascist activities,' I reminded him. 'And he was quite an attractive guy, in a wiry sort of way.'

'So was she,' said Nick.

'*Was* she?' I found that hard to believe. Short and stumpy was my impression.

'Stunning.' Nick had actually seen a photograph of her as she had been in the thirties. He described a classic beauty, slim and elegant in shoulder pads and pearls and one of those brow-baring hairdos, all blonde finger waves and combs. I was unsheathing my claws. Until he said that the Nazis wouldn't have been able to leave her alone.

'What do you mean?'

'There weren't many women prisoners at Buchenwald.'

'Oh God. They didn't . . .'

'Well they wouldn't touch the Jewish girls. They regarded them as animals. I mean literally. And it gets a bit lonely on guard duty up in those watchtowers.'

'Nick!' God, that was awful. Then I remembered something I'd seen on the Net. 'I thought they had a special hut of French prostitutes.'

'Really?' He sounded interested. 'You've been doing your own research by the sound of it.'

'I thought I'd make a start.'

But now he'd said it I realized he was probably right, as well. A pretty girl wouldn't have stood much of a chance. Two years of it. Jesus, I thought. And then to have her looks taken from her as well. Being the pragmatist she was, I'd guess Susmeta had taken the first female body that had come to hand without even considering the psychological effect of turning a lean and lovely ectomorph into a compact mesomorph. My heart went out to Ellen Sauerbruch, wherever she was. All she'd been through. It's your mind that gets fucked more than anything, I'd have thought. Being used like that. For two long years. It would unhinge a person, send them round the twist. If she hadn't already done away with herself, my bet was she was one crazy cookie.

Especially as Max hadn't even attempted to get in touch with her since the transplant. Or Axel. Fine friends they'd all turned out to be.

Nick said he'd get on to the Sophie thing straightaway. I flicked off the 'hands-free' and turned into this seedy little road off Wood Street.

The playground on that side was alive with surly kids, smashing footballs into the wire netting, flying alcopophigh on the swings, and eyeing my arrival speculatively. Interest definitely waned as they saw me remove my car radio and put on the steering lock. As I turned to check from across the road a dog was peeing against the front wheel.

I headed for the Arcade, to see my dad about Nan's birthday. It was empty, as usual, this Dickensian covered market, built into the bowels of a crumbling housing block. There was no shopping mall glitz and pizzazz; no W. H. Smith's or Top Shops or bright feeding stations, just cob-webby ceilings and old-fashioned painted signs and a lingering smell of bacon, and as my eyes accustomed themselves to the gloom, I clutched my purse tightly.

The shopfronts loomed out of the darkness like historic tableaux, the sort they have in museums, full of relics, dimly lit and dusty. I wouldn't have been surprised to find shopkeepers made out of wax.

The stamp shop's windows were stuffed with old albums open at pages of second editions and penny reds; next door a strange wedge-shaped shop was selling fireplaces, recently ripped from Victorian parlours and boudoirs. Stunned, they leaned together for support. *Buyer collect's* said the notice with an unnecessary apostrophe.

As I rounded a corner the pet shop erupted in screeching and squawking. Framed in millet and dog leads, the shop interior glowed with softly lit aquariums that did nothing to calm the seething emotions of those responsible – a couple of young women with a grievance, several children with special needs, one in a wheelchair, and Dave, the owner. I could see what they were on about. You couldn't miss it. An incredibly big, incredibly human-looking fish, was going glub-glub in a tight-fitting case of water. Two small children stood round-eyed before its ugliness, gather-ing fuel for wet nightmares. One had his hand down his trousers.

A pretty little girl, tugging at the T-shirt of one of the helpers said, over and over again, 'Wh-wh-wh-what's the fish looking at? Wh-wh-wh-what's he looking at?' And then, when she was given an answer, 'Why's he looking at me? Why-why? What's he looking at?'

Another boy rocked backwards and forwards, looking steadfastly at his fingers, which he flapped against the glass. Their carers were haranguing Dave for his cruelty. But you can't be cruel to a fish, he was saying. Cold-blooded creatures have no feelings.

'Well, you certainly haven't.'

'Eh? Whassat?'

'Look at his poor little face.' It was Charles-Laughton-playing-the-Hunchback, close-up and personal and it did have a certain poignancy.

'Oh sod off, why doncha? I'm fed up with yous lot coming round here making trouble.'

'He can't move, poor thing. He's in a terrible state.'

'So will you be if you don't get out my shop.'

'Yeah? You and whose army . . .?' But they turned to go.

'And get him away from my bloody fish,' he said of the flapping boy, 'He's scaring the shit out of them.'

'Thought you said the fish had no feelings?'

'Got more feelings than you have. Bringing poor kids out in public in that state. Shouldn't be allowed. If it was an animal it'd be put down.'

There was an incredulous indrawn breath, a lowering of voices.

'Ssshhh – they're not deaf, you know.'

'They've got just as much right here as anyone else.'

'Not with their problems. They should be locked up.'

'You're the one with the problem, mate. Bloody fascist.'

'Yeah, that's me. Reckon Hitler had the right idea, an' all. Do away wiv 'em.'

'Jesus Christ! Come on, kids, we're not stopping here.'

A parting shot, 'I'm reporting you, you horrible man. Don't think you've heard the last of this!'

'Wh-wh-wh-why's he a horrible man? Wh-wh-wh-what's the fish looking at?'

They emerged form the shop, pale and stricken. One of the women caught my eye as she heaved the wheelchair round, and shook her head, speechless. Could such monsters exist? Still?

The man came out to watch them safely out of earshot, then he said to me, as though I were a sympathiser, as though everyone must be, 'Either put 'em down or get a new brain, eh? On the NHS.'

'Don't you talk to me,' I said, with as much huff as I could muster.

His shop, 'Sid's', was plainly deserted. I tried the door and it was locked. *Just* locked, not shuttered and padlocked as you'd expect for works so precious. I made my hands into a gothic arch and peered through the glass. A glimmer of daylight outlined the bulk of furniture and the door to the back-room. It was ten past eleven. Perhaps he was in there asleep.

'Looking for van Gogh?' A crusty guy in rags and blankets appeared out of a miasma of bad, almost chemical, smells.

'Uh?' I gave him the benefit of my feeblest smile. Play along, I told myself.

'Gawn to cut 'is ear orf, heh, heh, heh!' The words issued from a wiry beard that seemed to move with a life of its own.

'God, I hope not!'

'Wally!' A fierce female came to my rescue, small and sharp, bony elbows akimbo. 'We don't want to 'ear none of that talk.' It was Adele from the train shop next door. 'You just run along, and leave her alone.' She turned to me, lowering huge specs and her voice. 'Don't you take no notice, duck, he's just a bit light, that's all. Ain't his fault. He should be on tablets. Fancy turning the poor bloke out to pasture at his age. Care in the Community, they call it. Fat chance of that round here. Community couldn't give a toss. How's he s'posed to manage, eh?' And to him, loudly, 'Be all right once you've had your brain transplant, eh, Wally?' It was certainly uppermost in people's minds.

He grinned into his toothless beard and, muttering imprecations, shuffled off to frighten the kids in the park.

She was telling me that Sid had just popped over the Post Office. 'He won't be long. You're Clare, ain't you? Seen you here before. You can wait in ours if you like. We was just having a cuppa. Want one?'

I accepted gratefully but the peat-brown liquid that steamed from thermos to tannic mug made me think again and when Adele stirred in a syrupy spoonful of condensed milk, I suddenly wasn't thirsty anymore. Thankfully someone outside 'Sid's' was wrestling with a sticky jamb and Adele went to see.

'He's back,' she swung in to tell me, then, 'Customer for you, Sid!' she carolled and winked at me. 'Don't forget your tea, duck. Take it with you.'

I needed his hug. If he was disappointed that I wasn't a customer he didn't show it as he squashed my nose against his turpsy shirt and dropped coffee and toast kisses onto my cheeks. Post Office, my foot: he'd been over to the café to escape Adele's tea. Mine was slopping on the floor. We stood apart, at arms' length, to check for damage.

'You're looking tired,' he said. But he always said that. He wanted me to stay a dewy ten year old forever.

'You're putting on weight,' I countered, patting his beer-gut. Mum had kept the cholesterol at bay with steamed vegetables and low-fat milk. But fat was the price you paid for betrayal.

'I like your hair.' This was the way to my heart.

'Don't like yours.' A sleazy rock-star's pony-tail. Was that to save money or to create an image?

'How's your mother?' At last.

'Bearing up.'

That was the formalities over. He really wanted to know if she was pining or embittered or if she'd found another bloke but if he couldn't bring himself to ask, I wouldn't tell. That was part of his punishment.

It was three or four months since I'd seen him and he was beginning to look like someone else. There was more grey in his hair, or maybe that was just because his side-burns were longer. His eyes were still strong but there were new puffs and pouches round them that didn't bode well and the creases between his eyebrows were worrying. The neckerchief was new, another affectation. He had a woman, I was sure of it. I could almost see her style, New Age and homespun.

'You going to drink that?'

'No.'

'Get rid of it then.'

I went through and tipped the slippery brew down the sink. He'd chosen the shop for its plumbing. One gritty brass tap gushing cold water. The other facilities were a bonus: a back room where a sleeping bag could be rolled out on a camp bed, an alcove where a broom-handle could be wedged to provide hanging space for clothes, a window onto the street to provide natural light to work by, a sill for jam jars, brushes and toiletries and snug space for an easel, a gouged worktable and a paint-spattered chair. The main requirement for an artist was water. And a drain. I know for a fact he peed in it. A case of having to, I'd have thought, in the middle of the night, when the shopkeepers' loo was twenty yards down the 'street' and accessible only to key-holders. They had a rota for keeping it clean.

He lived in a pigsty where the smell of oil paint and turps fought with the fug of old socks and beer-farts and take-aways, but that was his choice, his problem. He'd opted out of teaching years back after a particularly gruelling Ofsted inspection, managed to wangle early retirement, on grounds of ill-health (a non-existent dodgy back). The row had muttered around the house for weeks, with Mum drooping around, pale and red-eyed, and him hammering away on a garden sculpture. There were occasional flashes of temper: hers, mostly. It was the end of term, which didn't help. She had a hundred and eighty English essays to mark, plus all the précis and grammar stuff, and reports to write and he was being 'utterly selfish!' He could at least cook the dinner, run a vacuum round, hang the washing out, give Kate a lift to school. He'd gone out to buy some varnish.

The washing machine had been the last straw. Seventy pounds to replace the pump, and another seventy to clear the waste pipe. And hairgrips lined up along the draining board. He could have fixed it, Mum said, saved her the money, but where was he when he was needed? Down in his shed, welding dustbin lids together.

In the end he left.

He paid half the mortgage with his lump sum, and rented a 'studio' in Walthamstow. Nan wouldn't have him. If he was going to be an artist, a bohemian, rather than a daddy, she wasn't going to make it easy for him.

'How's it going?' I had to ask, coming out for air. There seemed to be more in the shop than on previous occasions. More stock, more quality stuff. A grandfather clock with a deep-throated tick, oil-lamps to lust after, a glass-fronted corner cupboard cluttered with good-looking china and knick-knacks.

'We-e-ell . . .' He was reluctant to admit it, afraid I might ask him for money, but his pride got the better of him. He'd sold a few pieces, he said. Word was spreading. He'd splashed out on a van and was able to go further afield, buy better stuff. Just last week he'd been up to a big house in Wickham Bonhunt, off the M11, got him a brass bedstead and a marble washstand and a few rather 'juicy' lots. I looked around hopefully but the bedstead had gone, he said, almost immediately. I spied the washstand, its iron knees buckling under a rickety tower of cardboard boxes: the 'juicy' items, presumably – what Mum used to call 'toot'. But when he lifted one down to show me, it contained none of the rusty light fittings and plug-less curling tongs that he used to fall upon in skips, uttering strange creative whoops. Here were carefully wrapped pewter goblets, pearwood candle holders, Art Deco masks, silver buckles to die for.

He saw my fingers twitching and, probably thinking I needed distracting, ducked through the door. 'Come and see what I'm doing now . . .'

From under the sink, where bottles of bleach and turps and Windolene lurked among the spiders, he dragged a heavy canvas, and bracing his knees, heaved it onto the draining board for me to view. It wasn't quite dry.

I licked my lips. Now that his *objets trouvées* were really rather tasty, I suppose you'd have to call what he'd made *riches arts* as opposed to the *pauvres arts* that he'd done before.

Gorgeous against the mossy window and its rotting frame, there swirled a textured sea of paint and cloth, drizzled with crystal beads and silver yarn, and threading through, a shoal of bright fish, which, it took me a moment to realise, was a set of silver teaspoons.

'This goes with it, you see,' he said, and leaving the sea propped against the sill, carefully angled beside it the depleted canteen of cutlery. The agate-handled knives, forks and spoons were in their places but risen up on end, bending, as though a current were passing through them.

They were plants on the sea bed and the black velvet hollows where they had nested were shadows. 'An integral part of the work,' he explained; 'a framing device.'

'Mmmm.' I rubbed my nose, doubtfully. I don't have my father's artistic genes, unless you call what I'm doing in television, art. I could see what he was getting at, but it just seemed sad to me, that he'd had to wreck a perfectly good canteen of cutlery.

That was the idea, he said. It was aggressive, challenging people's values.

'Oh,' I said. 'What's it called?'

'"*Why doesn't he use a spoon?*"' There was a note of triumph in his voice.

A twist of my face told him I didn't get it. It was a quote, he said. Lloyd George had likened negotiating with de Valera to attempting to pick up mercury with a fork. To which de Valera had replied, *"Why doesn't he . . ." etc.* Light filtered in and I murmured, 'Oh I see. It's a bit obscure, Sid. How's anyone supposed to know what Lloyd George said?'

'It'll be in the catalogue.'

'What?'

'The gallery's doing a catalogue. Tells you the references.'

'You're going to have work shown in a gallery?'

He wagged his tail. 'Trimble's.'

I'd never heard of it. 'When's this?'

'The opening's the thirtieth. It'll be on for a week.'

'This month?'

'Uhuh. Coming?'

There were prickings at the back of my mind, like a discreet pager. Something was happening that day. I knew I wouldn't be able to make the opening.

'Who was de Valera?'

'Clare!' But his disgust went over my head, for I had spied, beside the soap, a wiry black hairpin and, while he explained about some Irish nationalist Easter Rising, I was

173

hot on the trail of my father's secrets. One of the glasses on the window-sill, I now noticed, contained two toothbrushes; the other was smudged with lipstick. And a minute glint on the grimy ledge metamorphosed into a silver butterfly, the sort that fastens earrings and studs. I wasn't surprised or shocked. All the same my lower eye-lid began to tick.

'Do you get it now?'

'Uhuh,' I assured him. 'I suppose the fishes are meant to signify slippery customers?'

He dropped his head and spread his fingers, delighted with me.

I said I hoped he'd get as much for the work as he'd paid out for the canteen.

'Oh yesss!' He waggled his artful old head. It was a paying game – just a matter of finding discerning customers.

'You could give it to Nan for her birthday,' I said, nastily, 'if it doesn't sell.'

'Damn,' he said. He hadn't remembered.

'We're giving her a surprise party on the . . . ah . . . ' I bared my teeth in self-reproach because that was my prior engagement, of course. 'On the thirtieth.'

'Damn.'

'I thought I'd better warn you in case you'd arranged to take her out or anything. But, of course, you've already got something on.'

'I'm invited, am I?'

'Well, yes.'

'Your mother's all right about that?'

'Fine,' I said, lying through my teeth. She'd breathed fire. Said she wasn't having the selfish bastard set foot in the door. Then when she'd calmed down and only marbles knotted her jaw, she'd said she could behave herself if he could.

'And your sister?'

'Fine,' I croaked. My throat was dry with effort. Even

Adele's tea would have been welcome now. Why didn't I tell him that she'd promised to be polite for Nan's sake but that was it, that she'd refused point-blank to come with me to see him, as always? Why was I protecting him? It hadn't occurred to him to ask how Kate's end-of-term production had gone, whether she was still happy at the drama school; he wasn't interested in my job or Nick. He hadn't even offered me another cup of tea.

The tap squeaked as I turned it on, and water gushed into the sink. I sucked at it noisily.

'Oi, oi, oi!'

I was splashing the artwork, evidently. He pushed me away to twiddle the tap and I banged into the dividing door. A woman's crushed velvet hat fell down off the hook. He dabbed up the wet with a piece of rag whose pattern – pale green with pink stripes – cloned into a shirt I'd bought him with my first Christmas bonus. Not that long ago in the lifetime of shirts. Mum would never have let him tear it up for paint rags, even if it had grown too small. She was always very protective of our feelings.

There were tears clogging my throat as I backed out of the door.

I could hear him chuntering on about getting the work framed. He had an arrangement with a man on the Woodford High Road. Very reasonable. He was the one who'd advised him about treating the silver so that it wouldn't tarnish. Sensible guy. He'd do a good job, I could be sure. It was nice to have someone you could rely on.

12

Mum was having a major clean up. Not the weekly run round with duster and toilet brush. This was worse. Major major. Not only was there the added impetus of Nan's special birthday, *this* year, today, she had finally decided that every little reminder of Sid was to go. Every book, every button, every nail paring. Bin bags were piling up in the garage, cleaner spray filled the air and the cat scooted up the garden as fast as her arthritic old legs would take her. It was all my fault.

'Not even a cup of tea! His own daughter!' She couldn't cope with that. Tea was basic. She put her hand to her head, trying to fathom her husband's mind. 'Unbelievable,' was all she could say.

I shouldn't have said anything, but how could I not? Despite my family's professed indifference, one casual enquiry – 'How was the old bugger?' – led to another and, in a minute, I found myself being pressed for every detail of my visit, until, like a badly squeezed blackhead, I was weeping and sore.

My mother said she'd been a fool to wait this long, hoping he might somehow see where his real interests lay. But he was getting worse not better. She almost felt sorry for him and his pathological self-absorption. The bully.

'Bully?'

Pushing his daughter out of the way – you just don't *do* that. She fisted her palm, itching to land a blow. And as for reducing my Christmas present and my feelings, to paint rags – Ha! The cat had more consideration.

She'd sign those papers the solicitor had given her. If she

could still find them. Finish it. And if it meant selling up and splitting the proceeds, fine. She'd buy a house in Walthamstow. We might have to share a room but, what the hell? As for his stupid art show if he thought any of us would set foot – well, he could just whistle.

'Now, Clare, you can make a start on the garage.'

'The garage?'

No one *ever* cleaned the garage. Every time you'd been in there, for jam off the 'homemade' shelf or pickled onions, or to fetch a chicken from the freezer, or potatoes from the sack, anything, you wiped your feet carefully in case you'd trodden in something besides wellie mud, and checked you'd picked all the cobwebs out of your hair. It hadn't seen a car in twenty years or however long it was since we moved in. It was a tip. All the more reason to scour it clean, she said. If he was coming round to collect his rubbish, he mustn't see it in that state.

'No way!' I objected. 'I've work to do.' And my sister, taking her cue from me, wriggled away and closed her door quietly.

Lurking in my INBOX was a message from Barry. We needed to meet to discuss budget and crew and to time-table in a few shoots. He suggested Monday evening. We'd have a working supper and maybe a drink afterwards. If we got a wiggle on, it shouldn't take more than a few hours.

Dot, dot, dot, I thought. On your bike, Mr Giddings. Okay I needed to get it sorted before the summer break but one thing was certain. No way was I going to be alone with Barry for one split second. Nick would have to come with me. I sent him an e-mail to that effect.

Still no word from Ellen Sauerbruch. All the German Embassy could say was that according to the Birnbaums she had left her room neat and tidy, clothes in the ward-robe, personal items in the bathroom, soiled underwear in the linen basket. It looked as though she intended to return. In her waste bin they had found an envelope and covering letter from a travel agent, whom they had contacted. It seemed she had bought a single air ticket to Berne in Switzerland. What her business was there, where she was now, was anyone's guess. There were no personal documents left behind in the room, no passport, no cheque book.

I replied, thanking the embassy for their help, and asking them whether it would be possible to find out if Ellen had family or, even more unlikely, friends still living in Berne. A single ticket would seem to indicate that either she was staying there indefinitely, or that she was going on some-where else after completing business in the city. The Sauerbruchs were 'old money'. They might well have banked with the neutral Swiss given the uncertainties of war. What if there was money belonging to her? I doubted that, in those circumstances, the Birnbaums' lodging house in Cologne would exert much of a pull. She'd be off on a spending spree. I would. The interest over sixty years would be phenomenal.

The embassy said that they didn't have the facilities for pursuing my enquiries but that they would pass them on to the relevant authorities. And that looked like being the end of that. Banks never divulge clients' business. I felt I might have to write her off. Dear, dear, the Buchenwald Five were dwindling fast. I'd be down to three or four if I was lucky. Colin would be pleased.

The embassy also gave me Willi Greff's e-mail address. He was, they said, living with his daughter, Ottilie, and her family in the Austrian mountains and was eager for me to contact him.

I checked the newspage for mention of Friedrich Liebl. It simply repeated what I knew already, that his brain was one of eighteen buried by agents of the notorious Nazi doctor, Klaus Hofmann, beneath a second-world-war bunker in Berlin, that whilst waiting to be transplanted into a donor body it had been stolen from a repository in a private London hospital. It had not yet been recovered.

I keyed in Greff's website address. *Hello, Willi Greff,* rattled onto the screen, followed by all my usual introductory stuff, social CV and photograph, to which I added that I was making my debut as a TV director with a film about the Buchenwald brain transplants, generally buttering him up for interview. A fee was mentioned. I signed off and summoned the Babel menu, pulled the mouse down to German, and clicked my letter into cyberspace.

I spent the next hour working up my story. It was pretty thin at the moment, a clothesline with pegs at what I considered significant points: the economic crisis in Germany, Hitler's rise to power, the opposition of the left, including six million German communists (what happened to them?) the building of concentration camps, the incarceration of prisoners. Other strands concerned the doctor, Klaus Hofmann, his associate, Gisela Weiss, the inmates whose brains they'd stolen, the five who'd survived and all their baggage and, last but not least, Susmeta, who had put them back together again and sent them out into an anomic world.

So far the information hanging from each peg was a flimsy rag, just bits from the programme, plus what I'd gleaned from Doug Mallory and Axel Schlager. But as we gathered material so each item would grow; we would shape it, give it coherence and life. We were all researchers now and as I looked around the site I could see that both Jay and Nick had added to the file since yesterday, which was brilliant considering they weren't officially released to me from *Way of the World* until the end of the month.

Nick had nothing to report on the Sophie front. He'd reached a dead end in Germany. She'd simply disappeared, as Berthe had said, swallowed up in the Nazi atrocities.

Funnily enough, though, her father, Stefan Müller, was listed among the Auschwitz dead, and she wasn't. It could be that the records in the men's section were more efficiently kept. Or not. Anyway, he'd try another tack – immigrants into England from Germany in the pre-war/war years. He'd let me know.

PS. Been sorting through my gear for the Lakes. Remember I caught the tent on some barbed wire that time I did the Pennine Way. If I bring it over tomorrow, would you mend it on your mum's machine? Sorry about the short notice. Love you. Nick XXX

Shit. I really didn't want to be reminded of that sodding holiday. The thought of walking up and down mountains for a fortnight, humping a bloody great backpack and cooking beans on the old camp-fire, filled me with dread. As for sewing up the sodding tent – that was all I needed. I was supposed to be making a sodding film in case anybody remembered.

Jay's contribution was the text of an interview with a mate of a mate, a theatre nurse at Saint Meredith's who'd worked with Susmeta on a number of brain transplant operations, including those of Max and Willi Greff. In each case, he couldn't help but notice that the surgeon had deliberately tampered with the brain, once it was functioning properly inside its new skull, in the interests of research. In some cases she had succeeded in producing Alzheimer's, in others, Parkinson's Disease.

I sat transfixed before the machine, my eyes aching with the words. Little Miss Wonderwoman had experimented on living human tissue! If it was true it was dynamite. Jesus. Susmeta was a monster. Another Hofmann. My hand shook on the mouse as I scrolled down. I knew she was capable of it.

The rest of the report gradually swam into focus. The

aim of each experiment, the nurse said, had been to implant special stem-cells from other parts of the brain which would, in time, divide and multiply as cells do, repairing the affected part of the brain and curing the disease she'd introduced. Sadly, a couple of the more promising brains, all connected up and functioning properly, had had to be terminated, one because Susmeta had got the DNA recipe wrong, and one because the cells had multiplied out of control.

Nothing about getting the antidote wrong!

It occurred to me that anyone capable of carrying out her own research on living patients and of covering it up, was quite capable of falsifying e-mails. What if she had known about the antidote from the outset and had deleted it from the e-mail she'd shown me and Max? What if she'd lied to me? What if she'd been unable to account for the deaths of two, maybe more patients in any other way?

I picked up the phone. 'I can't use it, Jay,' I croaked. 'It'll ruin her. They'll never let her practise again. And it's the nurse's word against hers. If she sues us, where's our proof?'

'There's a video if we can get hold of it.'

'A video?'

'Closed circuit. It's normal procedure at Saint Merry's to record operations. The patients like to have them – beats holiday snaps for keeping guests amused after dinner.' I gave a horrified groan. He was winding me up, it turned out. The hospital kept them as teaching aids. And they were evidence in case of mishaps.

'What's his name, the nurse?'

'I said I'd keep quiet about that, if it's all the same, Clare. He likes his job.'

'Yeah, like I like mine.'

But Susmeta had risked hers. Sacrificed it for the sake of, what? Curing life-threatening diseases by stem-cell implantation, whatever that was. Shit. I mean, like that was so brilliant, wasn't it? I wondered whether the BMA would see it like that – the end justifying the means – or if they'd skin her alive.

My mind whizzed off to that Star Trek story, where Spock's brain has been recaptured from the Klingons, and it's down to Doctor McCoy to put it back in the skull. Spock's brain guides him by telepathy. Wicked. The dialogue's like, 'Now this should be the gagging reflex . . .' 'Wrong! That's my left ear lobe,' or, 'I still can't feel anything in my big toe.' If nothing else it pointed up the difficulties of transplanting a brain successfully. When you think – all the millions of nerves that have to be matched up. Susmeta was a genius. Could the BMA afford to lose someone so gifted? After all, the 'owners' of the Hofmann brains were long since dead. No one would miss them. Some might think she'd have been mad not to seize the opportunity. Pity the research material was not re-usable.

What to do?

I told Jay not to breathe a word, but, if he had the chance, to get hold of a copy of at least one of the incriminating videos.

Hello, Clare Russell. Willi Greff here. Please feel free to ask your questions.

Oh wow! My ears buzzed, my palms were damp. It was like picking up signals from outer space. I'd beaten the language barrier. God bless technology. Mundanely, I congratulated him on mastering the web in less than three months. He told me that Franz, his great-grandson, a computer whiz kid at fourteen, was leaning over his shoulder. He realised it was a required skill in the modern world and he was determined to have it.

Our communication may have been a little stiff and formal as a result of a rather literal translation of the German into English but I had the feeling that I was talking to a nice guy. He told me that his resurrection had been as much of a shock to the family Greff as it had been for him. But they were sensible about it and made him welcome on the clear understanding that he didn't think he was there for the ride. Never mind that they were multi-millionaires, Greffs were expected to pull their weight.

But didn't you start the firm? I asked him.

Ernst, my brother, and I, back in 1934.

They were both clever in different ways, Ernst with a flair for business and making money and Willi for breaking new ground in science. I'd already looked him up. In 1935 he was awarded the Nobel Prize for separating hydrogen from superheated steam. It was his refusal to put his later discoveries at the disposal of Hitler's war machine that earned him a place in Buchenwald. Wherupon Ernst Greff had fled to America, taking the two families and Willi's explosive research notes with him. Hitler was left with a lot of heavy water and not much else.

My poor boy. The letters translated slowly, painfully, on the screen. *We argued. The last afternoon we argued. Wilhelm did not want to go to America. He wanted to remain in Austria with his friends and be part of the glorious Third Reich. He did not understand me and my politics. At thirteen years old, he was convinced that Hitler would make Germany glorious. In 1941 this still seemed possible. This was my opportunity to do something important for the Fatherland and I was failing. I was a traitor and he hated me. We bundled him, kicking and yelling, into my brother's car. In the evening the SS came for me. He was not a bad boy. He just wanted to be like his friends. Like the rest of Germany he came to see the error of his ways and, so they tell me, never recovered from a feeling of guilt and loss.*

After the war, richer by several billion dollars, Ernst had returned to his beloved Innsbruck to take up the reins of Greffindustrie once again, with Willi's son, Wilhelm, as vice-president. But in 1952 Willhelm committed suicide. Ernst also was dead.

There was a long silence. He was waiting for me to reply but I couldn't think of anything to say. 'Rotten luck' seemed a bit inadequate. In the end I asked him who had taken on the presidency after Ernst.

Ottilie, my daughter, my sixty-five-year-old daughter. She has just retired, in fact, in favour of her son, Oscar, my grandson. He is the only member of the family I have still to meet. He is away on an extended business trip, visiting our branches in the Middle East – Arabia and Persia, exotic places like that.

Persia? Iran, he meant. Never mind. He had every right to be proud of his family's achievements. They had branches in every country in the world. Greffindustrie led the way in chemical research. The Americans and the Japanese didn't hold a candle.

It's a huge enterprise now, I observed, *world wide. You must employ millions of people, thousands of top class graduates. It must be hard to keep track of what's going on. All the different specialities – medicine, food production . . .*

Willi said he had a lot of catching up to do. There were so many new discoveries, new methods, but it wouldn't be long, he was confident, before he was making a proper contribution. I could quite see why Hofmann had wanted to preserve his brain. I wondered if Greff would be so confident if he knew that Susmeta had been playing about with it.

It's good to hear a success story, at last, I wrote. *Your fellow travellers seem to be finding it a tough and lonely road.*

Come to Austria soon, Clare, he said, *for the filming. The mountains are beautiful at this time of year. Come for a holiday. All expenses paid. Bring your walking boots.*

Thankfully he couldn't see the face I pulled. The Austrian Alps are steeper than any in the Lake District. But at least I wouldn't have to mend the tent and I could kill a few other birds while I was about it. I said I'd be delighted and gave him a date. I thought I'd wait to tell Nick in person.

The hoover was howling up and down the landing with the occasional suggestive bump against my door. I really ought to go and help. But, then again, I really was appallingly ignorant about the Third Reich. I couldn't possibly make a convincing film about the survivors of Buchenwald without knowing something of what they were up against.

I keyed in 'Fascism' for starters and summoned up a nightmare.

There were thousands of lonely websites, apparently, aching for me to visit them. All over the world. Morbid curiosity prompted me to download a few. And they were about what was happening now, not then. Today. In every part of the world. Some were in German, some translated from Italian, French, Serbian and Russian into English, some with American spelling, some unmistakably British, ungrammatical and loutish. If I'd had any doubts that fascism was alive and well and living just round the corner, they were utterly dispelled.

All their shoddy goods were laid out for inspection: membership packages, contact names, addresses, notices of meetings, adverts for Nazi memorabilia, fanzines, *Kraft durch Froide* ('Strength through Joy'), *Yah – Skin Reports,* calls to action, screamingly unfunny racist jokes.

And photographs.

Of buses carrying immigrant workers, with smashed windows and bruised and bleeding passengers, of young thugs in concealing balaclavas beating up Vietnamese on trains with hatchets and baseball bats, stoning children, torching hostels for migrant workers, kicking, shooting. I licked lips that were set hard in a grimace of distaste. And I realised that some people, thousands, if all those websites were to be believed, actually got off on this stuff. This was their pornography. If Hitler were around today he'd have no trouble mustering support. It would be an army of very sick people, but an army just the same.

There were articles, too, for those that could read, by 'good old boys', of every race, colour and creed. About sending asylum seekers 'home', and migrant workers. About dirty Poles-stroke-Turks-stroke-'Pakis'-stroke-Algerians-stroke-blacks-stroke-Jews-stroke-Rumanians-stroke-Croatians using the state to procure housing, employment, education, hospital treatment, unfairly, at 'our' expense (whoever 'we' might happen to be), bringing down standards, wages and property prices, creating unemployment and ghettos, corrupting 'our young women'.

The day was coming, according to one prophet, when nationals everywhere would rise up and take back what was rightfully theirs. *Courage, mes braves! Nil desperandum* and all that – a saviour was *'in the making'* who would lead his people to VICTORY! It was all very Messianic, with talk of second comings and transformations. When I discovered the site belonged to none other than our own dear Lord William Titherille, it made more sense. He was referring, I guessed, to his dream, that of his own rebirth through brain transplantation, as a younger and somehow more charismatic, leader of men. Poor, pathetic old geezer – he'd completely lost it.

Jesus, though, all that hate, all that ignorance! No wonder Max and his mates had been so utterly opposed to it. How could anyone with a spark of intelligence . . . I blew a cleansing breath. No more. I switched off the computer and picked up the phone. Thankfully research came in all shapes and forms.

'Hi Max,' I said. 'You free this afternoon?'

'Another rock concert?' He sounded amused and my heart strings twanged.

'If I can fix it how d'you feel about coming with me to see Douglas Mallory?'

He was all for it. So I phoned Douglas' number and got Sylvia, who was putting her smalls in with his to make the wash worthwhile. He was down at the polling station counting voters. Had I remembered to cast mine? Bugger.

Thankfully Max hadn't started out yet. 'Another time,' he said, regretfully.

So, in the end, there was nothing for it. I would spend what was left of the day lying in the sun with George Orwell, learning about the Spanish Civil War.

Some hopes.

Curtains and duvet- and cushion-covers twitched in a desultory breeze on both washing lines, while the lawn sprouted damp rugs and lampshades. Dirty water gushed non-stop down the drain. Folding chairs and tables dripped suds onto the patio, and the internal organs of the oven, tins and racks and baking trays, foamed caustically beside a notice, which advised 'Don't touch with bare hands'. I could hear the scrubbing brush hard at it on the back step and a drone of breathless singing. How was anyone supposed to relax under such conditions?

I dragged on a pair of Marigolds, grabbed a bucket and headed out to the garage.

13

The headlines caught my eye as I dumped the shopping on the kitchen table – FABS KILLED IN PUB BOMBING. I dropped into a chair amid a chaos of food processing and steak bashing, the words jumping before my eyes. *Killed!* I'd never had anyone of my acquaintance killed before, let alone so violently.

'Terrible, isn't it?' said Kate, laying down her mallet. 'They'd just called the meeting to order apparently – didn't stand a chance.'

'Shush!' I waved her away as I tried to read. Two killed and four taken to hospital with serious injuries. Even the barmaid downstairs had been cut by flying glass. George Paterson was unhurt but very shaken. Somebody else, the group's chairperson, had had to talk to the Press. '*One minute we were discussing the establishment of a permanent picket outside Saint Meredith's Hospital, next thing I was in the fireplace with blood running into my eyes. I don't think I even heard the bang! The meeting room looked like a battle zone – bodies lying everywhere covered in dust. Glass, lumps of masonry, splintered wood. Unbelievable carnage.*'

Unbelievable.

Who would do such a thing? Who would go to such lengths to destroy good people? Some absolute nutter. Christ, they were only worried parents when all was said and done. Poor old George. His troubles came in droves. First his son dying, then the shock of seeing him alive again on the box, then his wife going off her head, now people being killed. Peaceful protest didn't warrant such violence.

Who had access to bombs? What was the motive? It

seemed senseless. But then people get weird ideas, I told myself, imagined grievances. Delusion and obsession make them mad. Could there, I wondered, be someone who thought that the FABS might stand in their way of a brain transplant?

'Mum,' I said, when the racket of whizzing cream had stopped, 'you don't think Susmeta's in danger, do you? I mean, what if these terrorists forced her to transplant one of their brains? They could kidnap a member of the Government, like the Prime Minister and . . .'

'They'd have to kill her to keep her quiet,' said Kate, running her finger round the bowl and licking it.

'You don't kill the goose that lays the golden egg,' said Mum.

'They'd probably just threaten to cut off her nose if she – Ow! ' Mum had brought the rubber spatula down across Kate's fingers.

'If she what?'

'If she squealed.'

'Clare, did you clean up the paw-marks?' said Mum, dolloping whipped cream into meringue nests. (I'd carelessly let the cat in when I'd come in, dripping, from the shops.) 'And put paper down for people to walk on? Oh bugger, I put them out for the recycle man. Oh dear, why does it have to rain today of all days? Look, you'll just have to use today's, Clare. I won't have time to read it.' So that was the end of the news.

Cut to three-thirty and the sound of laughter, a babble of voices, the garden transformed, terrorism forgotten. Old people gossip under the trees, long-lost aunts and uncles turn up in the shrubs, surprising you with the Latin names of plants, young brown limbs sprawl on rugs, children sit on the wall and drinks are being downed. Summer wear, the occasional bright sari, men and girls in shorts, the rain

189

forgotten, except by the wearers of stiletto heels, who sink slowly into the damp lawn.

I'm in floaty sage chiffon and my hair's gone right for once and look who's here! Douglas Mallory and Sylvia!

'What are you doing here?' we all chorused.

'I live here,' I said.

'She lives here!' shouted Sylvia.

Douglas adjusted his hearing aid and between us we established my relationship to Nan and Mum and the house. Apparently Sylvia had known Nan for years. 'I'm a newcomer to the group,' said Douglas.

'East End Writers,' Sylvia explained. Of course, Nan wrote poetry. You forget.

'I didn't know you wrote, Douglas?'

'His memoirs,' Sylvia said, proudly.

'I'm no great shakes,' he said. 'It's just something for the grand-children to have when I'm gone.'

'Hey, what a great idea. I wish my granddad had done that. I mean it's where you're coming from, isn't it? Your roots. Perhaps I can get Nan to write hers.'

'You'll have her volumes of poetry,' said Sylvia. 'So Alice is your grandmother,' she mused. 'I had a feeling I'd seen you somewhere before.'

I was still puzzling over that as Douglas said hopefully, 'I suppose there's no chance of old Zeiler turning up.'

'Max?' It hadn't occurred to me to invite him. But it was an idea. Perhaps if I phoned . . .

'Ssshhh!'

I couldn't phone yet. Everyone was quiet, even the kids, listening to the car pulling up on the gravel. Mum had gone to the door, whipping off her PVC *What's for dinner, Mum?* pinny – orange sundress, dark hair curling on her shoulders, long brown legs, gold sandals – trying to appear calm for the first time in weeks.

From the garden we heard the doorbell ring, the latch

turning, voices in the hall. She must know, we thought. She must feel the air thick with bated breath, hear the grey grind of bone on arthritis, sense the excitement, she must smell the wine, the aftershave, the tobacco smoke, the barbecue. She must.

But, amazingly, she came to the back door and we watched as her face spread and softened in wonder. 'Oh,' she mouthed. And behind her Mum clasped her hands in glee. A moment of magic caught in time as flash-bulbs popped.

And we, so thrilled with our own cleverness and her delight, cried 'Surprise' and 'Happy Birthday', and broke the spell, while the neighbours either side hung out of upstairs windows to see. They'd come in later when things livened up. She trod the steps with deckchair legs, bending close to see who was here, who wasn't. Some she recognised straight away, some she had to search for among the wrinkles.

'It's John, isn't it? You know, Pam,' she said to Mum, 'I haven't seen this man in twenty years.' A few words, a squeeze of the hand, a blink of wet eyelashes and a creaky turn to the right. 'Mrs Patel, how lovely. What a pretty dress. Did you make it yourself? Isn't she clever, Pam? Ali, you kept that very quiet, naughty boy! Oh Mariam,' her voice caught, 'you brought the baby! What a sweetheart. Just like his daddy, eh? And the East End Writers! In force, to be sure.' Her little joke. She was addressing a tall policeman. I'm not hot on decoding pips but from his bearing and greying temples I guessed he must have been a chief inspector, at least. 'For all his fearsome looks,' Nan trilled, 'Owen's a honey. Can I tell them?' Owen shuffled his feet and blushingly agreed. 'He writes as Tilly Prentice.'

Oh wow. A published author. Romance wasn't my cup of tea, but Mum was bowled over. 'But – but I have all your books. I just love them. They were such a comfort to me when my husband . . .' Oh how she gushed. She'd never have thought Tilly Prentice was a man, could have such insight into the female psyche, could be so sensitive. In her experience men were total bastards.

Nan left them to it. 'Sylvia, I saw your poem in the anthology. I'm so pleased for you. And Douglas, how lovely! I say, IT'S LOVELY TO SEE YOU, DEAR.'

'Switch your hearing aid on, Doug,' said Sylvia.

We sat her down in her chair of honour under an awning where she wouldn't get baked, and Fred, Kate's new boyfriend from drama school, took photos with his digital camera as Nan's old friends came to talk to her. Kate and I swanned about with plates of this and that and bottles and glasses and believed them when they told us how lovely we were.

The music was incredibly naff, opera and stuff, but they were Nan's favourites and surprisingly pleasant on a hot afternoon. The wine flowed and a few of the wrinklies round Doug's table started nodding. More people arrived, others left to feed pets and babies or to start the journey back to distant parts.

Nick made it back from the cricket match, banging through the side door and tripping over the dustbin. 'Come on,' he beckoned to someone in the front garden, 'they won't bite,' and who should lurch into view, flushed with booze and embarrassment, but the man of the moment, Max Zeiler!

My heart jump-started and set my pulses racing. Look away, Clare, look away! But my eyes wanted to devour him, pig out. Nick had brought him to me, like the good retriever he was. Douglas Mallory was sitting up straight as a meerkat. Damn. There was never a camera when you needed one.

'Come in, if you're coming,' said Mum. I wouldn't have encouraged them if I'd been her. They were both lagered, more than somewhat.

'Clare, Clare, I've missed you!' cried my roaring boy,

192

smothering me with soft beery kisses. I had to stop him when he reached the nuzzling stage as the kiddies were becoming far too interested. Max had his head on one side, a small frown puckering his brow. He seemed to be wondering where he was and how he'd got here. I mouthed 'Hi', and Nick surfaced, pinkly.

'Poor old Max. Slow torture, wasn't it, watching Middlesex beat Essex? Bored out of his brain, weren't you, mate? So I thought well, I'd better make it up to him, bring him along to your Nan's do. All right? Oh, I've brought the tent,' he remembered, thrusting a tightly packed bundle at me. Poor bloke, he'd dragged it all around Valentine's Park, kept it by him during the match and, I imagined, with a great effort of mind over booze, had managed neither to leave it behind at the ground nor on the bus. Pity. I thought I wouldn't tell him about Austria yet. I gave him a dazzling smile, wondering how soon I could bin the tent.

Then Max was introduced to the birthday girl, and Nan inclined her head like the Queen, and said how delighted she was to meet Max, and she hoped he'd recovered from his operation.

'Mmm,' said Max, uncertainly.

Putting her misgivings aside, Nan patted his hand. 'Good, good. Now, I expect you're hungry, aren't you?' and sent Nick off in search of food, while Max fell into the chair I'd been patting beside me. It was then he spotted this wiry old gent, up on the top lawn, trying to catch his eye and beaming.

'Who is that?'

'Douglas Mallory,' I said, hugging myself. 'Small world, isn't it? I had no idea he was a friend of my Nan's.'

'Mallory!' He blinked through a fuddle of alcohol. 'But he is so old! Oh Clare.' He clapped his hand to his mouth and his eyes filled with tears. 'What am I going to say? It is not right.'

'Of course it is,' I assured him, surprised at how affected he was. 'He knows the score. It was his idea, after all. Just talk about the war, that's what he likes. Go on, you'll make his day.'

'Give me a minute,' he said, lighting a cigarette.

But a minute was too long. He'd reckoned without my dad and his bird.

She could have been the loveliest, sweetest, cleverest woman and we'd still have hated her. But she had to have sad kohl-blacked eyes and a flabby smile. The garden hissed and squirmed as they made their entrance. How could he?

Mum staggered visibly and Kate sat her down in the nearest chair. We stood guard, daring Sid to bring the seductress anywhere near her. Kate's fingernails were iridescent scarabs on Mum's shoulder, whose hurt, above my sister's raggle-taggle dreadlocks, was real and big and brown.

Nan only had eyes for her dear boy, who'd remembered her birthday for once. Wasn't that just blissful? She continued to grip his hand long after he'd kissed her.

He suddenly remembered and looked around. 'Phoebe?' She slid from behind him to press cheeks with my grandmother.

They knew each other, you could tell. They'd met before! How could she have kept this Phoebe to herself, given the plunging cleavage that had all the old men sitting up and taking notice, the intensely black hair from whose beaded curtains a dark-lipped vampire shyly peeked. A little cattiness on Nan's part would have made it all so much more bearable. But perhaps she'd been sworn to secrecy. Perhaps she'd wanted to spare our feelings. Perhaps she actually liked the woman. Mum struggled to her feet and rushed indoors.

'Talk to Douglas,' I told Max, and went after her. Kate came, too, and Nan. And Sid and Phoebe, actually, but they were only on their way to fetch something from the car, now that they had everyone's attention.

'That w-woman,' Mum managed.

I put the kettle on, not being able to get near her for all the patting and stroking going on.

'Pam, I'm so sorry,' Nan said, wringing her fingers, damp around the eyes, 'If I'd known you were going to spring a party . . . Oh dear, you poor thing, what a shock.'

'How long has it . . .' Mum faltered. 'How long have you known?'

She couldn't think. 'April? A long time.'

'Not that I care, really,' my mother said bravely. 'It was understood. I mean two years . . . We were free to have . . .' and burst into tears.

'Mu-u-um,' we moaned. Kate clicked her fingers. 'Kitchen roll!' I, who was nearest, tore her off a piece.

Mum blew her nose.

'More!'

I ripped off another square of paper and another. She sniffed and told Nan, 'I'm not jealous, you know. Not of her,' and dissolved again. I tore off five or six sheets, for good measure, but Nan bore the brunt of that outburst, and said that no way could any new romance of Sid's interfere with their relationship, hers and Pam's. (On good days, I thought.)

'But you never said anything, Alice. You might, at least, have told me.'

'It would only have made you miserable.'

'Not at all. I'm quite over –' Over what we never knew. Sid and Phoebe pushed into the kitchen humping a massive parcel wrapped in birthday paper. So, he hadn't bothered to look for anything else. There was just the slightest tinkle of cutlery to confirm my fears.

'What are you all doing in here?' he demanded, completely ignoring Mum's soggy face. 'Go on, out you go,

Mother, into the garden where everyone can see you. We have a presentation to make.'

'But –'

'Out!' He'd have clapped his hands if he could.

Like lambs we went, Phoebe making sad eyes at Mum, and Mum smiling quivery little smiles. Her life had just been turned upside down, but never mind – she mustn't make a scene.

Nan had to stand under her awning, the music had to be turned off, Max and Douglas had to stop talking, everyone had to wake up, the children had to come down from the trees for THE UNVEILING.

'Now then,' said Sid, 'where's that photographer?' Fred, he meant, who was a mate, not someone to be bossed. 'Come along, Mother, you over this side. Ready? Smile. Happy birthday, dear!'

Everyone was suitably impressed and Nan tried to appear grateful. She knew just where she was going to put it, where visitors would see what a gifted son she had. That was obviously the right thing to say. He whipped a table away from Mariam, who was breast-feeding her baby, and arranged his beautiful sea of spoons thereon, propped against the pergola. It looked like something you might see on the 'Help the Aged' stand at Chelsea, set off to perfection by late flowering clematis and 'Rambling Rector'. There was no card.

And then he announced that much as he'd love to he couldn't stop. He was on his way to a PRIVATE SHOWING. If anyone was at a loose end later on, they could do worse than spend an hour or two at Trimble's – High Street, Islington. We were all invited. Free drinkies. Or failing that it would be on for a few weeks.

Phoebe murmured in my ear the hope that we could all be friends. She mentioned words like 'civilised' and 'modern'.

'Sid,' said Mum, dodging his puckering lips – he was taking leave of everyone, continental style, once on each cheek, and back again – 'your stuff is in the garage. Will you take it with you? We need the space.'

He glanced at his watch. 'I'm a bit pushed at the moment, Pam. Next time I'm round, eh?'

'Next time, Sid? In *another* two years? The girls want the garage for their disco tonight. Take it with you now, please.'

'Late already, sorry, pet.'

'Do as you're told!' snapped Nan, and it was rather sad to see Sid framed in the back doorway, struggling to hang onto a binbag of clothes and books and bottles of stale aftershave, and attempting to wave a pompous farewell at the same time.

'He doesn't improve with age,' said Nan, shaking her head and sighing. 'It's your kids, Mr Larkin, that fuck you up. I apologise –' her scrawny arms encompassed all present – 'for what must, ultimately, be my responsibility. Now,' she said, 'I do believe there's some rather good champagne needing to be opened.'

After the toast and a top-up, she was ready to dish the dirt on Sid's new woman who, it seemed, ran the Victorian underwear shop in the Arcade. 'Oh that would appeal to him!' cried Mum. 'Lacy knickerbockers and stays! My God, he'll be in seventh heaven!'

Well, well – said Kate's eyebrows to mine, better than we'd hoped. Amazing what a few stiffening slugs of punch can do. I left Mum exploding into her glass while I went along to see how the old comrades were doing.

Fine, by the looks of it. Douglas was saying, 'No, no, you remember, old whatsisname with the cauliflower ears. Used to be a dab hand at Molotov cocktails, 'cept we didn't call 'em that in those days.'

'He had a Spanish girlfriend, you say?'

'Lovely little thing, black eyes, big whatsits. Married her, I think, lucky blighter.'

Until I sat down. Then the conversation switched to modern technology and how Max was coping better than Douglas, who still had to call on Sylvia to set his video. Not in front of the ladies, eh? How very boring.

There was a flicker in the trees that might have been a car's headlights in the back lane or, more likely, lightning, for at that moment a paper cup skittered across the lawn, and balloons and wispy white hair began tugging at their moorings. Sylvia looked up as ominous rumblings broke in on a chat she'd been having with Auntie Kath. 'God's getting the coal in,' she remarked.

Bare arms were goosy and the general consensus was that it was time to go indoors. Furniture and food were taken under cover and children made to say goodbye to everyone, to thank Auntie for a lovely party and to hurry up as the car was in the next street. Another sackful of coal in God's cellar, nearer this time, decided the waverers. Douglas and Max shook hands and promised to meet again soon. Those of us young enough to boogie crowded into a garage made eerie with a few dozen candle-lanterns. The music was turned up loud enough to drown the first heavy drops of rain and the tinkling of the piano in the lounge, where Uncle Ed was accompanying Nan and some of the ladies of the choir as they went through their repertoire of songs from the shows.

Nick had already donned his headset, deejaying, when I remembered Sid's work of art left out in the storm. I couldn't leave it there. The cutlery would rust. I grabbed the nearest strong man, who happened to be Max, and dashed out to the rescue. It was unwieldy rather than heavy, and difficult to balance. Rather than attempt to negotiate wet borders and slippery steps in my big heels we made for the garden shed where we eased the tinkling contraption gently onto the workbench, among Mum's geranium cuttings. Another vicious crack of thunder made me duck back inside.

'Wait a bit,' I counselled, as the rain slammed against the window and drummed on the flimsy roof and the wind puffed dust and seeds and straw up through the cracks in the floorboards. I pulled the door to, moved a watering can from one of Sid's homemade stools, overlooked in Mum's blitz, and sat down facing Max, who perched uncomfortably on a sack of potting compost.

'So,' I said, 'how'd it go, the reunion?'

There had been a lot of catching up to do, he said, on Douglas' marriage and children and grandchildren, and Max's operation and how he found life in the twenty-first century. They were just getting started on their mates in the trenches when it had started to rain.

'I came along, you mean. Put a dampener on things.'

He shook his head, sadly. 'But he should not be so old. Time is cruel.'

'We'll all be there, one day,' I said, tritely, trying not to notice the shed shaking, pulling at its tether like a wild horse. Any minute now, I thought, it'll be Goodbye, Buckhurst Hill, Hello, Glenda, Witch of the North. Alone with Max on the Yellow Brick Road. Scarecrow, Lion or Tinman, which would he be? Well, he had a brain, that was for sure – and his courage was beyond question. It was his heart I wasn't sure of.

'Not me,' he said, bringing me back to earth. 'I will not grow so old.'

'Oh I see, you plan on dying young, do you? Well, I call that ungrateful, after all the trouble Susmeta's gone to.'

He laughed. 'No, I suppose I cannot let the good doctor down. I had better try and live for ever then. Transplanted ad infinitum.'

'It might be lonely,' I said. 'Everyone you know will die.'

'I am used to that.'

There wasn't much room to move among the piles of flower pots and bags of Rooster Booster and blood, fish and bone, and just as well, or I would have got down there on the compost bags with him and given him a hug. Oh Max.

I knew I had to change the subject. I said, 'Did you read about the bomb?'

'The protesters?' he said, grimly nodding. 'The police came to the house late last night.'

'God! They don't suspect Susmeta, do they?'

He shrugged. 'We were each other's alibi.' When I looked incredulous, he said, 'They asked me questions too.'

'They surely don't think . . .'

'They have to check.'

'Max!' I was horrified. Poor guy. Fancy them thinking that he might, that he could . . . I leaned over and took his hand, stroked it. He slipped his fingers under mine and brought my knuckles to his lips. That's all. Just touched them to his lips, thoughtfully, as though they were his own; you could hardly call it a kiss. His eyes were troubled as they searched mine. No, I thought, and reluctantly took my hand away. Better not.

We bolted the door and splashed blindly, madly, back through the rain, through the puddles, to the party. Soaked. My lovely chiffon dress was wet through and clinging, showing every stitch and freckle underneath. My nipples were standing up like under-ripe blackberries. With hair dribbling down my neck and promising to frizz and a hot flush to beat any of Mum's I must have looked really tasty.

His eyes sparkled in the candlelight. His hand found mine, drew me towards him just as the music stopped, and Mum said from the doorway, 'My God, Clare, you look like a drowned rat!'

She wanted us all in the house. Now. Nan was going to open her prezzies.

There was some really sound stuff if you didn't count the subscription to *The Oldie* and the thermal undies. There was a purple evening jacket (how decent an interval could I leave before borrowing that?), a rum-pot of sloe gin, hand-crafted candles and a prehistoric tree fern for her garden. At last she came to mine and Nick's. It looked pathetically small, done up in a scrap of silver paper.

'Diamond earrings!' she breathed. '*Diamonds*. Oh my word, won't I be grand?' and among the gasps of delight and *you really shouldn't have*, tried to look about for the missing one of the pair, without causing alarm.

'It's a nose-stud, Nan,' I said, taking pity on her. 'There's only one.'

'Clare! Naughty girl – and Nick – you've called my bluff! Well, I'll show you. Mariam does piercing. She can do it tomorrow and I'll wear my diamond on holiday. They'll think I'm an author of note.'

Which prompted enquiries about the writing holiday she was going on with the East End Writers, and reminded Nick about the tent. What had I done with it? I seemed to remember stashing it behind the rockery. I thought it was time to break the news about Willi Greff's invitation to the Austrian Alps.

'Oh *what*! Nice one, Clare!' Nick swung me off my feet in a big, joyous hug, before leading Max and me in a riotous conga through the house, into the garden. The tail grew longer and longer, through the garage and out along the street. 'We're on our way to Telfes! We're on our way to Telfes! Da-da-da-dah, da-da-da-dah!'

The fact that it was research and film shoot all in one, that we'd be working our socks off interviewing, digging for information, getting the right handle on things, and the right camera shots, too, didn't seem to worry him. He probably hadn't thought about all the gruelling things we'd have to do, like looking round the Fuehrer Bunker and the freezer, plus I needed to get my hands on that letter. While we were in Berlin, I'd do a bit on Max's war work, go down into the sewers, maybe have a look for Grandma Wolff's suitcase. And get a few shots of the concert hall where Axel had played to packed houses. Visit his home in Hamburg, Ellen's in Cologne, the Sauerbruch factory, and the studio in Bavaria where Friedrich Liebl worked. They were a bit far-flung but if any of them were still standing, I'd have to check them out. I'd already put out feelers, trying to trace any surviving works of art by Liebl. So far, nothing, only the old photos they'd shown on 'Way of the World'. They couldn't all have been destroyed by the SS, surely? Then there was Buchenwald. I'd heard they'd cleaned it up, but even so . . . And the saltmines. The armaments factory.

All Nick could see were snow-capped alps looming up before his starry eyes. And somehow, I don't know how, he naturally assumed that Max would be coming too.

14

So here we all were, trudging along a zigzag track, halfway up a mountain with an impossible name, somewhere in the Austrian Tyrol. We'd cleared it with Barry, persuaded him that he really wouldn't enjoy toiling up mountains and was far better employed doing whatever it was producers do. *Way of the World* was finished for the season, so the film crew was up for grabs, until the autumn when their contracts were renewed. I'd been able to take my pick.

Nick and I had done all the groundwork, contacted the embassies, the museums, got permits to film this and that. But we'd come up against a brick wall in Berlin.

'What letter?' said the police.

'There must have been one,' I pointed out, 'or how would anyone know where the brains had come from?'

'You're right. We'll look into it. Get back to you.'

But no, there was nothing on record. Any communication from Hofmann about his brains had got lost. I'd have to make it up.

When I told Max he was beside himself. 'Lost it? They can't have! It's an important document! Imbeciles!' and other words in German which I didn't feel worthy of translation. OTT, if you ask me. I mean it wasn't that important. 'Who discovered the freezer?' he wanted to know. 'Who found the brains? Reported them to the authorities? They'd know if there was a letter.'

'What, you mean the contractors?'

'Yes, yes. The contractors. Who was working on the site at the time of the discovery? What did they do with the fucking letter?'

'Max, this was seven years ago. I'm not a detective, for God's sake. It doesn't matter that much.'

'It matters to me!' His eyes flashed. Uh-oh, I thought, this goes deep. It struck me he was like a foundling needing to have some memento, some trinket from his birth mother, to give him roots. He wasn't going to give up easily.

The contractors were a firm called 'Spitzy.' Richard spoke to the managing director who gave him the brush-off, told him that the gang were mostly casual labourers, impossible to trace now.

There must be payslips, some sort of record, for God's sake, I insisted. Or maybe he'd like me to get onto the tax people, find out that way. The guy took my mobile number and said he'd get back. I still hadn't heard, two days later, and it was bugging me. This man, the guy who'd opened the freezer, could be working anywhere in Germany, in the world, in fact. Or he might be dead of asbestosis or a bang on the head or a fall or whatever demolition men die of. Herr Felder might be trying to call at this very moment and how could he? It was notoriously difficult to get a signal half-way up a mountain. Following our leader, te tum, te tee – not Peter Pan, but our own Willi Greff, who never grew old either, in his hairy legs and lederhosen – I was cut off from all civilized means of communication. I felt helpless. Willi, on the other hand, was in his element, taking us on one of his favourite jaunts in the company of his great-grandson, Franz. The two seemed to have formed an alliance, in the face of the formidable grandmother, who obviously ran the household, if not the entire Greffindustrie, with a rod of iron. Hot on their heels was Max, blissful to be here. He had been to the area before the war, on holiday with his cousin, Harry Stevens. They had stayed at youth hostels in Innsbruck and all along the Stubai valley. So many happy memories. He hadn't stopped smiling yet.

Next in line was Nick, desperate to be in front but adhering to some unspoken boy-scout code about not overtaking the leader and giving me moral support as I huffed after him like a steam engine. He kept stopping on bends to snap views and flowers and butterflies and nipping back for ten second videos of Charlie and the team trucking along behind, red-faced and wheezing. He had this amazing new digital camera he'd bought at Heathrow and was driving me nuts with his constant demands to say 'cheese'.

Goodness knows where Jay had got to. When I'd left him he had been stripped down to his pink vest and shorts in the meadows, listening to the choughs and chaffinches, looking up gentians and orchids in his *Observer's Book of Alpine Flowers*, to all intents and purposes in his own serene little wonderland. But I knew my Jay. I could see Richard's lairy yellow beachcomber shirt on one of the lower levels. He'd come as the official interpreter. Who was pulling whom was hard to make out from up here.

And then, if you looked straight down the mountainside you could just make out the plodding bearers, laid on by the Greffs, emerging from the forested lower slopes, rounding the bends with tripods and cameras, lens boxes, sound decks, all the paraphernalia of a film shoot, and a couple of huge luncheon baskets provided by Ottilie, who, wearing stout boots, stout blouse and skirt and carrying an umbrella against the sun, brought up a substantial rear.

The day before, we'd filmed the Greffs at home in their mansion, taking breakfast in the breakfast room, coffee by the pool, lunch, tea and cocktails in various parts of the garden, dinner in the sumptuous dining room, and liqueurs on the veranda, as the mountains tucked their pink and gold heads under their dark duvets and snuggled down for the night.

Today we were to picnic in a favourite alpine meadow,

two thousand metres above sea level. It wasn't as bad as it sounded. Telfes, the village where the Greffs had their estate, was on a plateau a thousand metres up for starters, so we only had to climb another three thousand feet. The height of the lowest Scottish Monroe. Piece of cake.

We were already immersing sweaty bodies and throbbing feet in the icy lake, when Ottilie, the widow Richter, arrived, plod, plod with her servants, who immediately set to work standing bottles of Reisling in the shallows to cool, flapping out chequered cloths on the grass and laying out enough platters of cold meats and *wurst*, rollmops and smoked fish, cheese, bowls of salad and potatoes to feed an army.

While Max and Nick frolicked like dolphins in the water, Charlie and I set up a fixed camera and gathered eaves-droppings from the Greffs, who were, at first, too hungry to speak. It was a pleasant family picnic by the lake. But we were looking for undercurrents.

Ottilie was so pleased to see everyone enjoying them-selves. 'Eat!' she ordered, waving brawny arms. '*Essen!*'

Yesterday's talk had been about the past, about Willi's experiences in Buchenwald, and his family's exile in America, where Uncle Ernst sold his brother's notebooks to the US government, whose scientists were quick to recognise the enormity of Willi's discovery and its potential for both good and evil. In a war situation the latter was the more urgent need and, working on his formulae, they proceeded to develop nuclear weapons.

No doubt about it, science had been moving quickly, and Ernst wanted to ride on its back. He'd had vision and, after the sale of his brother's notebooks, money to invest in a top-drawer team of research chemists. The Greff family business began to prosper.

Ottilie's recollections had included schooldays in Man-hattan, her stormy relationship with her brother, Wilhelm, and fond memories of their mother. As she spoke I got

Charlie to zoom in on Willi, with the intention of recording, in close-up, the various sentiments that her words evoked. Yes, he was moved by mention of his wife and his son, to tears, actually. But it was the way he regarded his daughter, between times, that interested me. With caution. As though she were a particularly volatile experiment.

As she told us, in guttural English with a New York twang, of their return to Austria after the war, how changed they had found everything, his face hardened. It wasn't just that he was waiting for Richard to translate. His upper lip contracted in disgust and small muscles twitched around his eyes as though he wanted to turn away. It wasn't what she was saying – which he didn't understand until it was translated – it was the woman herself and her capitalist philosophy.

Europe was very poor in those early years following the war, unlike America. In Innsbruck there was hunger, homelessness, suffering. But that was to the advantage of anyone setting up in business. There was room for investment, for growth, and in no time at all, it seemed, their factory on Bahnhof Strasse had become too small. They'd had to expand and diversify. In the mid fifties, after Wilhelm's death, Ernst moved the business end of things to Julienstrasse, a more salubrious part of town, and put his own son in charge. He, himself, moved to the main industrial site at Munich. By 1960 Greffindustrie had become a corporation, manufacturing chemicals for industry and agriculture, plastics, pharmaceutical products and synthetic fibres. They now had branches all over the world, interests in every country.

Willi was looking distinctly unimpressed. So I asked, 'Where do you fit into all this, Willi? Are you preparing to take up the reins of management? Or will you go back to the laboratory?'

He was sitting on a rock, his bare toes dibble-dabbling in

the water, a plate of salad on his knees. He had grown a sandy beard as in pre-war days, and wore the same style of wire-framed spectacles and, as he considered my question, he pushed them higher up his long slippery nose and chewed quietly on his watercress. In fact, of all the transplantees, he was the one who most resembled his former self in physique, at least, being almost as tall and as spare. Facially he was nothing like. His daughter, he told me and Richard privately, took after his wife, a compact little woman, though in Ottilie's case, self-indulgence had coarsened her features. He could see nothing of himself in her, only in Franz, his great-grandson, who had the long face, the adolescent gawkiness of the teenage Willi, the same set of the eyes, and the same teeth. He would fill out as he grew older but would never quite lose that shambling gait, which Willi was now imposing on his new body.

We switched to a shot of the boy, never far from his great-grandfather, herding waves of grasshoppers to death by drowning. Willi spoke sharply to him, and the boy sat down, red-faced and sulky. Even so, he was interested in the not-so-old man's reply. Richard, on a neighbouring rock, translated.

'Not management,' he said. 'They would like him to continue where he left off.' By 'they' I presume he meant Ottilie, who sat staring out over the bright ripples, her fat legs stuck out in front of her, as she sipped her wine and ate her potatoes, shaded from the hot sun by her umbrella. Willi shot her a glance. 'I have to perform the miracle,' he said, wryly, 'of turning water into wine, or more specifically, sea water into energy by means of nuclear fusion.'

'Cheap,' put in Ottilie. I gathered she was referring to the cost of the project and not imitating the chaffinches that had come to scavenge our crumbs.

If it could be harnessed, Willi explained, the sea would offer a plentiful source of energy and there would be very little radioactive waste. Long ago by the world's reckoning, he thought he had found a way of doing just this, of separating hydrogen from superheated steam and, later, of converting that hydrogen into helium by fusion at high temperatures. Later research, based largely on his sold notebooks, had proved so expensive that America had withdrawn from international co-operation and cut its own fusion programme. But Willi was convinced they'd gone the wrong way about it. There had to be a cheaper method. In fact he'd almost had the answer within his grasp, when bloody Hitler . . .

As Richard turned this into English, Willi kicked the water in fury, raising eyes, hands and voice to heaven. Richard gestured for calm and explained that Hitler had interfered at the crucial moment. He had wanted Willi to turn his attention to the making of nuclear weapons. When he refused to do his Fuhrer's bidding he was carted off to Buchenwald, to ponder the error of his ways. But Willi declared he wouldn't make bombs for anyone, not just Hitler. 'He is a pacifist,' said Richard unnecessarily.

'I see,' I said. It looked as though Greffindustrie were onto a winner. Willi had been out of it for a long time and his notebooks had disappeared, but a mighty brain like his would have no trouble in picking up the pieces of his research and putting them back together, surely? Wasn't it like riding a bike? You never forget how. The way he jerked his head indicated that it might not be that simple.

Lunch over, we took a break from filming, most of us nesting on waterproofs in the prickly grass, some of us frankly asleep, lulled by the cry of the curlews, the thin air and the effects of a very heavy lunch. I had thought to do a little homework on the Spanish Civil War but found myself groping my way out of a pleasant dream to the rustle of maps and male voices plotting the route ahead, which would afford panoramic views and spectacular camera shots of the Stubai valley. A peak was mentioned, Elferspitz, accessible only by fixed ropes and ladders.

'No way!' I yawned. What was the point of all that lovely food and wine if we were going to do more climbing? Another thousand metres they reckoned. They had to be joking. 'You're not getting me up any fixed ropes and ladders.'

'They're put there to help,' said Nick. 'Easy, peasy. Think of the shot, Clare. Willi and Max, the Buchenwald heroes, standing together by the trig point, with a fabulous back-drop of mountain peaks and sky? Triumph over adversity? Looking down on Telfes, chatting about old times?'

'No.'

'You won't get another chance.'

I looked around for support but they were all dead keen to go. Even Jo was girding her dainty loins and telescoping a baby-legs tripod into her rucksack. Charlie reckoned we could manage the equipment between us, if we took the bare essentials and the lightweight VT camera, so small you could pop it into a pocket of your rucksack. In the face of all that enthusiasm what could I do? Grumbling to sour the milk I wrapped a couple of batteries in my spare socks, rammed them into the Karrimor and heaved it onto my complaining back. No one took the slightest notice.

Off we went across bogs, boulders and streams, beating off flies and mozzies as we went. There was no shade and vultures circled overhead. Our track was steep and stony when we eventually found it, a vandal's diagonal scratch across a green painted mountainside. I plodded, onward and upward, rarely raising my eyes from the boot in front as it showed me my next foothold. Sweat ran into my eyes and stung, my lungs were bursting, and my nose dripped continually. Pausing on a rocky bend to wipe it and to swig some water, I watched jealously, as down by the lake, siesta over, a microscopic Ottilie and her henchmen humped their baskets and our excess equipment back across the grassy cirque and disappeared, one by one, between buttresses of rock and down the way we had come.

Some way back along their path came two tiny walkers. I puzzled over them. We hadn't passed anyone. A flash of lairy yellow, the sun on dark skin and I knew. It was Richard and the pink-vested Jay, swapping recipes. 'Hey!' I protested.

The three in front stopped, pivoting one-footed to watch me jabbing the air and spluttering about defectors. Breathing hard and scrunching stones underfoot, Ez caught us up, with the news that Richard had been nursing a blister back at the lake. He'd slapped a plaster on it, struggled on to the foot of this climb and then decided that it would be foolish to go on. Jay had offered to keep him company.

'Why didn't you say so sooner?'

'Couldn't catch you,' he gasped. 'And Jo's on her way down, too, with the boy. She was feeling dizzy and faint. Too much wine at lunchtime, if you ask me.' Even as he spoke, we saw them, in miniature, as through a viewfinder, waving and feeling much better thank you now that they were on the way home.

So I was one of the hardier ones. Fancy! But I was very cross. If I'd known there were other wimps I'd have left the intrepids to get on with it. As it was . . .

Four of the party hauled themselves up ladders pinned to the rocks, with the fifth, me, rigid, squeaking with fright and refusing to move and the sixth patiently waiting.

'Let me help you,' said Max, placing my feet on the rungs.

'Give me your hand,' ordered Nick, above me. 'Clare, you're all right. Let go, for Christ's sake! Right hand, *right* hand! Got you! Now come *on.*'

But it wasn't him pulling me up that made my heart lurch, it was Max below with his hand warm on my bum, pushing. My knees gave way and I'd've sat right down on his head if Nick hadn't yanked me up and over the lip of the gorge with an oath to set the valleys ringing.

After that we had to clamber over the bleached boulders of ancient rock falls, with subterranean naiads and trolls gurgling beneath our thick soles. We crossed fields of shale where the path was the width of your foot and one slip would have sent you slithering down a fifty-foot slope of loose, flat, flakes of rock to certain death. We walked across a black moonscape where marmots called to each other with eerie voices and buzzards and red kites fed their young on precipitous ledges. We breasted a col and found ourselves in a land where the paths were almost level, cushioned with sweet-scented thyme and gritted with crushed quartz, where every jewelled surface dazzled with sun. I drank in the exquisite air and stretched my arms wide to encompass it all.

'Heaven,' agreed Max, in my ear. Spinning round I found his eyes hidden by reflective shades, his smile enigmatic. 'Or it could be . . .'

Oh God, oh God. I couldn't breathe. I couldn't throw myself into his arms, sink with him onto the glittering ground in thrall to ecstasy. I couldn't run away. So I stopped and sat down, on the pretext of removing a stone from my boot. He stopped, too. Ez and Charlie walked on by, talking hard. Now we were last.

I said, 'Max, I can't do this.'

'Do what? This bit is easy.'

'Oh, don't pretend. You know what's going on. You feel it, too.'

'I do?' And his grin was enough to drive me mad.

'Don't. Please. I can't deal with it now. There's too much at stake.'

He picked up my boot and banged it. No stone fell out, of course. 'It may be in your sock,' he said. Sock? We both knew the stone was a fiction. Nevertheless I took it off and before I could stop him he had turned it inside out and back again, my steamy, smelly sock, and held it to his face as though it were sweet with herbs.

'Ma-a-ax!' I giggled, appalled and delighted.

'We *must* deal with it.'

'N-no, Max.' I faltered because now my foot enclosed in his warm fingers. I gasped. 'I – I do love Nick, you know. He's, he's my best friend.' It sounded a bit inadequate. 'And he's so happy, Max, I'd hate to hurt him right now. Let's get the holiday over first. Please.' Took my sock from him and pulled it on.

'And then?'

'And then – I don't know. We'll have to play it by ear. For the moment just give me some space.'

Nick was coming back along the path to check on me.

'Space?' said Max.

'Leave it awhile. Wait.'

'Clare? You all right?'

'Oh hi, Nick. Yeah, I'm fine thanks. It's these little stones. They get everywhere.' I scooped up a few sugar-like lumps and put them in my pocket. Souvenirs of a moment.

I walked on ahead and left them to talk about walks they'd done or politics or whatever other interests they had in common besides me.

We were trudging through a snowfield when I found myself beside Willi. No Ottilie, no Franz: it was a chance to get him to open up. But all I could do was smile and wave my hands about and burble a grossly inadequate 'Wunderbar!' at the glory around us, cursing Richard and his sodding blister.

Our path to the top became a rabbit track that strung us out in single file again and we scrabbled to find holds in the grit and stones that would stop us sliding off heartstopping bends where the ground dropped away into whistling nothingness.

And then we were there, at the craggy top, and rewarded with breathtaking views of snowy peaks and turquoise glaciers and the blue sky of space. Down, miles down, was the entire green length of the Stubai valley where the river wriggled like a silver worm and people lived with their two feet firmly on the ground. The men were euphoric, banging each other on the back and shouting against the wind. You'd think it was Everest we'd climbed. We munched our Mint Cake and our glucose sweets and stuck our noses into thermos caps of sweet German coffee. Blood sugars replenished, Charlie set up the camera. Ez tried to minimise the buffeting but he didn't have Jo's know-how and it was impossible to hear what anyone said. The great dialogue between Max and Willi was a non-event. No one else knew German and in any case, Willi didn't seem to have a lot to say to Max or vice versa. I'd have to wait for the video and Richard's translation.

But they were pretty incredible shots, if I do say so myself.

And then – *then* they wanted me to take the short cut home, down the scree slope.

Oh no, I assured them. They were *not* getting me to slide down a mountain side of loose gravel, not even with two of them holding me every step of the way.

Willi assured me that he'd done this dozens of times. The DANGER sign (in three languages, with an emphatic skull and crossbones) was put there merely to discourage walkers from eroding the slopes. There really was nothing to fear. What appeared to be a precipice at the bottom was, in fact, the start of a gentle incline, where the scree petered out and a path led down to a forested area. Max seemed to remember descending by the same route five years ago, by his reckoning.

'No.' My centre of gravity was different from theirs. I was clumsy, gawky. I would lose my footing, and finish up dead. Buried. Under a ton of gravel.

The management huddled together and cunningly plotted while I continued my sit-down strike. I was familiar enough with the male psyche to know that they were planning to leave me no choice, and I was already on my guard as they proceeded to demonstrate how easy it was, stepping off into the breathless void, and then long-legging it down the cascading stones as though they were on an escalator, taking two steps at a time, and the train already in the station.

'Who-ho-o-oah!' they cried to show me how exhilarating it was, first Charlie, then Ez, then Willi whose exultant echo caught up with theirs and played leapfrog with the mountains.

That left Nick, Max and piggy in the middle. It was in their eyes, the signal, the urgency. I knew that whatever they were planning would happen any second. So I was ready when their hands made to grab mine and I startled backwards. My anticipation and their empty hands unbalanced them, and they were borne away without me. Max fell on his side, his outstretched arm dragging down the slope, his fingers clutching at stones. 'Bloody little fool!' he yelled up at me, slithering and throwing himself onto his back as he receded to specimen size. Nick wobbled but steadied himself, managed to remain upright. He was able to turn and plead, 'Now, Clare, now!' He looked as though he were riding a wave or a skateboard. Trouble was I'd never mastered either skill: I have the scars to prove it.

My mind wouldn't connect with my feet at all. I tried to tell him, but the only sound was the swish of stones as he slid further and further away from me in his own personal avalanche, getting smaller and smaller and disappearing over the edge.

The last stone rattled down after him and his voice wafted away on the wind, a feeble thing. I took a deep breath and prepared to begin the return journey.

Luckily the route was marked with daubs of red paint, all the way down. Thousands of people had been along here and they'd all got home, in one piece. I was a resourceful, intelligent girl. Why should I get lost? Or break a leg? I'd come up; I could go down. The relief of not having to ride the scree made me almost happy. Knowing there was no help for it, I shimmied down those fixed ladders lickety split, traversed those scrambly bits, on my bum mostly, and after a while began to relish the solitude, the freedom to look around, listen to the birds, see the marmots come out of their holes to discuss me with their neighbours. I stopped to pick harebells, sniff the thyme and the mint and watch the small puddle below growing into the lake where we'd had our lunch.

An hour later I was within sight of the village. It appeared every so often whenever the trees thinned. It was tiny, still four or five hundred feet below. But I'd done the hard bit. There was a wide forest path beneath my feet and I was feeling great. Knackered but happy. Then I heard this pant, pant, grunt, behind me and my heart sank. There was Nick, red in the face and fuming, come to rescue me.

The row was necessarily tight-lipped on my part as every ounce of my wit and energy was concentrated on trying to appear sure-footed and nonchalant. I didn't dare take my eyes off my feet for fear of tripping or slipping or sliding or twisting my ankle in a hole. Meanwhile he was telling me that my cowardice was dangerous, that I was irresponsible, I could have got people killed. Max's ribs were badly skinned where he'd slid down the scree.

'Tough,' I said. And when he looked at me in amazement, I pointed out, 'I didn't ask him to try and drag me down there against my will. That was his idea. And yours.'

'You're having a laugh, aren't you? What were we supposed to do?'

I shrugged. 'Indulged me? Come home the long way.'

His aggrieved expression told me he'd never actually considered that option. 'But that's . . .'

'Boring?' I suggested. 'And boys must have their fun.'

'You're so selfish, Clare.'

'Me!'

'Fuck off,' he said, and flounced down the path and out of sight. I knew he'd be waiting for me round the next bend with more complaints.

They'd hung around at the bottom of the slide, he said, sure that I would appear, that I would take a deep breath, hold my nose and do it. They'd waited. And then they'd climbed back up to where the ground dipped and they could see the top of the slide – I wasn't there. There was no knowing where I was. I could have gone back up to the top to wait for a helicopter, could have retraced my steps to the lake, *could have found the track round the scree slope and come down to them that way . . .*

'There was another way down?' I shrieked. 'You said it was the scree or go back the way we'd come!'

He shrugged. 'The scree slope was quicker.'

'Not in the long run,' I sneered.

'No, not in the long run.'

'You lied to me!'

'You screwed up.'

'You bullied me!'

'You're a pain in the arse.'

'I hate you.'

'I hate *you*.'

'Fuck off.'

'Fuck off, yourself.' And so on and so forth. When we reached the road I was exhausted and my legs were like jelly. I had to sit down on the first bench we came to and put my head between my knees.

After he'd given me the last of his boiled sweets, all warm and sticky, and let me drain his water bottle, he conceded that maybe the scree run hadn't been such a cool idea, after all. Just that he'd wanted to do it. They all had. He was a selfish bastard and he was sorry.

And then he said something wonderful, that made up for everything.

'I wanted to get you to myself,' he said. 'Tell you something tasty. I had an e-mail this morning, from the guys at the Ministry. Sophie Müller escaped the Holocaust. She was married to Max Zeiler in December 1938 at Mare Street Registry Office, Hackney.'

15

I was a few minutes late – a few minutes, for God's sake. I slipped into the huge dining room the way the maids came in and waited, not out of politeness but to get a grip on my anger. Ottilie was saying grace without me.

The table was magnificent: snowy starched linen, towering tureens and matching soup-bowls and side plates; silver and crystal-ware sparkling with privilege. Ranged among the candles and condiments, twin floral displays and baskets of bread, the heads of the diners were mostly reverently bent. A couple were new to me, married, I guessed, he, red-necked with a helmet of blond hair, she, a doughy Snow White. Two pairs of eyes were disobediently open – Max was scowling fit to kill, and Nick was looking at his watch and then, accusingly, at me.

Ottilie's flicked open on the Amen and beaded in on me skulking by the wall. 'Well, here she is!' she bawled in English. They all turned and stared. 'Come, Fraulein, come and sit down. I have finished now. We waited dinner as long as we could.'

I drew myself to my full six foot, in heels, tossed back my freshly showered frizz and attempted, with muscles that shrieked, a dignified progress across a wasteland of click-clacking ceramic tiles to an empty chair beside Nick. 'Thank you for waiting,' I said with teeth-rotting sweetness.

They fell upon me, then, like gannets. I'd done something very bad it seemed, giving them so much anxiety. I nearly laughed out loud at Max's reproachful glare and gave him a dazzling smile, brimful of promise. I couldn't wait to tell him, after dinner that Sophie was alive and well and living in Gants Hill. I felt like a kid at Christmas, bursting with secrets. Though, as Nick had said, if I was hoping to capture the lovers' reunion on film, I could think again. It would be traumatic for both of them. She was eighty-three. I had to be prepared for the fact that she might not want Max to see her old and decrepit. It didn't bode well that she hadn't come forward when the news first broke. There was an outside chance that she hadn't seen the papers or the telly – but he doubted it.

'Just as well Nick found you when he did,' Jay was saying.

'Why's that then?'

'Well,' he said, looking slightly puzzled, 'you could have been out there all night.'

'Is that what he said?' I bunched my mouth against name-calling. 'I was almost home, Jay,' I said indignantly. 'I wasn't lost. I didn't need finding.'

'They weren't to know that.'

'That was their problem, and entirely their fault. I took the red track,' adding cattily, 'followed you down . . .'

'Ah . . . ' His face darkened. Well may he blush, I thought.

'You should have said you were turning back. I'd have come with you.'

'You looked like you were enjoying yourself,' he said, in a sneaky sort of way, with an almost imperceptible sly flick of his eyes in Max's direction. Ouch. It was my turn to blush. Nothing got past Jay. Then he said with a shrug, 'It didn't occur to me, to be honest, Clare. Richard had a blister and couldn't go on, and, well, I thought I'd better give him a hand.'

'A hand,' I echoed dryly. 'I can imagine . . . Enjoying your soup, Jo?' I said, turning on the other defector, who was chewing bread ravenously. 'Feeling better, are you?'

She swallowed. 'I left you in the lurch, too, didn't I?' she said with a pretty pout.

'I felt a bit outnumbered,' I admitted. 'Men in packs are such bullies.'

'Bullies? How can you say that, young lady? I'm sure there are only perfect gentlemen around this table.' It was the man with the blond hair leering at me, mockery leaking from every pore. I hate that. Barry does it. The wife was forcing a wan, suety smile. I guessed she would know about bullies if anyone did.

'And you are?' I enquired of him, haughtily. Nick nudged me with his knee and glowered. My return knock was sharper. What?

Ottilie put me wise with a gloating introduction, 'My son, Oscar, just returned from his Middle Eastern trip, and his wife, Ilse. This is Fraulein Russell – Clare – who is directing the film. Your first, isn't it, Fraulein?' As she well knew, but she had to make the point.

'And none the worse for that, I'm sure.' Just in time I snatched my hand away from a condescending pat.

'Are we all going to be in it?' simpered the wife.

She had to be joking. I said the film was about Buchenwald survivors and so it was Willi I was mainly interested in. I hoped, by the way, that someone had used their initiative and captured the moment, on film, when Oscar ran out to meet his grandfather as he came down off the mountain . . . No? Well, we'd better mock it up in the morning – before we left.

'What!' There was a clatter of cutlery and a few splutters as soup went down the wrong way. 'But . . .'

But nothing. I hated it there. I'd had enough of the Greffs. Willi was all right, but he was a throwback, and watching him being manipulated by his scheming daughter wasn't nice. As for Oscar – my skin was already crawling.

'Yes,' I said, 'we're going to Buchenwald.' Max nearly shot out of his chair, almost as suddenly as the idea had jumped into my head. Now he was staring at me with consternation in his eyes.

I said, quickly, 'You don't have to come, Max. I wouldn't do that to you. We'll book you into a hotel here if you want to stay and you can meet us in Hanover next week. I thought we'd pop in and see Berthe while we have the chance, and have a look round some of your old haunts. But you're a free agent, of course. You do what you want.'

'I want to come with you.'

'Oh Max, it'd be fantastic if you would!' I must say, though, I was surprised. I thought it was the last place he'd want to visit.

'You will need me to show you around.'

Frau Greff expressed her feelings very forcibly. She had understood we were here for the week. This sudden change of plan was, well, it was, inconsiderate, quite frankly. She had invited people to meet us tomorrow. Tch!

I piled on the regrets. Wonderful hospitality . . . wonderful country . . . memorable stay . . . incredible footage . . . hated to leave but something had come up forcing us to rearrange our schedule. Our time was not our own, nor our budget. Had it been otherwise, blah, blah. But in spite of all that ingratiating eyewash she was still very huffy.

I had a splendid idea. Why didn't we finish our meal and the family Greff could adjourn to the terrace while we filmed them interacting and maybe playing Scrabble, like any normal family? I didn't dare look at the others. Willi had promised to take us down to the village tonight to sample the local brew. The general gloom reached out and pinched me, but I'd made up my mind.

While the crew set up and the Greffs did what they felt was necessary in order to face the camera, Nick and I took Max onto the balcony and broke the news about Sophie. He turned to us with unseeing eyes, his face a mask without colour or expression.

'Alive?' he croaked, leaning for support on the stone parapet. 'How can she be?' He shook his heavy head. 'My wife? Alive?'

222

Alarmed, I fetched a chair. He looked as though he was about to pass out. I don't know what I'd expected – not for it to be such a shock, at any rate. He must have known it was a possibility that she'd survive. He'd taken her to England, for heavens' sake, married her to keep her safe. But he sat down heavily, staring wildly, wincing a little, reminded of his sore ribs.

'Max?' I peered at him closely, for some clue as to his feelings. But he covered his face with his hands and his shoulders shook. He shrugged my hand away and Nick and I looked at each other. The poor guy was overcome.

A whisky helped. The colour gradually seeped back into his face and his eyes brightened. He began asking questions. Where was she living? Was she in good health? Had we spoken to her? Did she have any family? All we could give him was her address and telephone number. With that in his hand he began to smile, at last. He'd got used to thinking of her as dead, he said.

He'd written to her when he was serving in Germany, letters that disappeared into the void, that may or may not have reached their destination. Some did. He knew because he came back to London between missions for de-briefing, and was able to spend some time with her. She was very low, poor girl. Alone in a strange country, unable to speak the language, not knowing what was happening to her family back in Hanover. And then, one day, she wasn't home when he called. She hadn't been there for weeks. Missing believed dead, they said. Bomb damage all around. He'd gone back to Berlin in a daze. Dared all. Nothing had mattered anymore. Not long afterwards he was captured.

'Oh Max,' I said.

He looked up, and I saw myself swim into the dark depths of his focus. How he'd suffered, poor love. 'If I'd known that she was alive somewhere, I would never have . . .' He heaved a dismal sigh. Never have what? Gone down that sewer? Taken such risks? But I didn't probe. He could hang on to his secrets. For now.

The Greffs opted for Bridge, which had to be about as riveting as the shipping forecast. Apparently Willi and his brother Ernst had been grand masters before the war. I hoped Charlie had had the foresight to load an empty cartridge. We could save something.

Frau Ottilie G. Ein Karo.

Herr Oscar G. Ein Pik.

Herr Willi G. Ein Ohnetrumpf.

Frau Ilse G. Zwei Treff.

Frau Ottilie G. Zweimal Ohnetrumpf.

We were all yawning tears. Nick was sprawled in the armchair, frankly asleep. Max had gone to make some phone calls. Touching base with Sophie, I imagined.

Then came the interesting bit: the inquest at the end of the card game. Goodness knows what Willi had or hadn't done. Richard did try and explain to me that he'd made some appalling bids and lost him and Ottilie the game. I didn't need him to translate the insults, though. Even I knew what *Dummkopf* meant. I gathered poor Willi was nowhere near his old form.

Oscar regarded him anxiously. All through dinner I had watched him raising superior eyebrows, smirking and openly rolling his eyes at his mother whenever Willi said something old-hat or faintly stuffy. It wasn't the sort of behaviour you expected of respectful grandchildren, especially when the grandsire was a valuable resource.

We left them to it and went to bed.

I wasn't entirely surprised in the morning when Willi popped in on our crack-of-dawn breakfast to ask if he could come with us to Buchenwald. He hadn't been back yet and he wanted to pay his respects, he said. I said I was afraid it would be a squeeze in the minibus: nine of us *plus* all the gear. Willi suggested taking some of us in the Bentley and coming back on his own after Buchenwald. I was delighted. The long car journey would give me an opportunity to get him to open up, away from the influence of family and friends. Max seemed quite content to travel with the crew after I'd given him a thin wad of spending money and explained to him that Nick was going to share the driving with Willi and, in any case, I needed a researcher to ask the right questions. Jay was a bit miffed at being parted from Richard, but there really was no room and I needed Richard's linguistic skills clear and uncluttered.

How the other half lives – there was a drinks cabinet in the back and a TV. Suffice to say we were all nicely chilled out by the time we reached the border.

The conversation came around to the Austrian Freedom Party and how they'd risen to power in the last few years. Willi was naturally alarmed that the extreme Right was actually legitimised in Europe, given credence, that there was nothing the EC governments were willing to do about it.

'Well,' said Nick, whose turn it was at the wheel, 'every country has laws against racism. Like you can get done for making racist remarks. I mean you can get fined or dismissed from your job – very different from your day. But underneath it's, like, rife. And it's not just yobs looking for someone to beat up. You'd be surprised. It's old guys on my dad's allotment and mums collecting kids from school, guys in pubs – fairly intelligent people, you'd have thought. Oh, they lower their voices and look over their shoulders, make bloody sure they can't be overheard by anyone likely to give them a bit of verbal. Know what I mean? But it all comes out, all the old jokes, the old prejudices. If Hitler was around today, and he went about it the right way, he'd get a lot of support.'

'So things haven't changed?' said Willi.

'No,' said Nick, flatly. 'Britain is riddled with prejudice, and Germany . . . Well, you know, you've seen the news – the skinheads beating up asylum seekers. Like America's full of 'good old' boys and girls, not just the South. Just that Austria's a bit more open about it maybe.'

Willi looked glum. 'So many advances in technology and medicine and there are still people who cannot see beyond the colour of a man's skin.'

'Tell me about it,' I said. 'The Internet's swarming with racists.'

'So what is the use of all this technology if human prejudice will bring a country to its knees. Racism, xenophobia, is the canker that kills, that takes one people to war against another. You know my daughter, Ottilie, supports the Freedom Party?'

'I'm not surprised. You'll have to watch her, Willi.'

We were heading north to Munich through the mountains and gazing up at the remote tops. After yesterday's solo trek, I was feeling slightly more friendly towards those wild terrains, those unforgiving climbs through echoing forests and bleak snowfields. I could see what Willi was getting at when he said that up there among the eternal crags, roaming free, he could make believe his wife and son were still alive, waiting for him at home, and that Ottilie was the sweet little girl he once knew. He could even convince himself that his work would one day benefit mankind.

'It will,' I said. 'It has done.'

He sighed heavily, and a gravelly stream of German passed between him and the interpreter, with Richard becoming more and more agitated and Willi's face turning paler and stonier.

'Rich-ard!' I had to wail at last, 'what's he *saying*?'

'He is not a happy man, Clare. He feels that everything he valued is lost, his life being the least of it. He and his ideals were utterly betrayed by that brother of his.' So now we were hearing the truth. 'He would never have sold to America, nor agreed to his work being used to kill people.'

'Kill people!'

'He is sure his findings were used in the making of the hydrogen bomb.'

'Oh my *God!*'

Richard bunched his mouth. Willi must have been devastated. 'Nor would he have brought up his children to love capitalism. He says he'd rather have died in Buchenwald than have been born again into a family where his politics are considered quaint Utopian rubbish.'

'Oh Willi,' I said. I hadn't realised.

He shrugged. Richard said, 'And now he discovers that processing nuclear energy threatens the environment, that Germany is closing down its reactors in favour of "green" methods. Even his best intentions will harm the human race. He cannot, in all conscience, continue with this work.'

I didn't like to ask the obvious question: how was he intending to reconcile his principles with Ottilie's insistence that he add to the family coffers? Nick, thankfully, didn't have my scruples and Willi's reply knocked us all for six. Ottilie could insist all she liked, he said. Even supposing the flesh were willing, the mind was not what it was.

'What do you mean?'

'What I say.' Richard's voice trailed, half a sentence, behind the Austrian's. 'I am not the man I was when I won the Nobel Prize, intellectually, I mean.'

'You sound fine to me,' I said.

'I sound like a scientist who cannot make the necessary leaps of intuition he once could. I keep having to go back over old ground.'

'I expect you're just rusty, Willi. Out of shape. You probably just need a good workout, mentally speaking.'

'That's what I thought. But how do you give the brain physical jerks? Only by reading and puzzling. I have done that from the moment of my resuscitation. I have gone over and over my own work and that of others in the field; I have repeated all the experiments a dozen times, and still no enlightenment, no mental somersaults.'

'God, how are you going to tell Ottilie? She's got shares in you.'

'She will find out soon enough. I think my grandson already suspects after last evening's game of bridge. Ye gods, what a vile specimen he is! He takes after his mother.'

'Have you any idea what is causing it, this, em, deterioration?' I asked, earnestly, but even as I spoke Susmeta's green-gowned image swung into my head. Of course. She had done this. I was sure of it.

The brain is such a sensitive organ, Willi was saying, a simple blow to the head could cause concussion, memory loss, all sorts. Suppose the brains had been handled carelessly when they were transferred from the original container to the freezer, for instance? Though, in fact, it was anybody's guess. So many things might have destroyed the tissue, at any point in the process, from the poison used as a cryoprotectant to the extreme length of time the brains had been in the freezer. 'It would be remarkable,' he said, 'if in sixty years the flow of electricity beneath the Fuehrer Bunker was never interrupted, causing at least a temporary thaw.'

Nick said, 'When they found the cellar in '94 the bulbs were all blown but the cables were still live. The generators, powered by the flow of sewage, had never stopped turning.'

'Has it occurred to you that maybe,' I suggested, tentatively, 'the damage to your brain was done during surgery?' Suppose, with all her tampering, Susmeta had done something terrible, like undermined Willi's genius? She'd never forgive herself.

He stroked his long cheek and pursed his mouth. 'It has,' he said. 'I must also consider the possibility that the damage was not once-for-all but on-going.'

'Shit.'

He inclined his head, a wise old man of thirty-odd. 'I have a feeling that my brain cells are dying prematurely, that the damage is progressive.'

It was about then that we saw the train, snaking round a mountain and disappearing into a tunnel. The way Willi was rubbing his eyes and staring, it seemed he couldn't believe what they saw or perhaps the glare from the autobahn was making them smart. His face was creased in a grimace of pain.

Nick looked across at him, said gently, 'This is the way you came, isn't it, Willi? To Buchenwald.' It hadn't occurred to me. Nick was being sensitive again.

Willi clamped his lips together and nodded. There were tears in his eyes. It was a long time before anyone spoke – me, from the back seat, handing round the Polos. I'm a great believer in comfort eating. Willi took one and then began to speak.

He told us that it had taken the cattle train two days and a night to travel the five hundred and fifty kilometres from Innsbruck to Weimar. They were shunted into sidings and left for hours, while further contingents of prisoners were rounded up and loaded on. He remembered seeing suitcases lying abandoned, some that had burst open, dropped in the struggle to get on board, by people flinging up their hands to protect themselves or their children from the fists and goads of their guards. No time, no chance to go back for them. Hurry, hurry. *Schnell*! Push and shove, stumble up the gangway and into the boxcar, lowing and moaning like the cattle before them. The great doors slammed shut and were bolted on the outside. And there they had remained: the books and clothes, children's toys, toiletries, strewn over the rails like so much litter, in the roasting sun, while the train took on fuel and water, and the guards had a 'well-earned' break. I wondered about the Wolffs' suitcases. Had they been abandoned on the railway sidings, containing – what – the family silver? Presumably someone had found them, made off with the contents. And even if they'd managed to hang on to them, get them safely to the concentration camp, they'd have had to leave them behind when they went to the 'showers.' And then the likes of Max would have taken over, in the sorting sheds.

By late morning we were bowling along in bright sunshine through the green Thuringian countryside. It reminded me of parts of England, with its rolling hills and forests, its pretty rivers, its meadows dotted with cows and sheep. You could see why the intellectuals had loved it, Goethe and Schiller and the rest. It was so peaceful, so beautiful. A place to find yourself and be inspired. It was here at Weimar, the little capital city on the Ettersberg River, where the artist, Walter Gropius, had chosen to found his flat-roofed school of Arts and Crafts, the Bauhaus, with its distinctive emphasis on functionality and simplicity of form. Paul Klee was a master there, and Wassily Kandinsky; Marcel Breuer had fashioned the first tubular steel chair, back in the nineteen twenties, and Herbert Bayer had designed the Ten Million Mark Banknote, a nod to the inflated state of the German economy. It was to Weimar, also, that the government fled, in 1919, when Berlin became unbearable, where the constitution was drawn up that turned an imperialist and conquered nation into a defederalised republic – an inspiring spot.

While sitting beneath the shade of a favourite oak tree, overlooking the red-roofed town, Goethe is said to have told his friend Johann Peter Eckermann, 'Here one feels great and free.'

Here they built Buchenwald.

16

I was almost afraid to look. I don't know what I expected to see – human smoke and Nazis on lookout duty, I suppose, dingy huts and hollow-eyed prisoners, all in newsreel black and white. It was nothing like that, of course. They'd torn a lot of it down. Cleaned up the rest and sanitized it to take out the sting. I wasn't really surprised to learn that Max had gone off to look round on his own. His memories were so fresh it must have been sickening to see the green lawns and pink roses of the old girl's makeover. I caught Willi gazing doubtfully at the barbed wire fence as if to reassure himself that they hadn't turned the place into a holiday camp.

The watchtower clock had been stopped at 3.15, the time the torment came to an end and, below it, the massive iron-gate bore the legend *'Jedem das Seine'* ('To each his own'). I couldn't think how that was in the least bit appropriate to what had gone on here but Nick said that when the Soviet Army arrived in Weimar after the war, they'd seized on Buchenwald as the very place to punish a few of their own enemies, thirty thousand to be exact, and not just former Nazis, either. From 1945 until 1950 they'd imprisoned anyone who wasn't one hundred per cent with them: class enemies, counter-revolutionaries and social democrats. Tens of thousands of them had died of hunger and sickness. Some were buried secretly in the woods outside the camp and when their remains were discovered in 1983 the East German government had hastily ordered the grave, and the matter, closed. They didn't want to be reminded of the five years of tit for tat.

Originally, he said, the gate had told new arrivals that work would make them free: *Arbeit Macht Frei.*

'Dead, more like,' said Nick.

It was quite surreal, like we'd all held hands and jumped into Mary Poppins' land, with a perfectly blue sky and idyllic lawns speckled with daisies, fields, and hills upon hills, green upon green, as far as you could see. (The wicked wood outside, that gave the camp its name, belonged to another movie altogether.) Far from bursting into song, we trod the neat gravel paths gingerly, fearful of reawakening the past, and spoke in hushed voices so as not to disturb the ghosts.

Why couldn't they simply have left it as it was – the massive huts that slept vast hundreds in a battery of bunks stacked five or six high, the barracks, the hospital? Why couldn't they just have left people to wonder about the mind that could have devised that floor-to-ceiling brick frontage, the dozens of iron doors like the seals on a honeycomb, three rows high? These were not hexagonal cells to take fat bee larvae, these were Romanesque oven doors, two feet wide, two and a half feet high, with deep metal trays to slide out and in. Why turn it into something different? Just whom were we meant to glorify? Even our camera balked at the eighteen stone monoliths, put there by the Communists to commemorate each nationality buried in the mass graves. Nick had to go and stand beside one to give it credence. Such a small figure in the famous Street of Nations, where, in the days when it had been the GDR's 'Red Olympus', hundreds of thousands of East Germans had flocked every year on April 11th, summoned by the bell in the forty-five metre high bell tower. All day and far into the night, they would listen to rallying speeches, march in parades and honour the heroes of Buchenwald.

Unbelievably, one of the guards' barracks had been turned into a hotel for tourists. Four star. Breakfast-in-bed six Euros extra.

'And an 'I stayed in Buchenwald' sticker for your car,' said Jay. Willi looked up as though he might have believed it.

'Where's the golf course, I want to know!'

'Ah but they do have a Function Room,' Richard read from the tariff.

'Beautiful,' crowed Nick, going off on one. 'Hey, Clare, we can have the reception here! What d'you reckon? A wedding with a theme. Like, soak up the atmosphere, know what I mean? Tell you what, how about having the groom and the best man in prison stripes?'

'Tasty as, mate,' said Jay, wrinkling his nose.

I hit him in disgust. 'You're sick,' I said. 'Both of you.'

'Me?' He shook his head, his dark skin tinged with pallor. 'Jesus, this is as tacky as a chocolate crucifix.' As we filed through to the restaurant, he took the opportunity to murmur in my ear, 'So have you two guys, like, named the day?' thinking he'd missed something.

'No, Jay, it was a wind-up,' I said.

It was the old officers' mess. Heavily disguised and prettified, of course, the windows swagged with Regency stripes, chandeliers and mirrors twinkling in the afternoon sunshine, and tables dressed for lunch with crisp pink tablecloths and vases of flowers. While frilly waitresses scurried about with dishes of sausage, spuds and sauerkraut, there on the stage a woman in a posh frock was playing Chopin on Axel's grand piano.

My stomach churned; my back brain went into overdrive. I could almost see him there, in dirty grey and blue 'zebra stripes', a rapt look on his face, his fingers kneading the keys, the shabby string players scraping away for dear life, and no one paying them the slightest attention. No one listening. The voices growing louder, German voices, Nazi officers, raucously laughing over some incident on the parade ground, some gross mistreatment that had ended in death. Cutlery rattling, china clashing and doctors Hofmann and

Weiss raising their glasses to the success of their research. The smell of cooking overlaying everything – cooked meat, cooking flesh from the ovens, those sizzling oversized meat trays.

Voices, far away in the psychic fog. 'You all right? Clare?'

'She's gone a funny colour. Quick, Jo.'

But it was Jay who half-carried, half propelled me through doors to cool echoing tiles and mirrors and sinks, while some woman shrieked in German that this was the Ladies' and that young men were *'verboten'*. 'It's all right, babe, just let it go,' he said as my stomach clenched and my ears surged. My nostrils registered lemon loo-block just before I threw up into a toilet bowl.

When I emerged, shakily, with that poisonous taste of bile in my throat, I flopped down on the ground beside Nick, who groaned apologies. He'd also had to make a hasty exit, but discreetly, unlike some. Willi was sitting on a bench with his head in his hands. Charlie – he of the strong stomach – had gone foraging for sandwiches.

I breathed in the sweet air, freshly scented with cut grass, and tried to dispel the pressure at the back of my skull. As I became aware of a breeze, cool against my clammy face, I closed wet eyes and lost track a little. Became aware of hands stroking my hair. Let it be Max, I prayed. But Jo's little voice squeaked, 'Feeling better, now, babe?' like we had this sisterly relationship. Get lost, I thought. I am supposed to be the fucking director. Let's have a little respect.

A lawnmower buzzed in the distance and by my ear something was quietly rustling. When I opened my eyes I saw a worm, chopped in half by scything blades, writhing in agony.

Our first shoot, after forcing down a bit of lunch, was the sculpture Axel had told me about. I figured it might help to illustrate what Max, Axel, Willi and the others had been about. Huger than any photo could prepare you for; more substantial in bronze than in life, the thin figures made a statement that we hardly dared question. Fine upstanding German intellectuals, armed with not much more than a rifle, a communist banner and a lot of determination, had overcome their captors and led their fellows to freedom. We took wide shots and close shots, over bird-limed shoulders, and from the viewpoint of a little Jewish kid, who seemed to be tagging along on the end. The guidebook said that a story had been written after the war and become required reading for every schoolchild in East Germany, about this little boy who had been rescued in the course of the uprising. Some neo-Nazi visitors had recently sawn through the child's leg.

Whether or not the Uprising had actually happened Willi stood before the monument, moved to tears. I hoped, I really hoped, for his sake, and all of them, all the millions, that it wasn't just wishful thinking, and that some of the internees, at least, had risen against their captors.

Ernst Thälmann's cell was so dark we had to use spotlights and reflectors. I remarked that it reminded me of Our Lady's grotto in Lourdes with its eternal flame. Nick said it was a shrine, only instead of prayer candles there were all those dusty old wreaths and plaques, fraternal commiserations from political parties and trade unions.

'And not a drop of holy water to be had!' said Jayl in a very un-PC Irish accent. He caught my disapproval and protested, 'I'm allowed. Begod, darlin', you're forgettin' me mother's from County Wicklow, so she is.'

I glared at him. I knew he was trying to cheer me up but this wasn't a game.

'Ach, forget it,' he muttered.

The museum was on two floors of the former depot, very modern artsy with life-size cardboard cutouts of Nazi personnel and haunting collages of prisoners looming out of the dark. The display cases had been dressed by experts, scabby tin plates and tools and ragged articles of clothing draped and lit as aesthetically as a Selfridges' window. Atmospheric sounds played among the relics: shunting steam trains, barked orders, slamming doors, recollections recorded in a Babel of languages by former internees and their liberators, gun fire, strains of orchestral music, even Hitler addressing one of the Nürnberg rallies, accompanied by *'Sieg Heil'* adoration. But most effectively, there was silence, the sound of hate, the sound of starvation.

Max and Willi had both gone AWOL now. Just as well, I thought, as we changed cassettes among the glass-fronted cases. This would have been too much. Willi had managed a bit of a commentary earlier, about the parade ground and his memories of *'appel'*, standing there for hours, in all weathers, all conditions. He remembered a time, in 1943, when prisoners stood in thirty inches of snow. For some reason, no one understood why, the SS turned a hose on the prisoners. Many froze to death as a result. The bodies were stacked outside the barracks and later burned in the crematorium. When his voice became a growl of misery I thought maybe we had enough on tape. Told him to go and wait for us in the car. His daily routine, the appalling slops he'd been expected to eat, the food parcels that had saved his life, his attendance at secret meetings of the collective, varied little from the stories I'd heard from Axel.

Willi had worked in the foundry, outside the main camp, melting down scrap metal to make parts for the V-1 rocket. Accidents happened on a fairly regular basis, mostly through neglect and rough treatment, some when hopeless prisoners simply threw themselves into the troughs of white-hot molten metal. When that happened the rest of them would be systematically beaten, the idea being that would-be suicides would think twice, reconsider, if they knew their mates would be punished for their cowardice. But they didn't reconsider. They didn't care. They just wanted 'out'.

Towards the end of his time, Willi must have come to the attention of Klaus Hofmann, for without any sort of explanation he was taken out of the foundry and put to work in the main factory offices. Funny that, I thought, Willi was given lighter work just before his operation; Max, apparently, was transferred to the mines.

I was glad neither of them was here to see this particular section of the museum, a tasteful array of instruments of torture used by the Nazi inquisitors – pincers, electrodes, syringes, hammers and saws, clamps and drills. When I read the label properly they turned out to be medical equipment recovered from the hospital. This was probably the very saw, the very vice . . . My head throbbed with images. I could hardly look.

'Hey!' said Charlie, focusing on one of the exhibits and altering the lens for a close-up. 'Here's old Frankenstein himself!'

So it was. The man you love to hate, Herr Doktor Hofmann! It was a different photo from the one we'd shown on *Way of the World*; this was a group affair with his medical chums wearing white coats and superior smiles. There was the beautiful Gisela Weiss. Apparently, she and Klaus had had a bit of a thing going, though what she saw in him, heaven knows. Slightly balding, rather jowly, he must have been a good ten years her senior. I'd remembered him as having cold eyes but here he looked like someone's uncle – the one you'd put your money on if your pubescent daughter went missing.

The salt mines were further away than I'd expected – eight miles or so via the scenic route. I mentioned, brightly, that they would have had to make an early start, those prisoners who worked there. Nick soon put me wise.

'Oh you know the folks at Buchenwald – all heart! Let them have a lie in, poor buggers. Get them to dig their own underground caves and live on the spot. It doesn't matter if the sanitary arrangements are less than basic, if they get ill and die. Plenty more where they come from.'

'But Max,' I frowned, went on. 'We know that Max left for the mines every day. From Buchenwald. Don't you remember?' The script came back to me, Tom's voice intoning, *'One morning, instead of being escorted as usual to his work in the salt mines, Max was startled to find himself being marched in a different direction.'*

'Yeah, funny that.' He nodded slowly. 'I suppose he could have been some sort of foreman, got a lift out there every day with the soup and coffee. I'll check it out.'

I didn't know why he had to be so flip. I felt sick. I'd seen pictures, taken by their liberators, of survivors too weak, too thin to get off the floor, their poor feet eaten away by the salt, their throats parched to a whisper. Max might have been one of them if he hadn't been redirected, one morning, to the hospital. No wonder he wanted to be left alone. I shouldn't begrudge the poor man a few hours private grief. According to the car-park attendant, he'd already left for the mines with a coach-load of Germans. The message was that he'd see us there.

'Who'd have thought,' I said, as we drove away from it, 'that they'd tart up Buchenwald and make it a tourist attraction?'

'They had to,' Nick said. 'It was either that or pull it down. They couldn't leave it as it was.'

'I suppose,' murmured Jay, 'the idea is to warn us against repeating other people's mistakes.'

The idea was, I could have said, to make money for the tourist industry, but never mind. Perhaps school children and students could be taught something, but even then I was doubtful. The people who really needed to go there, like Willi's daughter, wouldn't, except to vandalize and deface monuments, spray graffiti, smash exhibits. By the busload apparently. It was a favourite day trip.

What had the world learned from Buchenwald, or World War Two, for that matter? Had Milosovitch thought twice, or Mugabe? Or Osama bin Laden or the born-again President of the United States and his British sidekick?

'At least they haven't gone down the road of dioramas and waxworks,' said Jay. 'God, some places even lay on authentic smells – wood-smoke and cooking.'

We drove westward through undulating fields, following the signs to the village of Neustassfurt, which we found nestling into the slope of a long, wooded hill. Arriving a few minutes ahead of schedule, we flashed our permits at the ticket office – the old mine office – and a sturdy-looking woman introduced herself as Helga, our English-speaking guide for the next two hours or so. Max had gone ahead, she said, with the German party. He'd told her he was with us and would meet us at the exit.

Helga made us all put on protective clothing and hard hats before we could take our seats on a rackety little train that reminded me of a fairground ride. Helga sat up front with the driver. There'd be nothing worth filming while we were on the train, she assured me, and we couldn't stop anyway because we'd hold up the train behind. 'And please not to lean out!' As she was speaking wooden doors in front of us swung open and we rode into the hillside, into total blackness.

I found myself ducking, thinking that surely the tunnel was shrinking, the ceiling getting lower. I have never been anywhere so dark. Even the Ghost Train at Southend gives you the occasional luminous skeleton to tell you your eyes are open and a blood-curdling groan for light relief. On this ride, the ghosts rode with us and the moans were our own.

There was no engine-noise. We were free-wheeling down-wards and the clickety-*clack*, clickety-*clack* became sinister somehow, inexorable, driving us deeper into something chilling and terrible. I began to panic. Would nobody speak? Or was this a trap and they all knew it except me, were all smirking secretly in the dark, knowing I would never again see the light of day? Before I went quite off my head, Helga began her little spiel and everyone breathed. I realized we'd *all* been holding our breath.

'Quite a frightening journey, as I am sure you will all agree. This is what the Buchenwald prisoners had to endure every day.' Max was one of them, I had to remind myself. Poor thing – this was one aspect of his internment he had never spoken about to anybody, not even Axel. I tried to imagine him on this train, sitting opposite me, where Nick was sitting now. What would he have looked like? Tried to remember the old photos, the other Max, in his striped pyjama two-piece, with the red cloth badge of communism, his thin, cropped head, stubbly chin, bitter, red-rimmed eyes. What would he have been thinking?

'Thousands made this journey,' Helga was saying. 'Most were hungry and exhausted, many were ill from vitamin deficiencies, lack of sunlight, infected lungs. Many were in pain from rotting feet or injuries received in the course of their work. We must not forget that salt stings raw wounds.' She reminded us that in the First World War English prisoners had also worked the mines. Many had died here.

'My great-granddad . . .' Jo's voice piped up behind me in the dark.

'What? Here?' She'd kept that very quiet.

Her voice came closer to my ear. I could feel her breath. 'Or somewhere like it.' Jack, a hefty guardsman, had been taken prisoner in 1917 and forced to work in the German salt mines until his release. 'It didn't sink in, what that meant . . . until now.' Her voice began to sound froggy and she gave a little cough to clear it. 'I mean I never knew him, just things my mum told me. About how he'd weighed six stone when he arrived back in England, and was given six months to live. But down here, it – it like, brings it home to you that these were real men. Family. You have their genes.'

A heavy silence hung over us, stifling the clickety-clack.

The train halted and we got out, blinking in the dim light. We had arrived at a wooden slide that descended perhaps twenty-five feet and was once used by the miners to get to work quickly. There was no way we could get the equipment down there so Helga summoned a lift for Charlie and Bryn. After warnings from Helga to keep our feet up, the rest of us shot down the two smooth wooden rails, shrieking like kids in the park as our stomachs were left behind. This was why we had needed protective clothing, we discovered, with reinforced seating! Down at the bottom was a small cinema, but there was no time to watch a film about the history of salt mining, we had to crack on . . . and on . . . and on . . . down more slides and lifts, through tunnels where seams of salt glittered in the dark rock, along galleries where the floor, ceiling and walls were as crystalline as quartz, down salty steps into grand halls and ballrooms hewn out of solid salt, with barrel ceilings and pillars like cathedrals. There was a Byzantine chapel, six hundred years old, where the sculpted effigies of saints sparkled into awesome life when we switched on our lights, and vanished into darkness behind us. Somewhere on this level, Helga brought us to an elaborate vault, divided into wood-lined chambers, where many of the stolen art treasures of Europe had been hidden by the Nazis. Buried deep underground, in perfectly controlled humidity, she said, they were safe from Allied bombs and prying eyes. I thought I could probably mock up some racks back at the studio, get the lighting right, prop up copies of a dozen or so well-known stolen masterpieces, like that Velasquez Helga was on about, and get some shots of a jack-booted *somebody* flicking through them, his peak-capped shadow falling across them. Wouldn't it be great if one of the pictures turned out to be one that the Wolffs had lost, or something painted by Friedrich Liebl? That painting could be super-imposed on a slowed-down film of his arrest, or the Wolffs' little boy being mown down by gunfire. And even as I was thinking that this would be a great moment in my documentary, another part of me was feeling bloody guilty. God, I was using them, these victims, these poor slaves, to further my own career! But, some other part of me argued, I was doing it for them too, wasn't I? Wasn't I?

As we went down to lower regions, the salt became so pure we didn't need the reflector screen to bounce the light, the air became strangely cool and tranquil and our voices echoed around the vast halls. I could only guess at the light show there'd have been, as hundreds of miners' lamps struck the glittering surface, and the percussion of as many mallets striking as many picks and wedges, as the slaves, with their poor bare feet and no protective clothing at all, marked out and split off hundredweight blocks of salt and the guards cracked their whips. Pity no one was there at the time, filming it. Hopefully there'd be something on Helga's video I could nick, with added sound effects.

As Jo switched off for the umpteenth time, dousing the place in darkness, she whispered to me that she couldn't help thinking that some of those pick-marks and grooves might have been made by her great-granddad.

'Or Max,' I said, in case she'd forgotten.

He wasn't where he said he'd be, waiting by the exit. In fact it was twenty minutes before he showed, huffing and puffing with exertion and checking his bare wrist for the time. Where his watch had been was a white band in the tan.

'Sorry, I hope I haven't kept you waiting.'

242

He'd got separated from his party, he said, and seeing my wry smile, admitted that he'd loitered with the sole intent of losing them. He shook his head. They could be so damn noisy, his fellow countrymen, laughing and yodeling and making silly jokes. And no, he hadn't got lost.

'Really?' Who did he think he was kidding?

Well, he conceded, maybe he had lost his bearings just a little. Thankfully he'd found his way to the lake. I'd seen it – an eerie underground Styx, man-made and totally clear and still, mirroring perfectly the craggy ceiling of the cavern. Once we'd set up, our guide, as a demonstration, had tossed a small stone into it. The stone had made the surface shatter, not with concentric ripples, but crazily, like a crystal plate dropped on a marble floor. Nothing behaved as it should have down there.

'You found your way in the dark?' Jo was full of admiration.

By chance, he'd had a torch in his rucksack. Fancy that. 'But I knew better than to go wandering about once I'd found the lake,' he assured us. 'I knew that a party of tourists would be along and I'd just have to follow them out.'

'How come your sleeves are all wet?' I enquired.

'Are they?'

'And where's your watch?' It was a good one. Some fan had sent it to him.

'Oh. Well, I confess I found the lake the hard way, by tripping over a rock. I put my hands out to save myself and . . .' He mashed his lips together and I touched his arm in sympathy. Poor guy, he was on the brink of tears. His nostrils flared as he inhaled. It would have made a fantastic shot. He said, 'I must have knocked the clasp undone. The watch fell into the water. I – I tried to grab it and, as you see, got wet.'

'Max,' I said, 'you could have been drowned. It's hundreds of feet deep!'

'Unlikely.' Nick shook his head in that superior way I was beginning to find really irritating. 'It's brine, like the Dead Sea – he'd have floated.'

'So why did the watch sink?' I threw at him.

'And Helga's stone?' added Jo.

'It's small and dense,' he said, stretching his mouth smugly.

Like you, baby Jo, I could have added. Instead I said quietly, hoping Max would get my meaning, 'You're all right, are you?'

'I am fine. Why should I not be?'

Because, I wanted to yell at him, it's where you spent the worst time of your entire life. It must have been fucking awful revisiting all those places, remembering all the things that happened, the things you were made to do. And honestly, there's no need to put such a brave face on it. We all understand.

The road to Berlin was long and hot and the van was stuffy after Willi's air-conditioned limo. He was on his way back to Austria, having given Max a lift to Weimar station. Max had changed his mind about coming to Berlin and I couldn't blame him. He'd had enough of memory lane. He was going straight to Hanover to spend some time with Berthe while we completed our tour of Germany. We'd see him there at the end of the week. I was taking my turn at the wheel and Nick was beside me. Everyone in the back of the van had fallen asleep.

Nick had been quiet for some time, thinking, I guessed, about how we were going to use the day's footage. Eventually he spoke. 'It wasn't exactly a waste of time, was it?'

'Absolutely not,' I said and started to tell him how I saw shots of the camp hospital and those antique surgical instruments tying in with a close-up of Max's mouth forming the words of his testimony at normal speed, then slower . . . slower . . . Stop. Silence. Then switch to a blank screen.

'That wasn't what I meant.' He was staring at me so hard I knew I was meant to be reading his mind. I felt my ears turning pink.

'What?'

'What do you think?'

'About what?'

'*You* know . . .'

I shook my head, pulled down my mouth. No idea.

'About getting spliced.'

Spliced? *Spliced!* God, that had been some sort of back-handed proposal. I'd never have known.

'What, at *Buchenwald!* '

'Ssshh!' He twisted round to see who was listening. I could see Jay in the mirror, his head on Richard's shoulder, wearing an *I'm-fast-asleep-and-not-hearing-any-of-this* look on his face. 'No, stupid,' he hissed. '*Would* I?'

I shrugged. I really knew him better than that, but I was playing for time.

'So, shall we?'

'What?'

'Clare!'

'Oh I dunno,' I said, irritably. 'God, Nick. We've just been to the most horrible place on earth, which I've somehow got to avoid turning into some dreadful melodramatic cliché. I'm driving a fucking great van on a fucking great right-handed autobahn. I can't get my head round things like getting *"spliced"*.' I ground out the word, hating it, hating him, his lack of style. I wanted soft lights, romantic music. I wanted Max. 'Ask me again, some other time.'

Jay's lips, in the back, in his sleep, imperceptibly tightened.

17

Ellen Sauerbruch is dreaming. A shadowy figure is running his hands over her glorious body. He lowers his head, nuzzling and nibbling, using his tongue to prise open secret places, to release a bubbling at her core, a joyful, rhythmic pulsing of nerve and muscle that floods her body with liquid heat. She sighs and rolls onto her back, her beautiful arms emerging from the hotel sheets to embrace him.

And finds herself looking up from an operating table. Mask in place, gloved palms raised, the surgeon is ready to begin. He inclines his head and they hand him a surgical saw, its cruel teeth glinting in the overhead lights.

She is woken by a soft-palate sound, an utterance she made, a scream or a snore, and grabs a pillow to stifle her moaning, to stuff between her legs as her despicable body continues to spasm, out of control. When it is over, this horrible orgasm, she lies shivering in the heat of her damp sheets, with beating heart and an ebbing pain in her groin. As she dares to open her eyes she gives thanks that the grey light entering her skull is only the dawn, and that the rain, throwing itself against the window, is not the sound that a saw makes.

She reaches for a cigarette and pauses with it on the way to her mouth. Today's the day, she remembers with a sinking heart, that Sophie Müller visits her daughter-in-law. Flicking her lighter, she sucks the smoke thirstily, deeply. Exhales a shuddering cloud of it as she thinks about what she has to do.

That old woman hadn't believed Max; when he'd called

to give her the good news that he was her husband, she'd called him a liar. She knew Bernard's voice as well as her own, she said, and he didn't speak German, for a start. In fact he didn't speak English any more. He was in the nursing home for Jewish Gentlefolk, babbling and dribbling, and she was just off to visit him.

'I don't know who you are, young man, but if you're about to try and sell me double glazing, you can go and take a running jump!'

Ellen's lips twitch as they had when he'd first told her his tale of crossed wires. He'd chuckled over the phone but, at the time, he said he'd felt like a child, cringing under Sophie's tongue-lashing. She had known some pretty devious sales pitches in her time, she said, but this was the cruellest by far. He should be ashamed of himself, playing such tricks on defenseless old women. She intended to write to her MP, she said, and slammed down the phone. He pressed Redial and quickly explained that he was her *first* husband, Max.

It was a few moments before she was able to speak and in the silence he worried that she might have passed out. Expected to hear the clatter as the receiver fell to the floor.

'Max?' Her voice was faint. 'How can you be Max? Max died in the war.'

He'd started to explain about the transplant but she'd interrupted, surer now and stronger, 'I know all about that. You think I don't read the papers? *And* I saw that programme. Set the video, even. What a let down. So. You are Max, are you?' She snorted derision. 'Do me a favour.' He said he could almost hear the curl of her lip. 'I have to tell you, Mister, you don't fool me for a minute. Max was . . .' She made a regretful kissing sound. '*Vibrant*, driven by his beliefs, his socialism. Such energy he had, such an interest in everything. And charm, you can't imagine. He had a way about him, a mischief; he was a naughty boy. Even in

247

those dark days he could make you smile. You aren't my Max. You want I should tell you why? Because you are a cold fish. I am sorry if that is not what you want to hear but I cannot say different. Warmth, caring, passion – is not there. I do not see you getting worked up about anything. You are too controlled, too careful. No, my Max is dead and you are a fraud. It is a wonder Berthe did not see through you. I wish they had asked me. I would have told them.'

How could he make her believe him? he cried, in desperation. He *was* Max! What could he do or say to convince her? Please. Should he tell her about the tooth marks on his right thigh where that dog had bitten him as a youngster, the collarbone that hadn't knit properly after that 'warning' by the SS? Should he tell her things only he and she could possibly know about? How they had had to meet in secret, the books he had given her, how beautiful she had looked in her wedding outfit, the silly hat, how she had wept the first time they had made love? Naturally he was not the young hothead he had been. All his youth, all that wildness had been beaten out of him. He had learned to be careful, to watch his words. Two years in Buchenwald had tamed him. It had tamed everyone.

He heard her draw in her breath. Knew she was listening hard to his echo in her head, asking herself, could it be true? Could it? He gripped the receiver tight, willing her to make the right decision.

Slowly she said, 'You know, I don't remember dog-bites and books and collarbones but I do want so much for Max to be there, somewhere, in your voice, you can have no idea.'

Ellen can almost feel sorry for the woman. As she flicks on the television for the morning news, she imagines Sophie, hunched forward in her chair, rewinding the video, playing it again, listening over and over to a sentence, a phrase, straining to hear, through the deeper register, something, some inflexion, some distinctive pattern of speech or accent, some gesture that would identify the speaker as the man she had known. Longing to be convinced.

He'd begged her to remember that his new body, new tongue, palate, lips, vocal cords, even his increased lung capacity, had changed his voice completely. It had come as a surprise to him. And his muscles still obeyed someone else's thought patterns. 'Let me come and visit you,' he suggested. 'Then you will know me.'

'No, Max, please.'

He couldn't help smiling. She had called him by name.

A slip of the tongue. She wasn't sure. And suppose he was who he said he was? 'You will make me a bigamist and my son, Maurice . . .' He heard her sniff. 'He will be a bastard. It would kill him.'

So that was it. Her reputation was at stake. It was not her fault, he insisted. No one would blame her for assuming he was dead, taking a second husband.

'You think so?' Her flat tone held no conviction. 'So enlighten me,' she said, heavily sarcastic. 'Why should you want to see me so very much? I am an old woman now, wrinkled and ugly. Not the pretty girl I was.'

Ellen knows how that feels. She suffers, too, and grieves for beauty that once was and can never be again. Life is cruel.

He tried telling her he was lonely, said he realised that they were years apart now, but for the sake of what they had had . . .

'What we had? What we *had!*' Her rage rattled down the phone. 'Max, we had nothing! I was another of your causes. Marrying me, getting me out of Germany was a political gesture, and you know it.'

'That's not true. I loved you, Sophie. In Buchenwald it was the thought of you that kept me sane.'

'Then absence must have made you sentimental. You only loved me for what I represented. In the little time we had together you were bored crazy. You know it.'

He sighed. Perhaps it was true. 'Oh Sophie, I need to talk to you.'

'So talk.'

'I have to see you.' Eventually she'd agreed. She'd continued to throw up every kind of obstacle, but she'd agreed. He'd be lucky to catch her in, for one. She led a full life. The next day she would be at the swimming baths first thing, then lunching at the pub with friends, bowls all afternoon and in the evening she went to china painting classes.

'Not Wednesday,' she'd said, 'that's Meals on Wheels.'

'But you'll be in?'

'I *deliver* the Meals on Wheels. There's no knowing what time I'll finish. They like you to stop and chat – they don't get many visitors.'

'Thursday?'

'Thursdays I'm at my daughter-in-law's.'

'All day?'

'Of course all day. She lives in Kennington. South of the river. It takes forever on the Underground.'

'You don't drive there?'

'At my age? Across London? What do you take me for?'

When he'd mentioned that the television might be interested in her story she'd shown more interest. The most convenient time was Monday week, after the cleaning woman had been. She only came once a fortnight. 'Not that I make much of a mess. I'm never in. But she does a bit of ironing for me and cleans where I can't. It's not so easy when you get to my age.'

He'd taken the details, her surname, Greene, and her address in Gants Hill.

Summer is drawing in its horns. Rain darkens the cobbles of the quayside and cafés close their doors. Chairs are tilted at tables against the wet, and sunshades and hanging baskets are brought inside. The boats rock on choppy water, their puddling tarpaulins pulled up tight, their sails furled.

With the windows shut, Ellen's cigarette smoke has nowhere to go. It layers the air and stings the eyes. But she chain-smokes nonetheless as she selects a raincoat from her wardrobe, and regards herself in the mirrored door. There is nothing, absolutely nothing, to be said for the longer style. Not that her shins and calves would exactly twinkle these days under the austere hemlines of wartime, but this volume of material makes her look as though one more puff of helium would send her skywards. She knows she must be inconspicuous, blend in with the crowd. If anyone can, she thinks morosely, *she* can. For his sake, she can.

Three seats along, Ellen can see her reflected in the dark window of the underground train, an old woman in a bright blue plastic mac, whose iron-grey hair distorts with the curve in the glass, grows tall, broadening her brow alarmingly, until it merges with its own mirror image. It reminds Ellen of a circus act, an elderly acrobat balancing her upside-down self on her own head.

Between them, a sleeping man, with a book open on his knee, and a black woman, meticulous in dress and jacket, busy with a file of papers, are oblivious of their own conjoined twins. As the train rattles through the tunnels her gold earrings glitter in the window across the aisle; his head nods towards Sophie's shoulder.

Opposite, two children play games to pass the time. As the train draws into a station, they vie to beat the recorded voice making the announcement: *This is Newbury Park.* Their grandmother smiles indulgently at the children's shrieking. The grandfather has the look of one of the guards at the camp. His lips are thin and sour; the lines scored deep into his skin are those of grimaces and scowls. He sits squarely in his seat, self-consciously bent at sharp right angles, drawing into himself.

Now and then the girl pillows her head on her grandmother's shoulder. There are sleep-starved puffs under her eyes but she's still alert and playing the game. *This is Wanstead.*

The boy, on the end of the row, is younger and unable to contain his excitement. The train is a novelty, a thrill laid on for his pleasure, the doors opening as wide as his eyes. His glance strays to the map over Ellen's head, to count the stations. He mouths their names, relishing the magical flavours of Leytonstone, Leyton, Mile End as they burst upon the tongue.

They'd been wet through by the time they'd reached the station: Sophie had braved the rain and walked to the station in her sandals and plastic mac and Ellen had had to follow. There had been a moment of panic when the old woman had shown a pass of some sort at the ticket barrier and gone through, leaving Ellen to queue for a ticket. As she'd rattled down the escalator, hearing a train coming in to the station, she'd moaned, 'Oh no, oh no. I *can't* lose her. I *can't*. Not now.'

Panting and hot, she had just managed to hurl herself onto the train as the doors closed. And there was Sophie sitting smug and safe, three seats along.

'Kids not back at school?'

No, Sophie, no! What are you *doing*? You must not attract attention! Must not! The sleeper jerks and repositions himself without waking. The gold earrings jangle.

'Say again?' The grandmother can't hear over the rattling of the train. Sophie is going to have to repeat her question. Louder.

'Still on holiday, are they? Kids round our way went back yesterday.'

The children kick and squirm almost in guilt. The old

man becomes rhomboid with embarrassment, but his wife expands, flows easily into conversation. 'Monday, they go back. Baker Day or summink. She can't take no more time off, poor gel, so they come to spend a coupla days with Gran and Pops, ain't you, kids?' They both nod, solemnly.

'Going somewhere nice?'

'Going up 'Amley's, eh, Gran?' The boy wants it confirmed.

'Madame Tussaud's first,' argues the girl.

'Well, aren't you the lucky ones!' says Sophie. 'Best time to go now. I remember, years ago, I took my grandchildren to Hamley's. Christmas time, it was. Oh dear, you couldn't move. Never again!'

They both agree they hate crowds, people pushing and shoving.

Between Leyton and Liverpool Street the two old women cover a range of topics, from the price of children's toys to her Bernard, in the rest home, and what her Maurice, the accountant, thinks about London Transport, shouting over the racket of the train, and making the old man cringe. Any minute now, thinks Ellen, she's going to tell everyone about her Max, with the transplanted brain. Ellen's eyes swerve to the advertisements but the witticisms elude her. How much longer? She could do with a cigarette.

'I'm hungry, Gran. Gran!'

The woman looks at her watch, shrugs and delves into her bag; finds chocolate, which she divides into quarters, and hands one each to the children. The old man, pre-empting her nudge, shakes his head vehemently and massages his chest. No fear. He doesn't want cholesterol or indigestion.

'Not you,' she says. 'That lady there. You'll have some, won't you, dear?' Sophie declines graciously. Her daughter-in-law is cooking lunch, she explains. She always overdoes it. In all the years Sophie's been going there on a Thursday she's never managed to clear her plate yet and still Rhona insists on piling on the food. 'Trying to finish me off, I shouldn't wonder!' It's a joke, of course. People all over the carriage are smiling at the absurdity of it, even the black woman lifts her mirrored head. Who on earth would wish this nice little Jewish woman dead?

'*This is Bank*,' the children shout in unison. The tape goes on without them. *Change here for Northern, City and . . .'*

Gran is saying goodbye to Sophie who, in a flurry of blue plastic mac, umbrella and shopping bag, presses a coin into each child's hand before letting herself off the train. Everyone is too astonished to pay any mind to the dumpy lady swiftly following, except maybe Pops who, scowling, draws back his twice-shined shoes to let her pass in her wet raincoat.

Sophie plunges through an opening and down a spiralling staircase into the bowels of the English underground system. Ellen tags after, so close that she could, at times, reach out and touch her. Past buskers and beggars and eye-catching posters, overtaken and overtaking, the plastic mac a squeaking vanguard.

When they arrive, the platform is already crowded. Their connection is going to be late, if it arrives at all. An electrical fault. The man on the tannoy recommends passengers seek alternative means of travel.

A few desperate people are persuaded to leave but Sophie is an old hand at this. She hovers, sighing significantly, beside a row of occupied seats, until someone gives in and lets her sit down. Invisible, Ellen leans against the wall, as more and more people arrive, dropping into spaces along the platform until, like water spreading and joining, they are lapping at the platform's edge.

Patience is rewarded at last. Train sounds fill the tunnel and a rush of air flutters hair and loose clothing. But Sophie doesn't move.

'There'll be a few along now,' she advises a neighbour, with acquired wisdom. 'Let this one go. No point in getting crushed to death.'

Ellen turns sharply to stare at her. But the choice of words was accidental. That look of bovine complacency was not inspired by images of Buchenwald. She wasn't even there. Only Ellen, out of all these people is reminded, sees what she sees, as the 'tube' train slows and stops. Sees solid, wooden doors sliding open and those pale passengers who can, struggling out. Those who can't may have to be scraped off the floor.

Ellen gives her head a shake but the nightmare persists; it has been growing all day, overlaying the present with the past. As Sophie predicted, the banked up commuters surge forward to squeeze in where others got out, cramming into the carriages, like fruit crammed into preserving jars, like the Jews arriving in Buchenwald from Auschwitz, packed into cattle trucks. Fatly it lumbers out of the station. There's another tidal wash to the platform's edge. The floodgates open: all colours, all races. The mix is unstoppable now. The Führer's worst fears realised.

Another train arrives and Sophie lets it go, too. And then she struggles to her feet, her joints stiff with sitting, as she heads for a space at the edge of the platform, the spot where, if she has judged it correctly, doors will open and she will find a seat. Horny toenails jut from her sandals to touch the yellow-painted hazard-line. She clutches her shopping bag to her like a shield, her umbrella a sword, ready to do battle for a seat. Her blue plastic mac is a flag beckoning Ellen across the platform.

More commuters pile in behind, late for work again.

The line crackles and clicks, crackles and clicks. *'Train approaching'* flashes across the information board. Sophie turns to face the draught, her red scarf waving, her plastic mac ballooning, and squints to see the destination come into focus as the black tunnel fills with the face of a train. She is leaning forward, stretching out her withered neck, trying to see.

Ellen is half a head taller. She sees the electric rail, slightly raised, slightly more shiny. Sees a mouse scurrying between the lines in dirty camouflage, and disappear.

She's up close now, close enough to smell Sophie's stale hair, see the pale skin through a combing of thinness. She holds her hands ready, feels warm plastic against her palms, and the sagging flesh of the woman's back. In her ears there's the roar and rumble of that other train, the teeth-skinning screech of metal on metal as the brakes bite, the hiss of steam, and then, the shooting back of bolts.

18

Just our luck, wasn't it, to arrive in Berlin in the middle of a cloudburst? The sewers were a complete washout, as manhole covers jiggled like pot-lids over the boiling rapids. Nein, Fraulein. It was not a good idea to go down while water levels were this high. And guess what they were building above the site of the Fuehrer bunker – a mammoth memorial for Jewish victims of the Holocaust. No way were we going to be allowed entry, leave alone search for a missing letter.

As a last resort I got Richard to phone Herr Felder at 'Spitzy' and, wouldn't you know? He was just about to call me. The man I wanted was Otto Pesch, now retired, but seven years ago he had been foreman of the team that found the brains. Pesch and his wife lived in a block of flats in what had been the Eastern sector, so I phoned to see if he was in.

An old man opened the door, wizened and bent, I thought, after a lifetime of physical labour, but he was only fifty-four, it transpired, and had retired 'on the sick' soon after the find. It had done for him. Couldn't sleep, see, thinking of those poor sods he'd found in the freezer, thinking of the Nazis and how his countrymen had given that bastard a free hand. He was shaken by an involuntary shudder. Mein Gott, you found some choice things digging out the Metro, but this took the biscuit.

'Was there a letter, do you remember, in among the brains?'

'Yeah, on the top, all done up with string and sealing wax.' He took off his glasses to rub his eyes, put them back on and stared more clearly into the past. 'I undid it, being nosey – I was expecting chocolates or fish fingers, at least – and there was this letter from someone at Buchenwald KZ.' I already knew that the letters KZ meant concentration camp. 'Give me the willies it did, just seeing that at the top of the page, and the swastika. Just had time to cast me eye over it – I remember there was this list of names and numbers – when the boy, Erich, opened one of the other things, one of the brains. I'll be honest with you, I was bad. Had to sit down, and I didn't know then it was still alive! But we got the police in straight away – they were hanging around outside in case we made off with any of the stuff out the bunker – and they took one look and cleared all us lot out, cordoned off the area. You'd've thought it was an unexploded bomb. Seen a few of them in me time, and all.'

So it was a nice little touch, the Pesch interview, and we got some good head shots of him describing his horror, but it brought us no nearer finding the letter. The Berlin police told me they didn't keep important documents like that. It must have been forwarded to the hospital in Hamburg, the guys who'd brought the brains and the other documents to England, who, when I'd contacted them, back in July, had at first denied all knowledge and then grudgingly admitted that they might possibly have sent it to the proper authorities.

'Who *were*?'

There'd been an interval filled with rapid keyboard tapping before my contact, Susmeta's 'bright spark', came on and said that they'd sent it originally to the Ministry of Health and Social Security, not really knowing where else to send it. It might have been forwarded to somewhere more appropriate from there.

The three ministries I'd tried, Health, Internal Affairs, and Defense, had been as much use as chocolate fire-guards. 'Most of our information is on computers, now.

Wouldn't know where to start looking for an original document.'

What is there to do, when you're fed up with being fobbed off, on a rainy afternoon in Berlin? Visit the War Museum, of course. An Aladdin's cave, as it turned out. They had everything we needed and more! Post cards, video film, which we were welcome to buy, except it was, disappointingly, the one we'd used in *Way of the World*, of the opening of the chamber under the bunker, seven years before. But what they did have was a replica of the freezer, newly installed, encased in concrete with the 'exact, same rust-stains', Richard translated from the placard.

'Oh cool, watch this!' yelled Jay, pressing a button to make the lid come up, with a puff of cold steam, offering a tantalising glimpse of mysterious cabbage-shaped packages inside. Charlie was all set to go and fetch the camera. Leave it to him. He could make that freezer speak . . .

'*Nein, nein!*' A man on sentry duty wagged his finger, pointing to a red deleted camera sign on the wall. Richard tried to explain to him that we were a TV crew, that this would be a film about the frozen brains.

'What frozen brains?'

'*These* frozen brains!'

He was adamant. *Nein.* Cameras were *verboten.*

And that was a crying shame, because there, oh there, in a glass case down the middle of the room, I'd spied something that made me salivate. With its waxed wrapper beside it, and dim lighting to preserve the lovely Gothic writing, was the letter. Hofmann's original! All spread out like a 'willing whore', as Nick put it. And beside it, unbelievably, were translations in French, Italian, and Japanese and good old plain English. In the third paragraph, after introducing himself, his little enterprise and a list of his unhappy victims (at least they got a mention), he described, in cold, clinical terms, how he had removed and frozen the brains. In the fourth, he drew to any future surgeon's notice the importance of administering the antidote to the poisonous cryoprotectant, in the correct proportions, before any attempt was made to resuscitate the organ. He described his own attempts to find an antidote, using three different chemical compounds. The last named was the one he'd found effective and in such and such a dilution. There it was, in black and white. He'd done all the work for her. Susmeta had lied.

Why hadn't it occurred to me at the time that emails could be doctored? And snail-mail letters selected? When Susmeta had brought in her file to show Max and me, she'd had plenty of time while we were talking to take out anything relating to that fourth paragraph. But why had she lied? Why had she wanted me, and anyone else who asked, to think that those poor brains had died because she'd been unable to find the right antidote to that dimethyl – thingy. I kicked myself. Because they'd died of something else, dope. Something she didn't want anybody to know about. It was obvious. Oh God, I had to have a photo of this fucking letter. Did they have a post-card? Fucking '*Nein*.'

What could we do? Well, thank God we were mob-handed, though Ez and Jo had opted to stay in the van and mind the equipment. We protested. We argued. We took the guard to one side and told him, in no uncertain terms, exactly what we thought of his unhelpful attitude and how, if he let us bring in the video camera he'd be contributing to one of the most important documentaries of the millennium. He wasn't working for the fascists, was he, by any chance? He wasn't one of these people who give the Germans a bad name because they're such fucking Jobsworths? Give him his due, he still said *nein*, but, by then, Nick had popped out his digital camera and snapped the lot.

Po-faced and sulky we sloped out of the museum, until we were well round the corner, when we broke into a run and dove into the van, shrieking and whooping. When Nick showed us his pictures in the viewfinder, we erupted again. Brilliant. We could put them straight onto the computer at work and print out the letter again and again, digitally altered or refined.

Our joy was short-lived. A few days later, Max phoned from Hanover to say that his sister, Berthe, had been taken ill. 'I am so worried,' he said. 'It was, I think, the result of eating boiled bacon and dumplings last night. She cooked it for me, remembering it was my favourite dish.'

'Are you all right?'

'Me? Oh yes, I am suffering no ill effects. I, or rather, my host body, has a fine, strong stomach.'

'What exactly is wrong with her?'

'I cannot tell. Vomiting and violent stomach pains.' (Not surprising, I thought – boiled bacon and dumplings sounded lethal.) 'She came down to breakfast this morning,' he went on, 'and had to go straight back to bed. She looked so bad. I am worried, Clare.'

'No chance of filming her, then,' I guessed. Bugger, bugger, bugger.

'*Nein*. I am sorry.'

There was a pause while my mind raced and the crew head-butted their annoyance and mouthed obscenities. We couldn't stay in Germany indefinitely, waiting for an old woman's stomach to settle. We'd done everything else we'd come to do. Found Axel's sheet music in Hamburg's main museum, with him on the front cover looking like Fred Astaire in bow tie and brilliantine. There was even some grainy film of him playing piano which would be stunning after some digital doctoring. We'd taken some really wild shots of the very room, in the very building, where the Gestapo had arrested him, which could be dubbed with the sounds of fists and boots and groans.

Cologne had been flattened by Allied bombers and built on. Nothing remained from Ellen Sauerbruch's time apart from the cathedral. Thankfully her father had been a patron of the arts, so there were photographs of their flat-roofed house, designed by Peter Behrens of the Bauhaus, with greenhouse windows that must have had everyone wilting on a summer afternoon. The factory had been made out of pre-stressed concrete, and was big and ugly, despite its light and airy working conditions. Herr Sauerbruch had been a kind master, providing housing for his employees, a social club, and an innovative pension scheme, which was still supplementing the income of some of his, then, younger workers. Nick managed to dig up some quavery recollections in a retirement home.

One old guy, in his nineties, remembered the daughter. 'A lovely girl,' he said, 'a real fashion plate, but with a heart of gold. When my little Franz was sick, she came to visit, paid for medicines. And when our street was bombed, she put on overalls and a tin hat and worked with her bare hands to pull people out of the wreckage.' I hated her, knowing that Max would have found her irresistible. Thank God she wasn't like that now.

The Birnbaums were worse than useless. They let us film her empty room but had no information for us. What were they to do with all her gear, they wanted to know – her clothes and toiletries? They needed to re-let the room. I didn't know what to say. After all, the poor girl could be wandering around with amnesia. In the end they agreed to hang on to the stuff for six months and then give it to Oxfam.

Nick splashed out on after-shave, hired a posh suit and took a trip to Berne, Switzerland. The story he spun the banks wasn't too far from the truth, that *Way of the World* owed Ellen money and, as she'd disappeared off the face of the earth we wondered whether we could pay directly into her account? The first five banks denied all knowledge but at Tourniers, the counter-clerk's eyes glistened at the prospect of a hefty deposit. Yes, Ellen was their client and yes, she'd been to see them recently to re-open her account. Her face fell rather when Nick made out his cheque for a paltry thirty quid. She hoped he hadn't made a special trip, she said nastily. Fraulein Sauerbruch was living in London. He could have popped the money round and saved himself the trouble. Further she would not be drawn. The bank was not at liberty to divulge clients' business. Still, it was something. Sourpuss was in London. I wondered if Max knew.

In Blenz, Friedrich Liebl's little village in Bavaria, all the old people had memories of him. They'd sat next to him in school (we took shots of the school), and fidgeted through his father's sermons (we took shots of the church and the triptych Fred had carved of the Holy Family). Some even remembered buying scythes and sauerkraut from his sister's shop, which she'd run until the late fifties. We filmed inside, outside and up the rickety stairs. They pointed out examples of his workmanship throughout the village: the war memorial in all its terrible detail, the coat of arms over the door of the sheriff's house, the hundreds of gargoyles carved into the walls and whittled into the benches and tables of the local hostelry. When money was worthless, he had paid for his beer with art. They showed us the site of his workshop, razed to the ground by the SS when they discovered the rude gesture he was making towards their beloved Fuhrer. The seditious statue had been hacked to pieces and burned but remained firmly fixed in the memory of the villagers. The offending finger, larger than life and slightly charred, had been rescued and was now housed in a glass case in the foyer of our hotel. I hoped they'd hurry up and find his brain. He sounded great.

But the budget wouldn't stretch to more hotel bills. Hanover was our last call. Our passage was booked on the evening ferry from Bremerhaven, and I was anxious to get back. Kate's year-group was doing 'The Threepenny Opera,' Mum was courting, and I was missing it all.

I said, 'How ill is she?'

'Too ill to be interviewed.'

'Have you called a doctor?'

'He is on his way.' He paused and said, 'Clare . . .' so gravelly and sincerely my heart skipped, 'I really should stay with her. She has no one else.'

'But you were going to show us around Hanover,' I whined, a petulant child.

'Even if I could get away there is nothing left to see. The Gratz Motorworks is a shopping mall. The street where we lived is a multi-storey car park. The dance hall, the church – there is nothing.'

'But we're halfway there . . .'

'I'm sorry. It would be pointless. Go home.'

19

The last thing I needed when I got back to England was news of the accident. First Berthe now Sophie – my supporting cast were dropping like flies.

There was a tearful message on the voice-mail from Rhona Greene, the daughter-in-law to whom Sophie had confided her secret before she died. 'Please,' she begged, 'tell Max Zeiler to stay away from the funeral. My husband doesn't want him upsetting the family.'

I returned the call, offering condolences. I also fixed an interview for that afternoon. If I couldn't have Sophie, the grieving family was the next best thing. Two days later, she rang again. I was alone in the office so she got straight through.

'Clare? Oh hi. I . . .' She hesitated. 'I don't know whether you'd be interested, at all. We've just been, em, going through Mum's things and there's, well, there's a couple of letters from Max Zeiler she kept from the war.'

'Oh *wow*!' I couldn't help myself. Very unprofessional, and unwise, too. Now she'd up the price.

'I was all for throwing them out, but Maurice said they might be useful for the documentary.' Valuable, she meant.

'How much, I mean – that's really great, Rhona. Thanks a lot.'

But thanks wouldn't suffice. Maurice was asking two thousand pounds, a thousand each!

'You're joking!' After a pause while I considered every angle, including theft, I had to say, 'Sorry, Rhona, there's no way I can afford that. We're working to a very tight budget, here. But thank you for thinking of me.' And reluctantly put the phone down. Five minutes later she was back. Maurice had been thinking. 'How much can you afford?'

I, too, had had time to think. 'Strictly speaking, Rhona, the letters are Herr Zeiler's property now. For him to dispose of, not you or me.'

'That man's never Max Zeiler. Sophie was a *widow* when she married Maurice's dad.'

'Yes, so you said in the interview.' I'd already edited that bit out of the videotape. 'I mean, she had to say that, didn't she? Otherwise her marriage wasn't legal. She knew he was Max, all right. Take my word for it.'

She muffled the receiver to pass on this information. I raised my voice. 'Rhona? Oh hi – look, I'm a bit pushed for time. Perhaps you could give me a ring when you've discussed this with Maurice.'

No need. Maurice Greene sold me the letters, sight unseen, for two hundred pounds.

The phone rang again immediately. Susmeta had been waiting in the queue, listening to *Mercury, the Bringer of Joy*. Not that he had. Nothing had, not since the pub bombing. She blamed herself. If only she'd thought of plastic surgery or face transplants sooner, there would have been no need for FABS, no need for meetings in pubs.

The police were still in the dark. The device was similar to one used in a bombing in Soho a few years before. That had been an anti-gay thing. Goodness knows what the motive was for this. She sounded even more mournful as she delivered her message. I couldn't believe what I was hearing. 'Berthe's *dead*?'

She sounded tight-lipped. 'Last night, apparently.'

'He phoned you?'

'Yes, just now. There was nothing they could do for her. She was unconscious for two days, apparently.' She sighed, 'He stayed with her to the end.'

'*Did* he? Well, that just shows you . . .' What it showed I

266

wasn't quite sure. Me in a not very good light, I think. All I'd been concerned about was the cost and inconvenience of a second trip to Hanover. It hadn't occurred to me that Berthe might be really ill, I mean, terminally. 'God,' I said. 'Poor Max!' and, to break the silence, 'What was it, food poisoning?'

'Something like that. She was severely dehydrated, he said, by the time they got her to hospital. They put her on a drip but she never regained consciousness.'

I exhaled hopelessly. 'So now he has no one. No wife, no sister.'

'Mmm,' she said.

Well he had me, I thought, putting the phone down. And I know it was very selfish when he was so sad and everything, but I couldn't help indulging in a little shiver of anticipation: because he was coming home, and because we could actually get cracking on making my film.

Since we'd been back I'd been doing my homework on the Spanish Civil War. I'd got a pile of old archive stuff that I needed him to talk me through. Douglas Mallory's version was already in the can but Max's eye would be fresher. A cut and paste job could be really effective.

A trip to Spain was a must, especially now we were losing so many people. I could see the pair of them, Mallory and Max, back at Albacete, reminiscing about their training days, when they had one real rifle between forty of them and broom handles substituting for the rest. And then I thought we'd go to Madrid, and relive desperate moments behind the barricades.

I'd dramatise the battle scenes, of course, hire a few extras and blacken their faces for the night raid on the Casa del Campo. Douglas had described that first action of theirs as madness. 'How they expected us to flush the buggers out of the mountains, *in* the dark, *in* the flaming forest, when you could only guess at their positions from the flash of gunfire. We were all geared up to fight the fascists, weaken their hold on the rest of Europe, but this was impossible.' They were all sick with fear, and with reason. A third of the volunteers had died that night.

'The racket was deafening,' he recalled. 'Bombs, machine gun fire, screams. Echoing among those eucalyptus trees. And blokes being blown backwards down the mountain like scrap paper, slithering to a stop in a pile of dead leaves, catching on the trees . . . dead and dying.'

I thought we could probably get away with filming that on Ben Nevis. Nobody would know the difference between Scots pine and eucalyptus in the dark. And the scrunch of the prickly holm-oak leaf litter that gave them away as they crawled up the mountain? I thought maybe holly leaves from Epping Forest.

A Max and Mallory voice-over would be great, Max cool as a reference book, Douglas with his colourful turns of phrase. He'd likened the rebels' subsequent occupation of University City to that of 'flaming cockroaches'. 'Of course,' he said, 'a lot of them had been students or lecturers at the university; both sides, Republicans and Franco's lot, knew the place inside out. Dear, oh dear . . .' He tutted at the memory. 'The things we got up to. But I suppose all's fair in love and war. We even sent bombs up in the lifts, you know, primed to go off when the doors opened. Exploded in the enemies' faces! And then, of course, our occupying the ground floor meant that they couldn't get down. They got so desperate for food they ate the animals in the research labs. We thought it was funny at the time but the poor buggers must have been desperate. The rabbits had only been inoculated with some disease, hadn't they?' He shook his grey head. 'Terrible way to go.'

I couldn't wait to direct the scene. The sooner Max buried his sister the better.

The letters arrived by special delivery next morning.

Barry tossed the packet on my desk after banging through the swing doors, with a bigger beer belly than ever, an unhealthy tan and a loud Hawaiian shirt. Suddenly work didn't look so attractive. A tête à tête with the producer was all I needed.

'I thought you were in France with Alison,' I said.

'Long story, long story.' He sighed dramatically. 'I'll tell you, if you've got a couple of hours.'

I smiled regret, indicating a throbbing computer and a clutter of papers and discs and tapes. He nodded understanding – he knew better than to interrupt a creative moment.

'So where is everybody?' he demanded, looking at his watch. I had to explain that because we'd worked our holiday Colin had given us time off this week, in lieu, though Nick was at home trawling the Net for information and I'd been coming in to try and make order out of chaos.

'Like you're not really here?'

'Won't be, soon as I can get this sorted. I have to be at a meeting.'

'Need me to come along, add a bit of weight?' My little heart went pit-a-pat: he was obviously at a loose end.

'No, I'm all right, thanks.' The meeting was a lie unless you counted what was occurring at the *Chain and Sprocket* later on. Thursday night was Irish night, and Nick, Jay and Fred were joining my sister and me for a bit of a shindig. I didn't think the Fat Controller would be comfortable at such a gathering, specially as Jay was bringing along the video, or rather the copy he'd made, of Susmeta Naidoo in her starring role as the demon doctor. I was leaving early to rummage round Oxford Street for a new top. But the less Barry knew about that the better. Luckily the phone started ringing in his office.

'Damn,' he said, 'I only came in to collect the post.' Then as an afterthought, 'Come and see me before you go, Clare. It's time you brought me up to date on our little enterprise.'

Little enterprise! This was my *pièce de résistance* we were talking about here, my rite of passage from apprentice to journeyman. And I didn't need his 'weight', so kindly offered. In any case, if I knew Giddings he had a very different 'little enterprise' in mind, involving sixteen stone of middle-aged flab and me on the casting couch. I'd have to keep my wits about me, and my rape alarm primed. He was ensconced in his office, feet propped on the desk, the telephone tucked under his chin, happily slitting envelopes. I was safe so long as I could hear the monotonous drone of his voice and the occasional ping of balled paper hitting the sides of his waste bin.

Meanwhile I had letters of my own to read.

Well, I had to check the contents, didn't I? Jiminy Cricket prodded away at my jugular with his umbrella, chirruping on about giving the jiffy bag to Max, unopened, but Jiminy was a minor irritation. I was media and the public's need to know was paramount. No, sod it – *my* need to know. I fancied the pants off Max. I had every right to find out what I might be getting into.

Two worn and faded envelopes fell out, both addressed to Frau S. Zeiler, 5, Mill Lane, Clatterton, Essex. The stamps were English, strangely, George VI penny reds and the postmarks Dover and London, WC1. I turned the envelopes for more clues, as you do. They were scuffed with long or frequent handling or with being carried around in a pocket or handbag until it was safe to post them. Yes, that was probably it. Max would have been working undercover by then, helping the enemies of the Third Reich escape to England. He'd very likely given them to his refugees to post on arrival, hence the English stamps. Alternatively, Sophie had worn them out with reading.

I couldn't get it open quickly enough, that first one, so old and worn, it was coming apart along the folds. I smoothed out the pages of faded blue script with shaking hands . . . and groaned. It was only written in German! Well, it would be. Sophie hadn't any English in those days. But that shut me out, good and proper. I was clearly not meant to pry into their intimacy.

I knew I should leave it, reseal the jiffy bag, save something. But I wasn't proud. I toyed with the idea of faxing it to Richard Cullen for translation, but I had a feeling he'd be with Jay and wouldn't want to be disturbed. It was his day off. Besides, this was something I didn't want to share. It was between Max and me. And there are more ways of killing a cat than choking it with fat-free yoghurt.

I scanned the contents into the computer, brought up the Babel menu and clicked on 'English'. Easy, peasy. Well, not entirely straightforward. Some sentences came up in jabberwocky, where I'd misread Max's gothic hand or the translation was too literal but, by messing about with the *Single Word* option back into German, and looking up similar spellings in the dictionary, managed to make sense of it.

There was no sender's address, very sensibly. You don't want to be traceable if the letter should fall into the wrong hands. It was dated March 1941 and began *'Dear Sophie,'* a tad restrained, I thought, for a new husband writing to his beloved but it took all sorts. The next bit was about how he had been thinking of her on her birthday and then a nice newsy letter:

> *'I have frost bumps . . .'* (Frost bumps? Was that goose pimples, by any chance?) *'in this dog weather.'* (*Hundewetter*? I looked it up: 'atrocious weather.') *'There is a raw wind off the sea. The fire gives out smoke but no heat as the coal is mostly slate. We have an electric fire but no electricity since the lines are down again. Oh misery. I am writing by candlelight and wearing two pairs of your thick socks, and the pullover, my greatcoat, a*

blanket, the muffler <u>and</u> the gloves, which might go some way to explaining the poor handwriting. Perhaps you are knitting, even now, beside the blazing log fire in Aunt Maud's front room. It does my heart good, if not my feet, to think of you tucked away in her little house in the country. They tell me London is suffering badly. I am glad you and she get on so well. As you observed she is very like my mother, though without her sister-in-law's abrasive wit! I am joking.' I was proud of 'abrasive', having gone through scrubbing brushes and scouring powder to find it. Perhaps I should take up this translation lark as a sideline. *'Give her my love. Has Cousin Harry been home on leave? The last I heard he was in Africa. At least he is warm! I am on guard duty, writing this while my friends snatch a moment's sleep. How they have suffered. They are terribly thin and quite exhausted. I am so glad we got you out when we did. Now they need all their strength for the rest of their journey. The voyage is bound to be choppy. I predict my lovely chicken broth will be making a comeback! Yes, I have learned to cook, but only chicken broth. It is nourishing for starving farmers.'* Farmers? Back to the German, I think. *Bauers.* I couldn't read his writing. More likely it was *Bauchs* – bellies. Yes, of course, 'starving bellies.' Poor people. *'But my part is done when I hand them over in a few hours' time. All I can do then is wish them luck. I will give them this letter and ask them to post it in a good red English letterbox.* Elementary, my dear Watson!

Take care of yourself. Max.

He could have been writing to anyone – any casual acquaintance. There were no endearments, no references to that last passionate night of love. No *love*. Not even a *Kind regards*. What was going on? And the other thing – Sophie hadn't been anywhere near London in the Blitz. She'd been staying with Auntie Maud – Harry Stevens' mother – all cosy in the country. So why the big fat porky about believing her to be dead? There didn't seem any point.

At any rate she'd had to wait nearly a year for her next letter, in January 1942.

'*Dear Sophie,*

Just to let you know that I arrived back in one piece. It was good to see you all at Christmas – a moment of sanity in my mad, cloak-and-dagger life. You almost persuaded me, you know, to ask for a quiet desk job in the War Office, translating or training saboteurs or doing some other useful work. But I am afraid I am a swashbuckler at heart. And in a matter of days, there I was, back on the plane, buckling on my ticket . . .' Ticket? Oh Max. That's one thing to be said for Leon Paterson's muscle-memory – it's improved your writing. Try again. If not *Fahrschei* what? Could it be *Fallschirm* – parachute? 'Buckling on my parachute' would make more sense, '*preparing to cheat the Fuhrer out of a few more victims. I must tell you, I had a small adventure today. We were on a train, my 'friend' and I, when I became conscious of someone watching me. It was our neighbour with the faded arm. Remember?*' (Probably not 'faded' but I couldn't be bothered to look up the precise disability.) '*My God, I was surprised to see him! And vice versa. It was the uniform of course. I had to play the part – told him I was on escort duty, taking my prisoner in for questioning, and it was hard when we had been so close to have him regarding me with such loathing. If only he had known that we were on the same side. I have no idea what he was doing so far from home. He muttered something about visiting relatives. It was clear to me that he thought I had sold out to the enemy.*

He got off at the very next stop, but it was a sticky moment. In accordance with your instructions I am eating properly and keeping fairly well, though I seem to have a slight cold and am feeling very sorry for myself. Oh for an end to this war. Again the letter ended far too formally. *Best wishes, Max.'*

What a star! I'd thought the sewer thing was pretty fantastic, apart from getting caught, that is, but dressing up in some kind of uniform, SS or Gestapo or something, and escorting refugees to freedom, right under the noses of the Nazis! I mean, that took some nerve. How many people had he got out of the country without arousing suspicion? Dozens? And each time the risk was greater. I'd never come across a real hero before. I mean Nick got his rocks off climbing up mountains, but he'd never done anything really brave, like outwitting the Nazis, saving lives. Oh Max . . .

I saved the translations, resealed the jiffy bag, and sent an e-mail to Nick, asking him to look out any anti-fascist-stroke-Jew who had escaped from Germany to England, by boat, 1940-41, with the help of a bogus SS or Gestapo officer, fitting Max Zeiler's description.

I was just getting ready to take my videos down to Editing when Barry called me into his office. I presumed the blinds were drawn against the bright sunshine, but it didn't do any harm to arm myself with a glowing cigarette.

'Clare,' he said, looking serious, 'I've just had Liz Turner's agent on . . .'

'Oh yes?'

'Come in, come in.' The door shut behind me with a click. His hand was warm and damp in the small of my back. 'He says you want her for the narration?'

'Be great, wouldn't it?'

'Would it? *Would* it? Come and sit down.'

'Oh absolutely,' I said brightly, remaining firmly on my feet. 'She'll set the right tone. A proper war correspondent. The thinking man's crumpet and all that.'

'That's Joan Bakewell, lovey.'

'Is it? Oh well, she's got street cred and a whole fistful of TV awards.'

'And she costs the earth.'

'Well, I . . .'

'And Turner's agent has just told me that it'll be twice the usual fee because she'd have to travel back from Hollywood. What is she doing in fucking Hollywood, I'd like to know.'

'She's in the new Kosovo movie.'

'Clare . . .' He shook his head in kindly, fatherly mode. 'Clare, you're not keeping me informed, honey.'

'You've not been here,' I pointed out, politely, I thought.

He waggled his head in an aggravating way and informed me that he'd told the agent her client was too expensive.

'You *didn't*! Barry!' I drew a despairing breath. 'Barry, I had that woman eating out of my *hand*!'

'I understand your annoyance.' He tried to pat said hand but I snatched it away.

'Annoyance!' I didn't quite screech but I do seem to remember my size seven stamping down on his plush shag-pile.

'Now, now. Believe me, kiddo – Turner's not right. Trust me. I've been in this game a long time.'

'But you said I had a free hand!' I sucked hard on my fag for control.

'Within the budget, honey, within the budget. Tom Farrell will serve you far better. He's relia –'

'*Tom*? Oh shit, Barry, I don't want *Tom*! Jesus, he's an old fart.'

'Tch,' he sighed, working hard at keeping a straight face, silver glinting in his designer stubble. 'Well, yes, but he's under contract, you see.' He put his arm round me and squeezed my shoulder. I jumped inches but you don't smack your boss, not for a friendly squeeze, not if you value your job. And I did value it. Oh I did.

'No, I do see your point, Clare,' he said, cuddling in close, a few fat fingers creeping down my bare shoulder to connect, casually, with my nipple. I froze. 'This is your first crack at directing and, of course, you want the best, the cream.' He pulled his earlobe with his free hand and eyed me carefully, as though weighing some sort of odds, which of course he was. 'I suppose I could *try* asking Colin for a few more shekels, though it might mean making a few compromises.' I could hardly breathe. What if I said go on then? What if I didn't?

I dared not move. Dared not give offence. Tried not to inhale his meaty breath as his mouth came closer. Pale powdery lips with dried spittle at the corners. I was suffocating. Simply *had* to breathe. *Had* to turn away to suck in good clean air and, in doing so, just caught the sound of a kiss vaporising beside my left ear.

He was only slightly put out and not at all deterred. Why didn't I make myself comfortable, he suggested, while he rustled up some coffee? Perhaps we could come to some sort of an arrangement.

I smiled like a simpering bimbo, took a last drag of my cigarette and tossed the glowing butt carelessly into the wastebasket. I knew, perfectly well, the sort of arrangement we'd be coming to, the toad. I looked at my watch and said, briskly, 'Actually, Barry, I do have this rather important appointment. I'll maybe pop in and see Colin myself in the morning. Thanks for your time.' With the smile fixed to my face, I concentrated on finding the doorknob one-handed behind my back and getting the fuck out of there, while he attempted to deal with the fire in the bin.

20

'Had a bad day, dear?' Mum's enquiry was muffled by my hug.

'That bloody, bloody man!' I growled, close to tears.

'Who's this, out of all the possibles?' said Kate, tucking a beaded pigtail behind her ear.

'Barry,' I whimpered, wiping my nose on Mum's shoulder.

'The groper,' Kate explained to Mum. She was lying on the floor, batting long eyelashes at the cat, with an open script between them, and an empty wineglass.

'Oh Clare,' gasped Mum, 'he didn't! Have some rhubarb wine, dear.' She poured me a generous glassful from a handy bottle. It was one of Nan's specials and came out on rare occasions.

I was too incensed to be curious – just sipped the sweet liquor gratefully as I told them just what he had done.

'You should have *said*,' Kate declared, 'I could have got you a dozen narrators,' scratching the cat under her pretty chin. 'Couldn't we, though, Perdie, eh?' Perdie got to her arthritic feet for more, her front legs trembling with effort. 'A dozen or more lovely voices. What do you want? Deep and mysterious?' She lowered her voice accordingly and waggled her eyebrows. 'Light and amusing?' said wide-eyed and winningly. 'Or sexy?' Lowered eyelids and a pout. 'We can offer posh Brian Sewell vowels, or your common Estuary-speak or a pretty Welsh lilt – whatever takes your fancy. We're versatile, we aim to please, and we're desperate. You could have us all for the price of Liz Turner.'

'You're not allowed, are you?'

'Well no, but I'm sure if we said it was an amateur venture – they wouldn't need to know you were giving us back-handers.' I stared as an idea slowly gelled. 'Just so long as we get the *Threepenny Opera* ready in time for Christmas.' She frowned, and blinked on some fantastic inner vision. 'You won't want us to sing, will you?' she enquired. 'We can, you know, in German, too.' She proved it by giving us *Und der Haifisch, der hat Zähne* . . . I only recognised it when she got to the MacHeath bit. She said, 'I'm sure Max would have sung it in the trenches.'

I couldn't imagine it somehow. I didn't think I'd ever heard Max sing. I said I thought I might have trouble with copyright.

She said, 'Well, anyway, I reckon if you asked them nicely, they could be persuaded to narrate your documentary between them.'

'I want Liz Turner,' I said doggedly.

'Well, You're going to need some actors, aren't you?'

My mind chugged slowly: Mum's rhubarb wine was lethal on an empty stomach. Kate was right – I was, too, going to need some actors. If I could use Kate's lot, I'd save an absolute fortune, with enough left over for Liz Turner.

'Leave it to me,' said Kate, scrambling to her feet, 'I know who's good.'

'Hang about,' I said, 'I need to think about it.'

'What's to think?' she said, making for the door. 'You need actors, we need the dosh. Honestly it'll be all right. Look, you won't even need a scriptwriter. Give us the scenario and we'll improvise.' I noticed she included herself. Maybe she could be the 1940's Ellen or that woman doctor, whose name always took a moment to call to mind. My mnemonic device was a flock of white geese coming into land on Connaught Waters. Though Gisela Weiss was a swan rather than a goose, judging from the photo we'd seen in Buchenwald. 'Just point the camera in the right direction,' Kate was saying, 'and keep it turning. Lots of directors work like that. And their dialogue is stunning.'

Yes, yes, it might work. It actually might. All these talented unknowns and an absolutely zingy script – I'd be made. Another Mike Leigh.

Her head re-appeared round the door, 'Hey, Clare, meant to tell you. Guess who I bumped into today in the Kings Road? The Bionic Man himself – Max Zeiler. I said I thought he was in Germany still and he said he'd just got back. He was with some people. You know that old geezer you had on the box? Lord Muck with the stately home?'

'*Tith*erille? What on earth was he doing with him?'

'No idea.' She began closing the door.

But she wasn't getting away that easily. 'Who else?' I insisted. 'You said "some people".'

'Oh just some dee-oh-gee. Weird looking bird. Nobody you need worry about.' She was gone, out to the phone, going, 'Look out, ole Mackie is back!' in fake and sinister American.

I found myself sitting on the arm of the settee, with a suddenly empty glass and a heavy thudding in my chest. Mum was speaking to me.

'Mmm?' I managed to say.

'I might as well save my breath,' she said crossly. 'You aren't listening.'

'I am, I am, I just . . .'

'And you shouldn't gulp wine down like that, you know. It's meant to be sipped and slowly savoured. It's strong stuff.'

'Sorry.'

'And what about poor Nick in all of this?'

'What do you mean?'

'I wasn't born yesterday, Clare. I should think very carefully before you go rushing into anything.'

I thought she was talking about recruiting the East London students and said something about auditions and sorting the wheat from the chaff.

'This Max business,' she said. 'You're obsessed. Look at you, glassy-eyed the minute his name's mentioned. You know nothing about the man.'

'God, Mother,' I retaliated, knowing there was no point in denying it. 'I know more about him than anyone on this earth! I've researched him to the nth degree.'

'Facts,' she said. 'They don't tell you what he's made of. I mean, can you trust him like you can trust Nick?'

'Oh, don't bring Nick into it.'

'Nick is integral, I would have thought. He is going to be so hurt, Clare. He worships you.'

'I know,' I said miserably.

'And does this Max feel the same way about you?'

'I thought so.' Without warning I crumpled, sobbed, squeezed out a tearful, 'He might . . . I don't *know*, that's the trouble. I don't know *how* he feels. He doesn't *talk* to me!'

'Hey, now.'

'Mum, he might have phoned. To let me know he was back! I mean, wouldn't you think?'

'Oh come on, sweetheart, let him have some life of his own.'

'No-o-o!' I wailed, quite beside myself.

'Oh dear.' She cast about for comfort. 'Have some more wine.'

After a hefty slug and all sorts of motherly advice (totally unconvincing) about letting things take their course, *che sera, sera*, it occurred to me that the bottle was almost empty. They'd been hard at it, she and Kate, before I'd got home. What was the occasion? I thought, at last, to ask.

'No occasion. Not really. Just . . . Well, the divorce papers came through today.'

And there was I, selfishly wallowing in my own troubles. Poor Mum. But she assured me that it was all right. The bottle had been cracked open in celebration. She was shot of the man finally.

'Oh Mum,' I said, not believing her at all. It was so sad.

She dabbed at her nose, and taking a tangential leap of thought, said, 'I didn't tell you, did I? Douglas Mallory's in hospital.'

He'd had a heart attack. And when I said I was sorry she sniffed and said, 'Nothing for you to be sorry about. It was your father's fault.'

'*Sid's*?'

'If he hadn't insisted everyone went to see his exhibition . . .'

'Mu-u-um!' I didn't follow this.

'You know how Nan's friends like to support the Arts.'

'Oh God, how embarrassing,' I said. I could imagine the old dears toiling round the gallery, at a complete loss. What were his pictures, after all, but montages of old junk, thickly daubed with paint?

'They may be rickety, her friends, but they're not feeble-minded. Some of them know a thing or two about painting.'

'I don't doubt it,' I said. 'They'll see through him sure as eggs. All his clever titles, they're just pretentious nonsense.'

'Well, *I* know that and *you* know that but Douglas and Sylvia thought fit to buy a picture between them. I must say I felt terrible when Owen told me what they'd paid.'

'Oh God.' It was all too difficult – rhubarb wine and divorce papers and a desperate need to phone Max, *and* Kate shrieking in the hallway, '*Yeah I know it's moonlighting – what's wrong with that? What? No . . .what? I can't hear a bloody thing . . . Well turn it off . . . So? You up for it or not? No, Fred – but Clare said . . . Well, of course she'll make it worth your while. Auditions on Monday.*' Where had she got that idea? My head was aching.

'I say "picture",' Mum was going, 'but it was more of an edifice – made of cogs and wheels and spindles and things, like the workings of an enormous clock.'

'Oh, don't tell me. Douglas carried it home.'

'No, of course not. It was far too big and heavy. Owen took it round in a surveillance van. No, the trouble came when they tried to carry it upstairs.'

'Upstairs?' (My mind was wandering. How long had he been back and what was he doing in Chelsea? Who was that damned woman?)

'They thought they'd put it on the landing where they could both see it.'

'No, I'm not hanging on. Mum makes me pay for these calls. Get them to phone back if they're interested.'

'Ri-i-ight.'

'And it was too awkward for anyone to carry, even Owen. Ridiculously tall and bulky.' I couldn't quite see what Owen's being tall and bulky had to do with anything. Meanwhile Kate was singing *Mack the Knife*, in her Louis Armstrong voice, as she waited for the phone to ring. 'Clare!'

I tried harder to concentrate. 'How tall?'

'Four or five feet, I suppose.' Not Owen, then. Was she talking about Sid's picture, maybe? 'The stairs in those places are so narrow. Of course, you'd know that – you've been there, haven't you?'

'Oh God, they didn't drop it?' She had my attention now.

'No, they put it on the stair lift.' I could only gasp. 'Oh they tied it on.' As though that were my objection. 'Quite securely apparently. Then they pressed the 'Up' button and off it went. But they hadn't reckoned on that low ceiling . . .'

'It caught?'

'It caught. And sat there growling away to itself and gouging a great hole in the plasterboard, Owen said. Then something twanged and great pieces of glass came slithering down the stairs. If Douglas hadn't pulled her out of the way, Sylvia would have had her legs sliced off.'

'My God!'

'They couldn't get to the switch, not with all that debris raining down on them – plaster and board, and cogs and wheels. It was on the arm of the chair, the switch, I mean. Anyway poor old Douglas was hopping about, you can imagine, a flea in a fit, and by the time the thing had ploughed its way to the top of the stairs and stopped, he was in the throes of a heart attack. Very grey round the gills. So rather than hang about waiting for an ambulance, Owen popped his blue light on the van, set the siren going and whizzed them through to Harlow in no time flat. Oh, it was very dramatic, Owen said. A mercy dash.'

'Fuck,' I said, miserably.

'Oh he's a lot better now. They're keeping him in to recover quietly. Away from Sylvia's fussing, if you ask me.'

'I'll pop in and see him.'

'Well, as long as it is just you and not the entire camera crew.'

'Mum,' I protested, 'I'm not a ghoul!' But she knew me too well.

'Oh, Clare, you'll like this.' She shook her head, grinning. 'When Sid heard about it he was round there, quick as a flash, picking all the pieces out of the wheelie bin!' She exploded with laughter. 'Waste not, want not, that's my Sid. Alice says he's put it all back together and renamed it *Lethal Automaton*.'

'That's a quote, is it?' Somehow I couldn't find it amusing, though I was pleased that Mum could. Owen Prentice had done a lot for her.

'Louis MacNiece, apparently.'

'Uhuh.' Another Mac, another Louis. Now the wretched song was lodged in my brain, I'd never shift it. But Max was no shark. If anyone had a jack knife hidden up his sleeve, it was Titherille. So what did Max want with the likes of him? I hoped he hadn't gone to him for money. Oh hell, I didn't like the look of this at all.

The phone rang. *'Yes? No, this is Kate. Oh hi, Max. Yeah, I'll just get her.'* My sister's head was round the door again, a bleached and shaggy mop. 'It's lover-boy. Get him to ring you back on your mobile, Clare. I'm expecting a very important call.'

21

The Chain and Sprocket was heaving. People were shouting their orders over a wall of heat and noise and ancient
bits of bike hanging from the ceiling. Standing room only
tonight. Rising above the hubbub, like a good head of
Guinness, was the piercing, plaintive wail of pipe and fiddles
and the clickety-clack of Mick, the landlord, on the spoons.
The rhythm was irresistible. Dribbling glasses were passed
high over bobbing heads. Boozy old men, rosy with sentiment, joined in their favourites with feet and fingers tapping.
Mick's black collie was scavenging around the table legs
for crisps and peanuts, twitching away petting hands like
flies. An elderly tart, with a clownish gash of Max Factor
where her mouth once was, danced a stiff, slow jig out of
time to the music. It was always the same on Irish Night.

We'd managed to get a table next to the band but while
everyone else paid attention to the music, my eyes kept
swivelling towards the door. Nick's arm round my shoulders
was hot and heavy and I shrugged it off, told him I was
tired, that Barry was getting me down. I blamed the heat,
and he swallowed it all with a mouthful of beer.

Kate gave me a long hard stare and turned to say something to Fred, who stopped bawling 'Paddy McGinty's
Goat' for a moment, cocked his head and stroked his chin.
When I crossed my eyes under his appraisal, he winked,
making me nervous.

My sister leaned across the table in a cloud of Calvin
Klein and said against my ear, 'You look ripe for plucking,
sweetness – quite stunning, in fact. I take it Max is expected?'

I warned her off with my eyes. She had been a tad

premature with her 'lover-boy' crack earlier on, but she was right. I had taken extra trouble tonight, letting down my marmalade hair and catching it up again with a swarm of tiny orange butterflies, to match my new floaty orange trousers and my skimpy pink top. Being of the ginger persuasion has never stopped me wearing hot colours. Pinks, reds, I love them, and if they clash so much the better. I still had a tan from Austria and had made up my eyes to look big and brown. Nick had made appreciative noises when he called to pick me up, since when I'd been horrible to him.

I really shouldn't have invited Max along tonight but how could I not? Susmeta had just broken the news to him about Sophie and he phoned, he said, to see how *I* was taking it. If that didn't beat all! I mean what was a lost interview against a lost wife? It had been hard enough adjusting to the fact that she was alive, he said; to learn that she'd been killed, in such a stupid, avoidable, accident, before he'd even had a chance to see her, talk to her, it was – it was a cruel twist of fate. The cliché rang false, but I guessed finding out that your wife has aged sixty years in six isn't the biggest turn on, especially when there's a nice young film director in the offing.

He was intrigued to learn that Sophie had kept his letters and seemed quite keen on retrieving them. Crossing my fingers, I suggested that he meet us at the Chain and Sprocket later on. I'd bring the letters with me. I didn't mention the other one, which had blown up beautifully from Nick's print. I wanted to surprise him, once I'd got two copies made, on Buchenwald headed notepaper, one the pristine version, for the actor playing Hofmann to sign in permanent blue ink and seal into its waxed wrapper, the other to be worked on by 'props' to show handwriting that had blurred and run when the frozen ink hit the air, several freezer burns and slight discolouration along the folds.

Plus someone, Otto Pesch, presumably, had managed to smudge part of the text when he'd brushed away the obscuring frost. It was legible, still, but quite distressed.

'Who's "us"?' he asked suspiciously.

'The usual – Nick, Jay, my sister, her boyfriend. People like that.'

'You're not going to surprise me with more of my old comrades?'

'*Moi*? Anyway, poor Douglas is in hospital.'

'What!' Occasional sounds of sympathy perforated the tale I told him. 'He is too old,' he said again. 'Heart attacks and frailty I do not associate with this man. He was strong and vigorous. A man among men.' I don't know where he picked up all these platitudes – not from me. He went on about life being unfair, old age being cruel. If I'd had a suspicion that maybe the friendship had been a tad one-sided, or that time was adding a touch of glamour to a relationship that hadn't been quite as Mallory remembered it, Max's concern dispelled it. He really cared about the old boy.

He established that Douglas was out of danger and where to send his 'Get Well' card, before allowing himself a small snort of laughter at the notion of one of Sid's pompous pretensions riding the chair-lift to disaster. I found myself smiling.

'So anyway Sid's repaired it for a small fee,' I said, coming to the end of my story.

'He's not all bad then, your father.'

'Oh he is. He's only doing it to curry favour with the old folks. They're the ones with the money.'

'Clare, he's your father – your flesh and blood!'

'I don't know why people say that. My blood's quite different. I'm just plain old O negative and he's AB negative . . .' I stopped. But the words were out. 'Don't you go telling Susmeta, will you?' I joked. 'I don't want her getting ideas about him and her Liebl project.'

He promised.

'No, we have nothing in common, him and me, apart from red hair. As for filial feelings, forget it. He forfeited any right to them when he ditched us for his career.'

'So you call him Sid, not Dad.'

'"Sid" is all he gets – more than he deserves.'

'I would like to meet him, your Sid.'

'Whatever for?'

'I think he is more like you than you admit. You, too, are single-minded. You go all out for what you want. That is what I like about you. One of the things I like,' he said in this very sexy, suggestive voice that had my head spinning minutes after I'd put the phone down. Too late I realised I hadn't asked him about his meeting with Lord Titherille.

The end of the set couldn't come soon enough. I was beginning to wilt – it was like a sauna in there, and my ears ached. Any more of that plaintive tin whistle and I'd ram it down the guy's throat. It was nine thirty and still Max hadn't shown. I was glumly surveying my empty bottle of Beck's when Jay, whose round it was, gave me the nod and said he'd see me outside. I elbowed my way through the sweating, grinning press, ignoring loose hands and mouths, and burst into the cool night air like I was drowning. Though the forecourt was floodlit and every table was full it was peaceful out there, cocooned by darkness and the looming forest on all sides.

I propped up the wall trying not to stare too hard at a couple of cyclists in Lycra who were trying to get down each other's throats, when Jay came out, balancing a brimming beer and a clinking gin and tonic in a glass beaded with condensation. I'd ordered another Beck's but this was wonderful. 'You looked like you needed it,' he said.

'Oh, Jay, I love you.'

'Me too.' His grin was a white flash in the dark. 'Look,' he said, fishing out a copy of the video from an inside pocket, 'I don't know what use this'll be. According to this guy, it won't mean a thing to you or anyone who isn't well up in brain surgery.' I slipped the tape into my bag, anyway. 'There's a few on there,' he was saying. 'Willi Greff I recognised and Ellen Sauerbruch. Some of it's kosher surgery, some is stem-cell implantation. Buggered if I can tell the difference.'

'I doubt if I'll do anything with it,' I said. 'I might just give it back to Susmeta. I mean she'll at least know then that we're onto her.'

'I wouldn't do that. She's a dangerous woman.'

'Susmeta?' I treated my burning face to the touch of cool glass. I generally trusted Jay's judgement but I thought he was wrong in this case. I was about to tell him that she was just ambitious, like the rest of us, when this very tasty green limo swirled into my gin. I had to lower the glass for a clearer view, and was just about to remark on the Chain and Sprocket's classy clientele when Max stepped onto the pavement and took my voice away.

He apologised for his lateness – he'd been stuck in a tunnel on the Underground for over an hour. Got out at Woodford and thrown himself into a cab. Some cab, I thought. The rank must be doing well out of the tube breakdowns.

'All you need,' said Jay, 'on top of everything else.' His face gentled. 'Bit of a double whammy, that – your sister *and* your wife. Can't tell you how sorry I am, mate.'

Acknowledgement was a jerk of the head, and a bunching of the lips that meant he didn't want to talk about it. He seemed pale and preoccupied under his tan, gazing at me as though I were something new and wonderful. And I lapped it up.

'What can I get you, Max?' offered Jay, and when Max

continued to stare at me, muttered resignedly, 'A Beck's'd be great, thanks, Jay.' Still Max ignored him. I flicked him a look of apology, but he had already turned away, shaking his noble head as he went back to the steamy bar.

'Where are the others?'

'Inside,' I croaked.

'What are you doing out here with, em . . .' He gestured towards the door as though he'd forgotten Jay's name.

So I explained, in case he was jealous, about Jay's mate, the theatre nurse, and what he'd told Jay about Susmeta's dubious activities. I told him how Willi Greff was worried that his mental powers were fading. I heard myself babbling but saw no reason to stop. This was Max, after all, standing so close his chemistry was in a double helix with mine, Max, massaging his lower lip so thoughtfully. 'She has discovered a cure for the trembling disease, you say?'

'And Alzheimer's. Which is pretty wonderful, actually.'

'So they were not for nothing, these experiments?'

'Well, no, but . . .'

'Would you mind if I borrowed the video, Clare?'

'Oh Max, I can't, I mean –' I huffed, and tried again. 'It was given to me on trust, Max. I'm sorry. In any case, you're not on there – just Ellen Sauerbruch and Willi Greff.'

His mouth pulled tight and I heard him say, 'She is the one I worry about. I had lunch with her today and she is very depressed.'

'Oh.' Needlessly I said, 'She's here in London?' my heart thumping. For if, as Kate had said, the 'dee-oh-gee' was nothing to worry about, why, as soon as his plane landed, had he headed straight for her? I mean, *lunch*, and he hadn't even phoned to tell me he was back. 'You think –' I squeaked and paused to clear my throat – 'You think Susmeta might have damaged Ellen's brain?'

'She has certainly damaged her psyche,' he said bitterly. 'Ellen was a pretty girl. She cannot adjust to being plain.'

I took a hefty slug of gin for courage, let it go down slowly. 'You're fond of her?'

'We worked together.' He flicked me a sideways glance. 'Closely.'

'I see.' Now my knees were trembling – a match for my cat's, any day.

'I thought you knew that,' he said, more gently.

'I didn't know you were like, committed.'

'Committed? Clare, she saved my life more than once.' He paused. 'There is a huge debt.' That sounded more promising. 'Debt' didn't sound like crazy with love. 'I must do what I can for her now. You know that William Titherille has gone into the cryonics business?'

'*Titherille*?' I'd forgotten he was there too. 'What are you doing, hobnobbing with *him*? He's a –'

'I know precisely what he is, Clare.'

I fussed and fumed but heard him out. As part of his plan to save England from itself the old fascist and his wife had had a long-standing arrangement with a cryonics group in America. On death, their bodies were to have been deep-frozen and thawed out again when some regenerative miracle cure became available. But Susmeta's groundbreaking neuro-surgery had rendered the freezing of dead bodies obsolete. Titherille had cancelled his contract and, indeed, persuaded the American company to come in with him on a new venture.

It was embryonic as yet. A few hundred surgeons had to be trained up in the two operations, brain removal and rehabilitation, but then it would be all systems go. Titherille had floated the idea on the Internet and already there was a long list of rich and eager subscribers. Saint Meredith's had been approached with a view to becoming the main UK treatment centre and were already buying in computers and storage units. All that remained was for Susmeta to see sense.

'She knows about the scheme?'

'She does indeed.'

'But she's not playing ball?'

'She'll come round.'

Dear me, I thought, things had certainly been happening while the mice were away. Trust old Tithers to spot a gap in the market. But I couldn't see why Max was involved. The old man stood for everything he hated.

He explained that Ellen had visited Titherille's website and e-mailed him. (Bloody Ellen, I thought. I would much rather she stayed plain and unappetising.) 'She is desperate, poor girl.'

She had to be, I said, to abandon her socialist principles. It just showed – when push came to shove . . .

Exactly, said Max. He had tried but she wouldn't be talked out of it. The best he could do was to insist on being at the meeting too. Someone had to protect her interests. Titherille was a shark of the deepest water.

'Oh, he's an absolute nutter, Max. Have you seen his stuff on the Web about the Fascist Uprising?'

'What stuff?'

'Once his brain is planted in a younger body, he is planning on leading the neo-Nazis to world victory.'

His laugh was derisive.

'It's not funny, Max. He's dangerous. He shouldn't be allowed anywhere near the operating table.'

Even my glass frosted with his reproof. 'I think I am able to judge for myself how dangerous he is.' Oops. He *was* touchy.

'So, what happened?'

He shrugged. 'She signed up.'

'So, sooner or later she's going to be beautiful again.'

'It would appear so,' he said and sighed a sigh that was deep, heartfelt and, to my sensitive antennae, more than a smidgen OTT. Prickles of suspicion ran over my scalp. For after all, he stood to benefit. They'd make a lovely couple. Slowly the words formed, 'Are you sure it's just Ellen who wants this operation?'

'Pardon me?' His frown was gratifying.

'Well,' I said, blinking in the sudden fluorescent glare of the truth, 'it can't be much fun fucking the back end of a bus. For what? For old time's sake? What do you do – shut your eyes and think of England?'

'Germany,' I should have said, but never mind, I'd got there at last. Spot on, I'd say, from the look on his face. 'Bitch!' he snarled and something in German besides. I dare say he'd have hit me if he hadn't noticed Jay standing by with a handful of bottles.

'Get stuffed,' I hissed. 'Oh and you'd better take your letters in case we never meet again.' Slammed them into his outstretched hand.

'You've read them, of course,' he sneered.

'They're in German,' I said, giving him my pissiest smile. 'I don't *do* German.'

Ignoring Jay in his fury, he flung off into the night. He wouldn't get far. There was no bus service and people round our way don't give lifts, even in daylight.

' . . .well shot of him,' a voice was saying.

'Bastard,' I choked.

'Oh sweetie.' Jay's free arm was round my shoulders. 'He's not worth it.'

'Oh Jay,' I wailed, 'what am I going to do?'

'The sensible thing would be to go back inside and be nice to Nick who would cheerfully lie down and die for you. Forget this guy.'

'But,' it occurred to my fuddled brain, 'I need him for the film.'

'Oh right, for all the fascinating insider stuff he's going to give us! Face it, Clare, he's full of shit. I mean it might be good shit, but he's keeping it well to himself, like it's all so terrible, we earthlings would never understand. He's not going to give us a flying fart.'

I almost managed a smile. Because it was true. Max was sewn up tight, unnaturally so. I'd thought I was getting close, thought I would be the one to help him unpack some of the secrets and pain. I hadn't known they'd include Ellen Sauerbruch, his partner in every sense of the word. Bugger the woman. Bugger, bugger, bugger.

'You coming back in?'

'In a minute,' I said.

It crossed my mind, as I swallowed what was left of my gin and stared mournfully at the slivers of ice that remained, that maybe I should have told him about Hofmann's letter and its meagre contents. I knew he'd have wanted to see it all the same, and now he never would. Because that was that. The end of a beautiful friendship. Of course he'd been fucking her, for whatever reason, pity, money. But I couldn't have been mistaken about that buzz between us. That look in his eyes. Suppose he'd just been keeping her happy. I thought of him now, wandering along the Epping New Road, wondering what to do. Stopping under a street lamp. He wouldn't be able to wait to read what he'd written to Sophie all those years ago. I knew them off by heart, the translations, knew he'd be whisked back to that desperate winter, the cold, the danger, the time when he'd been so brave and honourable. Who was he thinking of, as he held the shaking paper, his dead wife, his homely mistress, the man he used to be . . . or me?

I knew he'd have to come back to the pub to phone for a cab, or walk all night to Epping. I didn't have long to wait.

'Are you still here?'

'Where else would I be?'

There was no chance of getting lost. The forest was my backyard. I knew all the walks through it, short cuts across

294

it; I'd played there, climbed trees, made dens; I'd taken boyfriends there for picnics and romance. I'd gathered berries for jam and wine, sloes for gin. I knew the seasons and the people – the dog walkers, mountain bikers and the girls from the riding school. I knew the man who spiked up the rubbish after the weekend visitors, and his dog. I knew Roger the Ranger, Fred the Rambler, the woman with the ferrets and the tramp, though not his name, and Eric the Flasher, though not to speak to.

It wasn't that dark once you got away from the road. The trees thinned out to a broad green ride where Kate and I had galloped in our 'horsy' days, and 'sledded' on trays and plastic sacks at the slightest hint of snow, all the way down to the brook. The sky above the trees reflected London's streetlamps and office blocks and the red and white of car lights. There was a smell of honeysuckle in the air and newly cut grass. (The City of London, who owned the land, sold off the hay for winter-feed.) The sounds of the pub faded, superseded by small squeaks and rustles of night creatures, sleepy twitters, hooting owls and the eerie screech of a lovelorn fox. It was a starry night, I could see all around, and there was nothing to be afraid of. But my heart was in my throat as Max grabbed my hand and pulled me into the trees.

'No – not this way,' I said, but he took no notice, tugged my arm almost out of its socket and carried on. 'Max, wait, there's a path,' I cried, tripping on a root and cursing. I was sober enough to know that my new silky trousers were snagging on the brambles and I was getting scratched. There were boggy bits and I was only wearing skimpy sandals. The excitement was wearing thin. Why was he doing this, dragging me along? He needn't be so rough.

'Max, no, this is silly!' What was he trying to prove? He hadn't even kissed me yet. And then we hit the clearing, well out of sight and sound of the pub, and stopped.

'Jesus Christ!' I said, bending to examine my shoe, which was slippery with mud and felt as though a strap had broken. We were both sweating and breathing hard. Then he hurled me to the ground and fell on top. 'Max,' I giggled and tried to put my arms round him, to slow him down if nothing else, give me a chance to catch up, because I have to say, all that macho stuff was a bit of a turn off, but he was already tearing at my crop-top. 'Careful,' I said, 'this cost an arm and a . . .'

'Shut up,' he growled, without a trace of humour or affection, and my scalp prickled. As he wrenched my breast from my bra and stuffed it into his mouth I cried out, 'Max, you're hurting . . . Max, there's no need to . . . Ow! Look, let me undo . . .' But he wasn't listening, just grunting and sucking and licking and biting while his hands were busy with his zip. My treacherous nipple bounced up hard and eager, setting off immediate responses in my groin and I hooked my legs around him, the sooner to have him in me. His huge penis sprang free. And now he was tugging at my trousers, the waistband. 'Wait, wait, Max, don't tear it! You don't have to *rape* me, for God's sake!'

He looked at me then, sort of startled, and I saw reason sliding across his eyes in the moonlight. Without speaking, he lifted himself to one side.

'Do you have anything?' I enquired gently. As he continued to look blank, I explained, 'A condom?'

'Mein Gott!' His mouth twisted in disgust.

'Pass me my bag.' I'd actually gone out and bought some, thoughts of Polly Gross and AIDS and that lost weekend of his in my mind.

He growled. He literally growled when he saw what I was handing him and tossed the packet into the darkness.

'Please, Max. It's important.' But he wasn't interested. I thought it would probably be all right. Slowly I began unbuttoning my trousers but he couldn't wait and dragged at the zip, muttering, 'Come on, come on!' I slid out of my pants and trousers, onto the prickly stubble. 'Ouch!' I grimaced, trying to make a joke of it.

And he slapped the smile off my face.

'Shit, Max, that hurt! Max, stop! It's not funny. Stop, right now.' But he was already working his fingers into my vagina. I felt them inside me, hot and hard and insistently moving, causing muscles to soften and open and let go in spite of my fear. 'Oh yes,' I murmured against his ear.

'Over!' he rapped, Gestapo-like.

A pang of disbelief and I shrivelled inside, a sea anemone closing, a snail being sucked into its shell. '*What!*'

He jerked his head, meaning I should do as I was told.

'Oh Max, no – not this way. Not the first time. I want . . .'

'Quiet!' he said through cruel teeth. 'I am not interested in what you want.' His eyes were hard, the pupils pinpoints, his face gleaming cold silver as he spat the words, 'Turn over!' He yanked my shoulder and flipped me onto my front, knocking the breath out of me, reminding me of the gin I'd drunk.

'Ple-e-ease!' The word shuddered out of me.

'Up, bitch,' he snarled and yanked me up onto all fours.

'No, Max, please, I don't want – No!' I, who didn't cry, had tears in my eyes.

But by then he was inside, just about. He was too big and hard to go all the way, and I was too tight with fear, too dry with dismay. He grabbed my shoulders to pull me against him. It hurt. God, how it hurt. I gasped as he inched inside. I begged him to stop, said this wasn't the way. He reached underneath to knead my breasts, pinch my nipples hard to make me softer inside, more yielding. He stuck his finger in my arse, twisted it around savagely. Leaned over to sink his teeth into my neck. I yelped with pain and he slapped me round the ears, forehand, backhand, muttering, 'Shut up, shut up,' making my brains jangle. What was

297

I doing? How had I got myself into this mess – with a stranger? I found I was trying to crawl away, on all fours, with him having to follow after, on his knees. I've seen dogs in the same predicament. Oh God, oh someone, help me, I wept. As if. I found two large hands round my neck, squeezing, choking me. 'Stay still,' he snarled, and you know what? I stayed.

Little by little he forced his great prick in to the hilt. Then slowly withdrew and plunged again, holding onto my bony hips, digging in his nails to give him better purchase so he could pound deeper, into God knows what tender tissue. It scraped in, rammed against something so painfully I howled. 'Stop, please!' But he didn't. The sharp stubble stabbed my bare skin, and my breasts wobbled stupidly. I bucked, tried to shake him off and sobbed that I hated this, hated *him*. He grabbed me by the hair, twisting my head to hiss vile German into my ear, while tears and snot ran down my face and the pain went driving on. Saliva filled my mouth and dripped onto my hands as I felt him getting there, climbing the last hard stretch while I tried to contain my rebellious stomach.

He came, pumping into me and groaning, while I retched up gin and beer and disgust. Only when he pulled himself free did he realise I was lying in vomit. He muttered oaths. I rolled away. The forest was silent, listening with pricked ears.

He didn't apologise, check I was okay. Just lay there, panting.

I lurched to my feet, and nearly fell down again. My head throbbed as the blood returned. A sharp stone had buried itself in my knee. I was scratched and muddy, and chafed by stubble. My insides were mangled and my bones were bruised. I had hayseeds in my hair and semen dribbling down my leg. I'd been used like a dog and smelled of sick. And this was supposed to be the act of love! Jesus!

Nick knew how to make love. Nick was sensitive and sweet. But I'd ruined things with him – and for what?

I cleaned myself up with my pants, put them in my bag and pulled on my glad rags.

'Max,' I said when I was ready, 'the pub's that way. Follow the path – it's easier. I'm going home. I'm going to have to think about the film – whether to carry on. You've ruined things nicely.' His indifferent shrug told me that this was probably what he'd wanted. 'Oh,' as I turned to go, 'and just stay out of my life. I don't know what they did to you in that concentration camp but you're dangerous.'

I scraped together what was left of my dignity and went barefoot down the hill to where the trees were thick. I brushed myself down, put on my broken shoes and hobbled home, blubbering like a baby.

Mum looked up from a pile of exercise books in the kitchen. 'Hi,' she called, then as I tried to sneak up the stairs, remembered, 'Oh Clare, you had a phone call.' But the message was forgotten when she came out and saw the state of me. 'Clare! Oh my God . . .' She was up the stairs after me and cradling my head in her lap and rubbing my shoulders, before I'd even begun the story. Then I had to drag her, shrieking about German pigs, away from the phone. It wasn't rape, I insisted. The police wouldn't be interested – I'd led him on. It was as much my fault as his and, after a while, she calmed down and sat picking bits of hay out of my hair and crooning, 'Oh you silly, silly girl.' And later, when I was quiet, 'I'll run you a bath,' she said.

But as I shut the bathroom door, trying to avoid looking at the panda-eyed trollop in the mirror, I heard the front door go. I waited for voices, signs of life, and when there were none, realised she'd gone out. I was down the stairs in a trice.

'Mum! Mum, don't,' I yelled, heading her off at the corner of the street. 'Please!' I didn't know what she intended doing, with her sleeves rolled up and that look on her face, whether she was going to tear Max's eyes out, or make a scene at the Chain and Sprocket, or fetch my sister, or . . . or . . .

'Oh Mum, please don't tell Nick!'

She didn't deny it. 'Look at you with no shoes on! Go back home, Clare, for goodness' sake.'

'Please, Mum, let me deal with it. Mum, I'm a big girl. I can fight my own battles.'

'Looks like it,' she said. 'Look at you – ruined.' It sounded awful, irreversible. 'Let go of me, Clare! I'll kill that animal if it's the last thing I do.'

'I know. You mustn't. Please, Mum, it won't do any good.'

'It'll do *me* good.'

But she allowed herself to be led home, spitting and cursing all the way. At the door she moaned, 'Dear God, where's your fucking father when you need him?' The woman across the road slammed her window shut, thoroughly offended. Such language! From a teacher, too.

Mum had put Radox in the bath but I didn't relax. I scrubbed myself sore, then let the filthy water out and turned the shower on full force, as hot as I could stand. And I still wasn't clean. I didn't think it counted as date rape, not technically. I'd said No, but too late. It was unreasonable, maybe, to have expected him to stop then.

When I was ready, Mum came and sat with me. As she brushed my hair, I thought, yes, this is why I haven't left home yet. Though Nick would be as kind, probably – about anything else.

She said as she got up to go, 'I won't tell Nick, Clare, and I'd advise you not to tell him either.'

'Oh . . . right.'

A little later I heard Kate and Fred come in and the murmur of voices in the hallway. She came up and stood by my bed. 'Clare, you okay?' I heard her breathing, felt her warmth and concern, smelled perfume, smoke, booze. Kept my eyes shut as she switched off my lamp and closed the door too gently, not quite shut.

I heard her telling someone downstairs that I looked like shit. Was Mum sure I hadn't broken anything?

'God, those bruises! No wonder she threw up.'

Fred said, 'She must have been *well* lagered. I mean you just don't *go* walking home through the forest in the dead of night. She might have known she'd trip over something.'

'So long as it wasn't Eric the Flasher!'

Muffled guffaws and giggles and Mum going shush, shush, she'll hear you!

A throat was cleared and Kate said, soberly, 'Poor old Clare – rowing with Max must have really got to her.'

'What's this?' said Mum.

'Oh Jay said they were rowing over some woman Max was seeing. She gave him a right bollocking, apparently. Told him to bugger off, which he did.'

'Poor Clare,' said Kate. 'She really fancied him.'

'Old Nick is *really* pissed off – reckons he's had it with Clare.'

'Well, she asked for it, Mum. She treats him like shit, doesn't she, Fred? I mean you should have heard her carrying on when Max didn't show. Nick must have felt awful.'

I just lay there shivering, flipping the events of the night over and over, as sordid images came into my mind and my mind sheered away. Not me. It must have happened to someone else, not to someone as nicely brought up as me. It was all a horrible mistake.

It was past three when I remembered and I worked my way, with difficulty to the door, across the landing, down the stairs. It was on the newel post. They say bad things come in threes. But mine came in battalions. Bad sex in the woods, then Nick dumping me, and then, of course, when I looked in my bag, there were my soiled pants, making me heave, my purse, lipstick, tissues, comb – and no video. He'd taken it, the bastard, and how the hell was I going to get it back? I couldn't see any way, any hope, any point to anything. I just sat on the stairs and let the grief come down.

Mum was there in an instant, hushing me. 'Leave it now, Clare,' she said when I told her what else he'd done. 'Think about it in the morning. You look like death. Go on, up you go. I'll bring you some hot milk.'

As I made my way up the stairs, I remembered. 'What was that phone call about, Mum?' Perhaps it was something good. I needed something good to happen.

She said, 'It'll wait. Go and get some sleep.'

Not good news then. I sighed, 'Oh come on, let's have it.'

'Best not, Clare.'

'Mum!'

She sighed. 'Nan called tonight, from the hospital. She and Sylvia were having a nice visit. Douglas was so much better, and while they were off having something to eat in the cafeteria . . .' Her chin crinkled as she suppressed sudden tears. 'He had another seizure.' He was dead.

22

I must have slept. My eyelids heaved open, swollen and crusty with old tears, and my heart lurched as the nightmare began again – action replay, slowed down, speeded up, viewed from every lurid angle. It was real. It had happened. And it was no better in the light of morning. When I groaned my throat still ached, when I moved I was still sore and, in that other canal, the membrane was still inflamed, gritty as sandpaper, like a very bad yeast infection. And that nice old man was dead. Out of it. It should have been me.

Mum had left a note beside a cold cup of tea: *I've phoned your office – told them you'd had a bad fall and will be having a few days off to recover. Also made an appointment for you to see Doctor Hussein this morning – 11.15. Do go. There's some cold chicken in the fridge. Be home about five. Love Mum.*

There was still time if I got up now.

When, much later, she popped her head round the door, letting in a gust of cooking smells and normality, and said, 'You up to having visitors?' I thought, for one hectic moment, it might be Nick.

'Jay,' she said. 'You ought to see him. Tell him about the video.' When I groaned and pulled the sheet up over my head, she said, 'Please, Clare. He's come all this way. He's worried about you.'

'Jesus,' he said, putting down his cup when I came, gingerly, downstairs, 'you look like shit.'

'So they tell me.'

'You seen someone – a doctor?'

I shook my head. I'd already had an earbashing from Mum.

'You ought to. You might have broken something.'

'I wish.' Meaning my neck. Meaning to be flip and brave. But his frown of concern broke me up. Give him his due, Jay, he's the big sister I never had, but when all's said and done he's still a bloke. He managed a few tentative pats, but then had to pull away. Salt and saliva were the two things guaranteed to stain a navy-blue T-shirt.

Nevertheless he listened to my story with mounting horror and when, dry-eyed and weary I came to the end, he said, 'You're shitting me, aren't you?'

'No, that's what happened. He stole the video.'

'Forget the fucking video, right? I'm talking about the rape.'

'It wasn't rape, I keep telling you.'

'Oh it was, take it from me. Like you told him to stop and he took fuck-all notice?' He shook his head, grim-faced. 'I mean look at the state of you! We've got to get those bruises photographed and filed, *tout de suite*. I'm telling you, that guy has to be put away. Jesus, I mean what's the matter with him?'

'I goaded him. You were there – you heard . . .'

'Fucking nutter. He's dangerous. He could have killed you.'

'Oh,' was all I said, because that's what I'd thought when his hands were round my neck. I wondered what had stopped him.

'So, go and wash your face, get dressed.'

'What? Why?'

'*Why*?' He couldn't believe I'd asked. 'Because you and me are going down the cop-shop, babe.'

But I couldn't. Max was a hero. He'd suffered, died almost, been buried, and risen again. Everyone loved him.

'Clare, for fuck's sake – the next girl might not be so lucky.'

I trudged back upstairs.

'Only your face, mind,' he shouted up. 'They'll want to do DNA tests and things.'

Too late, too late. Next time I was raped I'd remember not to have a bath.

They managed to find something, they said, and the panties were helpful. In fact they were very kind, and they agreed with Jay that there was a vast difference between bad sex and rape. They took blood tests as well, for HIV and such. I said I was on the Pill so there wasn't much likelihood of my being pregnant. Ah, they said, and then told me that I was lucky to have such a kind and supportive boyfriend. Jay, they meant. I couldn't be bothered to argue.

When I phoned Nick he wasn't there. I must have left a dozen messages on his machine during the course of the weekend, telling him how sorry I was, that I'd been stupid, that we needed to talk, begging him to pick up the phone. His mum answered a few times and said he wasn't in but she'd get him to call me. He didn't. I guessed I'd really blown it.

The police said Max hadn't been back to Bayswater, and they didn't know where to start looking. That was fine by me. I hoped they'd never find him. The thought of washing my dirty linen in a court of law was a real downer. How could I hold my head up at work, always supposing I still had a job? Because that was the other thing. Barry would hate that sort of publicity. Not only that, the documentary was his bread and butter. If I couldn't work with Max he'd find someone who could.

Then the telegram turned up. It had been tucked inside one of the books Rhona had taken down to the charity shop. The woman from *Sense* had called the Greenes to ask if she should throw it away, a communication addressed to Mrs S Zeiler. They let Jay have it for twenty pounds, as it was very short. It was written in March 1942 and simply said that Max Zeiler was missing, believed dead. 'I wish.' I gripped the phone tight. The mere mention of his name sent shivers down my back. Four days on and I still couldn't understand how he could have treated me so cruelly. All my life good people had protected me from unkindness. I didn't know how to deal with it.

'I'll bin it, shall I?' Jay asked, gently.

'Right.' What use was it? Twenty quid down the drain, but hey . . .

My professional eye saw a young woman's hands, shiny new wedding ring in place, smoothing the buff paper across the screen. I was even toying with the idea of a close-up, a tear splashing onto the words *PRESUMED DEAD STOP*, Hitchcock style, when Jay broke in on my thoughts.

'Clare, while you're on . . .'

'Yeah?' No, not tears splashing. Terrible old cliché.

'We've had a call from Douglas Mallory's daughter, asking for Max's phone number. She wants him to say a few words at the funeral, as her father's oldest friend.'

'Oh shit.'

'I put her onto Susmeta.'

'Fine.' Susmeta would only tell her what she'd told the police – that she'd no idea where he was.

'Anyway, this bird – Felicity – she wants to talk to you. I said you were off sick but she said it couldn't wait. Something to do with the funeral service.'

She had a 'little-girl' voice, this Felicity – Daddy's little girl. He must have had her late in life. Breathily she told me that Nan was going to read a poem, Sylvia, too, and if I wanted to come along to pay my respects I would be very welcome. 'Daddy' had taken quite a shine to me. He'd been so looking forward to being on television, talking about his time in Spain. He was really very proud of having been in the International Brigade, fighting for what he believed in.

Her voice broke and there were tears in my eyes, too. I'd grown fond of Douglas.

Something wriggled, some lower form of life, and wormed its way out from under the slab where my career was buried. It *would* be a shame if Douglas's story were never told, if the interviews with Axel and Willi were never shown. The mountain scenes, the shots of Buchenwald, the salt mines and Friedrich's gargoyles were all too good to waste. Sod it, said the worm, gathering strength, you've got some great stuff there, Clare, the makings of a halfway decent documentary. You owe it to these guys. Sod it, I owed it to *me*. As for *his* side of it, I could use bits from the show, and there must be loads of Edit Suite snippets. We could shoot around him. And Barry would never get a whisper of the court case. There'd be no court case. All this wimping and whining! Big girls picked themselves up, brushed themselves down.

I poured myself another glass of rhubarb wine and asked Felicity if we could still use the film of her father's interview.

'Of course,' she said, sniffing. 'It's what he would have wanted. Actually,' she murmured brightly, and there was a single silent beat as she turned something over in her mind, followed by a decisive, 'No, perhaps I won't ask you to do that. It would be too intrusive.'

'What?'

'Well, I was wondering whether you might consider filming the funeral? Not the harrowing bits, of course, but the eulogy, things like that. It would round off his part in your story.' She was thinking like a director. I agreed, it would be a nice touch. 'And Daddy would just love it,' she went on, in her 'ickle' voice, 'to think that his passing hadn't gone entirely unrecorded. But it's not on, is it? I can't have you turning something sacred into a three-ring circus.'

'Sorry?'

'With the camera crew and all their paraphernalia.'

I said it could be done with the mini DV camera, so small and light I could hold it in one hand. Very discreet. I explained that it filmed better inside than out, where it tended to pick up traffic noise, but it would record anything inside the church perfectly well.

'I'd have to ask the rest of the family – and Sylvia. I believe you know her – Daddy's "girlfriend"?' She managed a schoolgirl giggle. 'If you're sure you could do it without being obvious?'

I booked out the DV and got Jay to bring it over. Luckily he'd thought twice about shredding the telegram.

I told the office I was working from home.

It rained the night before the funeral, ending the hot spell – the sort of storm where the lightning flash-flash-flashes like cameras at a star-studded premiere and it's not until later that the thunder kicks in, growling and barking for ages on end, at nothing, like an anxious old dog. I was awake most of the night, too hot, then freezing, with an ominous scratchy throat into the bargain. I was getting a cold.

Next morning, Tuesday, dawned grey and drear to match my mood. The last thing I wanted to do was go out, show myself to people who would see, at a glance, my shame lying on me like a dirty second skin. They'd know right away how I'd let myself be used.

Mum gave me a talking-to and her black polo neck to cover the bruises. Heavy makeup helped but I still felt shaky, kind of expecting *him* to be waiting round every corner. I dosed myself with Beecham's and caffeine and forced myself to think light settings as I drove round to Nan's, where I found her mourning her garden, smashed to smithereens by the rain. Rose petals littered the grass.

'If I'd known I'd have picked them last night. He admired my roses.'

We managed to salvage a few tight, un-sodden blooms and set them off with sedum and lovely purple-and-hot-pink fuchsia, twirling like puppet ballerinas from single strands. 'Not very funereal,' she said, wrapping them in pretty cellophane, 'but he'd have appreciated them.' She swiped at her nose, which seemed to have a constant dribble this morning and bloomed as red as mine. Emotional traumas – exams, or death, or rape – tend to lower the Russell resistance to colds.

The chapel was almost full. The East End Writers had turned out in force, and there seemed to be row upon row of Douglas Mallory's friends and relations, none of whom turned to stare at me. Some even smiled. Perhaps I didn't have WHORE emblazoned across my forehead after all.

When Sylvia introduced us to Felicity I was surprised to find a white-haired matron proffering her hand. Her lisping telephone voice had led me to expect sixteen going on seventeen, not sixty going on seventy. 'Dinky,' she smiled approvingly, batting black spider lashes. I couldn't think what she meant until she took the camera from me and weighed it in her pudgy hand. And then, straight to business: 'Now several people have promised to say a few words. I don't know whether you want to film them all.'

It was quite fascinating to hear that Baby Jane voice emanating from lips blanket-stitched with coral lipstick and teeth in-filled with tartar. I really had to concentrate hard on what she was asking me, said I probably would and edit it down afterwards. I warned her that there might not be much left by the time we'd finished.

'Oh. Oh, now that *would* be a shame. You mustn't throw it away. It would be the only record we'd have of Daddy's funeral and all the nice people who came. You will let me have a copy before you edit it, won't you?' Nan's elbow was sharp in my ribs, and her eyebrows were meaningful as Felicity turned away to waggle her fingers at some newcomers. Yes, I knew I was being taken for a cheap video, but what could I do? It was a moment before the rheumy eyes were on me again and I realised she hadn't actually stopped talking. The name, Max Zeiler, wafted to me on cashew breath and my heart stopped as I raked the room for him. Please, please, don't let him see me. But she was only saying that it was a pity Max Zeiler couldn't make it. 'That would have been a precious moment – an old comrade's recollections.' I shuddered.

Nan's brows contracted, out of loyalty to me, I thought. 'You weren't going to let *him* speak, were you?'

'It would have been *nice*!' she insisted before plodding off to twitter more baby talk to her guests.

Nan huffed and puffed and Sylvia patted her arm. 'Now, Alice, don't. Douglas wouldn't have wanted you to go into all that. Not here.'

Bloody hell, I thought. *Sylvia* knew – all the sordid details, about me and Max and my undoing in the woods. Nan had told her!

She dabbed her nose, avoiding my eyes. I dabbed at mine, shocked at her betrayal. I'd thought, at least, I could trust my grandmother.

Her poem was touching I had to admit. Called 'One of the Old School', it spoke of Douglas Mallory's kindness and tact and chivalry and it made me cry. Pity she couldn't have taken a leaf out of his book, I thought. I bet Douglas Mallory hadn't gone tittle-tattling to his friends about his nearest and dearest. Where was *her* tact when it mattered?

Then Sylvia waddled up to the front, pale under her rouge, in black Crimplene, but the lectern was miles too high after Nan, and she had to wait while they lowered it, casting a bright and beady eye over the assembled company. Her offering was pure doggerel, but no less moving for that. It told of the day she moved into Westering Park, when Douglas brought her tea and helped her put up her shelves. They'd remained friends ever since, loving companions.

> *'He sorted out my income tax*
> *I cut his hair for free*
> *I even cut his toenails and*
> *He did the same for me.'*

A spotty youth, daring to snigger, was hastily squashed. No one else laughed. The vision of devotion in the latter years was too poignant.

Another verse went like this:

> *Better far than wedlock was*
> *That friendship made in heaven*
> *When Douglas lived downstairs from me*
> *At number twenty-seven.*

When Douglas was safely laid to rest and rain had set in for the afternoon, we all trooped back to his flat, where Felicity had laid on sherry for the ladies and beer for the men, mushroom vol-au-vents and cakes and fancies from Douglas' freezer. Sylvia said he made them every year for the Westering Park Autumn Bazaar. He was a great pastry cook. Felicity had said it was a shame to let them go to waste.

My skin smeared with sweat as the cold kicked in and I felt distinctly spaced out, detached as a CC camera, watching Felicity stroking the leather settee, almost expecting it to purr or whinny. I guessed she was visualising it in her own front room, or that of one of her children. She was probably glad she had insisted on this colour. It was only two years old. Hardly used.

She grated on me – something about the way she smelled

– that smug fragrance of 'musk' with undertones of the real thing. I suspected the dislike was mutual. I knew I was the subject of whispers, as girlie-girlie clusters of guests turned to scrutinise me. God, I thought, suppose she had got wind of . . . Suppose Sylvia had . . .

'Stop glowering,' Nan muttered. We were alone in the conservatory with our butterfly cakes and the rain drumming on the roof. Sylvia had gone off to rummage through Douglas's drawers for his memoirs. She thought I might find them useful.

Glowering? Was I? I was feeling distinctly out of sorts. 'You did swear Sylvia to secrecy, didn't you? About me and – and *him*?'

Her papery brow creased in puzzlement. 'You and who?' She turned down her mouth and shook her head. 'Sorry, Clare, I'm not with you. Is there something I should know?'

Mum hadn't even told her. Oh, my lovely mother! 'I – I – something she said. Sylvia. I thought she . . . Oh, Nan, I'm sorry. I'll tell you about it later.'

'Whatever,' she said, in her modern way, and grinned.

'So,' I blundered on, 'what was it she said you shouldn't go into? It was about him, wasn't it?'

She raised her eyes to heaven and tutted loudly. 'Who, for heaven's sake?'

'Max.'

'Max? What's he been up to?'

'Not now,' I said.

She screwed up her face, eyes, nose and mouth, in an attempt to read my mind and gave up. 'It was nothing,' she said, at last, 'nothing at all. Just that Douglas thought Max Zeiler's brain might have been damaged in transit, as it were.'

'Nan! For fuck's sake! When did he tell you this?' She might have warned me.

But she'd only discovered the old man's doubts when

she and Sylvie had visited him in hospital, last Thursday night. He'd been in good spirits, expecting to be going home the next day. 'We got the impression from the nurses that it had all been a bit of a false alarm. No more than a bout of severe indigestion. He was quite sheepish, in fact, apologising for causing all the kerfuffle.'

'God, that was bad, wasn't it? For them to raise your hopes like that? I mean, it must have been a genuine heart attack. The second one finished him off.'

Her eyes filled with tears. 'I don't understand it, Clare. Before we went for our tea he seemed perfectly fine, sitting up, laughing, looking forward to the writing holiday. He was hoping to talk to someone there about self-publishing his memoirs. He only wanted a few copies, just for family, and friends . . .' her voice caught on a sob, her face crumpled and I held her tight, trying to still the shaking bones. I couldn't help wondering where Max figured in all this. 'Really, Clare,' she said at last, mopping her eyes with a tissue, 'we weren't gone more than twenty minutes and when we came back it was too late. We didn't even get a chance to say goodbye.'

'Oh Nan . . .'

'I don't know,' she said miserably, 'maybe we got him over-excited or something.'

'Oh don't be daft.' The thought of two silver-haired ladies getting the old guy steamed up almost made me smile. 'Talking about getting your memoirs published isn't going to set your heart racing.'

'It was what was *in* the memoirs.'

The war, of course, the Spanish one, where he'd been happiest, most fulfilled, fighting for a cause that was right, helping good people in their struggle against the forces of capitalism. Where Max had been his buddy, his pal, his partner in crime. His recall was so sharp the two old women had been transported into the thick of the battle, back to the smoke and dust and confusion, the crumbling masonry of Madrid's University City. They'd heard the crackle of artillery, the din of aerial bombardment, the curses and insults flung between nationalists and republicans, German voices raised in their version of the 'International.' Max had taught it to Douglas who, in turn, sang it to his hospital visitors, fisting the air in his pyjamas.

The funny thing was, Douglas had said, suddenly serious, that at Nan's party, when he'd reminded Max of this, his friend hadn't remembered at all. And when Sid's one-man picture show had whisked him back to the night he and Max had helped to rescue the Duke of Alba's art treasures from his burning palace, the German had looked politely blank, as though it was all news to him. Try as he might, he really couldn't recall the nightmare of lifting down hundreds of paintings from the smoking walls, some larger than life and twice as heavy, struggling with them through fire and falling masonry and flying bullets, and a constant din of bombs and burglar alarms. Yet it was imprinted on the old man's mind. The volunteers had been exhausted by the end of the night, fit to drop, but thrilled to think that they'd managed to lug all those pictures to safety, saved them for the Spanish nation. It simply wasn't the sort of thing you can forget. 'But they could be blotted out, if the bits responsible for memory – cells or nerves or what have you – had been damaged,' Douglas had said.

'And when you think about it,' said Nan, 'it would be a wonder if they hadn't been, somewhere along the line. Those brains were removed from people's heads sixty years ago, and we don't know what hospital conditions were like then. I mean germs could have got in during the operation, and I know you all say that Hofmann was a good surgeon, but he wasn't Superman; he didn't have computers to help him, and keyhole surgery. He must have got tired, severing all those millions of nerves; he might have got careless, missed a few. At this end, repairing all those nerve endings must have been a hell of a job. And supposing they got it right, made all the right connections, they couldn't put back what had passed between them, the electricity or chemicals or whatever. I mean that could be what memory is. I don't know, I could be wrong, but it seems to me we shouldn't be surprised if he's not firing on all cylinders, your Max.'

'Oh please, not *"my"* Max.' But she wasn't listening.

'And what about freezer burn? I mean, if I leave a piece of cod in the freezer for too long it burns – you can't eat it – and those brains were left for sixty years. Really delicate tissue. It's no wonder the man has blank spots. It's a crime, it really is, letting those brains loose on the world! Utterly irresponsible!' She was working herself up into a right lather.

'But what . . .' I began.

'I said to Douglas, far from bottling it all up, he probably couldn't remember much about the war and didn't like to admit it. Keeping the lid on that little honey must have been very hard. I always did think he was a bad actor. And Douglas agreed.'

I might have mumbled something. Her head came up, her diamond flashing in the brown flare of her nostril.

'And now he's done something to upset you, has he?'

'Mmm,' I nodded, tight-lipped. It was odd to think that at the very moment Nan had been talking in the hospital about Max bottling things up, he'd been spilling his venom into me. Well, maybe not quite at that moment, but soon after. I'd told the police I thought it must have been about ten fifteen when the rape took place; they like to know these things. Douglas had died at nine twenty, so the con-versation round the hospital bed had to have been much earlier, when Max was still stuck on the Central Line in a train going nowhere. So there was nothing odd about it at all. No connection. Except . . .

Something was bugging me. Something I'd missed and couldn't now put my finger on. What was it? I thought back. Pictured the cab sliding into my swirling gin, surreal and green, its flashing indicator light diffused among the ice cubes. Saw the passenger alighting. It must have been around ten when he'd arrived, give or take. And Douglas was already dead. So? I shook my head. What was I trying to fathom? Something . . . My poor befogged mind couldn't deal with lateral leaps today. My ears fuzzed and my forehead clumped over my eyes with Neanderthal throbbing. I held on to the windowsill to steady myself.

'You all right, Clare?' Nan's voice came from a distance.

'Just my cold. A touch of vertigo,' I said, pulling myself back to the here and now. I took a strengthening sip of sherry. 'Nan, you and Douglas, you could be right about M-M-Max . . .' I found I could hardly bear to utter the name, 'About him having some sort of brain damage.' I told her about Susmeta's experiments.

'You've seen the video?' asked Nan.

'Well, no, actually.' I skated around that one. 'But I know it exists.'

'Be careful, Clare.'

'What?'

'If that video were to fall into the wrong hands . . .' Her hooded old eyes held all sorts of dire warnings.

'Oh, I know,' I said hastily, thinking, Oh fuck.

All the same, she thought it unlikely that Susmeta would have risked her job and her reputation by producing flawed work. She'd have made pretty damn sure her creations were as perfect as she could make them. She'd have checked and double-checked for damage. Any damage, including freezer-burn. Which left the shorted electrical circuits theory to explain Max's blank spots. 'Either that or . . .' She hesitated, biting her lip, and her eyes narrowed in thought.

'What?'

But along came Sylvia at that moment, her brow furrowed under her tight new perm. 'I can't think what he's done with them, silly man.'

'What's that, dear?' Felicity had materialised beside us, with a plate of fairy cakes.

'Your father's memoirs. The drawer's empty.'

She wrinkled her nose in distaste. 'All that old stuff about the war? I threw it out. Nobody's going to want to read all that.'

We gasped in horror. Sylvia's mouth opened and closed soundlessly.

'That was his life's work, Felicity!' Nan scolded her.

She flounced, a petulant teenager. 'You can't hang on to every old scrap of paper. Good Lord, whatever for? Boxes and boxes of old toot he had, just gathering dust in his wardrobe. Labour Party pamphlets and union bumph. Legacy of a misspent youth,' she tittered. 'It would give quite the wrong impression to people thinking of buying the house. No, I sorted out the insurance policies and put the rest out for the bin men.'

'They haven't . . .?' I asked.

'Yesterday,' mourned Sylvia.'

'But, Felicity,' snapped Nan, 'he was hoping to get them printed up – for the grandchildren.'

'You're joking! Never known to open a book, my kids. No it's all computers and telly these days. You have to move with the times.' And, so saying, she shoved a fairy cake between her coral lips.

'More sherry, ladies?' It was Felicity's husband, Gus, with the decanter. 'You're all very serious out here? Why don't you come inside and talk to people? I'd like you to meet my son, Clare. Rob has this really exciting screen-play . . .'

We ignored them and tried to placate Sylvia who was having difficulty holding back the tears. 'I'll never forgive her. Never!'

'Let's get out of here,' Nan suggested.

We made our excuses and went up with Sylvia. Sid's picture was on the landing, looking too big and too loud. Two of the funeral guests were trying to make sense of it.

'What do you think? Worth a few bob, is it?' the man asked Nan, who cocked an eyebrow sceptically. She knew her son.

The woman said, 'They tell me he erected it from the wreckage of an earlier piece.'

'Overnight,' I confirmed. 'No sweat.'

'So would that make it 'found' art?'

'More like 'opportunist' art,' I said, as it dawned on me why he had rushed to fix the contraption to the wall on hearing of Douglas's death.

'*Really?*'

'It's not for sale, is it? Now old Doug's passed on.'

'No,' said Sylvia, bravely. 'It's not for sale. But I'm sure Mr. Russell takes commissions, doesn't he, Clare?'

'Oh absolutely,' I said. 'Isn't that what it's all about?'

23

Ellen Sauerbruch huddles deep into a fireside chair, its seating worn saggy by hundreds of noble backsides, its carved arms buffed to a shine by generations of idle hands. Opposite, in its twin, Lady Titherille gently snores, overcome by the wine at luncheon and the warmth of the wood-burning stove.

Chaotic images rear against Ellen's eyelids – a dark figure in the driver's cab, horrified whites of eyes, crowds of shocked faces, the sole of Sophie's sandal, a poster advertising insurance. Whatever sounds she made as she fell were swallowed up in a whinnying of brakes, metal on metal, in the shouts and screams, but Ellen heard them, hears them still. As she drifts into sleep there's the sudden in-drawn moan of fear, the clatter of a ricocheting umbrella, the crackle of plastic, the crunch of bone, the hiss of burning flesh. And her head jerks up, her heart hammering against her ribs.

She tells herself that the woman was old, living on borrowed time. The Nazis killed thousands, millions like her, and not so kindly. It had to be done, for his sake. But her finger-pads still tingle with the touch of flesh, warm and slack under rainwear, and the sweet smell of melting plastic follows her everywhere, spoiling everything.

He, too, is out of sorts, preoccupied and snappish. Understandably so: the waiting is over. Providing everything goes to plan they will soon realise their dream.

They are attentive, the old couple. They take her for walks when the weather permits, entertain her with tales of lords and ladies, teach her croquet and English history.

They give her the freedom of the library, the run of the music room, but how can she concentrate when her whole life is about to change?

After the storms of the past few days, bleak north westerlies stalk the fields around Ottley Place, picking up small dried leaves and seeds and husks and sending them scudding under the door and across the parquet flooring to snuggle into the fringes of an elderly rug. Ellen can only tuck her trouser ends in her socks, pull the collar of her sweater around her ears and think of the life to come.

She does not belong here, in this rarefied climate of manners and strained English vowels, though this room, in the draughty west wing of the house, provides a home for misfits of all kinds, everything that is unfit for the public gaze. Among the ancient typewriters, wirelesses and black Bakelite telephones, the untidy boxes of papers, is a large signed photograph of Adolf Hitler, a drooping flag bearing the sign of the swastika – a throwback, like herself, to an era best forgotten. The two old people seem comfortable here and thrilled beyond measure that once again the ancestral home is to play a part in history.

Things will be different, she tells herself, when she is beautiful again, when she can be herself and usefully employed. In the meantime she has too much time on her hands – to think, to brood, about ugliness and ugly deeds.

Last night they had all sat down to watch the stolen video, though the old man soon excused himself with paper work, and Edith fell asleep, as the scrupulous precision of laser surgery and Susmeta Naidoo's fluting commentary left them far behind. Ellen had not altogether understood what was happening, as streams of magnified cells whirled across a computer screen, but found it impossible to look away. When some imperfection or dysfunction was picked up by the technology, the Indian would pause in her journey through her patient's cerebellum to effect repairs, with almost invisible fibrous instruments. Nerves were connected, blockages cleared, electrical and chemical events set in motion, without a hand touching the patient.

Wartime surgery was never like this. Ellen could only marvel as the clumsy handiwork of the Nazi surgeons was made good. They could never have imagined when they froze the brains how their craft would have to be refined, how a mastery of mechanical arts and applied science would be necessary before the impossible could be made actual. But what faith they had had! What hope! As the camera moved away from the computer screen to a wider shot of the operating table, her heart had missed a beat. The patient was a woman! It was *her* body lying there – the body they had saddled her with. She reached for his hand, but he was too engrossed to respond.

The surgeon announced that she had one more repair to make, to the *substantia nigra,* which, she said, was suffering from dopamine deficiency. Left untreated the patient would return to the world suffering from advanced Parkinson's Disease. Ellen sat up staring, as the screen now filled with the moustache-shaped area. It was pale and it should have been black, coloured by melanin in the cells. He rewound the tape a metre or two and played it again.

'I do not understand,' she cried, no less puzzled on seeing the evidence a second time. 'I had no symptoms. When they took my brain it was perfectly healthy. My hands were steady.'

As if the camera had heard her it now focused on the patient's hands: Ellen's hands were visibly shaking with a sort of palsy.

He said, a sort of triumph in his voice, '*She* did that to you, my love. She destroyed the cells herself.'

'What!'

'You were expendable, *liebling*. We all were. She *gave* you Parkinson's Disease.'

'Why?' she managed to gasp.

'So that she could cure you. It is illegal to experiment on living patients. You were a convenient resource.'

Cautiously, Ellen stretched her fingers. Graceless and stubby they might be but they were steady as rock. Somehow Naidoo had managed it.

They were transfixed by the wonder of it, by the horror, as the surgeon continued to undo the harm she had done. Using her computer, and suction, she extracted special 'stem cells' from the frontal lobes. Neural stem cells, she explained to her students, have the special property of being able to mimic the development occurring naturally around them. 'They dance to the tune they hear,' she said. The theory was that, transferred to the damaged part of the brain they would think they were *substantia nigra* cells, divide and produce dopamine as cells in that region should.

'And when she woke up the Parkinson's was gone,' he smiled, indulgent as a father telling bedtime stories. Even so, she couldn't help fingering her skull, over the seat of the trouble. 'You realise what it means, my love?'

'Oh yes,' she said bitterly. 'Not content with giving me the face and body of a Neanderthal . . .'

'Not for much longer.'

'The bitch damn near made me a cripple into the bargain.'

'More importantly,' he said, 'she cured the disease. The woman is a genius. She is also ruthless in the pursuit of research – and we have the video to prove it. If the British medical authorities discover that she has been tinkering with patients' brains, taking them apart in the hope that she can put them back together again, like a clever child with an old clock, she will be struck off their register. Have no fear, you will be in safe hands, sweetheart.'

Ellen is not convinced, even now. The English have an adage: *You may bring a horse to water but you cannot make him*

322

drink. Suppose Naidoo is not sufficiently swayed by the threat of exposure to perform the operation? Suppose she allows the knife to slip? A shudder passes through her, as it did last night, when he had put his arm round her, squeezed her. 'Don't worry, *liebling*, soon you will be beautiful again.'

Please God. She must be rid of this frightful body before anyone remembers the chatty Jewish woman on the train and that other passenger who stared at reflections. And surely someone standing on the platform will recall a flurry of movement to which their eyes were drawn, surely they will have that dumpy foreign woman in a raincoat etched in their memory, the one who turned away from the disaster and fought her way through the craning crowd and out into the corridor? Someone was bound to have seen the fear on her face as she ran, helter-skelter, up the stairs to safety, is sure to connect her with a newspaper story, or a television piece. Ellen must disappear, her husk destroyed in a hospital incinerator. In her new disguise they will never find her. How wonderful to be sweet and young again, to be able to wear the silliest clothes and shoes, to have the looks he loves – she almost faints with longing.

Not long now. Things are already slotting into place. Lord Titherille had only to pay a visit to the man's workshop and flatter him a little, to have him netted and landed. He told him that he had visited Trimble's Gallery the week before and that he and Lady Titherille had been bowled over by the paintings. He was anxious to commission work. It might be helpful if Mr. Russell were to visit Ottley Place to see what he could use and to get a feel of the place. Why not come to lunch tomorrow?

Accordingly a van had trundled up the drive this morning and Ellen had been surprised to see a man in his early fifties being shown into the sitting room.

Somehow, from the way William had spoken about him and his strange lifestyle, she'd thought he would be younger.

But though he wore the ponytail and earrings of youth, his skin was weathered and his sideburns and unshaven chin were dusted with grey. He wore a shirt without a collar, a green corduroy jacket, yellow trousers and brown suede shoes. Clearly he wasn't a gypsy, more a striker of poses. She suppresses a smile. The new occupant of *his* body will have no difficulty playing this part, though the frugal life style might be temporarily daunting.

The visitor's braying appreciation had echoed down the staircase, as William showed him around. As he strutted into the dining room after his tour he was still raving about the family portraits, the edifying religious scenes and the landscapes. He actually seemed to know something about the paintings and their history.

'That anonymous job on the stairs,' he ventured, 'obviously Dutch – looks to me like it might be cut from a larger painting. Puts me in mind of Van Swaneveldt. He tended to do those lush Italian landscapes. Not that he ever went to Italy, of course. Painted in Paris and made them up. Well, why not? If you can get away with it?'

Over luncheon he told them that he had been a teacher in a large London comprehensive school for nearly twenty years. He trumpeted, 'Couldn't face another bloody Ofsted inspection, so I packed it in. "Call yourself an artist, Russell?" I said to myself. "Get out there, man, and bloody paint." Not that the wife was any too pleased. Threw me out, bag and baggage. But what can you do? Well, you only have one life!'

They had all looked at each other over forkfuls of quiche. One life and a short one, in his case, all being well. But the rest of them are hoping for at least one life more. Immortality, in fact. It all depends on the success of the mission this evening.

William has clearly taken to the man. It is late in the afternoon when his lordship comes in for his tea, having just seen his visitor off the premises. He closes the door on a flurry of leaves. 'He really does have some splendid ideas, you know. We should have called him in years ago or someone like him. Now you would know, Edith, m'dear, do we have a round shield tucked away somewhere? He's suggesting we make a feature in the armoury. Two dozen swords or so and daggers and suchlike, bristling like bulrushes around a shield would be rather eye-catching, don't you think? And he says he can do something rather splendid with the model trains at no extra charge.'

'No extra charge?' said his wife, concentrating hard on dissecting a jam sponge, 'William, the poor man isn't going to live long enough to lift a paintbrush. All this is merely so that he can explain his absence to his nearest and dearest.'

'I had to appear convincing. He'd expect me to haggle,' William mutters, peevishly. 'It wouldn't have hurt to delay things a week or two while Russell made us a piece for the front hall.'

Lady Edith is exasperated. 'You don't even like his work. "Phoney" and "passé" is how you described it, as I recall. It wouldn't be fair, in any case.'

'What wouldn't?' said William through a mouthful of cake.

'Having him do all that work for nothing. It's rather like stealing.'

'Goddammit, woman,' spluttering crumbs, 'it's hardly cricket, removing the man's brain! Hardly the last word in honourable behaviour.'

'And doesn't it worry you, William?'

'Of course it worries me, but it has to be done. I thank God that I have never shirked my duty, no matter how distasteful. If by one man's death we can save the world then so be it. Does anyone want that last piece of cake?'

William's man stops the BMW mid-terrace, and is attentive as they step out into the street. The very fabric of the tall,

Georgian houses breathes money and conservatism. Elegant railings and steps bring them to a door and a shiny brass keyhole into which he fits his key. This was Max's home, of course. He is easy here. Perhaps Ellen should have let him manage the business on his own, and not have insisted on coming too. But she is curious to meet her maker, the woman who deformed her. She steels herself as strange tinny music wafts out into the vestibule.

'It's you!' The Indian woman, half-naked in a silky plum sari, pads barefoot, from one of several cream-painted doors. She is flushed as she claws at his shoulders, her painted brow damp with exertion. She pecks at his cheek and her bare midriff brushes his shirtfront. 'I thought you said you'd be away. And who's this? Ellen Sauerbruch!'

Such a *little* hand takes hers. Warm and soft and sinewy, it is almost too small for the skill it possesses, the knowledge, the power to give life, take it away. With difficulty, Ellen resists an urge to squeeze that hand until the bones crack, until they are crushed to dust. She can scarcely contain her hatred, can scarcely smile.

'Good heavens, my dear! They've been looking all over for you,' the surgeon says, and Ellen's heart jumps. So soon? 'They need you for a film, you know.' She affects interest, hopes it conceals her relief. 'Where did you find her, Max? Does Clare know? Oh do come in. Please.'

They are shown into a large, high-ceilinged room giving onto a garden. Ellen's first impression is of soft lighting, a marble tiled floor, pale linen and green foliage. Gradually the brilliant rugs swim into focus, the cushions patterned with elephants, the fretwork and carving, the jade Buddha before whom joss sticks burn, giving off a sensuous and mystic perfume, the rippling music, and her nostrils flare with revulsion. Primitive idolatry – for all her western trappings the Indian cannot conceal her roots.

'I'll just . . .' The woman picks up a remote control and

stops the music, slips on a pair of gold pumps. She has been dancing, and not merely for her own amusement. There are two glasses on the low table, a dish of olives, and movement as an elbow then a face appear round the back of a large armchair.

'Axel,' she cries, 'look who's here! Or perhaps you don't recognise them. Max Zeiler and Ellen Sauerbruch.'

It is the pianist, Schlager, a contorted smile on his face as he rises to greet them. It isn't that the chair is enormous, but that he is slight, clownishly small. She can almost feel sorry for him. From the tall and willowy concert pianist, bowing to rapturous applause, he is reduced to this. No wonder he is anxious as she is for another transplant. They exchange pitying glances but avoid shaking hands.

Pouring them drinks and plying them with questions, Susmeta Naidoo is the perfect hostess, but Ellen, attuned to her tormentor by dint of long fascination, discerns agitation in her movements. The queen of the operating theatre, cool and self-assured, now appears unsure of her ground. Her eyes are hot and furtive, her hands fluttery. She is embarrassed that they have come upon her entertaining Schlager, dancing for him.

'Sit down, Susmeta.'

They are all startled by his abrupt tone.

'Max?' She is suddenly aware that this is not a social visit, but a conspiracy. Her ears prick back in alarm. 'What is it?' Her doe's eyes dart from one to the other. 'What's the matter?'

'*Sit down!*' he barks, his eyes blazing, giving her a push, and she does so, cowering, averting her face almost in shame. Schlager draws himself to his full ridiculous height. 'Steady on,' he warns, and Ellen, too, is puzzled at this display of anger and her reaction. And all at once she knows. This is why he has been so grouchy. He didn't want to leave Bayswater and his home comforts. He is jealous of Schlager, wants the woman for himself!

She sits down heavily on the edge of the settee, picks up her glass of schnapps. Greedily she sips, swallows, welcoming the prickling alcohol, eager for it to dull the hurt, blot out her fears. Schlager takes his cue from her and raises what is left of his drink in a silent toast. Their glasses click as they set them down on the table.

'You will come with us, Susmeta.'

'Come where?' The clever hands are gripping the arms of the chair, prepared to hang onto them at all costs.

'Just come. There is work to do.'

'What do you mean?'

It is incredible that she really does not know, when Max and she have talked about nothing else for so long. Surely this woman, so integral to the scheme, must have some inkling?

'You are going to perform a brain transplant operation. One that is long overdue.' He nods in Ellen's direction.

Her brow furrows prettily. 'What the hell are you talking about?'

He shakes his head, a sneer playing around his lips. 'No, you really cannot see it, can you? So immersed in self, so totally without pity. This was once a beautiful woman, Susmeta. Fair skinned and graceful. And you have condemned her to this – existence.'

Ellen blinks as her deformity is shaped by words, made flesh. She glares at the surgeon through hot tears of misery, and says, 'How would you feel, Mrs Naidoo, if someone had done this to you?'

The frown deepens. 'But I – I had no idea you felt like this.'

'What *did* you think, Mrs Naidoo?' she says boldly. 'That I was a prisoner of the Nazis, used and abused by them, and should therefore be grateful for anything, for your gracious gift of life?

The Indian breathes deeply before replying. 'I suppose . . . No.' She closes her eyes, briefly. 'It wasn't even that, my dear. Surgery is my passion, my life. You cannot possibly understand. I simply wanted to perform *surgery.*'

Ellen bristles. The condescending tone is more than she can bear but his scowling face tells her now is not the time to tell her so.

She is explaining that a female donor became available, a match for the frozen female brain – '*My* female brain!' Ellen wants to scream – and that was all that concerned her. 'Medically, she was perfect: the right blood type, the right age, and her physical health was excellent. What she looked like was of no importance. I was simply anxious to get on with the operation.' She glances up and softly says, 'I'm sorry.'

'Well, now you have a chance to put things right.'

'You want me to transplant the Sauerbruch brain into a new body?'

The Sauerbruch brain. Ellen sags. Yes, that is how the surgeon regards her – as an object, a brain, to be fitted into a skull and made to function. It's *that* impersonal. As impersonal as a flowerpot to a potter.

'You have a donor?'

He nods.

'I take it this is all part of Lord Titherille's crazy scheme.'

'Titherille is involved, yes, and Saint Meredith's.'

'Money has changed hands?'

'It has.'

'Pity.' She breathes hard through her nose. 'I'm not interested, Max. I told Titherille before. These operations have to have the seal of government approval. They have to be logged and approved by the proper authorities. Otherwise I could lay myself open to all sorts of trouble. As could any surgeons I train. All sorts of ne'er-do-wells could abuse the system, criminals wanting to escape detection . . .' Ellen bites her lip. 'No I'm sorry. I do commiserate, Fraulein, but unless you go through the proper channels I can't help you.'

'I think you will, Susmeta.' His face is impassive as he slips his hand into his jacket pocket and Naidoo gasps, thinking, perhaps, that he has a gun. Ellen wonders, not for the first time, whether a gun might have been more effective, but he was so sure. The video had somehow fallen into his hands and he was determined to use it.

As he tells Susmeta what it contains, what he and Ellen have seen, what the BMA and other interested bodies would no doubt consider compulsive viewing, a nerve jumps in the surgeon's hand, knocking the empty glass. It rolls off the table and smashes onto the unforgiving marble floor, as her face sets hard.

Yes, a gun might have been more persuasive.

24

My first day back was awful.

Nick blanked me at every turn. Whenever I passed his desk, he was glued to his computer screen or buried in a drawer. If we met in the corridor he just walked on by, leaving me staring after him, bottom lip wobbling. I didn't know what to do.

Jay said I was trying too hard. 'Chill out,' was his advice. 'He'll come round. You guys are an item.' Tell him that, I thought, next time he's chatting up the producer's new secretary – some twelve-year old with a blonde crop and big boobs, who bats her eyelashes like she thinks he's the best thing to happen since she passed her typing exam. And I'd brought it on myself; that was the galling thing. I'd betrayed him. He clearly hadn't gone for my falling-over-a-tree-stump story.

The documentary had died a death. One minute it was there on the bulletin board: *Buchenwald 5 – rehearsal – Studio 4 – 12.00 pm.* Then it wasn't. The slot was gone.

I was running around headless. I had a corridor full of drama students got up as Spanish freedom fighters, practising their glottal aspirates, and no one could give me a room or reasons. I got, 'Oh, don't know how that happened, you'd better see Barry', 'Not now, Clare, I'm run off my fucking feet' and 'Been a bit of a cock-up, has there, chicken?' Like it was down to me.

Barry could barely drag his eyes away from the blonde waif and muttered something about the sponsors withdrawing the funding – just like that. He didn't know why. Best go and see Colin, who'd be in a meeting all afternoon. Oh, and could I distribute these NO SMOKING leaflets?

Make sure everybody got one. Management was coming down on us like a ton of bricks since Maintenance had reported ashes in the bin. Anyone infringing the rules from now on was likely to find herself out of a job.

Meanwhile Kate was doing her drama queen bit, back-of-hand to brow. She felt so *responsible,* dragging all these busy people half way across London. They'd learned their lines, ransacked wardrobe, attic and charity shop, hung about all day without a bite to eat and for what? At least they were entitled to a day's pay and travelling expenses. They were act-*ors*, for heavens' sake, with union cards! My own sister this was, who, carried away by her own histrionics, flounced off, never to speak to me again.

I mean, a bit of sympathy wouldn't have come amiss. I'd had a rotten day, sneezing fit to bust and, with a head full of cotton wool, had no idea what was going on. I was hardly any wiser when I eventually got in to see Colin. Apparently one of the shareholders had objected to the way I was handling the material.

'What!'

'I warned you, Clare, no tub-thumping. This guy reckons your viewpoint is way too biased. I mean face it, girl, we're all Tories now, aren't we? We don't want to alienate every viewer in the land.'

'Tories?' I gasped. 'I don't *think* so.' Then it struck me. 'That shareholder – it's Titherille, isn't it? Jesus, I might have known!'

He wouldn't say, but it didn't take a genius to work out the Max connection. I'd wondered about their meeting in the Kings' Road. If Kate hadn't bumped into them he'd probably have kept quiet about it. He must have forged ties with the old bastard on our visit to Ottley Place and appealed to him now in desperation. Taken him up on his kind offer of patronage. I wondered if that also meant he was keeping his side of the bargain: trying to persuade Susmeta to play her part in the old boy's brain transplant scheme. And the penny dropped, setting the rusty cogs and wheels of my fuddled brain in motion. Of course! That's where the video would come in handy – for a tasty bit of blackmail. Oh bugger, and I'd handed it to him on a plate. Dumped poor Susmeta right in it.

Now Titherille was helping him to get his own back on me and it wasn't fair! But there was nothing I could say or do to sway Colin. It was out of his hands. Somehow I was going to have to break it to the crew that all we'd done so far – the research and the filming, the late nights spent down in the editing suite – had all been a waste of time and effort. I managed to get a token payment for my 'extras', as he insisted on calling them, but I emerged from his office in tears, like so many other directors before me.

In fact, having the project scrapped from under me probably saved me a lot of grief, though I would never have admitted it. It had been getting thinner and thinner. All my 'talking heads' had either died or gone walkabout; not only Sauerbruch and now Max, – I'd heard today that poor Willi Greff had been carted off by men in white coats. He was recuperating in a Salzburg sanatorium from a 'stress-related' illness. That was all they would tell me.

And then Susmeta phoned.

'Oh Mrs Khan, hi . . . I'm glad I caught you.' Her voice had that edgy sound you get on a mobile.

'You've come through to Clare, I'm afraid, but I'm glad I've caught you. Have you got a moment?' In spite of her *'Not really . . .'* I told her about Kate bumping into Max and Titherille in the Kings' Road, about Titherille's scheme for privatising the brain operation, about the video. I was about to tell her how between them they'd lost me my job when she interrupted.

'Yes, yes, Mrs Khan – it's most regrettable – but something unexpected has come up in that connection. It means I'm having to cancel all appointments for a week or more.'

'What's with the Mrs Khan thing? It's me, Clare.'

'I do realise that, Mrs Khan, but please try and understand.'

'Oh my God – he's there, isn't he? Listening to this?'

'That's right – a frightful nuisance, but there we are.'

'Jesus Christ! He hasn't hurt you?'

'No, not at all – and in the meantime, Mrs Khan, we have to think what to do about your father.'

'My father?' My brain was as stuffed as my nose. What was she on about?

'To be honest, Mrs Khan, I'm really quite concerned about his blood condition. I'm afraid it'll mean an operation if we don't act quickly.'

Blood condition? 'Sorry, I didn't quite . . .' And then it dawned. 'An operation? Oh my God! They're going to use Sid for a transplant! Whose brain? Oh no! Not Friedrich Liebl?'

'Just so, Mrs Khan.'

They were the thieves, Max and Titherille! No, maybe not Titherille – I couldn't see him climbing through hospital windows. That was more a job for his bullyboys, who had somehow managed to steal a swipe card. Jesus Christ, what a mess! And now they were ready to transplant, they had a donor, and it was my fault. I'd told Max about Sid's AB negative, hadn't I? I *told* him!

'Yes, exactly,' she said kindly and, in her best bedside manner, listened to my teeth chattering and various profanities as I attempted to hold my mind together after her bombshell. *'Perhaps you could put . . . in the pic . . .'* She was breaking up.

'What? I can't *hear* you! Oh Sid!' I cared, of course I cared. 'Susmeta? Are you there? Susmeta?' But the line had gone dead.

Sid wasn't answering his phone, either. Maybe they'd got to him already. Oh Sid . . . What to do? What to do? Everyone had gone home.

'Cla-are.' Mrs Robinson smiled weakly, putting her face round the door and flushing deep red. 'Out in the rain, dear? You'd better come . . . Well, no, actually, I – I don't know if he's in. I'll just go and see.' She said this over the roar of a stadium, the hysterical gabbling of a commentator and my beloved's voice egging on his side. 'Go on, go on, never mind him! Oof! Nice one. That's the way! Yes, yes, Ye-e-ess!'

'Excuse me,' I said, barging past his mum and into the front room where Nick was kicking his heels like a baby boy, nuzzling a can of beer and chortling with glee. I'd timed it badly. His face fell when he saw me.

'What?' He hardly flicked his eyes from the screen as some earless thug in a red shirt skidded on his chin over a white chalk mark in the rain.

'Switch it off,' I said.

'You what!

'You've got to help me.'

'Go and find some other sucker to do your dirty work,' he snarled. 'I've put in for a transfer.' His eyes were hard lumps of coal, wanting to hurt me as I'd hurt him. My sweet smiling boy of a week ago was long gone. This was some other.

'It isn't research. It isn't for me. It's for my dad and Susmeta.' His eyes were dead now – burnt out – his surliness complete. I forestalled the next 'Fuck off!' 'Hear me out, Nick. Please . . .'

I told him, over the defiantly burbling telly, that Max had stolen a video that incriminated Susmeta.

'Was this before or after you fucked him?'

'Forget it,' I growled, over a throat full of tears. 'This is no good.' I stumbled across the room. He continued to sit, staring at the screen, hunched into his self-absorption and hate. 'People's lives are at stake, you moron!'

I'd already slammed the front door when he came after

me, stopped me at the gate. The rain slid down my cheeks like tears. 'You say people are in danger?' This was his news hound's nose twitching, not his heart.

'My dad, for one. He's AB negative. Like Friedrich Liebl.'

There was a wafer-thin pause. 'Come back in,' he said.

'There's no time, Nick. Come on. We've got to warn him.'

'I'll drive, you talk.'

This time he listened. The phone call to Susmeta was fresh in my mind and it just spilled out, a nasal rant about videos and Mrs Khan and her father's blood condition. 'We've got to tell the police!'

'Whoa!' He was shaking his head, quickly, like a chemist shaking a phial, trying to get some of the words to gel, make sense. 'Slow down, for God's sake, woman. Start at the beginning. It'll be quicker in the long run.'

I stared at the windscreen, now clear, now blurred. Now or never. Truth or lies.

'Well?' He was waiting.

Mum had told me not to. Was she right? For all her kindness and wisdom, she'd lost her man. The lorry in front distorted with raindrops, its shape amorphous and confused; then, with a swish, it was sharp and bright, sparkling with clarity. The metronomic beat of the wipers kept time with my heart, my shallow breathing, my indecision. Oh hell, what did I have to lose?

The beginning, he'd said. Where was that?

I should have trusted my instincts, I told him. I hadn't liked Max at first, I'd found him cold and remote, but the more I learned about him, the things he'd done, the more I was drawn to him, this lonely, fascinating man who had been through hell. And when he showed a bit of interest in me, it turned my head, as Nan might say. I fell for his story first, not his looks, which I knew were nothing to do with him, nor his olde-worlde manners which he hid behind, but for that coat that he trailed, of heroism. I wanted my

336

film to plumb his depths; I wanted me to be the one that broke down his defences.

Nick murmured something I didn't catch.

'What?'

He shrugged, looking grim. I thought it might have been 'Bollocks'. He was steering deaf, dumb and blind past the lorry's spray, a drenching, drumming wash of surface water and sheeting rain. When we were through I said it was a bit like what I'd felt for Max – that emotional Big Dipper, crush, infatuation that had suddenly hit me. Now I was out the other side and it was over but, while I was in there, I couldn't think straight. I hadn't considered consequences, hadn't thought that far ahead.

It *was* 'Bollocks' he'd said. He said it again.

I said, 'I'm trying to be honest here,' and slumped into a depression.

He said, 'You were gagging for it.'

'Not *gagging* . . . I didn't know *what* I wanted.'

'Yeah, you did. Try harder.'

I sighed. 'Well, I suppose I wanted a fling, a bit of excitement. I'd had a lousy day with Barry. You were in my bad books – I mean you were such a bully . . .'

'A bully?'

'Yeah, making me go up that mountain. And then . . . and then . . . Well, you were always right, such a know-all and I . . .'

He said something like Tch!

'Plus I was more than a little lagered.'

He made a pretence of waiting, then, 'Anything else?'

'What?'

'Aren't you going to wheel out the old PMT, while you're at it?'

'Oh all *right*,' I snapped, 'I was up for it. At first. I soon changed my mind. It was horrible, Nick, really horrible.'

A sound escaped his lips, a cross between choking and scornful laughter.

'No really. Jay reckons it was rape.'

'Jay? Fuck, you told *Jay*?'

'And the police.'

'Jesus.'

I told him that, pissed or not, I'd soon realised I'd made a terrible mistake. Max was hateful, snarling, smacking me around, and . . . Well, he'd treated me like some sort of animal. It was vile, nasty. I'd begged him to stop but it was too late – he wouldn't. Or couldn't.

I told Nick Nan's theory about memory being an electrical charge or something that had got lost in the mending process, but that I didn't rule out brain damage of a more substantial kind. Max was so different from the man the Nazis had captured, who'd married a Jewish girl he didn't really love, just to save her from Auchwitz, who'd fought for the right of Spanish socialists to set up collectives, who'd risked his life to get Jews out of Germany. The guy we knew was a thief and a blackmailer, not to mention rapist. This guy was more likely to support fascism than take a stand against it. And anyone who could think about murder in such a cold premeditated way had to be mad. 'I mean, it wouldn't occur to a normal person to kill my poor old dad just to bring some defunct old German back to life.'

He didn't answer.

I related, more calmly, the details of Susmeta's phone call. I guessed she'd made it on her mobile from a car (the 'breaking up' must have been when it had gone into a tunnel), pretending that she had to break an appointment with Mrs Khan in order to allay concern about her absence. I explained the Titherille connection, how Ellen Sauerbruch had signed up to his cryonics scheme, how I'd found out that she and Max had been seeing each other.

My sweet boy hadn't said a word for ages, all through that whole degrading confession. While I stared out at the speeding North Circular, I could feel the distance between us quivering as it widened. I knew the moment when his breathing changed, when he adjusted his specs, when his grip on the steering wheel threatened to break it, when the muscles of his stomach moved with revulsion. I could smell his misery and disgust. When I dared to look, he was squinting through the rain, as though focusing on some tiny speck in the far, far distance.

Oh well, I thought, that's that. I should have listened to Mum.

'I wonder . . .' said Nick, finding his voice after industrial throat clearing. He cuffed his nose. 'Fuck.'

'What!'

'Suppose – suppose this guy isn't Max Zeiler at all.'

I couldn't help it – I snorted with laughter. And then I thought about it. Jesus. I supposed, I guessed, it *was* possible. Perfectly possible. They could have mixed up the labels or something. No, no, silly, there was his relationship with Ellen Sauerbruch. *She* wouldn't be fooled by any pretender. Unless they . . . Of course they could both be . . . Oh hell, where were my suspicions leading me? To a strange idea, which I shared with Nick – that they could both be impostors. 'Yeah,' I said slowly, 'you're right, 'cause they are definitely in cahoots. It's like they might have planned the whole thing, I mean, it's a crazy idea, wanting to be part of a freezing programme, but hey, Titherille wanted to do it, and there are plenty of others in cryonics schemes. Maybe there were these two lovers who heard about what Hofmann was doing and thought they might just beat the death thing by pretending to be Max Zeiler and Ellen Sauerbruch.'

He looked at me then, and I looked at him. 'Nah.' We shook our heads in unison. It was a preposterous idea. But it wouldn't leave us alone.

If they were impostors, we both agreed, it would be

have been really annoying to have old friends and family turning up who could blow their cover. Luckily, Ellen had no one, but Max had had Berthe and Sophie. Both of whom had been silenced.

'And . . .' I could hardly form the words. I swallowed. 'And what about Douglas Mallory?'

'But he had a heart attack . . .'

'Did he, though? Nan said the first one was a false alarm. He was talking and laughing, when she saw him, looking forward to going home. He should never have died. Shit, I mean I actually pointed Max in the right direction, told him where to find him.'

Saying that, I knew what it was I'd missed before. That night at the pub, the cab had pulled into my gin and tonic *from the left!* It had been the *right* indicator I'd seen flashing across the ice cubes. That BMW, probably no more a cab than my little Panda, probably Titherille's chauffeur-driven limo, had been heading *towards* Woodford, when it had pulled across the road to the Chain and Sprocket, and stopped to let Max out on the driver's side. If Max had left the train at Woodford as he'd said, and picked up a cab from there, the car would have been facing *the other way*. Max had come from Harlow, from the hospital! He'd killed Douglas and made it look like a heart attack.

'My God,' Nick said shakily. 'These people really are dangerous.'

'No one even queried the cause of death. He was that good. You see,' I said, making a sudden tangential leap, 'if they were prisoners, how come they knew so much about Max and Ellen. I mean they had their history off pat.'

'Like they'd had access to their files.'

I said, 'They are, aren't they?'

'What, Nazis, you mean?'

'Mmm.'

'I think so.'

'You don't think they could be –?'

'Hofmann and Weiss?'

'Mmm.'

'Can't be. Hofmann and Weiss were killed in the uprising,' he said. 'Their bodies were found, heads bashed in, brains dripping out.'

'Both of them?' I said, chewing my nail. 'Just a tad suspicious, wouldn't you say? I bet nobody thought to check that it was *their* brains.'

'Bloody hell.'

'Nick, they could have got other medics on the project to remove their brains, weeks, months before, when it looked like they'd lost the war. All they had to do was add them to the Berlin cache and put the bodies into cold storage. Then, when they knew the Yanks were on their way, their cronies tossed the bodies out into the camp, complete with brains. Any brains would have done, sheep, pig . . .' Another, more horrible option suggested itself to me, but I didn't dwell on it.

'Leaving the revolutionaries to take the blame,' Nick mused.

'Shit.'

I sat for a while, blinking at the windscreen, thoughts and images whirling about inside my head as I tried to fathom the man. He'd been so keen for me to make the documentary. What had that been about? Establishing his alias? Getting back to Germany? What was there for him? Just the opportunity to kill Berthe, or something else? And the letter? Why was he so keen to get his hands on that? After all, *he* must have written the damn thing. He must know its contents better than anybody. My ears rang with concentration but I wasn't getting anywhere.

I tried Sid's number again. He still wasn't answering.

'Nick, can't you go any faster?'

'Feeling suicidal, are we? Join the club.'

I clenched my teeth, muttering, 'Sorry.' I'd asked for that. Driving conditions were treacherous, but the journey was taking so *long*, and who knows what was happening to my dad. Without warning I burst into tears. He stiffened but fought against his better nature – didn't even give me a hanky.

'If you will go gabbing off to all and sundry about your dad's blood group . . .'

'Oh piss off.' I'd never forgive myself if Sid died, and he knew it. But he had to have his little dig. We were still not speaking when we reached Walthamstow. Then I had to direct him to Wood Street and the covered market.

It was still raining as we pulled up beside the park. The swings were deserted, the playground a wasteland of wet leaf litter and crisp packets. We ducked out of the car and fled across the road, but the market was locked up. They'd all gone home.

'They've got him, haven't they?' Misery crumpled my face. 'Oh Daddy, my Daddy . . .'

He stared at me, breathing hard, rain streaking his glasses. 'Don't,' he growled. 'Don't give in, for fuck's sake.'

'But what are we going to do?' I wailed.

'Not a lot, not on our own.' His teeth dragged at his lip. 'We're gonna have to go to the cops.'

'We don't have time, Nick,' I moaned, cuffing my snot. 'They could be operating right now! Removing his brain. My poor dad. We've got to stop them.'

'Come on,' he took my elbow and steered me, firmly, back to the car. Once we were moving again and I'd blown my nose thoroughly, he said. 'What's that geezer going out with your mum, Clare? The romantic novelist. He's a cop, isn't he?'

'Owen?'

'Do you know his number?'

'No, but Mum will.' We both grimaced in dismay but

342

what choice did we have? The police probably wouldn't believe us. Max was a national hero. At least Mum knew what he was capable of.

But she wasn't answering. She was probably on her way home from school and, upright citizen that she was, refused to answer her mobile while she was driving. We left a message.

25

Saint Meredith's hospital was under siege. Igloo tents and makeshift shelters of polythene sheeting snuggled up to the ramparts. Men and women in baseball caps and FABS tee-shirts peered out at the rain, fortified with mobile phones and headsets and tin mugs of tea. Beside the entry gates a few bedraggled individuals bearing banners sang 'We shall overcome' in reedy voices and handed sodden leaflets to visitors. I took one with fingers that refused to function, watched dully as the paper fluttered to the ground, neatly printed with photos of the Buchenwald Five. 'Sorry, sorry,' I muttered, feeling slightly sick.

The rain beat a ruffle of alarm on the car roof as they poked another through the window. Max Zeiler grinned out from the page. My hands were shaking, jiggling the words. I lay it on my lap to read. And, of course, it wasn't Max at all.

'*Pray for our children, the undead,*' begged a large bold font, above the hard-hatted winner of some horsy event. '*Leon Paterson, beloved son, killed when his favourite mount, Sweet Thunder, took a tumble at Gallagher's Brook.*' A silver cup nestled in his arms. My skin crawled and my stomach heaved. It was a nightmare in print.

Beside him was Axel, smiling down at a baby, his third child, according to the caption. Axel's former name was Darren Hooper. He, too, was beloved: '*husband of Ann-Marie, father of Josh, Brig and six-month-old Charmian. Fatally injured in a car crash.*'

Down the page, Ellen, as Carla Perez, beamed like a Toby jug under her mortarboard on graduation day, flanked by her equally squat but very proud parents, Ramon and Irma. She was a dearly loved daughter, working in her father's firm of solicitors when the tumour was discovered.

Next to her was a photo of Willi Greff, aka Lawrence Peters, standing on the steps of Saint Michael's, Braintree, arm-in-arm with his new bride, Hannah, who was thankful for those *'blissful few months, before the stroke took him away.'*

Very different people, they had all carried Donor Cards affirming their last wishes: 'to help someone to live after my death.' Had any of them imagined when they signed their names to Section 'B', that they would be *'doomed'* as the leaflet put it *'to roam the world possessed by the spirits of others'*? It went on, *'This evil practice must be stopped. Surgeons cannot be permitted to play God.'*

And now Sid Russell would be numbered among them – my poor old dad. I wondered how they intended to explain away his new personality – if they would bother. Perhaps he would be seen boarding a plane to South America and that would be the last anyone would ever hear of him. He would change his name, book in for a facelift and virtually disappear.

Rain was coming in, spattering the leaflet, bringing me round. I sneezed; realised Nick was speaking. If these protesters were to find out that another transplant operation was about to be performed, they'd be outraged. We should get them on our side. I agreed; we needed all the help we could get. We signed their soggy petition but, instead of going straight through the gates to the car park, asked be taken to their leader.

The security guard must have taken a lot of flack one way and another, with the theft of the brain and the demonstrators setting up camp outside, threatening all sorts of non-violence. Although he remembered us from the Max Zeiler show, he couldn't take any risks.

I said we were following up with a piece about the new brain transplant scheme, as seen on the Internet. I had the mini DV slung over my shoulder, and my clipboard, which I waved about to add credence. Perhaps we could speak to the manager?

Mr. Bradley, looking dapper in a light grey and tastefully pink-striped suit, came down to investigate, rubbing dimpled hands at the prospect of free publicity. I said we were doing this off our own bat, having had a whisper that Saint Meredith's was going into the brain-transplant business in a big way. If the producer thought we had a story, big guns would follow. There aren't many who can resist the siren call of television and Mr. Bradley was as charmed as any, ushering us through to the foyer with rosy smiles, offering us refreshment and any assistance that was within his means. It was almost too easy.

So we took some footage of the security guard, whose name was Winston Ball, and the receptionist, who was painting her nails, altogether enraptured by someone on the other end of the phone. She acknowledged us with a nod and a fan of wet fingers until she realised we had the camera trained on her, whereupon she became ever so efficient. Nobody questioned our presence, as we sashayed around wards and corridors, filming patients at supper, doctors in conference, the refurbished plastic surgery suite. We were even encouraged to put on masks and gowns and enter theatres, but saw no one we recognised on or off the operating tables.

We had plenty of questions to ask Mr. Bradley, who plied us with sherry and crisps, obviously delighted with his improved prospects and with our part in providing free publicity. In the few months since our programme, he said, he had been inundated with enquiries about transplants. Inundated. Thanks to *Way of the World* Saint Merry's could look forward to a constant flow of patients, *rich* patients, wanting new bodies for old.

In his opinion, the protesters out there by the wall were fighting a lost cause. What was done couldn't be undone. Though, it had to be said, salutary lessons had been learned. In future nothing would be left to chance – his eyes lit up with religious zeal – you'd be able to choose your new body on the Internet, dictate your needs in terms of cosmetic surgery, and the families of donors would be generously compensated. One day, he was sure, when the government pulled its finger out, there would even be brain transplants for children. Strictly between ourselves, he confided to the camera, he could tell us that the number of enquiries from parents of severely physically disabled children was substantial – quite substantial.

I didn't dare look at Nick. I could feel him twitching. This was what fascism was all about, wasn't it, a healthy mind in a perfect body? And to hell with those that didn't match up? I was only guessing but wouldn't it be heartbreaking if your brain-dead child were resurrected only to call someone else Mummy? A bit like the end of the world, I'd have thought. And what about the poor kid seeing someone else's face in the mirror? He'd grow up a psychological wreck.

No, it was a rotten idea, mind-bogglingly evil, and would therefore appeal to all sorts of dirty dealers – babysellers, kidnappers, murderers. They'd crawl out of the woodwork. I said I thought it would be a long time before the government gave their consent to *that*.

He tapped his nose and looked cunning. 'We'll see, we'll see . . .'

We learned a lot. That there were scores of surgeons treading on Susmeta's heels, boning up on her methods as fast as they possibly could. 'Some of them, indeed, will be even better than she is,' he said. 'They'll be ready by the time we are.'

'Oh,' I said. I hadn't realised. 'So how many surgeons will you need?'

'How long is a piece of string?' He chuckled hugely, showing his fillings, his eyes disappearing between pudgy lids. Then, as if a switch had been thrown, his shoulders stopped shaking and he was very serious indeed. 'We are making provision for an extra forty beds. I'd say we'd need a dozen neuro-surgeons under contract to be on the safe side. A dozen, at least.'

'You can *afford* that?' Shit, we were talking millions here.

'Yes, we can. I dare say that, in time, as improvements are made, so our costs will go down. Turnover will be speeded up, no doubt about it, and each surgeon might manage two operations a week. Maybe more.' He flashed his teeth at the camera, unaware that I'd zoomed in for shots of the dollar signs in his eyes and his fingers drumming greedy sums on the blotter. He allowed himself a speculative nod or two and sighed, polishing his glasses, which had steamed up with avarice. 'It's a sound investment,' he said, with another fatuous smile, 'if you have a few shekels to spare . . .'

'And tonight's transplant?' I couldn't stop myself, heard Nick suck his teeth in dismay. 'How much are you making out of that?'

'I don't know what you're talking about,' he said quietly. He put back his glasses and moved his chair away from the desk.

I took no notice of Nick, who was making mad faces at me – shut up, shut up – and said, as calmly as my hammering heart would let me, 'People are going to ask questions about what happened to the last Buchenwald brain. They have a right to know.'

'I'm sorry?' Now his smile was puzzled but still pleasant. 'You must be aware that the brain was stolen from here some months ago. The police have not recovered it, as far as I know.'

'So how is it, Mr. Bradley, that a surgeon in your employ

is going to perform a transplant operation, using that very brain, in this hospital tonight?'

He stroked his chin. 'I don't know how you came by your information, young lady, but I can assure you that you are quite mistaken.'

Nick shrugged. I think he believed him. He believed everyone except me. And he *was* plausible, this amiable Mr. Pickwick. He'd been so straight about everything else. I wondered if I could be wrong? Could I have misunderstood Susmeta? Perhaps the lines had been crossed and she really had been talking to Mrs Khan. Or perhaps she'd been stoned or something. Out of her mind. Perhaps I was. I said, 'I want to believe you, Mr. Bradley,' thinking that maybe he'd been duped, as well.

He said kindly, 'Perhaps it would be a good idea to switch off the camera and you can tell me what exactly you think is going on.'

So I did. And at that moment the door opened and Winston was there, along with another uniformed gorilla and a man in a white coat. Bradley must have pressed some sort of panic button under his desk. The mask of geniality came off at last, revealing the tight, cold anger of a snake poised to strike.

'Now then, children, *I* have some questions for *you*. Close the door, Ball.'

My cold is worse, much worse. It clogs my ears and nose with a dull roar. There were voices, familiar voices, but they are long gone. Let them go. Right now I need to breathe. It's imperative that I breathe. How, though? My nose is so stuffed I can't feel it. Without warning my mouth sucks open and my lungs fill and fill. I'm alive then. I was beginning to wonder. But how come my eyelids don't work? They're heavy – glued in place. And I can't lift my head off the pillow. Someone, not Mum, has tucked me in so tight I can't move. Minutes or hours go by before I have the energy to try again. It's only when it dawns on me that the pillow is as hard as the floor that my eyes fly open at last – to sheer black terror.

I remember.

I remember a fist smashing into my face. Sudden awful pain, across my nose, cheeks, teeth, and tears streaming. Like I'd walked into a lamppost. People don't *do* that to me. To anybody I know. I remember shouting – about Sid, I think, about them being about to operate on him, turn him into a fascist. I seemed to think that if Winston knew this he'd stop hurting us, he'd listen to our story and help us. I remember Nick telling them to leave me alone, just before that hammer blow to his stomach that left him groaning and retching for breath.

Nick! What have they done to you? I try to get my tongue round his name but there's no voice. Where is he? I can – I *will* turn my head as . . . far . . . as . . . as . . . a pencil line of light around a door. It takes me a few seconds to work out why my line of vision is level with its base.

So how come I'm laid out cold on the floor? It wasn't the beating. Something happened afterwards. Those voices . . . Think, Clare.

People came into the room bringing the outdoors' air with them. Who? I knew them then. Just can't seem to put a name to the face now. That tall blond man, with a scowl like Michelangelo's David, who made my insides shrivel with revulsion. It's on the tip of my consciousness, like a word that won't come. Go through the alphabet, A to . . .

'Ladies and gentlemen, give a special 'Way of the World' welcome to Ma-a-ax Zeiler!'

Welcome, indeed. My fingers curled in hate, my black-enamelled nails unsheathed. I believe I actually growled like a fighting cat, and shrieked as I hurled myself at him, blindly tearing at his face and neck, ripping the delicate fabric of his shirt, streaking it red. Only when they hauled me off did I have eyes for the others: Susmeta, Ellen Sauerbruch and old man Titherille. But where was Sid? What had they done with my dad?

'On a trolley, young lady, out to the world.' Who told me that? Whose voice was that smooth and smug? It'll come, if I concentrate.

'Do not worry, Clare, he will not feel pain.' Oh yes, now I know that voice; remembering it turns my stomach.

That was the moment when Nick struggled for his turn at the enemy, but Winston held him from behind. 'Bastard!' he managed to snarl before Max beat him to the floor and kicked him repeatedly.

Susmeta was in tears, saying she was sorry, sorry. Well, bully for her.

Sauerbruch was angry at what they'd done to my face. 'How long will it take to heal?' And why the hell should she care?

Nick knew. He raged like a cornered beast, said he'd see her in hell first, said they'd never get away with it. People knew we were there and why. If we went missing they'd know where to start looking.

Bradley, the smoothest of managers, didn't seem bothered. 'Oh you won't go missing, sunshine, rest assured.' He signalled to the man in the white coat, who produced a hypodermic needle, removed its paper packaging, squirted it free of air bubbles and stuck it in Nick's arm. Who simply slumped.

'No-o-o!' I was jumping about, yelling that they were monsters, before they did the same to me.

Feeling was coming back into my face, like when the numbness wears off from having a tooth filled, not that I could touch it and see, but one lip could feel the other, and I knew my nose was sore and probably swollen. I still couldn't breathe through it and my throat was dry. My tongue stuck to the roof of my mouth, which tasted like the inside of an old and smelly trainer.

But I was alive, opening and shutting my eyes and wiggling my toes and fingers. I could turn my head from side to side, get my bearings. There was a grey slatted window half way up one wall, shut tight – the draught came from under the door on the other side. Slowly I rolled my head again, over cool linoleum tiles, revelling in sense returning . . . and froze. How did I know about the tiles, their slick texture? It was too dark to see; my sense of smell was kaput, so how?

I knew, or rather my head, my scalp knew, the size and shape of those tiles and exactly where the edges butted. How come my scalp was so acutely sensitive, so tactile all of a sudden, and so conscious of the draught under the door? It was almost as though . . . as though there were nothing between my skin and the elements.

Jesus Christ, I was bald! They'd shaved off my hair! Like for an operation. But I couldn't get my head round the rest of it, the brain removal bit – it was too busy exploding, teeming with madness, white panic. Fuck. Jesus. Me. They'd done it to me!

It took a while for common sense to filter through, for my heart to come down from my throat, slow down. They hadn't got that far. This was still me thinking, blinking, swearing like a loony. So what were they waiting for? Were they coming back?

Eventually my fingers unclenched, making contact with some loose cottony material, not my jeans. My knees were cold, and my bum. They'd taken my clothes and put me in one of those awful hospital gowns that tied up with tape. But why? Why me? I wasn't AB negative. I was . . .

I was handy, that's what. O negative – the universal giver of blood. Ellen F. Sauerbruch was after my body! That was why she'd been cross about the splattered nose. That was why they hadn't killed me. They'd trussed me up like one of those chickens in French markets, barely alive and ready for plucking, except they'd plucked me first. It must have been a toss-up as to who went under the knife first, Sid or me, and he had won by a whisker. Oh Sid. I had to get to him.

I attempted a sort of sit-up, but fell back weakly, banging my poor naked head on the floor and jarring every nerve. Oh wow, hot tears. I could feel them on my face.

'Nick!' I croaked over a throat clogged with floor sweepings. I could hear again too – that there was no reply. I listened hard, holding my breath. A radiator was ticking; there was a rattle of rain against the window, the slash of car wheels along a wet road, muffled voices and footsteps in the corridor outside. If I shouted who would come in, friend or foe?

'Nick!'

No answer.

What if – Jesus, suppose they'd taken *his* body. Suppose they'd decided that things were getting too hot for Max. Suppose *they'd* matched blood-wise. Nick would make a good disguise.

I had to get out of this. Had to, or I was dead. 'But I can't move,' I heard myself whimper.

'There's no such word as can't!'

God, they come back to haunt you, those maxims. I didn't know whose voice was in my head – Nan's or Mum's or even Sid's, but I got the message. Stop feeling sorry for yourself, child, and *think*.

Re-cap. I could turn my head. I could bend in the middle, both ways. I could bend my knees, too, ignoring scabs and old bruises, bring my feet up behind to meet my stretching fingertips. Long, skinny legs have their uses, and no bum to speak of. What was it they'd used round my ankles?

Bandage? Surgical tape? No – it had a shiny feel. It was sticky tape, the big brown stuff they seal boxes with. That must be what was pinning my arms to my sides, as well. In normal circumstances (God, would things ever be normal again?) when I needed a length of the stuff to remove cat hairs from my clothes, I'd rip it with my teeth. But my teeth were a long way off, and chattering. Sharp, I needed something sharp, or failing that the hard edge of a radiator.

I rolled and wriggled across ten miles of linoleum to the window, without encountering a single stick of furniture or my boyfriend. My ex-boyfriend. I did find the radiator. I needed to be upright for this. By squirming and shuffling I managed to prop my head against the nearby wall; another shuffle backwards and my shoulders were there; a bit of a hump and I was sitting up. I brought my knees up, and digging my bare heels into the floor, pushed against the wall for leverage. After struggling for a while, I was up. Exhausted, but up. My hurt face was throbbing. I felt sick. I needed a cigarette. But I couldn't think about any of that. They could be coming for me any minute.

I squeezed in close to the radiator and found my hand would just fit flat between it and wall so that the tape between thigh and wrist was pressed against the vertical metal flange. Carefully I bent and straightened my knees, down up down, in best horse-riding fashion, rubbing away at my bonds, hoping the squeak of friction didn't travel along the pipes to the next room, that I wouldn't overbalance and crack my face on the adjacent wall.

Shit. Someone was coming. There were voices at the door, shadows under it. A key turning in the lock. I was already rolling across the floor to what I hoped was the position they'd left me in. Kept my eyes closed as light came flooding in and leather soles were squeaking on lino.

'Still out cold, boss.' It was Winston's voice.

'Mmm. It should be wearing off about now. Fetch the

anaesthetist, Ball. If he gives them a top-up we can all sleep tight 'til morning.'

'He's gone home, boss.'

'Gone home? What's the time then? Good Lord, ten past eleven! And they're still in theatre? Well, bring whoever's on duty now. Better let me talk to him first – put him in the picture. Hurry up, man, it's been a long day.' The door closed. A muffled voice, 'And I expect you want to get off, don't you?'

I lay still, as the footsteps departed in different directions.

Them, he'd said. *Give them a top-up.* Nick was here too, then, somewhere. Thank you, God. I thanked Him again, as in desperation I jerked my hand hard – and the eroded tape snapped. I had one hand free and, in no time, had peeled the tape from the other.

Just my legs to do. But they were fastened tightly together, from ankle to knee. A mermaid's tail. Fingernails were no good, even strong black lacquered ones. I slapped my gown for anything useful. Loose and sharp objects had been removed, along with my clothes and shoes and bum bag. A hairgrip might have worked, but alas . . . no hair.

There was one last hope. I touched the place on my nose gingerly. And caught my breath, finding what they had missed among the dried-on blood and snot. It nearly killed me taking it out, but there it was at last, pinched between my trembling fingertips, my nose-stud, tiny and blunt and smelling of blood or rust, but nevertheless, a distinct possibility, if I . . . didn't . . . drop . . . the wretched thing. Concentrating madly, I forced the pin through the layers of tape and dragged it to an edge as through butter. I couldn't believe how easy it was.

The light flicker-flickered when I switched it on, revealing poor Nick, flinching from the fluorescence, slumped in the corner of a bare room and wound about like a mummy, with tape over his mouth. I guessed they hadn't gagged *me* for fear I would suffocate, my nose being in the state it was.

A combination of teeth and nails and my magic nose-stud tore him free, too. He groaned, 'Oh, baby, what have they done to you?' We found his glasses in his pocket and he was able to tell me that they'd painted an iodine skull-cap on my bald dome. I rushed to the window and pulled the blinds to examine my ruined reflection. The boiled egg look did nothing for me. Okay, it was probably what the fashionable young body-donor was wearing to the operating theatre that season, but for me it was the last straw. As terror struck I started shaking, my knees crumbled and I sank to the floor.

'Hush, Clare.' Nick laid his hand on my lips. I must have been making some sort of noise. His touch was unbearable. I gazed at his face, dark and unreadable against the light, my eyes brimming with love, my lips puckering against his fingers, blindly, reflexively. When he snatched his hand away, I closed my eyes, shamed by rejection, and bit back the tears. And then I felt his lips touch mine, cool and questing. Such a soft and tentative kiss, it didn't hurt at all.

Next moment we were in each other's arms, hugging bone to bone, so close, so part of the other's flesh there was no room for doubt or guilt or sorrow, just bottomless gratitude and relief. No need for words. This was where we belonged. So close, I could feel his heart beating, his love flooding through me.

'All right?' he whispered, pulling away and examining my face for lingering signs of despair, thumbing away the tears. 'Come on, hon – we aren't out of the woods yet.'

Back to earth with a bump. He was right. They would be here in a minute. What were we going to do? There was no escape from the room. The door was locked and the window was on the fourth floor. In any case we needed to be on the inside, not out, if we were going to rescue Sid.

It was time to call up the troops.

Out along the perimeter wall bonfires were burning. I hoped they were still watching for our signal, hadn't gone to bed. I switched off the light and flicker-flickered on again, off . . . on, off . . . on. Someone out there, on lookout, noticed, thank the Lord. An answering torch flashed on and off.

Someone was coming – footsteps and voices. Not too many, hopefully. If there were two we stood a very slim chance; more and we'd had it. Nick helped me untie the tapes on my nightie and, carefully, took off his tee-shirt. He was too hurt to fight. We had to count on the element of surprise, took up positions behind the door.

Winston was first in and started fiddling with the light switch.

'This the right room?'

'Yeah, why?'

'There's no one here.'

Now they were both in the room, Winston and a wiry little Asian in a white coat. I guessed he was mine. It was relatively easy to pop the nightie over his head, impossible to tie it, especially when his instinct was to pull it off, but I managed to twist it tight enough for him to think he was being strangled. I suppose I intended pulling him backwards, off balance. But he wouldn't go down. He kept treading on my bare toes and we finished up in a tangle of legs and feet on the floor, with him butting the back of his head into my bare stomach. I was only vaguely aware of grunts and thuds against the opposite wall, but suddenly Nick was leaning over me, punching the anaesthetist where he thought his jaw might be under the gown. He slumped in a dead weight from which I crawled, clutching my gut. We found the syringes in his top pocket, ripped off the packaging by the light from the door, and jabbed them home.

I tried to speak, gagged and puked up in the corner,

sherry and crisps and all the blood I'd swallowed, while Nick kindly held my head. With the anaesthetic out of my system I felt a bit better, though my knees were trembling.

Nick peeled a rather bloody T-shirt from Winston's battered head, and I was about to slip into my guy's white coat when he stopped me. 'I'll be more convincing,' he said, clipping the stethoscope round his neck and I suppose he had a point, not to mention the hair for the part. 'You put your thingy on again and I'll go and find a wheelchair.'

So we left, locking the door behind us, a white-coated doctor wheeling his helpless patient back to her ward, albeit with borrowed underclothes beneath her theatre gown and a pair of sweaty, oversized trainers on her feet. We dropped the key in a fire bucket, as a couple of late visitors passed us *en route* to the lifts, and it said something for our disguise that they hardly spared us a glance. With no one on the main door when they let themselves out the FABS would let themselves in.

'Which way?'

'Has to be on this floor, doesn't it?'

It didn't actually – there were operating suites on every floor and neither of us remembered a thing about the journey to Room 311, whether we'd gone up or down in lifts after being given the pre- med – but it seemed logical that they'd have shoved us in the nearest available empty room.

And this floor's operating theatre appeared to be busy, the red light prohibiting entry to unauthorised personnel, likes of us. I was halfway out of the wheelchair when Nick shoved me back, swung away into the lift alcove, and pressed for a lift.

'Wha-a-a?'

'Bradley and Tithers!' he hissed. 'Keep your head down.'

Moments later, deep in conversation, they tip-tapped smartly past us in their well-heeled shoes and down the stairs. Thanks to Nick's quick thinking they'd only seen the back of us as they'd closed the theatre door behind them.

'*I would advise you to stay exactly where you are!*' My heart jumped as the pompous tones spiralled up the stairwell. I thought for a moment Bradley was talking to us. '*This is a hospital in case you've forgotten. There are sick people trying to sleep.*' The ensuing hubbub told me that the FABS had met with an obstacle. Any minute now Bradley would press a panic button and the place would be swarming with heavies.

'Come on, Nick. Let's go.'

'Hang on a minute, babe. We haven't thought this through. I mean what are we going to do when we get in there?'

'Stop them! Switch off their computers. We'll think of something.'

'Clare, they'll knock us aside like flies. And if they haven't finished the operation we could do more harm than good. Better wait for the others.'

I knew it, knew, too, that if we pulled the plug on the Liebl brain, my dad, or rather the last vestiges of my dad, his body, would die, his last chance gone. But I didn't want to wait. That was my dad in there.

'Think,' I said.

'I'm thinking.'

'What's in your pockets? That anaesthetist will have had a key or a swipe card or something . . .' Both, as it turned out, the key handily labelled 'Drugs.'

'*Open Sesame,*' he whispered.

'Dad!' I mewed, seeing him through the window, stretched out on the operating table like that, his bare big toe just needing a mortuary tag. I thought I was prepared for it but my knees sagged anyway and I might have passed out, if Nick hadn't been there, holding me up. God, it was horrible to see him like that, minus strut, minus arrogance – quite, quite helpless with his head inside a sort of incubator, sprouting fibre optics instead of red hair. His skull just above the eyebrows had been prised off like the shell of a hard-boiled egg and his brain protruded obscenely. No, not his brain, by now – Friedrich Liebl's.

Masked figures in theatre greens bustled about tending monitors, checking pulses and pressures, testing reflexes and muscle movements while Susmeta, pale and drawn, directed operations from a bank of computer screens, with Max Zeiler breathing down her neck, on guard duty, presumably. Only he might know if she put a foot wrong, or removed the patient's understanding of language, or his sense of taste or connected x to y. She must have been tempted.

Unlike the monitors in the control pod at *Way of the World*, the screens in front of Susmeta showed various parts of the brain, coloured like a Kandinsky landscape in vivid yellows and pinks and purples. One zoomed in, as we watched, on a swarm of plankton or brain cells or something, which connected or sprang apart as her hands guided two pinpointing devices on the bench in front of her.

We attracted scant attention, in our theatre camouflage filched from the adjacent dressing room, until I stood beside Max with my primed syringe and smiled, 'Hi.'

With Nick and I both pumping him full of morphine he didn't begin to count back from a hundred. Meanwhile all hell had broken loose outside. The 'peaceful' protest had beaten a path via lift and stairs to the very door of the operating theatre, whopping their assailants with walking sticks, tent mallets and umbrellas, giving as good as they got.

'Come on, Suse,' I said, picking up my syringe, and pulling the trembling surgeon to her feet. 'It's okay – it's empty. Act frightened but don't struggle – I'm too knackered to fight.' Outside in the corridor Bradley called off his thugs when he realised that I was about to fill his golden goose full of something nasty and things were just chilling out when the lift doors opened and Owen Prentice stepped into the corridor, followed by a half a dozen uniformed police. Good old Mum – I bet she was waiting in the car outside. I looked around for old man Paterson, but he'd disappeared, probably slipped by me through the open door. 'Oh God,' I thought and dragged Susmeta back into theatre, hoping I wasn't too late.

Ellen Sauerbruch, ridiculous in bath hat and green coveralls, was throwing a wobbler, stamping her feet and screaming about doctors and removing brains. 'He is the one!' she cried, catching sight of Nick and stabbing him with a stubby finger until he backed away, clutching his chest. The police, who had managed to quell the riot, thought they could see an operation in progress and hovered just inside the door, loath to put a patient's life at risk.

Ellen had no such qualms as she clutched at Nick's arm. '*Die blutgruppe*,' she yelled, 'it is the same for him, for Max! *Schnell, schnell*, hold him, please! Open up the skull!' Her eyes were wild and desperate as she turned to plead with the stunned-looking theatre staff. 'Now. We must do it now! We cannot let him die!'

I didn't understand. Max was unconscious, not dying. I needed him to stand trial. So what was Sourpuss's hissy fit all about? Was she completely off her head? And where, oh where, was my VT camera when I needed it?

She stomped over to Susmeta, took her by the shoulders and began to shake her. 'Kommen Sie, Fraulein!' She slapped her face, 'You, do something!'

'Hey!' I protested as Susmeta wearily held up her hands. No, no more. But a couple of policemen were already on the job, prising Ellen off my friend and telling her to stop this, madam, there was nothing to be gained by violence. One of their mates was putting handcuffs on George Paterson who seemed to be giving him no trouble at all. What was going on?

Sourpuss was struggling wildly. 'You do not understand,' she insisted. 'We can save him. Du lieber Gott! Get him on the table.'

For God's sake, I thought, don't let her near my dad. But they, very sensibly, refused to release her, and she began to sob, loudly, gustily, 'You are killing him!'

An older woman, small and South American, ducked under the police cordon, ran up to Ellen and tried to embrace her. 'Carla, Carla, darling. Mama's here, don't distress yourself. It'll be all right.'

But she backed off in horror. She was only interested in saving her beloved Max. It was all that mattered. And with surprising strength and agility, she twisted free of her captors, grabbed a scalpel from the tray, and made straight for Nick. I leapt in front but (and not before time, I'd say) another officer produced a can of CS gas and squirted it. Sauerbruch stumbled back, dropping the blade, hands tearing at her eyes, gasping and choking and crying with pain and frustration.

And then, as they dragged her away, I saw the reason for her distress. Max lay on the floor in a spreading pool of blood with George Paterson's walking stick impaled in his chest. In lieu of a wooden stake, I would guess.

26

The credits roll.

'Yessss!' squeals Kate, bouncing on the settee as her name comes up, and spooking the cat. 'Making her debut, lovely newcomer Kate Russell! Rumour has it we shan't have too long to wait before we see this talented young actress on our screens again.' As the beaded locks fly Nan holds her champagne flute aloft to save it.

'Narrated by Liz Turner'

'At great expense,' I mutter, 'and worth every penny.'

*'Other parts were played by students of
The East London Acting School.'*

'Available for after-dinner speeches and children's parties,' says Fred.

Nick's name scrolls around, one of our two official researchers, and we applaud him frantically, then it's hooray for Jay on the production team, and for the Camera crew, Sound, Music and Lighting; even Barry gets his five seconds of glory. Finally come the magic words:

*'The Buchenwald Project' was
'Written and Directed by Clare Russell.'*

'Woo-woo-woo!' they go, throwing cushions in the air. It's heady stuff, success and, easily moved these days, I'm in tears on Nick's shoulder. There are bits I wish I'd done

363

differently, edited more stringently, but it's too late now, and everybody else seems to think I've done wonders, made my mark. Not that it was difficult. All I did was change it from a story about five Buchenwald internees and their resurrection to one about the Nazis' attempt to infiltrate the twenty-first century. Colin liked it much better.

The neighbours knock on the wall to show their appreciation. Mobiles and fixed phones ring and Kate and Mum and Nan take messages from Sylvia, down the road in Loughton, and Jay and Richard in their flat in Tooting, Mariam in Walthamstow, Uncle John in Richmond, Nick's mum and dad, Jo and Ez, my aunt and uncle in Newcastle and everyone else who knows me, including Sid who, strangely, seeks no accolades for his own part in our little drama.

'Well done, Clare,' he says. 'Chip off the old block, eh?'

We refill our glasses, and Nick with his arm round me, squeezes tight. 'Bloody great,' he says in my ear.

It's a double celebration. Nan's letting us turn her upstairs into a flat, since she can't manage it any more and doesn't fancy a stair lift. We're going to Homebase tomorrow to buy some paint and a king-size bed. Mum won't miss me, she says, not if I come round as often as Nan does. In any case, she has Owen to keep her company now – she's helping him write his next novel about love in the comprehensive, trying out the moves.

'Was I really all right?' says Kate, stepping off cloud nine for two minutes to grab a handful of peanuts.

We all agree that she was fantastic: me to a T, disconcertingly so. And she didn't have to shave off her mop after all – we gave her a bald wig and airbrushed out the lumps. Mine has grown again in six months. Darker, but only because it's winter still and doesn't have the sun to give it brightness. It'll soon be ginger again.

The trial scenes were brilliant, say so myself. We couldn't

take cameras inside the courtroom, obviously, so I hit on the idea of animating the court artist's drawings, with the help of the computer, and feeding them into the drama, as and when, breaking it up nicely, along with flashbacks and footnotes. There was my dad, large as life and twice as objectionable, strutting about in his designer-stubble, telling everyone how he fell into the Titherilles' clutches. The film includes a snip of a scene in his studio, making great play of him working on yet another masterpiece. Least I could do. His constructed paintings are in great demand following the piece the *Sunday Times* did on him, and Wood Street Market is fast becoming a cultural Mecca, colonised by wannabe artists.

Luckily they managed to keep his body alive on life support, but the brain, Liebl's brain that Susmeta had been forced to put inside Sid's skull, was in a bad way when it came to her. Stolen from the hospital on a hot day, transferred to Ellen's ice box at Chelsea Harbour and then removed to Ottley Place, where it had suffered a partial thaw when the power lines came down in a storm, it was scarred with freezer burns and almost beyond repair. The break in transmission when we invaded the operating theatre had just about finished it off. If he'd lived, Liebl would have been a drooling idiot. That's her story, anyway. It's now preserved in formaldehyde in the War Museum, in pride of place and stone dead. So she was able to reunite Sid's body with *his* brain, which she had taken the precaution of treating and freezing in time-honoured fashion within seconds of its removal.

'I told you not to worry,' she said, when I fell into her arms after his operation.

'Did you?'

'Yes, just before you hung up.'

'I didn't hang up. You broke up.'

'Did I? Oh dear. No I told you – told Mrs Khan – not to

worry, we'd do everything we could for her father. You were meant to take comfort from that. Goodness, Clare, I had no intention of being accused of murder, on top of everything else.' She stretched her lips, but her eyes didn't smile.

'Shame Liebl didn't make it, whoever he was,' I said, fishing.

'We'll never know now,' was all she said.

But as Nick pointed out, it was probably all for the best. If it was you-know-who and he'd survived to stand trial, albeit in an altered state, all the neo-Nazis in the world would have taken it as a call to arms; there'd have been real trouble.

Max wasn't so lucky. He recovered. George Paterson hadn't been in the best of health when he attacked him and could only force the walking stick's spike a few centimetres into his chest, splintering a rib but doing no real damage.

He pleaded not guilty, which was hardly surprising, and Nan, seeing this for the first time, wrinkled her nose in disgust. 'Bastard,' she spat, with venom. What she'd have said had she known about the rape I dread to think.

When he took the stand he said he been aware for some time that vast tracts of his memory were missing. Now he was having blackouts. Only a few days before his arrest he had found himself wandering around Epping Forest in the middle of the night, with no idea how he had got there, what had happened. He had eventually stumbled upon a road and flagged down a passing lorry, which had brought him back to London.

Now it was Mum's turn to mutter obscenities and wring her hands as though wringing his neck. I'd heard his denial many, many times and still I shook my head in disbelief. Nick took off his glasses and rubbed his eyes. He hated this bit.

Nan shook her head in disbelief, 'Tch! He could be *reading* his lines . . . Dreadful, dreadful! Didn't I always say he was a terrible actor? Does he really expect anyone to believe him?'

'He's desperate, Nan.'

'We all wanted to believe him, that was the trouble,' said Nick.

'Not me,' she insisted. 'I didn't trust him an inch.'

Actually I do remember her saying that. But we don't take any notice of what our grandmothers say, do we?

When Max said he couldn't remember, either, what he was doing at Saint Meredith's Hospital on the night in question, and suspected that, like me, he had been lured there as a potential body donor, my family responded with jeering and variations on, 'Yah, boo, sucks!'

He said he had reason to believe that his brain had been tampered with, irreversibly damaged, during the transplant operation and, on cue, Exhibit A was shown to the court, the famous video, in which delicate tapering fingers were seen playing video games in someone's brain. Zap! Zap! Another top neuro-surgeon told us what we were seeing, cells being destroyed in the cortex, the region most associated with memory. Replacing or repairing those cells, as happened later on in the tape, could not restore the memories that had been permanently eradicated.

Nan rolled her eyes comically because, of course, this was her theory, though she maintains she had another all along: that he wasn't Max Zeiler at all, but someone else using the alias. Had she shared this with us, who knows – we might have been saved a whole lot of trauma. And I'd probably have pooh-poohed it, anyway – soppy old Nan with another of her crazy ideas.

Of course, the patient on the operating table in the video wasn't Max, but Willi Greff. Nevertheless, as Susmeta admitted tampering with all her Buchenwald patients and Greff was now in a sanatorium, suffering from a nervous breakdown caused by memory loss, it followed that there was reasonable doubt that Max could be held responsible for his actions. It all sounded so plausible.

Exhibits B, C and D, produced by the prosecution, were printouts of emails sent to and from Max, using his own and a computer at Thurwell. (Lord Jerry and Polly Gross both milked their encounters with the 'headcase' for all the publicity they could. Polly even wrote a song about it, which will feature on her new album.) The emails erased any doubts about his part in plotting my downfall and Sid's. Get Sid and I'd follow. That was why they'd pretended to go along with Susmeta and her 'Mrs Khan' phone-call. She'd played right into their hands.

> Confirming your booking for the 19th September.
> Both patients will require full hospital
  accommodation and nursing
> care for seven days following transplant operations,
> to be carried out by Ms Susmeta Naidoo. Then as I
> understand it, you will make provision for their
  transfer
> to Ottley Place, for convalescence and subsequent
> air passage out of the country.
> Received: the sum of €500,000. Thank you for
  settling
> payment so promptly.
> Dennis Bradley

Max had taken the precaution of clicking on *Delete* but the police computer experts were easily able to recover them from his Recycle Bin, along with Exhibit E, a record of his dubious Internet activities. He'd visited some pretty unsavoury websites, catching up on ways and means of dealing with unwanted ethnic minorities by means of a worldwide network of 'good old boys'. I guess if I hadn't introduced them he and Lord Titherille would have found each other anyway. This didn't prove anything, of course. A cat may look at a king and, in any case, Max, conveniently, had no recollection of any of this computer activity, not even of the stories he'd downloaded of Jewish attempts to escape Germany. One particular story seemed relevant, contributed by an Isak Wolff, who described an escape through the sewers of Berlin. Helped by partisans he and his family had reached England in February 1942, though not without casualties.

Exhibit F was another email, recovered from the 'Sent' items.

> My dear William.
> Mission successfully accomplished I see.
  Congratulations.
> Let us hope that the fools against body snatching
  will take
> warning. Time is a-wasting.
> My own task, concerning our little surgeon, is
  proving more
> difficult but not impossible. Having come so far,
  I will
> not allow our project to be jeopardised
> by a woman's scruples. Our friend
> in the freezer would not thank me, I think.
> Max.

It was sent the morning after the pub bombing, just before he went to the cricket match with Nick.

That was when they wheeled out the closed circuit video. Thank God Susmeta had left the CCTV running. She said she wanted to record the fact that she had been coerced into performing the operation. I recovered the rest of the day's filming from Bradley's desk drawer but neither the trial nor the documentary would have been the same without those shots of Ellen and Max having a stand-up row, with sub-titles. (I'd thought long and hard about dubbing and voice-overs, but decided they'd detract from the drama.)

He insisted that Liebl should be transplanted first. The world could not wait. Ellen stamped one flat foot and then the other. She jutted her chin at him. S*he* couldn't wait – not one hour, not one minute longer. This ugliness was sending her mad. 'It is horrible, Klaus, hell on earth!'

The prosecution insisted on rewinding the tape, playing it again. She had definitely called him 'Klaus.' Not Max. Klaus as in Hofmann. And when, in her despair, she accused him of not caring, not understanding her feelings as a woman – How could you? You're a man and the worst sort of man, an obsessive. All you think about is your damned experiment' – a tremor went through the courtroom.

Nick held me tight. I couldn't help it. Suddenly I was shaking, sobbing, beating him off. I couldn't bear him to touch my dirty flesh. It had suddenly hit me, I suppose, what had really happened in the forest. I'd let a mass murderer fuck me, a man without a heart, who had cut up Jews and other helpless innocents just to see what would happen. Luckily I wasn't the only one making a fuss. As the implications sank in – that we'd brought back the Beast, himself, given him life, taken him to our bosoms – the small disturbance became pandemonium. People cried out, fainted; some actually spat at the prisoner in the dock; threw things. The judge had to bang his gavel for order, threaten to clear the court unless people behaved themselves.

Eventually they restarted the video and any lingering doubts the jury may have had faded as 'Ellen' continued her tirade, oblivious of the camera's red eye trained on her. Closed circuit television wasn't something a person coming from the middle of the twentieth century would know about, necessarily, that Big Brother was recording her display of temper and would use it in evidence against her.

'You couldn't care less what you look like, just so long as you can do your work, but I turned heads! I had style! I even managed to make that wretched Nazi uniform look like something out of *Vogue*. If I'd known I was going to look like a hobgoblin I'd never have agreed to take part in the project. Never! I'd as soon have taken my chances with the War Tribunal, never practised surgery again! Please, Klaus . . .' There it was again. 'Liebl won't know any different, let him wait. We have the girl sedated already – why don't we just get on with it?'

When she understood what Ellen wanted, Susmeta stormed, 'I'm not doing it! I'm not killing Clare! Just for your convenience, for your stupid vanity. Do what you like with the video – I'm out of here!' And shaking her head vehemently, she would have pushed through the swing doors if *he* – whom I would now have to get used to calling Hofmann – hadn't grabbed her and slapped her face.

'Oh no, my lady,' he said as she burst into tears. 'You will do as you are told or we shall have to test the extent of *your* vanity. A little disfigurement might be just what you need. Oh not your hands.' As if this would be her first concern. 'I was thinking more in terms of rearranging the facial features. I have always had a notion to try plastic surgery. Or perhaps some sort of internal investigation, something that wouldn't necessarily show but would cause considerable pain . . .'

She dashed away her tears and crept quietly over to her computer chair to consider her choices, while they continued wrangling. The stocky little Fraulein suggested that Klaus only stayed with her because she had money and Klaus said he didn't need her money, thank you very much, he had his own now. He stayed with her because he loved her.

'You really do?'

'Gisela!' he reproached her. And the jury nodded, gratified on two counts.

'Then let me have the first operation.'

He gave in, and they summoned nurses to fetch me, undress me and shave my head. Like I'm on this trolley in the anteroom, nose spread all over my face, completely out of it. And right on cue, I sneeze!

My temperature was up, apparently, and the chill of a bare head must have reminded me, through the anaesthetic, of my condition. Thank God it did. Everybody knows you can't perform major surgery if the donor has a cold.

It wasn't funny, in the least. I'd nearly been killed, for fuck's sake. But up in the public gallery my so-called friends were laughing their socks off. Jay, Charlie, Jo, Ez, Fred, Kate – hooting, splitting their sugar fat sides. Mum was dabbing her eyes – tears of mirth. Hardly the caring, sharing support group. As I told them.

Nick said it was relief after the tension. The grand build-up and then the sneeze! Great stuff. I was still tight-lipped. 'Oh come on, Clare,' said Nick, trying not to smile, 'even the judge is laughing.'

It bothered me for ages, that boast of Hofmann's, that he had money of his own. Where had it come from? He'd been desperate for money just a few weeks before and yet here he was, paying two lots of hospital fees, in advance, and would presumably be footing the bill for convalescent care and those long-haul air flights. I guessed he was planning to accompany his colleagues into temporary exile, and you'd need some pretty substantial dosh for something like that. I thought, at first, that he must have stolen it from his sister – from Berthe, I mean. But she was a poor old thing, living on a pension, and, it occurred to me now, he'd been able to pay his return flight home, no probs. I hadn't subbed him that many euros in Austria, probably just enough to cover fags and food for the journey to Buchenwald and get him a train ticket to Hanover. I'd assumed he must still have the money Susmeta had given him or that he'd cadged some off Willi before they parted. But he might not have had to. If he was Klaus Hofmann and had planned his escape into the future, surely he would have made provision for his return, as other fleeing Nazis had done? Some, like Gisela, had made sure they could draw on deposits in Swiss banks, others had buried money and valuables in out of the way places, dropped packets wrapped in oilskins into mountain lakes, down wells or even . . . or even sewers. (What was that – a red herring? Surely a clever man like Hofmann wouldn't have risked his nest egg being washed away in a flash flood?) What else then, for a get-rich-quick X marks the spot? Well, they'd heaped up art treasures in salt mines, most of which had been found – but he must have known that. And still he'd shown an inordinate interest in the mines and he hadn't even worked there.

Aha.

All that time he'd spent messing about on his own, getting 'lost', getting his sleeves wet . . . *'Do you get the feeling we're being watched?'* she'd whispered. What if Jo had been on to something?

I ran the tape of our journey, whizzed through to the mines and stopped at the shoot of the salty lake, all lit up ready for Helga to throw her stone. Okay, now slowly, slowly, I told myself, scan the beach – we're looking for someone lurking. He came out of the mine after us with the next party, and 'got separated' from the group ahead of us. So he must have been at the lake round about the same time as us. Wouldn't have wanted us to see him, though. No way, José. So, is he hiding behind a crag, a column of salt? Can't see, can't see. I had to stop. Needed a fag. Took a deep lungful of concentration before nudging the cursor around outcrops and into rocky clefts. Where are you, you bugger? Zoom in. Into the darkness. Lighten it. 'Come out; come out, wherever you are, And meet the young lady . . .' What's that over there? Zoom in again. Something on top of that boulder. A reflection on something wet. No, too close – it's out of focus. Digitally enhance. Slowly. It's coming clearer. A hand, a wet hand, caught in our light! Gotcha!

But now Charlie had changed to a close-up of the splintering of the water as Helga's stone hit. There wasn't another long view. Play it again, Sam. And again. And . . . whassat? There, just in the frame, I'd caught a gleam that wasn't crystalline. It was smoother, metallic. Zoom, zoom, zoom. Adjust the focus. Oh cool! It was a watch, a man's watch. The one he was supposed to have lost. It hadn't fallen in the lake. He'd taken it off and lain it flat as you do when you're about to plunge your arms into deep, salty water. He must have forgotten to put it back on when he'd finished. When he'd found what he was looking for.

When I showed the video to Owen, he passed the word along to the German police, who found the watch, complete with Susmeta's inscription 'To MZ from SN, with love' and a twenty-metre length of rope floating on the water, still perfectly preserved after sixty years.

Whatever he had fished out had been his sole purpose in coming to Germany. Probably the entire film idea had simply been a ruse to get down into the mines to recover it. And, I didn't flatter myself, I guessed he'd wanted me to direct it because he knew I'd be putty in his hands.

Further investigation uncovered a bank account in Hanover that had recently been opened in the name of Max Zeiler. But it wasn't money he'd deposited, it was gold, several ingots of gold, to which Max Zeiler had the title deeds, dated the 5th of January 1945. Presumably they'd been wrapped up inside some sort of waterproof bag. It didn't take much of an imagination to work out where that gold had come from. A surgeon? A corrupt surgeon? In a concentration camp? Whose job it was to pull thousands of teeth? No wonder he'd been huffing and puffing when he came out of the mine. His rucksack must have weighed a ton.

After they'd heard this evidence the jury was in no doubt that the defendant was the Beast of Buchenwald, a psychopath, who had maimed and killed untold numbers of prisoners and who was probably also indirectly responsible for a recent pub bombing where two people were killed and several injured. The verdict was unanimous.

When Gisela's turn came she changed her plea to guilty, having already inadvertently outed herself. I think she hoped that the judge might take a more lenient view if she told the truth. She described how Klaus Hofmann had discovered that he was suffering from stomach cancer and had hit on the idea of having his brain frozen as a means of cheating death. When, towards the end of the war, certain high-ranking German officials were desperately seeking a way out of a 'no-win' situation, some committed suicide, some booked their passage to South America, some volunteered to be guinea pigs in Hofmann's Project. In the end fourteen Nazis offered their brains for removal and, fingers crossed, subsequent rehousing, including the man they called 'Liebl'. It was a gamble they were willing to take. There was room for two more in the small freezer that was their time machine, beside themselves (Gisela, of course, intended to stand by her man), and so, on a whim, Klaus decided to include Willi Greff and Axel Schlager, Axel for his music, Willi for his science. Neither had known what was happening to them. Loyal assistants, fully conversant with the doctor's methods, had operated on the two surgeons when the time was right, frozen the brains, now tagged with the appropriate aliases, and repacked them, as per instructions, so that the latest additions were on the bottom layer. Presumably there had been no mishaps on the journey to Berlin, and they had been settled safely into their underground home for the duration. Friedrich Liebl's brain was to have been added to the cache at the last minute, if all else failed.

More than that she wouldn't say except that their bodies, hers and Hofmann's, must have been frozen separately and thawed in good time for it to appear that they had been killed by the inmates during the Uprising.

'There was an Uprising then?' The barrister narrowed his gaze.

'Presumably.' She frowned as she attempted to read his mind.

'Professor Weiss, perhaps you can help clarify a point. When the Americans entered Buchenwald on that day in April 1945 there was evidence of a recent inmates' rebellion. It appeared to have been a sudden, spontaneous attack taking advantage of the panic and disarray engendered by their own imminent arrival. It didn't last long, just long enough to litter the place with dead prisoners, a few guards and a number of hospital staff, yourselves included.'

She inclined her head.

'Your associates must have had great presence of mind, in the face of such an onslaught, by desperate men armed with primitive weapons, clubs and knives and suchlike, to remove two bodies from the freezer, arrange them to look as though they had been battered to death and then shoot themselves in the head.'

Still she said nothing, though her knuckles whitened in her lap.

'By the time the Allies found your bodies, on the floor of the operating theatre, they'd had time to thaw out and bleed. Now I'd imagine the thawing process would have taken some, what, twelve hours? More?'

By now, at least one jury member was doing sums based, probably, on defrosting a chicken.

'Professor, it would seem to me that the perpetrators of this deception, your 'loyal associates' or whoever was behind the project, were extremely lucky to have an armed rebellion to explain away your death. Extremely lucky! It might almost have been laid on for them . . .' He smiled a foxy smile, paused a little, before saying, 'I have to tell you, Fraulein, that I don't believe in luck. I believe that your being seen to have died was so important to the success of the enterprise that the Uprising was cooked up by the authorities to provide a plausible reason for two surgeons having their heads beaten in. I believe it was part of the plan. And I believe that you were in on it.'

It was true. The internees' plot had been exposed back in 1944 and most of the rebels taken out and shot, among them Max Zeiler and Ellen Sauerbruch – a few more deaths to add to the long roll for which the two surgeons were responsible.

Speaking of their work in the hospital, Gisela admitted that before Hofmann had hit on a successful freezing formula, it had been necessary to experiment on scores of unwilling victims, all of whom had been Jewish. She confessed, in tears, to pushing Sophie Greene under a train. Klaus had made her do it for fear that Sophie would know him for an impostor. She was so sorry. She had taken no part in the other murders.

'What other murders?'

Zeiler's sister and the old man – she'd forgotten his name.

'Douglas Mallory?'

Yes, that was it. She wasn't quite sure how Klaus had managed it but she imagined he'd injected the patient with something that had stopped the heart. She had been in bed when the car arrived back at Ottley Place. He hadn't come in to her and hadn't wanted to talk the next day. He was clearly very upset at what he'd had to do.

So upset, I thought, that he'd stopped off at the Chain and Sprocket and raped me for good measure. The green BMW that had taken him to Harlow and back had belonged to Lord Titherille.

His testimony was a joy. He described how proud he was to number Klaus Hofmann among his friends. The man was a genius and should be recognised as such. Lauded, in fact, fêted. Given the right backing, the right opportunities, he could easily become as great a surgeon as the little Asian, better, in fact. This man soaked up knowledge. He had already mastered much of the new technology required by modern surgery, as had his associate, Gisela Weiss. This trial was a farce, sheer hypocrisy. Why didn't the Home Secretary, or whoever was running the show, face up to the fact that only a fascist regime could generate the medical advances that lily-livered democracies could only dream of? Give the man free rein. The woman, too. Such rare gifts shouldn't be thrown away lightly.

Lady Edith closed her eyes in silent despair.

Next.

Axel Schlager really was Axel Schlager, the concert pianist. He proved it by finishing his opera and having it performed at the Almeida. It was generally reckoned to be a work of chilling beauty. The libretto, written by Shimon Grosman, the poet, himself an erstwhile Buchenwald internee, was described in the *Times* as 'unsentimental and gritty and consorting wonderfully with the full-blooded naivety of the music.'

He didn't know why Hofmann had chosen to preserve him. Sentiment, perhaps? Susmeta was more determined than ever to find him a more suitable donor. It was she who persuaded me to use a couple of his arias as themes in *The Buchenwald Project*. I would see, she said, repetition of the themes would get people humming, and before we knew it they'd be asking in shops for the CD.

Cursing her carelessness in overlooking an area of dying cells when she operated on Willi Greff's brain first time round, Susmeta is, at this moment, treating him with stem-cell therapy in his sanatorium in Salzburg, but whether he goes back to work for Greffindustrie when he is cured or finds some other form of employment is a matter for conjecture.

The Titherilles were charged with harbouring stolen goods (that is to say, a frozen brain, purporting to be that of one Friedrich Liebl), and, more seriously, were implicated in Douglas Mallory's murder. This they both denied. The car and driver had been put at Hofmann's disposal. Where he went in it and what he did when he got there was no concern of theirs. The fact that they had been planning a *coup d'etat* was incidental. Their involvement in the pub bombing wasn't proven, and their defence lawyer got them off with a caution. The interest engendered by the affair, and coincidentally, by my film, has been such that they feel constrained to keep Ottley Place open all year round and to hell with the heating bills. Their Nazi memorabilia draws particular attention. It has been gathered together in an eye-catching piece of constructional art taking up their entire entrance hall, and now includes personal items belonging to doctors Hofmann and Weiss, such as shower cap, lipstick, T-shirt and bed-socks. Photographs of the old couple and their famous houseguests have been mounted in a colourful decoupage, with a cutout of 'Friedrich Liebl's' brain, at its hub. The artist has chosen to remain anonymous, but we can guess, can't we?

I had a visit from a very intimidating couple of men in suits. I guessed they might have been MI5 or 6. They didn't beat about the bush. It had come to their notice that I was in possession of a letter, written by Klaus Hofmann. They'd seen the rushes for the film and were afraid they couldn't allow that particular scene to be shown. The letter was thought to contain important secret information, which was, of course, why Max had been so keen to get his hands on it.

It was only a copy, a mock up, a prop for an important scene, I pointed out. The War Museum in Berlin had the original. Not any more, apparently. Not since Max Zeiler's true identity had become known.

I gave them everything I had with the letter on, deleted it on hard disc and floppy, and promised to be good. They apologised for putting me to the trouble and spoiling my film. It didn't matter, I told them, cheerily – I had another opening up my sleeve. After they'd gone I phoned Nick and checked he still had the original disc.

The next day he came over and we worked on it together. While the letter was printing I told him my theory that, like Max and Ellen, every one of those Buchenwald fugitives would have had something put by for the future (except for Axel and Willi who were expected to fend for themselves), and they'd have known exactly where it was and gone straight to it, if they'd been able. But when it came to party funds, I said, there would have to have been some separate arrangement, something only one or two would have needed to know about.

'Yeah, like I wouldn't trust that bunch of psychos with a money-off voucher for cat food.'

I allowed myself a grin as I picked up the English version of the letter. 'This is one way he could have sent that sort of information into the future.'

'Who, Hofmann? You think he'd have altruistically popped some money in the bank, Nazi Party for the use of?'

'Maybe not him. He was only a corrupt doctor after all. No, the one with money to spare was Liebl.'

'Whoever *he* was,' he reminded me. It was true. There'd

been a lot of wishful speculation but no one had ever proved that Friedrich Liebl was anyone other than himself.

'Okay. Well, let's just suppose that someone, some Mister Big, could have given Hofmann the account number and got him to put it into his letter in code. Then if it went astray they'd know who to come to.'

'To draw money out of an account you'd need identification. Gisela Weiss was lucky Ellen Sauerbruch's dad put some money away in his daughter's name.'

'They forced him, I bet.'

'Hmm . . .' He made a face. 'I think it's more likely they buried it.'

'Oh right . . .' I stabbed at the list of prisoners' names. 'So what's this lot then, map references?'

'Clare, you're a genius!' But he didn't throw his arms round me in a passionate embrace. Instead he stared closer at the letter, pushing his glasses up to meet his scowl. 'I bet I know what he's done. Listen, do we still have the *Way of the World* video, the bit showing those CVs?'

He meant the aliases that had been wrapped around the brains, and we did. I read out the eighteen serial numbers, listed in Hofmann's letter, and he checked them against the numbers on the CVs. In several cases there were slight discrepancies. Now were these the careless typos of an uncaring man or the deliberate mistakes of an amateur encrypter? We got Richard to ask Axel for the number that had been tattooed on his arm. It was the same – 31450 – as the one given in the CV. Hofmann's letter recorded it as 31430. Yessss! The five and three had to be significant. Max was listed in the letter as number 21552 and, in the CV as 25152, so one and five were the numbers I noted down. In the end we had a string of eight pairs of meaningless numbers, which, with the help of a map we downloaded from the Internet we eventually rearranged into two likely map references – 53 30N 13 44E which turned out to be a lake near Strasburg and 48 75N 15 02E another salt mine, in Bavaria this time, near the home of Friedrich Liebl, coincidentally. But salt mines and lakes can be huge sites, kilometres wide. How would we know where to dig or drop anchor? I had another look at the translated letter but there was no mention of crossed trees or important landmarks. I left Nick trying to fathom co-ordinates while I went and placed a call to the Austrian embassy.

The lake turned out to be an old stone quarry and a favourite hiding place for Nazi fortunes. Divers had recovered gold bars and hundreds of thousands of English pounds back in 1957. The treasure had been in strong boxes and chests and submerged to a depth of seventy-five feet. Men had died trying to discover if any further treasure remained – it was not to be recommended.

Nothing had ever been found in that old Bavarian salt mine. If there had been any secret caches, the Nazis or other treasure seekers had removed them years before. Now it was used as a landfill site. Hundreds of thousands of tons of rubbish had been tipped down there in the last forty years. Foiled again. Or fobbed off again.

I guess the MI5 'suits' got in first. Still, it's got to be worth checking out. Much as I hate the idea of picking over a rubbish tip, or dredging a lake all next summer, and more so, the thought of crossing swords with 'suits,' a documentary about the Nazi spoils of war is definitely on the cards, especially now we've worked out the co-ordinates.

In the light of her incomparable skill, the contributions she has made to medical science, plus the invaluable testimony she gave during the trial, the British Medical Association declared itself prepared to overlook Susmeta's aberrations. In other words, she is far too valuable a resource to be dumped. However, there was one final service the Home

Secretary asked her to render the State, if she would. Or two, rather, *two* final services, if she would be so kind – namely, the removal the brains of the guilty parties from the bodies they had usurped, for re-freezing.

There was an outcry. What a crap decision! They must be destroyed, surely? And seen to be destroyed. There must be no risk, *no* risk at all, of such evil ever being embodied in flesh again.

But the judge was adamant. The UK had abolished the death penalty long ago. It would not, could not, be resurrected for any reason, ever.

Accordingly Susmeta removed and froze the living brains of Klaus Hofmann and Gisela Weiss, and they were placed in a deep refrigerated vault in a bank known only to the Home Secretary. On the same day Leon Paterson's body was buried with full ceremony, next to the casket containing his brain. Carla Perez was cremated.

Nick is worried. He is perfectly sure that somehow, some way, the neo-Nazis are going to get their hands on those two frozen brains.

'I doubt it,' I say, reckless on champagne.

'What do you mean?'

I say, with my newly acquired suspicious nature, 'I wouldn't be surprised if there aren't at this moment, deep in some medical research station, far away, two new doctors beavering away at some knotty problem that's been bothering the government for yonks, like cancer or muscular dystrophy.' I thought for a moment. 'Or more likely, the common cold.'

'You're joking,' says Nick, lowering his glasses to see me more clearly. 'Clare, tell me you're joking.'

ABOUT HONNO

Honno Welsh Women's Press was set up in 1986 by a group of women who felt strongly that women in Wales needed wider opportunities to see their writing in print and to become involved in the publishing process. Our aim is to publish books by, and for, women of Wales, and our brief encompasses fiction, poetry, children's books, autobiographical writing and reprints of classic titles in English and Welsh.

Honno is registered as a community co-operative and so far we have raised capital by selling shares at £5 a time to over 350 interested women all over the world. Any profit we make goes towards the cost of future publications. We hope that many more women will be able to help us in this way. Share-holders' liability is limited to the amount invested, and each shareholder, regardless of the number of shares held, will have her say in the company and a vote at the AGM. To buy shares or to receive further information about forthcoming publications, please write to Honno:

'Ailsa Craig'
Heol y Cawl
Dinas Powys
Bro Morgannwg
CF64 4AH.